Annie shook her head slightly as she muttered to herself. She hated being so cowardly and sickened by a little blood.

"I'm sorry, sir," she said to the soldier lying on the porch floor. "Can you unbutton your jacket for me?" Modesty kept her from touching his clothes.

The Union officer blinked to clear his eyes and focus. "Yes, of course, miss." His voice was hoarse and small. "I'm sorry to be troubling you with this at all."

With a grimace, he undid the long row of brass buttons and tried to ease the blue jacket off his left arm. The motion caused a little gusher of blood to spurt up through his torn shirt.

"Oh, dear." Annie plopped to the floor, her brown muslin skirts popping air out like a blacksmith's bellows as she landed on her bottom. The house whirled. Her stomach lurched. Annie couldn't believe that not only was she having to tend to a Yankee, she might retch right there in front of him.

Also by L.M. Elliott

FLYING SOUTH
"Poignancy, humor, and history."
—*School Library Journal*

UNDER A WAR-TORN SKY
"Packed with action, intrigue, and suspense."
—*ALA Booklist*

Annie, Between the States

L. M. Elliott

SCHOLASTIC INC.
New York Toronto London Auckland Sydney
Mexico City New Delhi Hong Kong Buenos Aires

ISBN-13: 978-0-439-89630-6
ISBN-10: 0-439-89630-4

12 11 10 9 8 7 6 5 4 3 2 6 7 8 9 10 11/0

Printed in the U.S.A. 40

First Scholastic printing, October 2006

Typography by Larissa Lawrynenko

For my beautiful family:
Megan,
Peter, and John

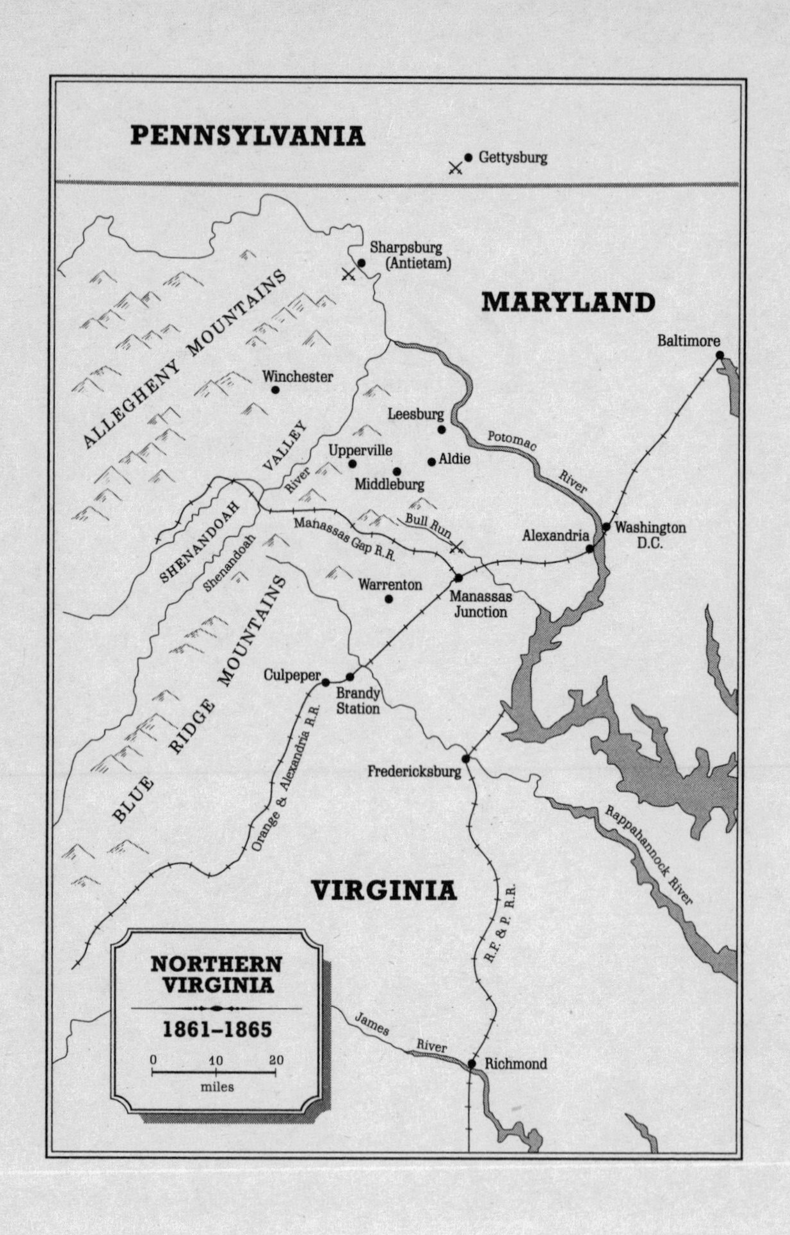
PENNSYLVANIA
Gettysburg
Sharpsburg (Antietam)
MARYLAND
Baltimore
ALLEGHENY MOUNTAINS
Winchester
VALLEY
River
Leesburg
Potomac
River
Upperville
Aldie
Middleburg
SHENANDOAH
Shenandoah
Manassas Gap R.R.
Bull Run
Washington D.C.
Alexandria
Warrenton
Manassas Junction
BLUE RIDGE MOUNTAINS
Culpeper
Brandy Station
Orange & Alexandria R.R.
Fredericksburg
Rappahannock River
VIRGINIA
R.F. & P. R.R.
NORTHERN VIRGINIA
1861–1865
0 10 20
miles
James River
Richmond

Annie, Between the States

CHAPTER ONE

July 21, 1861
Manassas, Virginia

Stop being such a pea-wit.

Annie shook her head slightly as she muttered to herself. She hated being so cowardly and sickened by a little blood. She squeezed the ball of lint in her hand to quiet her trembling. It was simple enough to do. The lint would help the wound clot. All she had to do was stuff it in. Taking a deep breath, Annie knelt down and tried again.

"I'm sorry, sir," she said to the soldier lying on the porch floor. "Can you unbutton your jacket for me?" Modesty kept her from touching his clothes.

The Union officer blinked to clear his eyes and focus. "Yes, of course, miss." His voice was hoarse and small. "I'm sorry to be troubling you with this at all."

With a grimace, he undid the long row of brass

buttons and tried to ease the blue jacket off his left arm. The motion caused a little gusher of blood to spurt up through his torn shirt.

"Oh, dear." Annie plopped to the floor, her brown muslin skirts popping air out like a blacksmith's bellows as she landed on her bottom. The house whirled. Her stomach lurched. Her ribs heaved against the wall of her corset. She fought to pull in the hot, dusty air. But it only made her feel more nauseous. Annie couldn't believe that not only was she having to tend to a Yankee, she might retch right there in front of him.

BOOM-BOOM-BOOM.

The windows behind her rattled hard and the floor quaked. Annie forgot her queasy stomach. *Lord save us.* Those were closer—she was sure of it. She was no expert; she'd known the sounds of war for only a few hours now. But she was learning fast.

When she'd first heard the cannons at daybreak, she'd thought the noise was way-off thunder, a squall line gathering itself up against the Bull Run Mountains. She'd prayed for rain. The cornfields and hay fields needed it badly. But her naïve thought lasted only a few minutes. There had been skirmishing recently at Blackburn Ford, a mile or so away. Annie had mistaken that artillery fire for distant thunder. This morning, Annie quickly realized that it was guns, and the beginning of something horrible.

It'd have to be, given all the soldiers who had swarmed the area. She'd stood by the gate with Aunt Molly's brood of children, watching Confederate troops pass by. Their cannons were pulled by burly plow horses that strained with the weight. They were thick black barrels, menacing and cold-looking, almost as long as train cars.

"Great God Almighty, Annie, look at them," her little cousin Will had breathed in awe. "They could blow down giants. Do you suppose the Yankees got guns like that?"

"I don't know, honey," she'd said, putting her arm around him. "General Beauregard's waiting for the Federal invaders at Bull Run. And General Johnston's on the way from the Shenandoah Valley. They'll take care of things."

BOOM-BOOM-BOOM.

Cannon answered cannon. Yes, clearly the Union had guns just as big.

Annie thought of her brother, Laurence, good, kind Laurence who'd taken his two best thoroughbreds and joined Jeb Stuart's 1st Virginia Cavalry. Would Laurence be in the fight? What would she and her mother do if Laurence were hurt or . . . or

. . . She couldn't allow the idea. Defensively, she replaced fear with anger. South Carolina had gotten Virginia into this mess, South Carolina and six of her Deep South sister states. Ever since they had seceded in the winter, Confederate men had swaggered about, shouting about states' rights and the fact that the Federal government existed only by the consent of the governed. They'd seemed to want the fight, as if it'd be fun, a good frolic.

And the North was no better. Rather than letting states leave the Union as the Constitution guaranteed they could do if they no longer agreed with its policies, President Lincoln declared war and called for seventy-five thousand volunteers to put down the insurrection—eight thousand recruits were required of Virginia, he said. That was when, in May, Virginia finally, reluctantly, opted to secede from a government that demanded it wage war against its closest friends. Arkansas, North Carolina, and Tennessee did the same, and the Confederacy held eleven states. Everyone started wearing rosettes and singing songs of glory.

Both sides expected quick, easy victory. The nearby village of Centreville was clogged with senators and people from Washington who'd hired carriages, packed picnic lunches, and traveled thirty miles over eight hours to watch the battle as if it were a Fourth of July celebration. Those guns certainly didn't sound like a picnic to her.

BOOM-BOOM-BOOM.

Annie covered her ears. She shouldn't be trapped, smack-dab in the middle of a battle. She wasn't supposed to be here. She should be home, safe in Upperville, west toward the Blue Ridge, shielded from the advancing Federals by a long, thick line of Confederate brigades. She'd just been on her way home from school and gotten stuck.

Annie attended Baker's Seminary for Young Ladies in Alexandria. Well, she had until the Union bluecoats crossed the Potomac River and occupied the town in May. Then she and most of the other girls had left. Usually, she would have ridden the train out the Orange & Alexandria Railway to Manassas Junction and spent the night with her aunt, who lived just a few miles away. But the Federals had shut down the rail line. She'd had to beg a carriage ride from a classmate and then walked the remaining distance from Centreville. Her mother, Miriam, had come in their rig to fetch her home. During their visit, Aunt Molly came down with measles, a gift from the Confederate soldiers camping nearby. Several neighbors caught it, too. Miriam insisted they stay to nurse Aunt Molly. And so here they were, sitting on the edge of Hades.

Mother never thought of such things. She was always taking care of everybody else but herself. This time, though, she'd dragged Annie into her dangerous do-gooding. It was selfish, is what it was, Annie fumed.

She looked over to her mother, who was bandaging a mud-slathered Yankee. He lay among a dozen Union soldiers who'd been carried in on stretchers and were being tended by a Federal surgeon. No apologies or asking permission. The Union army had just taken over Aunt Molly's yard with their wounded. They'd run off with Mother's carriage horses and the few work horses Aunt Molly had, too. Something about the cavalry and preserving the glorious Union. How would Aunt Molly travel now, or bring back supplies from town? How would she and Mother get home to Upperville?

Of course, the absolute worst part of all this was the fact that her mother was insisting on helping the surgeon—and making Annie do the same. Most true ladies would never dream of facing so much blood and horror. Ladies were supposed to be delicate and dignified. If her classmates at Baker's could see her now, it would confirm their cruel whispers that she wasn't as well bred as she pretended to be.

"Miss." The hoarse voice from the ground jerked Annie back from her frightened and angry thoughts. "I can probably do it myself if you hand me that lint."

Long before they knew there was like to be a battle to defend a critical railway juncture where the Orange & Alexandria line tied in to the Manassas Gap line, Annie and her mother had joined other Confederate women in scraping petticoats and bed linens for lint to stuff into wounds and staunch the bleeding of their soldiers. They hadn't planned on using it for Unionists. But the Federal surgeon had only what bandages and medicines he could carry in his saddlebag, hardly enough to treat five men, much less twenty. Evidently, the Yankees had left the majority of their medical supplies back in Centreville. And they had just a few ambulances to carry the wounded back to their encampment.

How could they be that foolish? Annie wondered. Or maybe it was plain arrogance, figuring they'd scare off the Confederate army with nary a scratch to themselves. Well, they'd misjudged Southern boys, for sure. And they'd obviously misjudged what slaughter their weapons could bring.

The officer tried to sit himself up. He fell back with a thud.

This was simply too much. Annie knew entire sections of Milton's *Paradise Lost*, how to play the piano, some French, all the psalms in the King James Bible, even a little botany. She didn't know anything about keeping a man from dying from a battle wound.

"Mother!" Annie wailed. "Mother, please come here. Please. He's dying. I just know it."

Miriam Sinclair reassuringly patted the face of the boy she was tending before standing and sweeping across the lawn to Annie. How did she always look so calm? Annie marveled. Her anger vanished. Even though she was fifteen years old, she just wanted her mother, wanted her the way she had when she was little and woke from a bad dream.

"Annie, darlin,' don't be silly now. You'll be scaring the lieutenant." Miriam's parents had been Irish immigrants. Even though Miriam was Virginia born, her parents' old way of talking now and then slipped into her speech, something she typically squelched back home in the Anglican stronghold of Fauquier County. Annie's father, Thaddeus, had ignored his social standing when he'd married the beautiful but Irish-Catholic Miriam. She tried hard during his lifetime to shed her heritage for him, even dropping her heartfelt religion to become

Episcopalian. But Miriam's roots always showed when she comforted someone.

Miriam undid the officer's shirt and pulled it back. As a mother and the head of a large working farm, she'd nursed too many to be squeamish about propriety. Annie gasped when she saw the ugly gash along the officer's side. She turned her eyes away and covered her mouth.

"It's just a flesh wound," Miriam said after a quick assessment. "I can dress this easily. See, Annie. It's not even as bad as the time your brother ripped up his leg when he fell off that firebrand stallion of his."

"Are you certain, ma'am?" the officer murmured as he turned to Miriam. He had that look of relief all sick people did when Miriam got near them. "The doctor left me. I heard him say that he couldn't treat a wound to the body, only the arms and legs. I thought . . . I thought maybe he'd given up on me . . . left me, you know, to . . . to . . ."

"Hush, now, son. It's really just a deep scrape. Look here." She held up a thick book that had fallen out of his jacket. The volume was in shreds, blackened and singed. "I do believe your book saved you. It must have deflected the bullet so that it just skipped along your side as it went on its way. Best be telling your surgeons to take a closer look next time if you Yankee boys are going to insist on this foolishness." She smiled down at him as she spoke.

He smiled back sheepishly. "Yes, ma'am."

With surprise, Annie picked up the book. Poetry by John Keats. She loved Keats. She didn't think a Northerner would like such gentle verse. *Beauty is truth, truth beauty,—that is all / Ye know on earth, and all ye need to know.* She looked at the young Union officer more carefully. He had dark, questioning eyes, and a lean, clean-cut face with none of the bombastic whiskers so many of the men grew that made them look like walruses.

He was trying to say more, but his voice was getting fainter. "Cannon explosion killed my horse. . . . Beautiful horse, called him Ulysses . . . perhaps not the most auspicious name, after all . . . Rolled over on me when he went down. . . . I think maybe a rib or two is broken . . . but I can breathe all right. . . . Must not have punctured the lung . . . "

"What's your name, boy?" Miriam interrupted.

"Thomas. Lieutenant Thomas Walker, from Massachusetts, serving with Palmer's cavalry battalion."

"That's fine, Mr. Thomas Walker from Massachusetts. No more talking. Don't worry. This cut isn't much at all, and ribs mend themselves if you give them time. Later you can write home to your mother and tell her all about your misadventures. Don't forget to write her. She'll be worrying.

"My name is Miriam Sinclair and this is my daughter, Annie. You are enjoying the hospitality of my sister, Molly, whose lawn this is. There now, we've been properly introduced."

Miriam reached over and squeezed Annie's hand. "There, you see? It's all right, child. Now fetch me a bowl of soap and water and a clean needle and thread. A horse hair would be better, but they've taken the horses, haven't they? As if they didn't have enough of their own to be stealing poor Molly's old horses. Well, a thread will do. See if Molly keeps some crushed yarrow or garlic to help this heal. And then draw some fresh water for these other boys, Annie. This heat is awful." Fear shadowed her face for a moment, and she whispered, "Don't forget to say a prayer for your brother." Then she went back to business.

Annie was grateful for the walk to the well in back of the house. She fanned her face as she went, knowing from the hotness she felt on it that her cheeks were flushed as red as her hair. She pulled up water, cool and sweet, from the dark deepness of the earth, and cupped some on the back of her neck. If only she could slip down to the branch and wade into the water that splashed along rocky shoals there, the way they had as children. Maybe later. Maybe later all these soldiers would be gone. Surely Laurence and his friends would run them off. Laurence. She closed her eyes to recite, "Dear Lord, in all your mercy, protect our boys in their hour of need. Grant them . . ."

BOOM-BOOM-BOOM.

Annie covered her ears against a long, screaming whistle and then another deafening *BOOM.* There was a crash and a lightning spark, and the top of one of the walnut trees at the bottom of the lane exploded and cracked down to the ground.

BOOM-BOOM-BOOM.

A black comet sliced the air and landed in the cornfield, hurling up dirt and smoke and shattered stalks.

Frozen, Annie watched the ten-acre cornfield and its shoulder-tall green stalks. On the far side, it seethed and smoked, as if it were coming alive. The writhing rippled forward toward the house, closer, closer. Then she heard it. The crack of muskets firing, men shouting, screams, explosions, horses neighing in fright.

A Union soldier popped out of the corn, looked back, stopped, fired, then ran on. Another dashed out, suddenly splayed out in a spasm, and fell. A third bluecoat stumbled out of the stalks, crawling, screaming, moving on all fours. Then there were five more, six, ten.

The battle was coming straight at her.

CHAPTER TWO

In her mind, Annie was running, skirt hitched up, feet flying across the lawn, into the house, fast as a rabbit.

In reality, she was rooted.

This can't be happening.

Annie opened her mouth to scream. Nothing came out. She couldn't hear a thing, just a roaring in her ears, like high winds. Her body swayed with the violent thumping of her heart.

Faintly, Annie heard a voice, like a whisper, far away: "Run! Run, miss!"

Another Harpylike whistle through the air, a black ball hurtling into the cornfield, a shock, a volcano of cornstalks, and screams.

Crack-crack-crack.

Up from the corn, coming toward her, billowed a wave of blue-clad men, panicking, crying, many dropping rifles and ammunition, throwing everything overboard so they could move as fast as possible. They jostled one another. Some fell and were trampled. Others stooped, picked up the fallen, and dragged them along.

A rider crashed out of the cornfield. His chestnut horse reared and pawed the air as the officer yanked him to a stop. "Stop, you cowards!" he bellowed. "Turn and fight!"

A few slowed, looking nervously back toward the officer. One small, thin soldier actually stopped, loaded his gun, and aimed toward the field, ready. But most kept running, ducking their heads lower.

"Stop or I'll shoot you down!" the officer shouted, and fired his pistol into the air.

Annie felt herself inching back, back, back.

She could see faces plainly now as they swept up the long hill toward her. Young faces, old, dirty, bloody. She heard the voice again. "Run, miss, run! There are a thousand men behind me!" Finally, Annie focused on a Union soldier at the front of the pack, waving his arms at her.

His urgency kicked her into action. Annie turned and ran. Now she could hear their feet, crashing along the ground, coming up behind her. She looked toward the house and saw her mother rushing down the steps, searching the sea of confusion, calling for Annie.

"I'm here, Mother," Annie gasped. "Here." She raised her hand to wave, and as she did, she smelled something smoky and sweaty. A grimy hand reached up and grabbed her arm, swinging her around. She almost fell with the wheeling motion, but the hand held her up.

A face loomed over hers. A face twisted up in terror. "Which way to the road? Please! What will take me back to Centreville?"

Annie choked, frozen by the fear radiating from him.

The hand shook her. "Which way?"

"Let go of my child!" Miriam was there, pushing the man away. "That way. Past the house, down the lane, onto the road, then three or four miles east."

As Miriam spoke and pointed, a half dozen boys swarmed her and the man. "Which way, ma'am? Which way?"

The man whose face had been savaged with fear now looked ashamed. "I know. Follow me, boys. Best get back to the house, ma'am." Then he darted off, dogged by the others.

Miriam and Annie huddled together, unsure how to reach the house without being knocked down. A storm surge of Union soldiers broke around them and washed on. More were coming.

"Annie, take my hand. We need to get inside." Miriam pulled Annie along behind her as she dodged and skittered among the running men.

"Water, ma'am. Please, I've got to have some water."

The plea was echoed, and once again Miriam and Annie found themselves stopped and surrounded by frightened, shaking, panting men. Annie looked down and realized that she still clutched the water bucket. Her skirt was drenched, but there was some water left in the bucket. She put it on the ground, and the men dropped to it. She and her mother waded on and reached the stairs.

The Union surgeon had managed to move all the wounded onto the porch. But the house was no island. Several of the fleeing soldiers scrambled up the steps and raced through it and out the other side.

Miriam spoke firmly. "Molly and the children are down in the cellar, Annie. I want you to go there, too."

Annie finally found her own voice. "What's happening, Mother?"

From the floor came her answer. "It's a retreat, miss," the Massachusetts officer said with disgust. "And a disorganized one. See that officer down there?" Annie looked to the rider, who was still shouting and circling his sweat-lathered horse. "His men aren't listening to him at all. If he can't dissuade these men from running, no one can. There must be something really fierce chasing them. Our cavalry should be protecting their rear. But perhaps they're engaged with Confederate riders. It looks as if everyone is mixed in together. I'm afraid you're not very safe at this moment, miss. You should go below in the cellar."

Annie nodded. "You, too, Mother. Please."

"Yes, soon, darling, I just want to make sure these boys . . ."

At that moment, Thomas Walker's prediction came true. Out of the corn burst twenty horses, kicking and snorting, hot to race on. Their Union riders fought to control them and regroup, waving sabers in the air, a few aiming pistols.

From deep in the corn welled up a horrendous, wailing shouting—a sound that made the hair on Annie neck's prickle and Thomas Walker prop himself up. "What in God's name?" he murmured.

It sounded to Annie a little like the baying men

did during foxhunting, but it had a haunting caterwaul to it, a shrieking aggression like that she imagined of Indians on the warpath. It carried a chilling abandon as if the men making the cacophony knew it was a death cry, perhaps a foretelling of their own end, and they both welcomed and mourned it. The Rebel yell.

The Union cavalry horses reared and bucked in reaction to the sound. Only a few of their riders managed to fire off shots before they, too, turned their mounts and fled, catching up with the soldiers running on foot.

Crack-crack-crack. Little puffs of smoke popped atop the corn as whatever was hidden answered fire. Something glinted in speckles of hot silver. Sabers. The Southern cavalry was coming.

"It's our boys, Mother. Oh, hurrah, we're saved."

BOOM-BOOM-BOOM.

An ancient maple tree guarding the corner of Aunt Molly's lawn sparked, lit up, and shattered, hurling shards and beam-sized pieces of wood into the air. A thick branch spun round and round to the ground and crushed a young man beneath it.

"Sweet Jesus, have mercy! That poor child." Miriam started down the steps, as if she were going to try to lift the log off the broken boy.

"Mother, no!" Annie grabbed hold of her mother's skirts.

"Annie, that could be Laurence. Oh, my God." She struggled to pull free.

It was the Union surgeon who stopped her. He spoke brusquely. "Ma'am, you must go downstairs. That soldier is dead. Do you want your daughter to be hit next?"

"Mother, please." Annie pulled her along a few feet. "It's not Laurence. He'll be all right."

Miriam finally turned to Annie. Annie could see the grief in her mother's face and knew she was also thinking of three other sons—brothers Annie barely remembered, two older than Laurence and one younger. All three had died with their father in an epidemic of scarlet fever that had decimated their household years ago. At the time she'd been six years old and her little brother, Jamie, had been four. They and Laurence had been sent away to avoid the sickness and survived. But afterward, the responsibility of being the eldest, of helping to run their farm, and of coaxing their mother out of her sorrow and self-recrimination had dropped like a stone on Laurence. Overnight he had become solemn and trustworthy. He'd been only twelve. He was precious to Miriam, very precious, more than

Annie or Jamie could ever hope to be. Annie often resented that fact, but today she understood. Laurence being safe meant that he'd be there to keep them all safe.

Crack-crack-crack. A crest of Confederate gray riders plunged out of the corn. Spurring their horses on, they caught up with the last of the blue cavalry. Riders skirmished in a jumble of horses, plumed hats, gold epaulets, flashing steel, pawing hooves, and curses. A shot. A horse stumbled and dropped to the ground as his rider jumped aside and landed on his hands and knees. He rose, only to be whacked on the head with the butt of a pistol.

Enough. Annie suddenly felt some strength. It was insane to remain in the middle of all this. "Mother, Laurence would be furious with you right now, to see you endanger yourself and me this way. We could be killed by a stray shot. Come downstairs."

The potential of angering Laurence did it. Miriam nodded, took Annie's hand, and followed.

The earthy coolness of the dirt cellar instantly calmed Annie as she shuffled her way down the dark steps. Miriam closed the door and bolted it. The shouts, the gunfire, and the cannon explosions became muffled and distant. *Thank God.*

There was one small, dusty window that spread enough hazy light to see by. In a corner next to the vegetable bins, Aunt Molly lay on a straw mattress Annie and Miriam had dragged down for her when the shelling had started. She coughed and wheezed. In the gloom, the fire-red measles rash on her face couldn't be seen. But Annie knew it flamed there and that her aunt's horrible fever had broken as a result. She'd be all right. But Annie still didn't want to get too close to her—she hadn't had measles, and many a person died of it. Aunt Molly's three children huddled way across the cellar as well. Miriam had forbidden them to have contact with their mother until she was recovered. They immediately jumped up and clustered around Annie.

"Is it those gigantic cannons we saw?" Will tugged on Annie's hand, his eyes big and worried. Annie nodded.

"Miriam, what's happening? It sounds like the Coming of the Lord out there." Aunt Molly's voice was thin and frightened.

"Part of the battle has moved right into your yard, Molly." Miriam sat down by her younger sister and took her hand. Her voice had a false singsong cheeriness about it. "But it will be all right. Our cavalry is here now, chasing the Federal invaders off. You'll see. It'll be over within a few minutes, I imagine. And just think, darlings"—she turned to Annie's cousins—"you'll be telling your children that the war was won right in your front lawn!"

But it wasn't over in a few minutes. The sporadic fighting went on and on. Explosions continued to rock the house, shaking buckets of dust out of the exposed beam ceiling down on them. Several times they heard doors open and bang against walls as heavy feet pounded the floors above them. Outside the window, hooves thundered by, canteens and muskets dropped, clods of clay were kicked up against the panes.

Annie paced, running her hands along the shelves that held dozens of canning jars filled with peaches and blackberry preserves. The apple crates were empty, awaiting the fall picking, but the sweet smell of dried apples still lingered from the winter. She thought of home and the wealth of stored food there, and couldn't help but feel a little bit superior and sorry for her aunt and her cousins. They had to work so hard to scratch out a living. The soil around Manassas was poor and overtilled. Her uncle John had a good job as a supervisor in one of the nearby grain mills, but the garden and orchard they kept on their thirty acres was small. Their cornfield was their one large crop. They had only a few hogs, chickens, and one milk cow. Annie prayed that the marauding Yankees hadn't found the cow Will had tethered in a thicket in the scrubby pine forest.

No one had realized until that week that a war would mean armies could come and encamp on their fields or in their houses and simply take whatever they wanted to feed their troops or haul their wagons. Annie felt a resentment and hatred building against the Union Yankees that she'd never felt before, not even as she'd listened to family and neighbors decry Washington's imposition of high tariffs on their exported crops and imported goods, its political policies fashioned by smug Northerners living hundreds of miles away. Not even as everyone she knew prepared for a fight.

Will and Sally, the oldest of her cousins, took Annie's hands and walked the cellar with her. They were only seven and six years old. What would happen to them if Uncle John was killed? He'd joined the 8th Virginia Regiment and was definitely in the fray. Aunt Molly certainly couldn't take care of all of them. It had been different when Annie's father had died. Their home, Hickory Heights, wasn't huge, but it had been in his family for several generations and was well established on the rolling, fertile hills of Fauquier County. They had a herd of cattle, sheep, and fine horses, abundant wheat fields, and large orchards. Unlike her aunt's, their home had many outbuildings—barns, a separate meat house and potato cellar, an icehouse, plus a summer kitchen. There were servants to help tend and plant. It took clever managing and persistence, but Hickory Heights could thrive without an adult male running it. But here? She glanced over at her aunt, weak and sick, lying in the dirt of a cellar. She wasn't sure. Annie squeezed Will's hand. He wasn't like Laurence. Such a little boy, in such a terrible time.

It was getting darker in the cellar. Twilight was coming. Annie went to light a lard lantern hanging from the ceiling when she realized that it was suddenly quiet, very quiet. "Mother?" she whispered. "Do you think it's finally over?"

They all stood still, hushed, straining to hear.

"What's that jingle?" Will asked. "Hear it?"

They did—a steady rhythmic clattering. Annie slowly guessed at the sound: trotting horses, with scabbards, muskets, spurs, and canteens gently jostling against one another. She took in a deep breath and held her hand to her heart. She turned to her mother, who looked awash in relief as well.

But the question was: which army was it?

"Annie, can you see out the window?" Miriam asked.

Annie pressed her face through cobwebs to look out. Nothing but muddy boots and horses' legs. She rubbed a circle clean in the dust and peered harder. She could see uniformed legs, but in the growing darkness, there was no way to distinguish between blue and gray cloth.

"I can't . . ."

"Shhhhh, listen." Miriam held up her hand to stop her.

Many feet were climbing the steps to the front porch. Voices, low, calm. But the words, the accents, were muted by the thick fieldstone walls of the cellar.

Annie began to tremble. Dared they hope? If it was Union soldiers, if they'd managed to retake this position, how much revenge would they want, given all their wounded and dead?

Someone was running through the house, making the floorboards creak and groan. The feet reached the cellar. The door rattled.

Miriam moved to the steps, holding up her hands to keep everyone else in place. "Don't move. Don't make a sound until I know who it is," she breathed.

The door rattled again hard.

"Mother? Aunt Molly? Annie? Where are you?"

Laurence. It was Laurence!

Annie felt the world weave and her knees give out as the floor came up to bang her head.

CHAPTER THREE

"Is this the same sister I had to pull out of an oak tree because she'd climbed up so high to look in an owl's nest? The same tomboy who dared to ride the wildest horse in my herd because I'd told her that he was too much for her? Where's my fierce Annie?"

Annie felt herself surface to consciousness, following that gentle, teasing voice. Her eyes opened and she saw Laurence bending over her, her mother and cousins bunched up around them.

"Here, drink this, child." Her mother held a tin cup of water toward Annie, as Laurence propped her up. Her head pounded and her hands shook as she reached for it. "You must be ashamed of me," Annie mumbled. "I don't know what happened."

"Tsush, Annie darlin', such a day we've had. It's no wonder."

They pulled Annie to her feet and brushed the dirt from her flounced skirt. Annie longed to pull off the clammy drawers that clung to her legs with perspiration. She tugged at the high collar of her blouse. The air was stifling. Suddenly the cellar felt more like a tomb than a sanctuary.

"Can we go outside for some fresh air, Mother, please?"

Miriam and Laurence exchanged glances. "The Black Horse, Radford's 30th Virginia cavalry, is outside, Annie," Laurence began. "They're good boys, a lot of them from back home, in Fauquier. They weren't going to let any bluecoats in their sight stay put. The Federals are in complete disarray, fleeing to Washington. Colonel Stuart is anxious to continue pursuing them and end this nonsense right now. But he's bogged down at Sudley Springs with all the prisoners we caught. He said I could come ahead and check on Aunt Molly and you. There are a lot of wounded outside, Annie. Are you sure you want to go out just yet?"

No, Annie wasn't sure. Within this one day she'd seen more ugly, frightening things than she ever could have imagined. But she wanted to breathe in some cool night air. She wanted to hear the peeper frogs singing. She wanted to look for a falling star in the wide, purple-black sky, and forget the killing and bleeding and mayhem she'd witnessed. Besides, she didn't want to admit being afraid. The corset had just choked the wind out of her, that's all. Such a ridiculous thing to have to wear. Her aunt didn't wear one. Why did she and her mother have to?

Annie felt her jaw jut out a bit as she pulled away from her brother and mother. "Of course I'm sure, Laurence. Why would I be afraid of some of Virginia's finest gentlemen and the Yankees they've captured?" She forced a smile.

"That's my Annie," Laurence answered. He held out his hand. "Perhaps, if we are fortunate, Colonel Stuart will ride forward and I will have the honor of introducing him to my beautiful sister."

As they climbed the cellar stairs and walked through the small frame house, Laurence told her more of Stuart. "He is absolutely insane and brilliant at the same time, Annie. Amazing valor. Three weeks ago, near Falling Waters, we had a merry little skirmish. At one point, Colonel Stuart found himself separated from us and completely alone right by a group of Federals. The bluecoats stood behind a rail fence staring at him. Like so many of our officers who left the U.S. army when Lincoln declared war on their kin, Stuart still wears the U.S. blue uniform while he awaits new gray cloaks to be made. Seeing that the bluecoats thought him a Union officer, Stuart roared at them to take down the rail fence as if to prepare for a charge. He was so commanding, they did it. Then Stuart told them to throw down their arms, or they were all dead men. All by himself, he captured forty-nine men from the 15th Pennsylvania Volunteers. Can you imagine?"

He stopped by the front door to light a lantern to carry with them. As he struck the flint and the flame flared, Annie looked at her brother's fair, fine-boned face, before always so quiet and contained, now flushed with excitement. Still very young-looking at age twenty-one, and yet there was a man's self-assurance in his large, hazel eyes. Laurence had always had a mature, almost princely air to him, which had been forced upon him by circumstances. But this was something different. Annie wasn't sure exactly what it was, but it inspired and saddened her at the same time.

Miriam came up behind them, and Annie could tell her mother sensed a new resolve about him as well. "Was it hard today, son?"

Laurence began to speak, stopped, then began

again in a hushed tone. "It . . . was disturbing, Mother, I'll not lie. We were ordered into battle several hours after the fighting had begun. Colonel Stuart ordered us to attack where the firing was hottest. As we rode through a valley, we passed surgeons at work with hacksaws on our boys . . . great heaps of arms and legs lying about. . . . I . . . I'm afraid I was sick from the saddle as I passed." He rubbed his forehead with his hand and sighed. "A blue haze of gun smoke confused everything. We found ourselves in the midst of a large regiment of men in blousy pants and red-tasseled caps. The Colonel figured them for those bodacious, Moroccan-styled Zouaves from Louisiana. He called out, 'Don't run, boys, we're here.' Well, it turns out they were Zouaves all right—but Zouaves from New York. They opened fire on us, at rather close range."

Boyishly, Laurence took his mother's hand. "I was frightened. But I remembered what Colonel Stuart had said just a few days before when we were outnumbered. He said, 'A good man on a good horse can never be caught. Cavalry can trot away from anything. A gallop is a gait unbecoming to a soldier unless he is going *toward* the enemy. We gallop toward the enemy, and trot away, always.'"

Laurence was quiet a moment, in thought; then

another of his heart-stopping, dimpled grins lit up his face. "And we know, don't we, Mother, that I have a *very* good horse."

Annie laughed. Laurence's pride in the horses he bred and trained was one of his few real faults.

"So we held firm. The Zouaves put up a good fight. According to some we captured, they're a regiment of volunteer firemen from New York City, so they're tenacious and not afraid of a bad situation. But we rattled them, and eventually they ran. All the Federals ran. Looks like some ran right through here." He lowered his voice. "I'm afraid Aunt Molly's corn is ruined. Has there been word of Uncle John?"

Miriam shook her head. "I need help getting her back upstairs to bed. Do you suppose some of your friends could carry her?"

"Of course, Mother." There it was. That quiet, responsible look Annie knew so well. "I'll see to it. And I'll check on Uncle John. I think the 8th was on the right flank, where fighting was not as fierce. We can hope that God spared him."

Laurence turned back to Annie. "To fresh air, sister."

Outside, Annie was startled by the crowds. Everywhere were huddles—of men talking and laughing, of doctors leaning over soldiers, of horses grazing. To the side, a large group of prisoners sat on the dew-covered ground, guarded by a few Confederates holding shotguns. Some of the bluecoats kept their heads bowed. One played a mouth harp. Several played cards. A few chatted easily with their captors like classmates in a school yard during recess.

Young Confederates scampered from one mass to another, carrying messages, carrying water, carrying questions—"Ain't we going to ride on? Those bluecoats are just down the road, begging to be caught, like fat partridges." "What should I do with this man, doctor? He's bleeding bad." "What should we feed all these prisoners?" "Did you see how they ran, by God, did you see? They're no match for Virginia boys, I tell you!"

Down by the ruined corn, campfires burned, and the smell of coffee and salt pork frying in thick grease drifted toward Annie. She hadn't eaten since early morning. But the smell of such coarse food was hardly appetizing.

Yip, yip. Yehaw. Whooee. Yesssss, sireee! In thundered a dozen riders, yelling and whooping in triumph.

They reined their horses in hard, and the leading officer shouted, "Look here, boys, we've brought you a feast. The Federals were expecting to celebrate tonight and made themselves a mighty fine dinner. But guess what! They forgot to take it with them when they skedaddled home!"

The men cheered and collected to see the cache: champagne, boxes of lemons, cakes, beef tongue, smoked fish. There were also boots, blankets, trousers, and new accurate-firing rifle-muskets. But the cavalrymen grabbed first at the rich food.

"Where is Colonel Stuart?" the leader called.

A soldier answered through a mouthful of cake. "He's waiting to move on, if given the order. Beauregard's meeting right now with General Johnston and President Davis. Seems General Beauregard had the chance to follow them, too, but he received a report that some Federals were recrossing Bull Run. A rider came through just a moment ago and said that Beauregard turned his flank and found it was actually our boys. I think someone needs to suggest we all wear the same uniforms instead of each regiment having their own styles—handsome as they are, sir. It's too confusing. We've plenty of Federals to fight without shooting at each other by mistake."

The officer petted the neck of his sweaty horse as he listened. "Let us hope there's no need for coordinated uniforms, that today has finished it," he answered. "There's enough dead out there on the field as it is. Many more than any of us anticipated."

"Amen to its being over," Laurence muttered. "Stay here on the porch a moment, Annie. I'm going to see if I'm needed. I'll return."

A soft, damp night breeze brushed Annie and cooled her. She looked up to the sky and tried to close her ears to the sounds around her as she searched for constellations—Orion, the hunter; Draco, the dragon; Gemini, the twins. There. A thin ribbon of golden light streaked the blackness. She closed her eyes and made a wish on the falling star, a wish for things to be normal again.

"*She walks in beauty, like the night / Of cloudless climes and starry skies* . . . although it does look like it's beginning to cloud up a bit."

Annie jumped at the sound of the soft voice behind her. Half lying, half propped against the wall, was Thomas Walker of Massachusetts. She'd almost stepped on him. She'd been so preoccupied by Laurence and the scene on the fields before her, she'd missed the fact that there were still wounded men and the Federal surgeon on the front porch—now, however, carefully watched by a Confederate soldier.

"Sir . . . forgive me. I didn't see you."

"It's all right, Miss Sinclair. I know you were rejoicing in your brother's safety."

Annie felt herself blush. He'd heard everything, of course. She wasn't offended, simply embarrassed. Her mother and her schoolteachers had drilled manners into her, and it was extremely rude to have completely missed his presence. "Do . . . " She was unsure how to proceed. Lord, how topsy-turvy the world had become; this certainly wasn't a social situation her etiquette classes had ever mentioned. "Do you need anything else?"

"No, thank you. I feel much better. I've had water and a little corn bread. One of the youngsters brought it to me." He gestured to the lawn, and Annie saw Sally carrying a tray of corn bread. Mother must have seen to that. Again she was embarrassed—she should be helping. "It was very tasty. You have been very kind to us, miss."

Annie nodded. She started to go down the stairs, but curiosity got the better of her. "What was that verse you spoke? I'm not familiar with it."

"It's Byron. Lord Byron. I'm afraid I have a weakness for England's Romantic poets. Not something I spoke much of while I attended West Point."

"Do you know the rest of it?" she asked. "I

love Keats. I haven't read this Byron."

He nodded and recited:

> *"She walks in beauty, like the night*
> *Of cloudless climes and starry skies;*
> *And all that's best of dark and bright*
> *Meet in her aspect and her eyes. . . ."*

He paused. "I could write it down for you, miss, if you have paper and ink."

"Oh, I'd love to have it. It's beautiful." Somehow poetry had normalized the strangeness of their meeting and conversation. For a moment, Annie forgot that this man was a declared enemy of her family, her homeland, her way of life. She liked him. And then she hated herself. She should be helping her Confederate protectors, not mooning over some Unionist, no matter how much poetry he could recite. She gathered her skirts and stepped backward down the stairs.

"I should see to our soldiers, sir. I wish you a speedy recovery."

"Thank you, miss."

She walked a few paces and heard, "You know, Miss Sinclair, those constellations you were looking at . . ."

Annie stopped. "Yes? What about them?" She hoped for another verse of poetry.

"Well . . . one of them is very important. The Little Dipper. Slaves call it the Drinking Gourd. I've read that they follow it—the North Star is the tip of the handle—over the Mason-Dixon Line to freedom."

Annie stiffened and her voice became icy. "My brother does not fight to keep slavery, sir."

"No? Are you sure, miss? Do you have any slaves?"

Annie's face grew hot. They did, but it wasn't the way Northern abolitionists portrayed it. Hickory Heights' servants were like family almost. There were seven of them, living in decent cottages with their own vegetable plots and flocks of chickens, which they could sell to make money of their own. Against Virginia law, Miriam taught them to read. She tended them when they were sick. One, "Grandma Hettie," had been retired for years, living in leisure and health, visited daily by Miriam before she died last year at the age of eighty-two.

It seemed to Annie that their servants were better treated and cared for than the factory workers in the North, many of whom were immigrants, paid next to nothing and then cut off and cast aside to starve in city slums once age or illness or injury made them useless to the rich factory owners and merchants. But . . . Hickory Heights' servants weren't exactly free. It was something Laurence had spoken of doing as soon as he came of age and could legally do it. That had been in May. The war had simply interrupted all his plans for the farm.

"It really is none of your business, sir," said Annie primly. "We are not like the cotton plantations or the cane-brakes down south. We are good to our people. We take care of them. My brother's man begged to follow him into battle, he loves him so. Laurence and he grew up together. What we fight for is our freedom, our ability to govern ourselves in a way that answers our needs, not those of Boston shipbuilders." She couldn't help a final dig: "Besides, there are still many slaveholders within your sanctimonious Union. Slavery is still legal in the city of Washington, and in Maryland, Delaware, Kentucky, and Missouri. Lincoln's own in-laws own slaves. I read that many of your generals and senators do as well. What we can't abide about you people is that you don't practice what you preach."

Thomas Walker smiled and nodded. "You're correct. Our mission right now is simple: to save the Union. President Lincoln has not outlawed slavery. Four of the states in the Union still condone it. Probably some members of President Lincoln's cabinet own slaves. But someday this war will also be about slavery. You'll see. And I sense a great kindness in you, miss, if you don't mind my forwardness. I'm afraid bluntness is a New England trait. I think it will eventually strike you that fighting for your freedom while denying others theirs is unconscionable."

Annie could barely breathe, she was so angry—angry because she knew that no matter how kind their family or friends might be to their servants, it would never make up for the horrible fact of slavery. Angry because Northerners assumed everyone in the South mistreated slaves and wanted slavery to continue, while the reality was that the overwhelming majority of Southerners, like her aunt Molly and uncle John, had none. Angry because in her heart, she knew this Yankee was right. It was unconscionable.

Slavery was not what her brother fought for. He fought to protect his family and his farm and because Virginia was his country. And yet, his valiant courage would always be tainted by the assumption.

"I hope . . . I hope they lock you up for a long, long time," she finally sputtered as she turned and fled into the night.

CHAPTER FOUR

For the next few hours, Annie fell to helping Confederate soldiers with a vengeance. She brought water. She served corn bread. She tore Aunt Molly's cotton bedsheets into bandage strips and walked among the soldiers awaiting medical attention. She held the hands of the young and thanked the older ones for defending Virginia.

Well past midnight, she pulled a jacket over a slumbering boy who had fallen asleep in the middle of telling his battle experiences. He was that weary. He'd been one of the lucky ones, just scratched up and scared. Looking at his face at peace, Annie reckoned him to be about her age. Risking his life before he'd even lived it. And here she was, talking poetry with a man who might have shot the boy down.

She stayed kneeling beside him and bowed her

head in prayer. The battle had raged on a Sunday and the irony of all this killing on a church day did not escape her. Her prayers felt hollow, and Annie looked down at the boy again. His forehead was awash in perspiration. Funny, it hadn't looked like that a minute ago, and the night was a pleasant one. Annie put her hand to his head. It was hot as a stovepipe. "Good Lord," she murmured. He was burning up with fever. No wonder he fell asleep mid-sentence. Remembering her mother's care for her, Annie doused a linen scrap in water, squeezed, folded it, and pulled it gently across his throat, cheeks, and forehead.

"Sweet lady, I hope if I fall in battle, you are there to nurse me."

A pair of thigh-high riding boots with spurs stood before her. In the moonlight, a saber scabbard gleamed alongside. Annie looked up at one of the hairiest men she'd ever seen. Even in daylight it would have been hard to make out his features behind the thick beard that stuck out a good two inches from his face. Still, his voice marked him as a gentleman.

As the man bowed, sweeping his arm out before him like a courtier of old, Laurence hurried up behind him.

"Colonel, I'd like to present my sister, Annie." Laurence helped Annie to her feet. "Annie, this is Colonel James Ewell Brown Stuart."

So this was the man, known as Jeb Stuart, whom her brother so admired. He was much shorter than she'd imagined, but quite broad across the shoulders, giving him an illusion of great stature. "It is an honor, sir. My brother has spoken so wondrously of you and your influence on your men."

"Yes? Well, that's fine. Corporal Sinclair is a good lad. Excellent horseman. But of course, your brother is a Virginia boy and we're born in the saddle, aren't we? If he keeps things up, he'll be a colonel himself before long. Do you ride, miss?"

"Oh, yes, sir." Annie thought of her beloved Angel Wings, her ink-black mare with the long white stockings that accentuated the delicacy of her legs as she trotted. She'd give anything to be home and heading out riding the next morning instead of here.

"Actually, Colonel, my sister is quite the equestrian. And a daredevil." Laurence smiled. "I wanted to give her one of my brood mares when she was about ten years old, but she'd have none of it. 'Too poky,' Annie said. So she picked the wildest mare I had. Beautiful mover, but a mind of her own, very forward under saddle. Fast as Mercury.

"Well, the two are peas in a pod. Angel—a ridiculous name for that horse, given her temperament—won't let anyone ride her but Annie. Together, she and Annie lead the hunt. She shows up some of the men dreadfully who don't ride half as well as she does. My mother despairs that Annie will never attract a husband, embarrassing all the county's bucks as she does. And I don't know how many times my mother has asked that Annie not jump the orchard fences—they're close to four feet high—and how many times she's done just that despite my instructions."

Annie blushed. Must Laurence always talk about her headstrong misbehavior?

"Really?" Stuart took off his hat in salute. "You must do me the honor of riding with me one day, Miss Annie. I have a wonderful mare myself—Skylark's her name. I wager she could jump an eight-foot ditch for me if she had to. We'll bring along your brother to tell us which fences we're allowed to jump, eh?" He laughed, a loud, hearty sound that caught the attention of a crowd of nearby cavalrymen.

"Hey, Colonel." "Congratulations, Colonel." "That was a rousing day, Colonel." "On three, boys, hurrah for Virginia! One-two-three: Hurrah!"

Under that mop of beard, Stuart smiled. He waved.

"Come taste this fine Unionist champagne, Colonel!" one man shouted cordially, holding aloft a bottle.

"Not I, boys. I promised my dear mother when I was twelve years old and left for school that I'd never touch liquor. I'm twenty-nine and I never have. Never will. I'll have coffee instead," Stuart called back.

"Yes, sir. I'll fetch some. We even have some sugar to sweeten it tonight, Colonel."

"Excellent," Stuart roared. "I'll join you in a moment." He bowed again at Annie. "My apologies. I must leave you to celebrate our victory with our boys. But never forget that it is for ladies such as you that we fight and we die." He leaned closer and said in a theatrically loud whisper, "I wouldn't worry about a husband. If they can't ride to keep up with you, you don't want them. And by this time next year, I imagine you'll have collected a dozen marriage proposals. You'll break all our hearts, Miss Annie, when you accept one."

Stuart strode off, his steps long, athletic, and powerful. Laurence watched him go, his face beaming with admiration. Annie felt breathless—as if she'd just been waltzed around a ballroom.

Stuart sat around the campfire for a long time, orchestrating a steady rise and fall of laughter and jokes. Musicians who traveled with him—a banjo picker, a fiddler, and a bones player—joined the circle. The men began singing jaunty Stephen Foster tunes such as "Oh! Susanna," "Camptown Races," and "Ring, Ring the Banjo."

Around midnight, as Annie slipped into the room she was sharing with her mother and girl cousins, the songs turned melancholy. She went to the small window. "*A hundred months have passed, Lorena / Since last I held your hand in mine . . .*"

Miriam came into the cramped bedroom, sighing with fatigue. As she undid her gray hair, beautifully thick and long, she joined Annie at the window and listened to the last words of the sad song: "*'Tis dust to dust beneath the sod / But there, up there, 'tis heart to heart.*"

She put her arm around Annie. Suddenly, Annie was crying.

"I'm sorry, Mother. I don't mean to be so weak," Annie mumbled into Miriam's dress.

"It's all right, child. It's just letting go of it now, you are. Go ahead and cry."

Annie's sobbing woke little Sally and Colleen.

Rubbing their eyes, they padded across the floor and hugged Annie's knees. The three girls, tall and tiny, clung to one another, and somehow Miriam managed to get her arms around them all.

"There, there, girls, it's all right. It's over now."

But somehow, in her soul, Annie knew it was not.

CHAPTER FIVE

September 11, 1861
Lewinsville, Virginia, just outside Washington, D.C.

Annie was sitting in the parlor of her father's cousin, trying to pay attention to a cake recipe. She and Miriam were houseguests in Cousin Eleanor's home in Lewinsville, just across the Potomac River from Washington, D.C. They were on their way home to Hickory Heights, but Annie and Miriam had traveled twenty miles in the opposite direction first to say good-bye to Laurence. Colonel Stuart's camp was just down the road in Falls Church, on a ridge that offered a distant view of the U.S. Capitol building. The carriage ride from Manassas had been long—almost five hours—and required an overnight stay.

Annie had argued mightily with Miriam over the choice of Cousin Eleanor for their host. Annie was frightened of the rather stern older lady, who clearly didn't much approve of Miriam. To make it worse, she was a staunch Unionist. Her husband, Francis, was a lawyer and often argued cases in the Federal court in Washington city. He'd joined the U.S. army in the spring and had been put to work in the quartermaster general's office making sure the army was well fed and outfitted with shoes and blankets. As a clerk, he would never aim a gun at Laurence. But Annie still couldn't believe that Miriam seemed so comfortable sitting and drinking tea with someone committed to crushing the Confederacy.

"It's not like that," Miriam had said the night before. "This war will put all of us in strange positions. No matter what happens, we are family. I myself would have preferred that we stayed in the Union, darling. There were many Virginians who cast their voices against secession, you know, when the legislature called for a popular vote. But ultimately Virginia felt it could not fight against its closest neighbors, that it could not stay without dishonor. Meanwhile, Annie, we will not forget our manners, especially toward a lady who is showing us kindness."

Annie had nodded silently, recognizing that Miriam was repeating many of Laurence's sentiments. He had expressed little confidence in the political party that had advocated secession, calling its leaders erratic, unprincipled, bombastic men. He felt it a bitter tragedy that the government created by fellow Virginians—Jefferson, Washington, and Madison—was being torn apart. And yet, when the breakaway politicians held sway and Virginia voted to secede, Laurence joined ranks immediately. "Virginia is my country," he'd said simply.

And in truth, things had become strangely quiet since the Battle of Manassas in July. Perhaps Annie's foreboding had been wrong. The Federals had settled quietly into their camps and the Confederates into theirs in a seemingly peaceful standoff. Right this very moment, Union troops were guarding the Chain Bridge, not five miles from where Stuart and his cavalry sat.

Oh, there had been the terrible cleanup of the Manassas battlefield. The Federals had left their dead behind, lying where they fell in the fight, expecting the Confederates or the locals to bury them. July downpours had made the work harder, more time-consuming, and more gruesome. And there'd been the sad funeral for Mrs. Henry, an eighty-five-year-old widow. She was bedridden and had refused to leave her home atop the hill named for her family. That hill became the center of fighting, a perfect landmark for the artillery of both sides to sight their targets.

More than a dozen cannonballs had crashed through Mrs. Henry's roof. Windows shattered. The house was riddled with bullets. A shell explosion had killed her.

This peaceful September morning, Annie refused to remember the revolting horrors she'd seen on her way to Mrs. Henry's funeral. Instead, she pictured the beautiful hedge of althea that circled the Henry house and had miraculously survived the battle. Annie had gathered an armload of the crimson-and-white blossoms to put on Mrs. Henry's coffin. As they'd crossed the fields in procession, Miriam had found several letters littering the ground, including a beautiful one written by a Northern lady to her husband, George. It had a return address. Miriam sent the touching letter home to the woman, with a note explaining how she'd found it and that she hoped George had survived the battle.

These were strange times indeed.

Annie shifted in her needlepoint chair and tried to focus on Cousin Eleanor. Now she was talking about how long the cake needed to bake. As if she really did the cooking. Cousin Eleanor had three freed Africans working for her—a cook, a gardener, and a driver who minded their carriage horses. Lizzie was a superb cook, but she didn't like visitors to her kitchen. Not like Annie's cook, their beloved "Aunt" May, who always had sweet tidbits hidden in the cupboards and who had encouraged Annie and Jamie to play marbles on the kitchen floor as she worked. Aunt May's hugs always left them dusty with flour.

Annie settled down to listen dutifully by reminding herself that the next day she'd be heading home to Aunt May, to Angel, to the hills, to the wind clouds that slid up to rest against the Blue Ridge. She'd even be glad to see Jamie, that rapscallion brother of hers, who was as full of himself as only a rooster or a thirteen-year-old boy could be. He evidently had tried to saddle up and head to Manassas when news of the fighting reached home. Fortunately, Aunt May and her husband, Isaac, had locked Jamie in his room.

Without realizing it, Annie giggled at the thought of the scene.

"Annie?" Miriam's gentle voice jerked Annie back to the parlor. "What's so funny, dear? Cousin Eleanor can surely use the benefit of something amusing."

"I'm sorry, Mother, Cousin Eleanor, I was . . . I

was just thinking about . . ." Annie stalled for time. Somehow she didn't think her prim, Unionist cousin would be amused by Jamie's antics. "I was just thinking about . . . that scene!" Praise God, Mr. Burton's literature class came back to her. "That scene in *Hamlet*, where the gravedigger pulls up Yorick's skull and . . ."

Miriam looked shocked. "A gravedigger? Mercy, that doesn't sound particularly amusing." She crossed herself superstitiously and then flushed at Cousin Eleanor's look of disapproval for her papist gesture. Miriam made her try-to-think-of-something-more-ladylike expression at Annie, a look Annie had seen a hundred times, then turned to Cousin Eleanor. "This"—she gestured toward Annie—"is my best-read child. I so wish her father had lived to enjoy her conversation. Thaddeus read everything. I'm afraid Annie is beyond me."

"I can see that, Miriam." Annie caught the contempt for her mother in Cousin Eleanor's remark. Why did her mother tolerate such things? But Annie's anger vanished at her cousin's next statement: "I have a great many books, child. Your father often lent volumes to me when we were younger. Would you care to pick out something to read this evening?"

"Oh yes," said Annie. She couldn't help swallowing the invitation whole, as a greedy duck would a June bug.

Cousin Eleanor's stiff skirt rustled as she led Annie to the next room, which was only a little alcove really, a circle of windows and a huge bookcase.

Annie ran her fingertips along the leather-bound books. So many of them—Shakespeare's tragedies; sets of poems by Robert Burns and Francis Scott Key; Sir Walter Scott's Waverley novels. Nathaniel Hawthorne's *The Scarlet Letter* and *The Blithedale Romance* surprised her a bit. They were recent Yankee novels, but she supposed that made sense given Cousin Eleanor's politics. Curiosity got the better of her, and she pulled *The Scarlet Letter* from the shelf.

Cousin Eleanor smiled—yet another surprise for Annie. Maybe the old lady wasn't really so bad. "You remind me of your father, Anne. I was quite fond of him really." As she turned, she murmured more to herself than to Annie, "Such a pity that hair is so red."

The ragged-edged pages were thick, the printing fine. This was a costly edition of the novel, Annie knew. She came to Hawthorne's description of Hester Prynne emerging from jail, holding her baby and stunning a jeering crowd with her dark-eyed dignity and the defiant, richly embroidered letter *A* on her clothes that branded her an adulteress.

Annie let out a schoolgirl's sigh. "How romantic and strong Hester is."

She stared out the window, daydreaming. After a few moments, Annie looked over her shoulder to make sure Miriam and Cousin Eleanor were still caught up in their conversation about household arts. She could hear Miriam worrying over the fact that Annie could never seem to complete a sampler. Annie rolled her eyes. "God save me from such conversations and concerns."

She reached into her pocket and pulled out an envelope. Her hands shook a bit as she unfolded a stiff piece of paper. It was a poem about Annie. And it was written by Colonel Jeb Stuart.

We met by chance; yet in that 'ventful chance
The mystic web of destiny was woven:
I saw thy beauteous image bending o'er
The prostrate form of one that day had proven
A hero fully nerved to deal
To tyrant hordes—the south avenging steel.

*

The handwriting was elegant, strong. No inkblots, no corrections. His signature was bold and large. It was a mild, Indian-summer morning, but Annie felt hot and jittery. Surely this was just a crusader's poem dashed off to honor a lady's youth and face. There is nothing to it, she cautioned herself. Just like you, Annie, to lose your head over nothing.

The day before, when visiting Laurence, Annie had seen several young women at the camp Stuart had set on Munson's Hill. Escorted by their mothers or brothers, the girls were all aflutter with the colonel's compliments and patriotic excitement. The colonel was even planning to award one pretty girl named Antonia Ford with a commission as an aide-de-camp in thanks and praise for the daring she had shown in delivering to him useful information she had overheard being discussed by Federal troops occupying her hometown, Fairfax Courthouse.

"He is forever swarmed by ladies," Laurence told Annie later. He grinned as he spoke, but there was a touch of disapproval in his voice, too. "He suggests we cultivate ladies to keep an eye on troop movements," Laurence continued, "but I don't like the idea of endangering them. We have plenty of scouts to do that job."

Stuart had presented his poem to Annie when Laurence was with Miriam, as if Stuart knew that Laurence might not like her receiving such attention.

Sitting in the alcove, Annie closed her eyes and relived what was surely the most exciting moment of her life.

Stuart had been dressed in his finest attire that day. His gray coat was slightly unbuttoned to reveal red silk lining. Huge gold braid climbed up his sleeves from his wrists in showy epaulets. A tasseled silk sash was tied about his waist. Tucked into it were white buckskin gloves. And his eyes—she hadn't been able to see them before on that night of Manassas—his eyes were shockingly clear, bright blue against his sun-browned face and his bushy beard.

Annie remembered the scent of well-worn leather as he leaned over her hand to kiss it. She felt him squeeze her fingers, felt the warmth of his breath against her glove. He had pressed the envelope into her hand as he straightened up. His jovial blue eyes never left her green ones as he spoke.

"This is a token of my appreciation of your devotion to our country, Miss Annie. Please accept my pledge of lasting friendship." His gaze made her quivery, and he laughed gently as he stepped back, clearly aware of his effect on her. Yet there was no flirtation in what Stuart said next. His voice was matter-of-fact. "You don't know it yet, but you are a soldier's dream. As this war goes on, you will serve as inspiration to our men. Not all our ladies will prove as true. Take care of yourself."

He'd walked away in that bold stride of his, followed by his two setters, Nip and Tuck, calling out to a ventriloquist who'd come to entertain the camp. Annie's heart kept pounding until he was out of sight, swallowed up by the carnival-like crowd.

Now Annie sighed again, and read the poem to memorize it.

I saw thee soothe the soldier's aching brow
And ardent wished his lot were mine

. . . .

And fortune smile upon thee ever,
And when this page shall meet your glance
Forget not him you met by chance.

Restless, Annie wandered out into Cousin Eleanor's garden for some air. Hundreds of pink rosebuds paraded along the white picket fence. Annie bent to inhale their delicate scent. She cupped her hands around some of the blooms, as if they were a bride's bouquet. A honeybee crawled off a rose onto her hand, and its hairy legs tickled her before it drifted off. Annie could see the white beehive in the back of the garden and knew it was probably stuffed with honey.

Inside the fence, lima bean, squash, and grape vines, plus currant and raspberry bushes, were already picked clean. Only the pumpkin vines were still thick and green. It was a tiny garden by Annie's standards. Clearly her cousins depended on local markets for a great deal of their food, something she would find alarming. Hickory Heights' fields and livestock filled almost all their needs.

As she lingered, Annie heard voices. At first, she thought nothing of it. Cousin Eleanor's house was near the road that ran from Langley to Falls Church. The dirt byway was often traveled.

But she also knew that Stuart placed pickets along the road, men hidden behind trees and bushes, to watch for possible Union movement. Laurence had told her that they were constantly sending out scouts to check on the whereabouts of the "bluebirds," as he called them. Federals did the same. Could these voices be such a reconnaissance group? She stood frozen in stillness, straining her ears, wishing a cat-bird would shut its beak and stop singing!

She could hear horses kicking up stones as they trotted. They must be coming up the road from Falls Church. Stuart's boys? Annie straightened her skirts and pinched her cheeks to make them pink. But as she put her hand on the gate to swing it open and to step out to greet them, the sound of their voices stopped her.

One was calling into the woods along the road. "Captain wants you back right now. How many did you see?"

"Must have been fifty, camped out for the night. Maybe a hundred. Maybe more. They took off lickety-split all right."

"Confound it, man, how many was it?"

Another voice interrupted: "You mean they saw you?"

There was a silence and then: "Suppose so, sir."

Annie felt a tingling up her spine. There were no drawls in those voices, no soft rounded *r*s. The voices were clipped and nasal. The last voice she'd heard like that had belonged to that insolent Thomas Walker, the Massachusetts man lying on Aunt Molly's front porch.

Annie hurled herself behind the veil of grapevines that had been trained to grow up a trellis. The men weren't coming along the road. It sounded as if they were moving through the woods to conceal themselves.

"There was an exchange of fire between a handful of Stuart's riders and some of our Vermont boys as they came back from reconnaissance. We're bringing out more artillery guns, cavalry, and three regiments of infantry from Camp Advance right now. Upward of eighteen hundred men. The plan's to go ahead and occupy Lewinsville today. Five roads cross here; they're important."

As the man talked, Annie felt them pass along the length of the garden, hidden behind a thick grove of trees.

The voices were getting fainter. "There's an engineer officer with the expedition, says he was a classmate of Stuart's at West Point. You know, it seems they all know one another from there. 'Old Beaut,' the officer said, 'is just like a cat. Curiosity will get him. He won't take time to figure our number. He'll just ride out.' Then the officer told us not to hurt him any; he wanted to treat Stuart to dinner in Washington. . . ."

Annie could hear no more. It didn't matter. She was going. Going to warn Stuart and Laurence.

CHAPTER SIX

Annie didn't stop to consider how dangerous warning the Confederates would be or what might happen to her if she ran into Union troops. All she knew was that her brother and that dashing Colonel Stuart were in peril—that the Federals were heading her way *again.*

How could she stand by like a simpering coward and let her countrymen be overwhelmed by greater numbers? Perhaps if she forewarned the Southern cavalry, she could somehow prevent a skirmish from happening at all. Maybe if he knew how many Federals were coming at him, Colonel Stuart would withdraw to a safer area. It would mean that Lewinsville, Annie, and her mother would be engulfed within enemy lines. But that was all right, because they were leaving for home tomorrow anyway. Just as long as there wasn't some terrible battle to witness and more dead to bury afterward. Annie would do anything to avoid that nightmare again.

No, the only questions remaining were: How would Annie get to Stuart's men? And should she ask permission from her mother first, before leaving? The second question Annie dispensed with quickly. Her mother would never let Annie go on such a bold errand. She'd have to leave without being seen by Miriam, Cousin Eleanor, or her servants.

The first question was more of a dilemma. Annie could walk the three miles, but it would take way too long. She couldn't hitch up the carriage. She didn't know how, and it would be too obvious on the road. No, she'd have to ride one of the carriage horses.

Annie scampered to Cousin Eleanor's small stable and peeped around the door. She didn't see Cousin Eleanor's man. She tiptoed in, her carpet slippers making no sound.

The horses were munching on hay, swishing their tails against flies. They looked up at her sleepily. Which to pick? She didn't know any of them. The Union forces had stolen the carriage horses that Miriam had brought from home. The two she and Miriam had used to travel to Lewinsville had been replacements, given to Miriam from the many left behind in the retreat. They were steady, but old and slow.

Cousin Eleanor's pair were better fed, and had sleeker coats, no obvious scars or bangs on their forelegs. One had kinder eyes and welcomed her petting his soft, whiskered muzzle. He'd do.

Annie looked at the tack hanging on the wall. It was almost all carriage harnesses and reins. There was only one saddle: a man's saddle. She hadn't thought about that. Cousin Eleanor clearly didn't ride. There was no side-saddle for Annie to use.

Annie's face flamed in frustration. If she was caught riding astride the horse, she'd shame her family yet again. Curse propriety. Sidesaddles made no sense at all anyway. It was ludicrous trying to jump fences with both legs pinned on the left side of a horse—there was no way to balance, no way to stay on except sheer determination. The best riding she'd ever done was bareback when no one was looking, her legs wrapped around Angel's rib cage.

For pity's sake. Annie steeled herself. You are wasting time.

She grabbed a bridle. At home, Annie rarely tacked up Angel. Their groom, Gabriel, did it. But she knew how. Annie struggled to pull the bridle over the huge horse's head. He didn't like the bit and stamped his feet impatiently.

"There, boy, it's all right, good boy," Annie crooned, but the horse continued to pace and rustle.

Bother, Annie fussed at the noise. I'll be found out.

Pop-pop-pop-pop.

The horse yanked up his head and pricked his ears nervously. His nostrils flared wide, trying to smell what he could hear.

Annie heard, too, and recognized it immediately. No more mistaking the sounds of conflict. Manassas had taken that innocence from Annie. It was gunfire, still far off, but shots answering shots.

No time left. She'd have to do without a saddle.

Annie pulled the horse out of the stall and found a mounting block outside. As she hurried, her ruffled petticoat caught about her knees. What a nuisance. The layers of flounces would make her slide all over the horse since she wouldn't have stirrups to steady her. Without hesitating, Annie did another scandalous thing—she reached up under the skirt of her mauve-colored visiting dress and pulled off her petticoat, leaving only her knee-length drawers as undergarments. She left it there, a perfectly round circle of lace. She grabbed hold of the horse's mane and jumped on, bundling her silk skirts up around her thighs.

At first the horse just stood, dumbfounded at the feel of a person rather than a harness on his back. But he was a willing sort and gladly lumbered away without the weight of a wagon behind him.

Annie moved into the woods, paralleling the road. She remembered that it led directly to Stuart's camp. She kicked the horse into a jostling trot and gritted her teeth as she banged against his spine.

Hurry up, you old thing, she muttered. She goosed him into a canter. This was a smoother gait, but the speed was risky through the woods, where low branches and hanging vines of Virginia creeper blocked her way. Branches and briers scraped her face and tore at her sleeves. But Annie was unaware of the scratches. Her skirt billowed up and down like a sail as the horse surged on, obviously happy to be out and moving freely.

Pop-pop-pop-pop-pop.

Gunfire again.

BOOM-BOOM.

Now cannon fire, too. But it was farther behind her now. Annie was definitely making distance. How much farther? she wondered. Maybe fifteen more minutes. Could the horse keep up the pace? She patted his neck and listened to his heavy breathing.

So far it was even. She knew better than to push an out-of-condition horse this hard, but she had no choice.

"Come on, old fellow," she spoke, and he lifted his ears to listen.

Annie ducked and leaned and threaded their way through thick pines and tall pin oaks. The ground was uneven with roots, and Annie tried to avoid fallen branches, figuring the carriage horse hadn't jumped anything in ages. They careened down a ditch and scrambled up the other side. Annie reached up to push her hair off her face—the jostling ride had knocked loose her hairpins. And that's when she made a mistake. She didn't see the fallen tree.

"Oh, my Lord," she breathed as she felt the horse pull himself into a massive ball of muscle and then spring up and over the three-foot log.

At just the right instant, Annie grabbed hold of his thick mane. She lifted up into the air, but her hands held firm and pulled her back down onto his back as he landed, panting, on the other side. Her neck whipped around and her bottom hurt mightily where it had banged hard against him at the landing, but she was still on him. "Good boy!" she gasped, and patted him. She fought the urge to let out a whoop of satisfaction. That had been something! What a ride.

As the two stood panting, the horse snorting and shaking his head, Annie heard leaves scattering. Squirrels darted up trees, spooked by something coming along the road. She listened harder and recognized the jingle and clatter of cavalry.

This *had* to be Laurence coming in that direction. Still, to be certain, Annie peered through the trees. She saw a huge group of horses and riders in Confederate gray uniforms. Awash in relief, Annie completely forgot her concern for propriety. She kicked the horse on. They popped out of the woods and slid down the embankment in a tumble of branches and loose stones and old leaves, the huge horse skittering to a gawky stop in the middle of the road.

The neat column of gray-clad riders jerked to a halt. A few of the sleek thoroughbred horses reared, startled by Annie's sudden and loud appearance. Some of the riders instinctively drew pistols or swords. For a long moment, they stood still eyeing Annie, Annie looking at them, her heart pounding, her hands shaking. Praise God! She'd found them. Oh, they'd be so glad to hear her information.

"The Federals," she croaked, for her throat was parched, her mouth full of dust from her helter-skelter ride. Annie pointed back behind her. "They're coming with infantry and guns. . . ."

No one moved. None of them seemed to understand her. They were looking at her as if she were a madwoman. With a horrible realization, Annie's hands flew up to her hair. It was half up, half down. Twigs stuck through it. Her face was damp, and when she pulled back her hands, she saw a smudge of blood on her fingertips. She looked down and saw that one pagoda sleeve was torn, lace dangling. She'd even lost a shoe.

Tears of embarrassment filled her eyes. "The Federals . . ." She tried again but could say no more. The vision of the horsemen blurred. Through her mist of tears, she saw one detach from the group and ride closer. She blinked to clear her vision and saw he had on a hat with a fluttering plume. As he got closer, he began to roar with laughter. "Miss Annie!" he called. "As I live and breathe . . . Miss Annie . . . You are like Liberty herself riding to our aid." An aide shadowed Jeb Stuart as he trotted toward her.

Hastily, Annie did her best to calm her hair and wipe away her tears. Stuart reined in his horse beside her and grinned. "You absolutely awe me, Miss Annie." The aide behind him did not look as impressed.

"Colonel Stuart," she began breathlessly, "please forget my appearance right now, but I had to warn you. Warn you about something I overheard Federal troops saying as they passed by my cousin's house three miles back." She turned and pointed. "They were saying that they're going—"

"To bring up an entire brigade?"

Annie gasped. "Why, yes, exactly."

"I know." Stuart smiled at her.

"And guns and—"

"And reinforced cavalry." Stuart beamed at her. "Yes, I know. My scouts brought back the news about an hour ago. We're heading out now to scare them off."

"But Colonel, they will so outnumber you. They said they'll mass eighteen hundred men. And, sir, I can't see all your riders, but it looks like you have only . . ." Annie tried to count Stuart's horsemen.

"About six hundred." He interrupted her again. He seemed greatly amused by the whole thing.

Annie shook her head. That meant the Union had a three-to-one advantage over the Confederate riders. She couldn't understand why Stuart wasn't turning them around.

Stuart spoke quietly to his aide. "Go back and find Corporal Sinclair and ask him to come forward to me."

The aide shot Annie one more disapproving

look and clucked to move his horse away.

Stuart pulled from his waistcoat a monogrammed handkerchief. He opened his canteen and doused the cotton square in water, handing it to Annie. "You've scratches on that beautiful face, Miss Annie. Best wipe it clean."

Annie took the handkerchief. "Colonel," she tried again, "there'll be too many of them."

"Tut, tut, Miss Annie. Don't you worry." He stopped smiling and became earnest. "If we oppose force to force in this war, we cannot win. You are right. Their resources are greater than ours." Then he leaned back in his saddle, putting his hand on his hip, and grinned again. "We must substitute esprit for numbers. We can win through our spirit of the chase."

He turned in his saddle, the leather squeaking as he did. He called back to his riders, "We're off to hunt bluebirds, eh, boys?"

"Yeeehaw, Colonel," some called back. "Let's ride!"

At that moment, Laurence rode up on his favorite dappled gray horse, Merlin. The shocked, then embarrassed, look on his face when he saw Annie about broke her heart. She hung her head.

Stuart caught their exchange and spoke loudly

enough for his riders to hear. "Now, Corporal Sinclair. I have found Lady Liberty on the road here, and she is in need of an escort. She rode out to warn us of Federal movements. I am giving you the honor of seeing this lady to safety."

"Come, boys." He lifted his hat in salute to Annie. "Tip your hat to the lady as you go." He spurred away.

Annie tried to smile at the hundreds of faces as they cantered by, hats held aloft, some smiling, some just staring, some sniggering at her.

Then she turned to face Laurence.

For an awful pause he said absolutely nothing. Then he held up his hand to silence her. Annie knew that look of carefully contained anger. "Do not speak to me," he said as he took his horse into a slow trot.

Annie dutifully followed. But her horse was tired and no longer excited about his adventure. He wanted to walk and kept breaking his trot. The road was tough going now, pitted by the hundreds of hooves that had just thundered through. Within a few minutes, Laurence was well ahead of her.

"Laurence," she called. "Wait!" Suddenly Annie was afraid to be alone. All her courage was used up.

Atop a rise in the road, Laurence turned his horse to a halt. He sternly waved at her to hurry up. Annie booted her horse into a disgruntled trot and bounced, bounced, bounced up to Laurence.

As she reached him, she saw a glimmer of a smile on his face. Then he snorted and dropped his head, shaking it. The laughter started in his shoulders, and pretty soon his whole body was rocking with it. He actually had to wipe his eyes as he finished laughing. "Lord, Annie, you are hard to brother. What a mess you look. What am I to do with you?"

Annie smiled back. How many times had they had a conversation like this? "I'm sorry if I embarrassed you, Laurence. I know I look ridiculous. But I couldn't stand by and do nothing."

Laurence's amusement disappeared. "Yes, Annie, you could have and you must in the future. Think what might have happened to you if you'd been caught. Right off to Old Capitol Prison, I imagine."

Annie pursed her lips. How could Laurence not understand?

Laurence softened. He'd never been able to lord it over Annie for long. In truth, she knew that he was usually proud of her gumption. That's what had made it possible for her to take his reprimands in the past. She knew that for the most part he said them because he had to, not necessarily because he believed them.

Her brother laughed. "Prison would probably be good for you." Then he grew serious. "Think, though, Annie, the worst thing would have been if you'd gotten caught in crossfire between us and the Feds. Some boys would have shot first and looked to see who you were later. You're our only Sinclair girl, you know. You're precious. How d'you think Mother would survive your getting killed?"

Annie started to say that she expected Miriam would take it a lot worse if Laurence were killed, but then a different thought interrupted her. "Oh, no. Mother." She looked down at her dress and its torn sleeves, the dirty skirt, her bare foot. "How am I going to go back to the house looking like this?"

"How, indeed?" asked Laurence with a grin. "Come on." He turned his horse. "We'll figure out something as we go."

As they rode, the sounds of battle began to greet them. Not as loud or constant as Manassas, not at all. But there was a definite scrap going on, not far off. Laurence grew impatient. "I should be with my men," he muttered. "We need to hurry."

They darted into the trees before they got to Cousin Eleanor's house. Everyone was on the front porch, their backs to Laurence and Annie, looking toward the sounds of fighting.

Laurence turned to Annie. "Here's what we do. Just like that time you fell in the pond and I had to distract Mother while you got inside the house and changed. Remember?"

Annie nodded.

"I'm going to ride in as if I'm carrying messages from camp to Colonel Stuart. You creep in the back way. Put that horse in the stable. And get inside. Throw a shawl over those sleeves, fix your hair, and maybe you can get away with it. Ready?"

She nodded.

"Next time I see you, miss, I want to see a proper lady." Laurence winked.

"Heeyaw." He took off his hat and whacked his horse with it, sending them racing toward Cousin Eleanor's house, kicking up mud and rocks. Annie dropped off her horse and quickly led him toward the stable.

Laurence wheeled to a stop right in front of the group, bringing a dramatic cloud of dust and debris up behind him, momentarily fogging everyone's view in a perfect screen for Annie. She slipped into the stable, left the huge horse gratefully drinking water in his stall, padded silently upstairs, found her evening shawl, pushed her hair back and pinned it tight. She even had the foresight to grab the book she'd been reading as she passed on her way toward the open front door.

Annie appeared just as Miriam was saying, "I'm so worried, Laurence. I can't find Annie anywhere."

"Here I am, Mother. I'd sat down by a shade tree at the edge of the wood to read and I must have fallen asleep."

"With all this noise, darling?" Miriam looked at Annie with complete disbelief. Annie fidgeted. She saw the growing look of suspicion on her mother's face. And then—horrors—her mother's eyes fell to her feet. Annie had forgotten her missing shoe!

Fortunately, Cousin Eleanor was looking at Laurence. "Are you riding out to join them, Laurence?" There seemed to be no conflict between them, despite her loyalty to the Union.

"Yes," Laurence answered.

"Be careful," Cousin Eleanor said quietly.

He tipped his hat. "Yes, ma'am, I will."

Miriam simply held up her arms. Laurence leaned over and kissed her. "It'll be all right, Mother. Stay in the house." Then he rode away.

Annie had seized the chance to tuck her foot carefully up under her skirts and even to slump a little so that her hem touched the floor. Walking in such a manner, she managed to conceal her bare toes for an hour. She was convinced that Miriam had forgotten what she'd seen.

That night news reached Cousin Eleanor's house that the skirmish was over quickly. Even though they had the greater numbers, the Federals had been completely flustered by the surprise charges of Stuart's riders from the woods. Assuming Stuart had more riders than he actually did, given their bold attacks, the Federals broke rank. They eventually re-formed, only to withdraw back over the Potomac River to Washington. Not one Stuart man or horse was hurt.

Annie silently reveled in their victory. She hadn't really had anything to do with it. Colonel Stuart had already known everything she'd ridden out to tell him. But she was pleased with herself all the same. She was especially smug about the fact that she'd managed to keep her ride a secret. That hadn't been easy to accomplish, either. It'd been a long time until Annie had been able to slip upstairs and grab another pair of shoes and a clean petticoat. Getting back out into the garden to retrieve the one she'd left behind was impossible. Miriam wouldn't let her out of the house again for fear of soldiers.

As she crawled into bed, Annie resolved to wake up before dawn and retrieve her underwear from the garden before anyone else was awake. Then her subterfuge would be complete! Annie flopped over and closed her eyes with a self-satisfied smile on her face.

The door clicked open and Miriam tiptoed into the room. Annie sat up. She chirped: "Good night, Mo—" But she didn't finish, clapping her hands over her mouth.

In Miriam's hand was Annie's telltale petticoat. Her mother dropped it on the floor and gave Annie that raised eyebrow look she knew so well.

Annie scrambled to explain.

"I don't want the details, child," Miriam silenced her. "I know how many times you and your brother have conspired against me. I trust Laurence to know what he's doing. And you"—she kissed Annie on the forehead—"I trust you will have *all* your things put together before we leave tomorrow morning. I don't think Cousin Eleanor needs to know of any shenanigans."

CHAPTER SEVEN

December 24, 1861
Hickory Heights, between Middleburg and Upperville, Virginia

"They're pulling in a Yule log the size of a hog," Jamie said as he reached for the raspberry preserves. "You seen it, Mother? It'll burn all twelve nights for sure."

Gently, Miriam laid her hand over Jamie's. "Don't reach across the table, son. Say, 'Please pass the preserves,' and then wait for us to do so."

"Aw, for pity's sake, Mother, no one cares about manners in these times. There's a war on! Besides, I'm the man of the house nowadays. Laurence says so, until he gets back. You can't go correcting the man of the house, you know." Jamie swelled himself up like a turkey about to gobble.

"I certainly can if that man acts like a baby and

leans over the table for sweets. Now finish your breakfast, darling. I want you and Annie to collect holly for me to put on the mantelpieces. The servants are busy stacking wood and preparing the feasts for us and for them."

Jamie made another unhappy face and slumped in his chair. Annie rolled her eyes. Jamie had been near impossible since they'd returned home. The idea of spending an hour in the woods clipping holly branches and listening to his complaints didn't sound like much fun at all. Whenever he had Annie alone, he'd start in on her about wanting to join up as a drummer boy like one of his schoolmates at Middleburg Academy had done. Miriam, of course, would have none of it. Annie agreed with her.

"You don't know anything about how it is," Annie had told him.

"Oh, and you do, I suppose?" he'd snapped back.

"As a matter of fact, Mr. Smarty, Mother and I both saw what a battle is like, and it's no place for a child, especially a hothead like you, Jamie."

That's when he'd thrown a checkers piece at her. She'd hurled one back and they'd both ended up in their bedrooms for the rest of the day with only bread and milk for dinner.

"Doesn't Miss Miriam have enough to worry about without having two varmints for children?" Aunt May had scolded them when she'd brought their dinner trays. "What would Mr. Thaddeus have said? Don't you be shaming his memory."

Annie didn't know which was worse—a tongue-lashing from Aunt May or her mother's quiet look of disappointment. On Christmas Eve she wanted to be a help, not a nuisance. "Mother, I can gather the holly myself," she offered. "I'll enjoy the walk. It's not so very cold today. Give Jamie some other chore, something appropriate for a man of the house." She smiled at Jamie to reassure him that she wasn't goosing him with sarcasm. She meant it as a compliment.

"Thank you, Annie," said Miriam. "But I'd rather Jamie go along. I worry how safe the woods are these days."

"But Mother, it's safe as can be. General Stuart is encamped in Centreville along with Johnston's infantry. That's several thousand men in gray. The Federals aren't going to get past that to us."

But Annie knew what was worrying Miriam. Stuart had suffered his first real defeat just a few days before in Dranesville. Word had spread like a forest fire through Fauquier and Loudoun counties, from which so many of Stuart's riders came. While escorting Confederate army wagons out foraging for food, Stuart had stumbled onto three thousand Union soldiers doing the exact same thing. Stuart had only twelve hundred men. Stuart held on against two and a half times his number for two hours, but finally had to withdraw when the Federals brought in three more regiments from their nearby camps. Against such odds, Stuart amazingly had lost few men: only twenty-seven men killed, about a hundred wounded or captured. But Annie and Miriam didn't know for sure yet that Laurence had survived the fray safely.

Miriam shook her head at Annie and her voice was shaky as she said: "I'll feel better if you have him with you, Annie."

For once, Annie knew better than argue. She looked at Jamie and used what little big-sister authority she had. "We'll leave in an hour, Jamie. Let's wait until the sun's a little warmer."

Jamie actually agreed, obviously satisfied with the notion that he was to be her protector. As if he and his freckles could do anything to fend off a bunch of Yankees.

Upstairs in her room, Annie found Rachel changing the linens. The daughter of Aunt May and Isaac,

Rachel was three years older than Annie. She was a beautiful girl with huge dark eyes and a slender build. Laurence's man, Sam, was way sweet on her. Annie was sure they'd marry someday. Since Rachel was the only other girl vaguely her age at the house, Annie easily shared her thoughts with her, just as she had with her closest friends at school. Rachel, in fact, was the only person to whom she'd shown Stuart's poem. Miriam had taught Rachel to read, often alongside Annie, and Rachel had a hunger for pretty verse as well.

"Those are some handsome words, Miss Annie," she'd said.

Annie had flinched that time when Rachel had said *miss*. Ever since her heated exchange with the Massachusetts man, she had felt a new unease about her relationship with her servant. Annie considered Rachel a friend, family almost, but did Rachel feel the same?

"Rachel?" Annie began.

"Yes?" Rachel muttered. She had a pillow tucked beneath her chin as she pulled a new pillow-case on it.

"Have you had word from Sam?"

"No." Her lovely face clouded. "Maybe Gabriel could go into the village to find out?"

Annie nodded. "I'll ask Mother."

Annie pulled on two shawls, a cape, and a hand-knitted hat and mittens. She teased, "I'm heading out to pick holly. Should I find some mistletoe in case Laurence is granted a pass and Sam is here for Christmas?"

Rachel whacked Annie with the pillow. Annie grabbed another and whacked Rachel back. *Whack-whack. Whack-whack.* The girls giggled as goose down flew.

Falling onto the bed, gasping, Annie gave up. Rachel fell down beside her. "Get the mistletoe if you want, Annie," she whispered, "but be sure to invite that General Stuart of yours."

Annie sat up, instantly red-faced. "It's not like that, Rachel," she cried. "Not like that at all. He's just like . . . I don't know . . . like Ivanhoe and Rebecca. He's just gallant enough to compliment a lady's devotion to soldiers."

"Who?" Rachel looked at Annie blankly.

"Ivanhoe." Annie jumped off the bed and went to her dresser. There were three books atop it. "Here, read this." Annie held out Sir Walter Scott's novel.

"I can't take that."

"Yes, you can, Rachel. I know you can read this.

We've read harder things together. I can explain some of it as you go, if you need."

"I mean I can't take that out of the house. Missus Miriam never gave me a book to read on my own. What if I got caught with that?"

"What do you mean?" Annie couldn't understand Rachel's having such a fear at Hickory Heights. "I'm lending it to you. Don't be silly, Rachel. You know Mother wouldn't mind."

Rachel looked at her skeptically. Annie took her hand and put the book in it. "It's fine. Please read it. I think you'll like it. It'll be lovely to talk about a book with someone. Poor Mother is too busy, and you know Jamie. I'm not sure he knows his ABCs."

Rachel sat looking at the book, running her hands along its smooth cover. She nodded.

"Good. That's settled." Annie left the room. Seeing Rachel hold the novel as if it were a jewel made Annie's face flush with embarrassment.

It hadn't really occurred to her before that Rachel might long for books of her own or feel that Annie and Miriam would begrudge her borrowing them. But of course, she would, wouldn't she, Annie puzzled out. We gave her the education to relish books, but not the means or environment to go out and buy them herself. Nobody in the area would sell

Rachel a book if she did manage to save enough money through selling her own chickens or vegetables, as Miriam allowed their servants to do. No matter how progressive they were at Hickory Heights, the general outside culture in Virginia was not.

Annie knew that Miriam considered Rachel part of the whole of Hickory Heights, her health and happiness Miriam's responsibility just as much as Annie's well-being was. And yet it was a second-class existence, the life of her servant, wasn't it?

Annie welcomed the cold air outside that shocked her brain clear of such troublesome thoughts. It was a beautiful December day with a cloudless sky, the blue made sharper by its being a backdrop to the black latticework of bare trees. As Annie waited for Jamie to come out the front door, she took in the sight of her home. Since returning in September, she'd so relished being there. Perhaps it was because she'd arrived just as the hickory trees surrounding the house flamed golden for autumn. Perhaps it was because she now knew there was always the possibility of losing their home if the war came their way. Nothing could be taken for granted these days.

Hickory Heights had been built in the late 1700s and had spread itself out as her ancestors had grown in number. The kitchen addition was constructed of clapboard over logs. But the main part of the house was made of the dark gray fieldstone that surfaced everywhere in the surrounding foothills as they rolled themselves up to build the Bull Run Mountains to the east and the Blue Ridge Mountains to the west. In fact, Hickory Heights sat near three important westward passages to the Shenandoah Valley, the breadbasket of the Confederacy—Snicker's Gap, Ashby's Gap, and Manassas Gap. Laurence had worried mightily over this fact before he left, sensing that the gaps were dangerous back doors for Union troops. But so far the gaps had remained quiet and safe.

Annie could almost see Ashby's Gap from her bedroom window. Her room was in the back of the house—the northwest corner, from whence came the coldest winter winds. But though it was often frigid, the view was magnificent. Jamie's and Laurence's rooms were in the front, where it was sunniest, claiming the view down their lane to the main road, almost half a mile off. They had the advantage of looking out to see what visitors had arrived. Miriam had given up that master room to Laurence when he was eighteen years old and taken the other small, back bedroom beside Annie's. None of the four bedrooms were that big, and Annie marveled to remember—vaguely—how crowded the house had been when her three other brothers and her father had lived.

Jamie appeared at his bedroom window. She waved at him to come on. She could feel her nose beginning to numb. She imagined his route. Knowing Jamie, he'd slide down the banister and run into the parlor to kiss Miriam, who was undoubtedly figuring accounts or writing a letter at the corner desk. Then he'd run through the dining room and out the kitchen, hoping to steal another biscuit on his way.

She laughed out loud as he predictably popped out the side porch, holding up two biscuits like stolen loot. Some things the war hadn't changed.

Annie led their way past the herb gardens, the smokehouse, the icehouse, the chicken coops, and the stable and carriage house. She thought about riding Angel later. Her horse would be frisky in this cold.

Jamie tossed the remainder of his biscuit into the hog pen.

"You could have given that to me, you know,

little brother," she chided.

"Don't want you fat like some old lady," he joked. Womanly roundness was the fashion. Miriam was always complaining that Annie was too thin.

They passed the fenced orchards and the stubbly brown hay field, shorn of its timothy. Jamie scraped a stick along the fieldstone fence, scaring up into the air a covey of small brown quail. They paused to fill their basket with some chestnuts fallen to the ground, their prickly casings popped open. "We can roast these tonight," Annie suggested. "Let's try to be good for Mother. It's Christmas Eve, you know, and she's worried about Laurence."

"I know that," he said defensively, and then shrugged. "I can do that." He squared himself up and added: "And this!" Reaching underneath his coat to his back belt, Jamie pulled out a gun, aimed, and fired, knocking off a thin branch from a nearby dogwood tree. He staggered several steps from the explosion and coughed from the stench of burned powder.

The blast and the surprise of it knocked the breath from Annie. "Good God, Jamie!" She held her hand to her pounding heart. "What are you doing?" She reached out and grabbed the thing from Jamie. "Are you mad?"

The gun was hot and heavy, and she almost dropped it to the ground.

Jamie started laughing. "You're such a girl, Annie. That's why I'm here to protect you."

"Oh, Jamie, I could tell you . . . you . . . " She ached to tell him about her ride to Stuart. She was better than most girls. She could do a thing when she had to.

"Tell me what?" he sniped.

She started to tell him exactly what, but the thing in her hand stopped her. The heaviness of it—at least two pounds, maybe more—made her look down at it. There was a naval scene etched on its cylinder, a long barrel, and a walnut handle. But it was the cylinder that puzzled Annie. It looked as if it rotated and could hold more than one bullet at a time. Laurence didn't have anything like this gun. "Jamie, what is this? Where did you get it?"

He smiled slyly and stuck his thumbs in his pockets the way gentlemen did as they discussed politics in front of a fireplace. "I have my ways, little lady."

"Jamie, stop it. This isn't a game. This is real. Where did you get this thing?"

"I bought it off Edward for a gold piece. He'd ridden down to Manassas to look for souvenirs and found this lying by a dead Yankee. Edward took some of his buttons, too, but I didn't want any of those." Jamie jerked the foot-long gun back from Annie. "Edward came home with four of these—.44 army Colt revolvers. It's a six-shooter, Annie. I aim to use it myself to pick off as many of them Yankees as I can."

"Oh, Jamie." Annie felt sick. "You mustn't think that way. If you could see the misery these guns do to the body. You're just a boy, don't . . ."

"*Just* a boy." Jamie stepped back from her. "You wait and see, Annie. It'll be 'just boys' who'll save this country. Mother will be proud of me, if you're not. She'll finally think me as good as Laurence. You'll see."

"Jamie." Annie laid her hand on his shoulder. She hated hearing his jealousy of Miriam's affection for Laurence, because it reminded her of her own. And she was ashamed of it. Put into words, the thoughts sounded so petty and selfish. But they were there for both of them; she couldn't deny it. She recited to Jamie things she often said to herself: "Laurence is already a man; that's why she admires him so. When you're grown, she'll feel the exact same way about you. You'll see." But how could Miriam? Laurence was so fine. How could she and

Jamie ever compare?

Jamie shrugged her off and took aim again, this time back toward the house.

"Don't shoot again. You'll scare Mother silly," Annie cried, and pulled on his arm.

And just in time.

Over the knoll struggled Aunt May's husband. "Miss Annie? Master Jamie? You all right?"

"See?" Annie shook his arm as she let go. "You could have killed poor old Isaac."

"It'd serve him right for locking me up in my room when I wanted to get to Manassas," Jamie muttered as he thrust the revolver into his belt and covered it with his coat. "Oh, I don't mean it," he added when he saw Annie's shock.

He waved to Isaac. "We're down here. We're all right. I just tried to get us some squirrel." He whispered to Annie, "And someday I will, too. I could shoot the hat off a galloping Yankee with this if I had to."

CHAPTER EIGHT

Christmas Day, 1861
Hickory Heights

Annie sat up, shaking all over. She forced her eyes to clear and scan the blackness, her ears to listen carefully to the silence. Nothing. No cannon. No broken bodies rushing at her. It'd been a dream. Manassas again.

Wrapping her arms around her legs, Annie pushed the nightmare from her brain with daylight thoughts. How cold was it, anyway? Annie breathed out a thin vapor of steam. Frosty. She shuddered as she jumped out of bed and bundled herself in her quilt. Her feet ached at the bite of the cold pinewood floor. It was Christmas Day, and except for fixing meals and feeding the livestock, the servants were off work the twelve days of Christmas while the Yule log burned. Rachel did not have to help Annie kindle her bedroom fire this morning or the next eleven.

Annie blew on the embers of last night's fire. She slowly added wood to bring it to a full blaze and backed against the screen to stop her shivering. It was still dark, and the flames lit her room with a rosy, dancing light that cheered her. In preparation for the cold, Annie had carefully laid out her clothes to warm by the fire. Once she donned all the layers, she'd be fine, but getting them on would be a race against the chill. She puffed out some air again. This time she couldn't see mist from her breath. Time to dress. No dawdling.

Hurriedly, she pulled on wool stockings plus ruffled drawers cinched at her waist and below her knees. On top of her shift she fitted her corset. That, at least, would not have to be tied so tightly today, since Rachel wasn't there to yank the back draw-strings to strangling. Still, it was a day for fancy dress, and Annie dutifully stepped into her cagelike crinoline—a bell of oak-split circles and spines flaring out from the waist to make her hoop skirt four feet wide in diameter at the floor.

She was dressed enough now to survive washing. On the marble-top table beside her bed was a porcelain pitcher full of frigid water. A blast of wind rattled her windows. "*O Wind, / If Winter comes, can Spring be far behind?*" Annie mumbled a line from the poet Shelley as she scrubbed her face and brushed her teeth with a hog's bristle brush and ground-up charcoal from the fire ashes.

She picked up her favorite outfit, a dark green princess dress, a one-piece cashmere gown with straight, tight sleeves and a line of buttons from her throat down to the floor. It was one of the few dresses Annie wore that made her truly proud of her red hair and her green eyes—coloring that usually called out "country Irish" but in this dress looked elegant. Along the collar, cuffed wrists, and hem were lines of crimson roses Miriam had embroidered. It was beautiful work, displaying her mother's needlework artistry.

" 'Twould do you well, darling, to be learning the craft yourself," Miriam had said the first time Annie put it on and *oooh*ed at its prettiness.

As Annie leaned over to fasten the final ten buttons, her corset cut off her breath. She straightened up sharply, feeling light-headed. As her head cleared, Annie caught her image in her bureau mirror. "Oh, no," she cried, and stepped forward to look again.

She'd grown. Her wrists were well exposed beyond her dress sleeves, making Annie appear even ganglier. She looked to the floor. The hem was too short as well, but at least the edge of her petticoat made it look finished. She sighed. She didn't want to change her clothes. It wasn't Christmas without wearing this dress. How could she have gotten taller? She was going to be sixteen next month, a complete adult. She even knew of a few of the county girls who'd married this year at sixteen, worried their beaus might be killed in the war. And here she was still sprouting like a toddler.

If you are such an adult, find an adult solution, Annie could hear Miriam say. She thought for a moment and then turned down the sleeve cuffs, hiding her wrists but her mother's clever stitching as well. Can't be helped, thought Annie. Still, her eyes filled with disappointed tears. There'd be no replacing this dress, not for a long time, not until the war and the blockades were ended. Things just weren't as she'd expected them to be when she became old enough to have such pretty garments. She'd so looked forward to barbecues and picnics and Christmas balls and courtship walks with bits of recited poetry. There were no balls scheduled for this holiday. All the men were gone. There might be some smaller gatherings that she would enjoy. But it wasn't the same.

Annie brushed her waist-length hair for ten

minutes to make it gleam. It helped that she had already washed it twice that month with an herbal rinse to make it shine. With Rachel's help she might thread colorful ribbons into the two thick braids she'd make from the sides of her hair before looping and pinning them like a garland at the back of her head. As it was, she'd just do the usual everyday hairdo of Southern women.

Sometimes Annie wished that she could just let it hang down, loose and free, like Angel's magnificent mane and tail, but society had required Annie to put it up ever since she was a child. She dutifully parted her hair into three sections—straight down the middle toward her nose from the crown of her head and then side to side behind each ear. The back part she gathered and coiled into a tight chignon at the nape of her neck. The two front sections Annie braided and then rolled back to wrap around the bun. Most women had to tuck ratts—wads of hair the size of small potatoes created from strands left on hairbrushes—underneath the side braids. This was to add fullness to what could be a severe hairstyle, to frame and flatter the face. Annie didn't need such false additions—her hair was thick and full and, except for the color, a source of some vanity for her.

Taking one last look in the mirror, Annie slipped a prettily carved tortoiseshell comb into her creation. She smiled. Thank God, she hadn't inherited those carrot-colored freckles that Jamie had. Her skin was alabaster pale unless she blushed. In terms of looks, Annie was somewhere in between Laurence's fair gentrified elegance and Jamie's leprechaunlike wildness. She would do. She threw a chenille shawl across her shoulders and gently pulled open her door to keep it from snapping and awakening Miriam.

"Christmas gift!" a merry voice whispered.

Annie let out a little shriek before recognizing the figure in the dark. "Laurence! Where did you come from?"

"Oh, none of that, Annie. I caught you at Christmas gift." Laurence referred to the tradition of slaves being given special treats if they surprised their masters on Christmas Day, a game that had become part of white families' celebrations as well. "Now you owe me a present!"

"Oh, Laurence, we were so worried about you." Annie flung her arms around her big brother. He was covered with dust and his gentle face was bristly with an unshaved beard, but he was about the best Christmas sight she'd ever had.

"You and Mother have to stop worrying about me so," Laurence told her in the parlor as they sat in front of the fire. "There are going to be more battles, and ones a lot worse than that little exchange in Dranesville. I won't always be able to get word to you that I'm all right."

He turned to watch the fire. The Yule log Isaac had lit last night had been soaked in herbs and wine, and it filled the room with a wonderful musky smell. Dawn was just beginning to seep through the sky. They were the only ones up. Exhausted, Laurence had barely touched the bread and milk Annie had brought him. He and Sam had ridden most of the night to get home in time for Christmas morning. Laurence was thin and ashen, despite his joking and holiday cheer. "There's camp fever in Centreville," Laurence told Annie. "Measles, mumps, and typhoid. It was good to get some clean, cold air in me."

Sitting beside the fire, Laurence had begun to slump and his eyes to droop. He was falling asleep. Annie crept up to him and tried to pull off his boots so he could rest in comfort. His eyes popped open. "You don't need to do that, Annie," he mumbled. "Can't sleep on picket duty."

Annie couldn't tell if he was talking in his sleep or not. "Let me take care of you for once, Corporal Sinclair," she whispered. She jokingly adopted an old-world accent as she pulled. "What would Mother be saying if she saw you here in your old filthy boots on a Christmas morn."

His eyes were shut but he smiled wanly as he responded, "That's *Lieutenant* Sinclair to you, Lady Liberty. Made second lieutenant after Lewinsville, when they made Stuart a general. I think your antics had something to do with my promotion. Not again, though, Annie, you hear? No more of those . . . " Laurence was softly snoring.

Annie settled his boots by the fire and covered him with her shawl before she tiptoed out of the room to wake Miriam and give her the good news.

Miriam was dressed in fifteen minutes and down by the fire, sitting opposite Laurence as he slept, tears of relief slowly seeping down her face.

"Now, about that gift you owe me, Annie." Laurence leaned back and put his arms behind his head. "I did catch you at Christmas gift, you know."

Annie laughed. It had been a lovely Christmas dinner, even though their "groaning board" didn't groan with as much weight this year. They'd feasted on wild turkey, cranberry sauce, pigeon pie, rice, sweet potatoes, and turnips. They'd used their last bit of sugar for a cake. Now they sat around the Christmas tree with its decorations of bright ribbons, paper dolls, candles, and popcorn strings that she, Rachel, and Miriam had made. Miriam had given all the servants their Christmas presents—ten dollars apiece and bolts of new calico she had somehow managed to find and buy—and sent them off to enjoy the eggnog that Aunt May had made for them. It was time for presents.

But did Annie have to go first? The shirt she'd made for Laurence's uniform was far from perfect. She'd sewn the pockets on upside down at first and even stitched a sleeve closed somehow. Miriam had had to finish it for her. "Well, it's not much, Laurence," she said as she handed him her package.

Laurence was out of his dirty uniform, dressed instead in his Sunday best: cravat tied at his throat, silk waistcoat, and long coat with tails. He looked quite the country gentleman. The checked flannel shirt she'd made for him looked completely wrong. But he seemed to love it. "It's cold out there in camp, Annie. Thank you. I need something like this."

"Can't they keep you warm, son?" Miriam asked.

"Well, we're all huddled together in log cabins

in Centreville, about the worst construction you've ever seen, Mother, all slapdashed together by people like me who haven't the first notion of how to build them correctly. Entire forests were leveled and some of the boys took fence rails from the surrounding farms to build them. I'm afraid Aunt Molly's fences were torn down and used before I arrived in camp. General Beauregard wasn't exactly subtle with the locals. He ordered the muddy roads corduroyed after Manassas. They did it mostly with townspeople's fences and boards from their barns. I'm glad he's not in charge anymore."

"Poor Molly. That's shameful behavior," said Miriam.

"Yes, ma'am." Laurence nodded. "We just weren't prepared for all this, Mother. The Confederacy is still trying to get itself ready for a real war. Oh, we're doing fine in cavalry skirmishes because we all grew up riding and we know this country. But we're not ready for the big gun battles that are coming. Why, we don't have half the arms we need. Do you know what we have put up to guard the Centreville fort? Quaker guns. Know what they are?"

Miriam and Annie shook their heads.

"Logs cut to look like cannon from a distance. We're hanging on through clever deception. Do you know how Stuart confuses the enemy sometimes?"

Again they shook their heads.

"By having us cut trees and branches and drag them behind our horses, so the clouds of dust we cause make it appear as if there is infantry marching with us." He laughed. "Old Jeb, he's a clever one. But we can't fool them like that forever." He grew quiet and added, more to himself than to them, "And my saber isn't much good against their revolvers and carbines."

That's when Jamie jumped up and ran from the room.

"What's that child up to now?" Miriam asked. Jamie had been unusually quiet all day, shadowing Laurence wherever he went.

Annie had a pretty good idea of what he was doing, and she knew Miriam would be horrified. But just as she was about to tattle on him, Jamie dashed back in, holding aloft the revolver.

"Here, Laurence, I have a present for you, too. Something that will help you win this war against the Northern invaders." Jamie had obviously built up a speech as he ran to his room to retrieve the six-shooter. He was all puffed up about it.

Slowly, Laurence stood. His voice was low as he asked, "Boy, where did you get that?"

"Off a dead Yankee. Isn't it grand?"

"Jamie!" Miriam gasped.

"Oh, I didn't see him, Mother. Edward went to the battlefield and collected all sorts of things—hats, insignias, buttons, and four of these revolvers. Take it, Laurence. Kill some Yankees with it for me."

Jamie was too impressed with himself to really notice Laurence's face, but Annie did. She'd never seen it look so cold or so disgusted. "You mean to tell me, James, that Edward scavengered these things from fallen soldiers?"

Jamie stopped prancing and waving the gun.

"Like a buzzard? He cut buttons from their uniforms as they rotted? For souvenirs? Boy, I don't want you ever playing with this Edward again."

There was a long pause of silence while Jamie's face turned purple. When finally he spoke, there was a schoolyard hatred in his voice. "I'm not a *boy*, Laurence. And I don't *play* anymore. You are not my father. You can't tell me what to do. And when I join this war, I bet I kill a lot more Yankees than you do. Have you even killed any?"

"Jamie!" Miriam was aghast.

Laurence shoved his hands into his pockets, as if to control them. "This is not a contest, boy, between you and me. And you have no idea what killing is about. It's not something you aspire to, James. If you were a real man, you'd know that." Laurence rubbed his forehead and seemed to recognize the harshness of what he was saying. "But then, you're only twelve. You don't know any better."

"Twelve? I'm thirteen, brother, fourteen come March. But you've never paid attention to things about me, have you? A real man? I'll show you, soon enough, who's a real man." Jamie stormed from the room.

Miriam stood to follow.

"Leave him, Mother." Laurence held up his hand. "He'll sort it out."

But Annie knew Jamie wouldn't. He'd always been brimming with melodrama; that'd been the fun of him as a child. Introspection and careful thinking were unnatural for him. What really frightened Annie, though, was that the merriment was leaving Jamie. War rhetoric was twisted inside him, pushing him into that black-and-white kind of thinking that poisoned a person's ability to consider other opinions.

Laurence motioned for Miriam to sit. "I haven't given out my presents yet, Mother." He handed Miriam two small things.

Miriam sat looking at them for a moment, trying

to regain herself. She looked up at Laurence, who nodded at her. "It's all right, Mother. I was a fool myself at that age."

"No, darling," Miriam answered, "you were never allowed a foolish time. You've had to act like a man since you were a baby, haven't you, burying your father and brothers and convincing me to come out of my darkened room and breathe again. I'm sorry, son. I wish I had been stronger. I wish I knew how to manage Jamie. I wish . . ."

Laurence kissed the top of Miriam's head. "It's all right, Mother," he repeated. "Open your present now."

It was coffee, a tin of oysters, and a pound of sugar. Gratefully, Miriam held the package of ground coffee to her nose and inhaled the aroma. "We haven't had any of this for weeks, Laurence. Thank you."

For Annie, Laurence had a *Harper's Weekly* newspaper from last Christmas. "One of our pickets exchanged tobacco for it with one of their pickets. And he gave it to me for oranges I had bought from a sutler's wagon for you. I thought you'd prefer the magazine."

Inside was a drawing of a family toasting one another and another drawing of people in repentant prayer. Best of all, though, was an installment of

Charles Dickens' *Great Expectations*, and the conclusion to his Christmas story *A Message from the Sea.*

As Annie turned the pages, Laurence kept talking. "They do that all the time, you know, the pickets, sitting across a creek or a field from one another. A few days ago, we heard two of them singing Christmas carols together in the night—a Southern boy and a Union boy, both just wanting to be home for Christmas." He shook his head. "A voice in a bush on one side of the border and a voice in a bush on the other side, joined to sing 'It Came upon the Midnight Clear.' We all stopped to listen. And then it was quiet again, back to the business of waiting and watching for a time to shoot at each other."

The fire crackled as Laurence fell silent. After several moments he shook himself from his thoughts.

"I stopped to see Aunt Molly on my way home, Mother, and a package for you had been delivered to her. It's probably best that Jamie isn't here to see it, given his hatred of all things Yankee. It's from Massachusetts. He might figure you to be consorting with the enemy." He handed it to her with a quizzical look.

"Massachusetts?" Miriam undid the string. "Why, that's even farther north than New York, isn't it? What in the world could it be?"

The brown paper fell back to reveal a bolt of beautiful midnight blue velvet, a book, and a letter. "Oh, my," breathed Miriam, "what gorgeous material." She opened the letter.

"Who's it from, Mother?" Annie asked.

Miriam turned over the paper. "Saints preserve us. It's from the mother of that Union soldier we helped at Manassas. Do you remember, Annie, that lieutenant the Union doctor had foolishly left?"

Annie certainly did remember Thomas Walker. His dark eyes and words still plagued her.

"Read it, Mother," Laurence suggested.

Miriam held the letter out at arm's length and read:

"Dear Madam,

"My son Thomas has written and asked that I send a letter of thanks to you. He is currently a prisoner in Libby Prison in Richmond, but he hopes to be exchanged soon, and perhaps he will be home for Christmas. I understand that I might be able to see my dear son because of you. He says that you saved his life and treated him with much kindness in the middle of a terrible

battle in which his men bombarded your farm. I wish our men had the same breadth of mercy you have, Madam, for then perhaps this war would not have happened at all. Thomas tells me you also have a son fighting. So I know you feel the same worry I do. I will pray for your son's safety and a speedy end to this conflict.

"I read that your people have difficulty procuring fabric these days. I thought you might appreciate having this velvet for Christmas. Perhaps it can be a dress to wear when this cruel war is ended and our loved ones return home safely to us. I send it with the most profound thanks. I gave Thomas life but you kept it flowing in him. No matter what side we stand on, I consider you a sister in sorrow.

"Please also find enclosed a book Thomas specifically asked that I send for your daughter. He asked that she forgive him some rudeness he wouldn't describe to me—and I hope you believe, Madam, that my boy usually has the best of manners. Thomas wrote that your daughter had been interested in this verse. I must tell you that it is

one of my favorite volumes, one Thomas has oft read aloud to me at eventide. I hope your daughter enjoys it as much as I have.

"Yours with the most heartfelt gratitude,

"Katherine Walker."

Miriam handed Annie a thick book of marbleized paper and a stained leather cover. She opened the front to a portrait of an intensely Romantic-looking young man, Lord Byron, the very poet Thomas Walker had quoted to her on that awful night of destruction and death. It was a beautiful book, published in 1836, including all Byron's poems and a sketch of his life.

Annie was speechless.

Finally, Laurence spoke. "This is why this war is so hard. There are many gentlemen and mothers on the other side I'm sure I'd like a great deal if things were different." He shook his head solemnly. Then abruptly he laughed. "We better find Annie a Confederate beau quick, Mother. Whatever you do, don't tell our firebrand, Jamie, about this. He might come after Annie with that revolver!"

CHAPTER NINE

March 14, 1862
Hickory Heights

"Steady, Angel, steady."

Annie leaned back slightly and straightened her spine to slow down her horse. It was a cold March day. The ground was muddy from thawing and unusually late snows melting. Angel was spooking at most everything, lurching suddenly to the side and prancing. She'd even throw in a few good back-legged bucks to protest getting her hooves so wet and sloppy.

Annie couldn't help laughing at Angel's antics. The bucks weren't serious, just the flourish as of a high-strung horse, excited to be out no matter how much she thought she didn't like the mud. No jumping Angel over logs or fences today, though. The footing was too slick and the mare's attitude too feisty. Annie had that much sense.

Still, she was up for a good canter to let the cold air whip some life into her. It'd been such a long, boring, anxious winter, shut inside the house, playing old maid with Jamie, or worse yet trying to help him with his studies. His school was closed, the headmaster and teacher off with General Johnston, and Miriam had insisted that Annie be his tutor. The only thing he would pay attention to were stories of wars, so Annie set him onto Homer's *Iliad* and *Odyssey* and Vergil's *Aeneid.* But the epic poems only spurred his restlessness. This morning he'd thrown the whole table over and stalked out to Lord knows where. In truth, Annie was delighted with his tantrum and disappearance. They meant she could slip out for a ride.

"Come on, girl, cannnn-ter," Annie sang, pulling out the first syllable of the word *canter* and lifting it on its last. Angel instantly and lightly responded to her voice command, waltzing through the open, greening fields in a graceful one-two-three rhythm, as smooth and steady as a rocking horse. Oh, it was glorious. Annie scared off some deer and a pair of pheasants. She even saw a hint of red tail disappear over a fence. "Don't worry, old fox," Annie called out with a laugh, "you're safe today." Annie had never enjoyed the catch of foxhunting, just the sport of riding through the countryside amid a crowd of horsemen. It was the closest she could come to the sensation of being part of a wild herd of horses, free and spirited, racing as one being.

Reluctantly, Annie slowed Angel down to a trot and then a walk. She'd come down a hill to bottomland, and Angel could slip on the mudflats and pull a muscle. Carefully, Annie guided Angel over the tentaclelike roots of a walnut tree to the steep banks of Panther Skin Creek. They scampered down the slope, and Angel gratefully stuck her muzzle into the rushing water. This was one of Jamie's favorite places to fish, sitting on the rocks, hidden from view by the high embankments. Fishing, of course, was better in still water. But Annie knew that Jamie didn't really come to catch dinner but to skip rocks and splash about. She'd even caught him swimming naked down here with Gabriel. Now that had certainly brought a stern lecture from Aunt May!

Annie's thoughts wandered to less amusing thoughts. There'd been all sorts of terrifying rumors and news the past few days. Now that spring was coming and traveling was easier, Federal General McClellan had his Union soldiers on the move. It looked as if he was trying to head toward Richmond, by taking troops down the Potomac River, east, out into Chesapeake Bay, and around Virginia's northern neck peninsula. In response, to shadow McClellan, General Johnston had evacuated the Confederate stronghold at Centreville. He ordered Stuart to burn what could not be carried before he followed the infantry south. Because of the hurry and lack of wagons, the cavalry had had to torch railroad cars full of clothes and ammunition and mounds of bacon as high as barns stockpiled at Thoroughfare Gap. Smoke and the scent of cooking meat drifted several miles to Haymarket.

It was a horrible waste, a horrible situation. The northwest corner of Virginia—where she sat—lay completely open to Yankees now. Infantry from Pennsylvania had already come from Harper's Ferry and taken Leesburg, only eighteen miles away. There was word of all sorts of Federals along the Blue Ridge from Snicker's Gap south to Manassas Gap. How could General Stuart abandon them like that?

Annie thought of those blue eyes, that bold walk. She remembered the beautiful, patriotic words he'd written to her. He couldn't have liked those orders at all, she told herself. Laurence wouldn't either. She knew Richmond was the capital of the Confederacy and had to be protected at all costs; but to withdraw—without even a murmur of a fight or a warning to the inhabitants, leaving them undefended—well, it just was frightening, confusing, unchivalrous, that's all.

Annie urged Angel up the banks, noticing that spring beauties were trying to push their way up through the frosty mud. Normally, Annie would have been gladdened by the sight of their tiny purplish buds, but a melancholy line of Keats came to her instead: *Where are the songs of Spring?* and then another: *Woman! when I behold thee flippant, vain / Inconstant . . . .*

Was she inconstant, vain? Annie had been so pleased with Stuart's poem, him calling her Lady Liberty. But she'd also been flattered by the Massachusetts man. Truth be known, she had passed many a dark and dreary winter day happily by reading his collection of Byron that had arrived at Christmas. She could still see his frightened face relax as Miriam had tended him, could still hear his voice and the words that had so disturbed her. Thomas Walker. "I hope they keep you in prison forever," muttered Annie. "Meanwhile, I'll enjoy your book!"

Turning for home, Annie caught a strange sound on

the wind. She pulled Angel to a halt. The horse obviously sensed something, too, for she began to tremble and twitch her head about, ears pricked, turning to find the direction of the sound so that she could run in the opposite direction.

There it was again. Now it was gone.

A funny rattle. Very rhythmic.

Not guns. Too constant, not like a conversation of fire and answer. Like a humming almost. Annie closed her eyes to concentrate. But the wind kicked up enough to sweep trees into a swirl, making the world resound only with the *swoosh* of rushing air. Annie clucked Angel into a trot up the hill, where she could hear for a mile, where sound carried on the vaulting crisp air as easily as a hawk coasts clear heavens.

She came to the crest and reined in. Annie could see a corner of the road through the hills and glades and traced it north, little bits and pieces of it popping into view among the dips and rises of earth. There was nothing along it, and yet that sound somehow told Annie to watch the road.

Da-da, dumm, dumm, dumm, dumm, da-da, dumm, dumm, dumm, dumm.

Good God. It was a drum cadence. Annie couldn't believe it'd taken her all that time to figure out that obvious fact. But now that she had, it was as if she'd ridden out purposely to scout for troops.

There! There was a glint of something in the faraway distance. Sunshine off metal. She squinted her eyes and yes, in that turn of the road, maybe a mile off, she could see a mass of blue, heading for her, slowly, evenly: hundreds, maybe thousands of men.

Annie stood up in her saddle and scanned the earth in all directions. Any gray crowds, any Confederate champions to meet them? Nothing. Angel began to snort and dance, echoing Annie's instinct to run. But she lingered, trying to assess where they were heading. West toward Paris and Ashby's Gap? East toward Middleburg? Or south to regain the Manassas Gap Railroad? In any of those scenarios, they'd use Ashby Gap Turnpike. And that would take them near . . . home.

Oh, my Lord. Annie had learned enough from their experience at Manassas to know that the Federals could pick Hickory Heights clean, like a flock of starlings landing on a cherry tree. They'd need to hide the horses, the hogs, and the chickens—fast!

She turned Angel toward home, but another sound stopped her. It was the sound of a voice, urgent, shouting. Annie looked down the hill, looked left, right, and there was Gabriel, yelling up into an oak tree. What in the world was he doing? She looked up into the branches and saw red, a knot of bright red hair. Jamie! Jamie was lying flat along a high limb. What a time to be playing games, brother!

Annie sent Angel flying down the hill. As she came closer, she realized that Jamie wasn't playing a game. He had that fool revolver in his hand. He was lying in wait to shoot at the coming Union troops! One shot from Jamie and a thousand rifles could be turned on him, killing him before they even saw he was just a child.

"Jamie!" Annie shouted. "Jamie, come down this instant! They'll kill you certain. Come down!"

Jamie ignored her.

Angel slid to a prancing stop by Gabriel. The young groom held up his hands in dismay. "I been trying, Miss Annie. I can't get him down. He say he's gonna ambush the soldiers. What we going to do, Miss Annie? I can hear them coming."

The drums were louder, closer. Indeed, the wind now carried snatches of voices, the sounds of wagon wheels creaking and shuddering along the roadway. They would pass the crook in the road within ten or fifteen minutes.

Annie was panting from the pell-mell dash

down the hill. "Gabriel, have you tried climbing up after him?" Gabriel was fifteen years old and strong, much bigger than Jamie.

"Yes, Miss Annie. He done push me off the branch. Scraped me up good." He held up his right arm, and Annie saw his ripped coat sleeve and a long scrape along his face.

"Oh, Gabriel, I'm sorry." She looked back up at Jamie. He'd always been spoiled with their servants. He deserved a good hiding, really. He needed to learn a lesson about treating them with kindness. But not this way. This lesson could kill him.

"Jamie, get down out of that tree! What possible good do you think you can do? There are a thousand of them, at least, Jamie. I saw them from the hill. They'll knock you out of that tree with hot lead, Jamie. It's not a game!"

"I'm the only man left around these parts to defend us," he shouted down at Annie. "And I aim to do it!"

"Jamie, this isn't defending anything. It's suicide. It's crazy. Think of—"

"Miss Annie," Gabriel hissed, tugging on Annie's riding skirt. "Hush up, Miss Annie."

Startled, Annie looked down at the groom's face. "What's the matter with you, Gabriel? I've got to get

Jamie down before he does something . . ."

Gabriel shook his head at Annie. Something about his eyes stopped Annie and filled her with dread. Slowly, she turned.

Three Federal riders sat within a hundred feet of her. One was pointing a carbine straight up at Jamie.

CHAPTER TEN

"Interesting fowl they have around here," said the man pointing the gun. He pulled back the hammer with a loud click. "Should I shoot it down for dinner, sir?" he asked the officer who sat staring at Annie.

"I don't know. Given what we've overheard, you could. But it depends on what this girl has to say."

The man's eyes were cold, his voice strangely accented. A Dutchman perhaps. She'd heard tell of them. Jamie's life hung on her words. What should she say? What were these people like? Did they value family? What would inspire his pity? Seeing how still the horses stood, the Yankees had obviously been sitting there for a few moments. But for how long?

How could she not have seen them coming?

Her questions raced around and around in her head and her throat went completely dry. Annie began to speak, but it was as if her tongue had hardened to the roof of her mouth. No words came out.

The officer glanced up at Jamie—who for once was silent—and then back down to Annie. A nasty smirk crept along his face. "Brother and sister, no doubt. Cat got your tongue, miss?"

"I . . . I . . . "

"I'd say he's a bushwhacker, sir, and we ought to pick him out of that tree. I've got a nice clean shot at him."

Whether the soldier really meant to fire or simply to terrify, Annie would never know. Gabriel stepped forward.

"No call to shoot that boy, master," he said in a low, quiet voice. "He ain't right." He tapped his head. "He's forever climbing that tree. Today's no different. He wouldn't know that you were coming. If you know what I mean." He tapped his head again.

Annie watched warily. If Jamie could hear what Gabriel was saying, he'd probably shoot all of them. But the real question was: Would pretending Jamie was addled work with the Federals?

The officer shifted in his saddle and eyed Annie carefully. "This true?"

What should she say?

Gabriel nodded at her. "It's all right, Miss Annie. I know it's hard on you and Missus Miriam. But it's for Marse James' own good that these soldiers know the truth."

Gabriel had always known how to handle even the wildest, stupidest horses. He, Laurence, and Sam just seemed to have an instinct for it. Gabriel's father had been able to talk a horse down from a fit just with his voice. She'd seen it as a young child and always remembered. Gabriel had the same gift. He was using it on her now. Annie played along.

"Well, it is embarrassing, Captain," she began.

"Sergeant," he corrected her.

"I'm sorry . . . Sergeant. I'm afraid I just haven't gotten used to all these ranks and handsome uniforms." Annie was choking on the syrup in her words, but if it would save her brother, she was willing to play the simpering belle. "Gabriel spoke correctly." She lowered her voice to a lilting whisper. "Jamie isn't quite right, ever since he fell from that horse. He can be quite muddled. Half the time, he's just playing games that make no sense. My mother and I simply despair sometimes. But we are hoping that he'll grow out of it." She smiled. Surely this man couldn't hold a boy accountable for such tomfoolery.

"Humpf," the sergeant snorted. He looked up at Jamie. "Get down out of that tree, boy. Or I'll shoot you, your sister, and your slave. Understand? You have to the count of ten." He counted off matter-of-factly, "One . . . two . . . three . . ."

Jamie scrambled down. He glared at Annie and his freckles flamed. Luckily, his anger kept him from speaking. He still clutched the revolver.

The third rider jumped from his horse and snatched it from Jamie. "Where did you get that, boy? This belongs to the U.S. army."

Annie spoke before Jamie could. "It belongs to me. A gift of sorts, Sergeant. I was staying with my aunt in Manassas, and her house became a makeshift hospital for your troops after the battle. There were several cavalry officers there. One gave it to me as he died, in thanks for nursing him." Good Lord, the lie rolled off her tongue so easily!

"Poor lad," Annie added. "A cannonball crushed his legs. There was nothing the surgeon could do. He's buried in my aunt's apple orchard. He was from Massachusetts, I believe." She'd have to take extra time over her prayers that night.

Again, the sergeant snorted. "I think we'll hold him for questioning, just the same." He motioned to the soldier who'd been keeping Jamie under gunpoint. The soldier lowered his carbine and roughly pulled Jamie onto the horse behind him. "He might be tricked into divulging the whereabouts of some of Stuart's cavalry, if he's truly not right. We hear there's a small band of them somewhere in these hills. But we can't get anyone to confirm it. All the residents are secessionists. Take him back to the colonel."

The soldier wheeled and rode off with Jamie toward the sound of the coming drums.

"Jamie!" Annie cried out. But again, Gabriel silenced her by putting his hand on her stirrup. He clearly sensed something she didn't. Annie trusted his judgment. He'd always been right about hidden dangers in horses.

The sergeant noticed Gabriel's nudge. "Why are you loyal to this woman?"

"Sir?" Gabriel asked.

The sergeant shook his head and muttered, "What they say about the stupidity of these people must be right." He raised his voice and slowed his speech as he spoke to Gabriel—as if Gabriel were a slow-witted child. "We have a number of contraband following the infantry. You may join them."

"Contrabrand?" Gabriel asked.

"Slaves that ran away and follow the Union army.

They cook, clean the officers' uniforms, and tend our horses in exchange for food and our protection."

Gabriel was silent.

"Think it over." The sergeant turned to Annie. "I was scouting ahead, looking for any Rebel cavalry. Colonel Geary's troops need a place to camp for the night and the colonel requires a house. You must live near here. Take me there."

That night, the fields of Hickory Heights blazed with campfires. Two thousand Pennsylvania infantry had taken over the Upperville area. Several hundred of them camped at Hickory Heights. The officers' horses crowded the Sinclairs' barn and devoured their corn. The sergeant and a dozen other staff officers were bedded down in their hayloft. The colonel and his staff were inside, enjoying an enormous meal they demanded that Miriam serve them.

One major even had his wife traveling with him. She had arrived in men's clothes. She came down to dinner in one of Annie's two dinner dresses, a plain skirt of green apple silk, the bodice and sleeves made of puffed white muslin, accented with strips of black velvet to match the waistband. Annie consoled herself that it did nothing for the Yankee woman's sallow coloring.

"You don't suppose they'd poison the food?" the

major's wife had whispered to her husband as Miriam carved and served the roasted hens Aunt May had prepared.

Annie had been preoccupied with worry about whether any of their precious chickens had survived this invasion. Somehow Isaac and Bob, their field head man, had managed to hide most of the horses and hogs in thickets at the far corner of the farm. But their sheep and cows were still in easy view. Would they end up slaughtered tonight to feed all those men? At least they hadn't yet planted the fields. All those tents and feet would have mashed everything dead. But would the soldiers steal their seed corn and wheat?

The question about poisoning stopped Annie's thoughts. How dare this woman suspect them of something so underhanded? The nerve of these people! She fumed. Arresting a thirteen-year-old boy; taking over their house, their barns; stealing their food; wearing her clothes; insisting they eat dinner together. But she had to behave. Jamie was still being held somewhere. Miriam and Annie both knew it was up to them to plead his case.

They said next to nothing during dinner. The officers mostly ignored them, only occasionally asking questions about the weather and what crops thrived in the region. Miriam's answers were short and painfully polite. She even managed to smile graciously when Aunt May brought out a cake for dessert. Annie knew that cake had taken every granule of the Christmas sugar Laurence had brought.

As the Union staff stood to leave the table, Colonel Geary remained seated and waved off his companions. "I wish to speak to Mrs. Sinclair and her daughter. Now, madam," he started with Miriam, "where is your husband?"

"My husband is dead ten years now," she answered quietly.

"Really? I saw men's clothing upstairs."

Annie held her breath angrily. So not only had that woman put on one of Annie's best dresses without asking, they'd been snooping around all their bedrooms.

"Those would belong to my son, Laurence. If you wish proof of my lost husband, I can take you to our family cemetery tomorrow morning, sir. There you'll find my husband and three of my boys, all buried within the same month. Of course, you'll need to be directing your soldiers to move their things so you can see their graves. I note that some of them blasphemed and used the headstones as supports for their guns and saddlebags."

Annie was proud of her mother's grit.

"I see." The colonel nervously pulled on his whiskery sideburns, but he made no apologies. "Where is the son?"

"He rides with General Stuart's cavalry. He is a lieutenant with the 1st Virginia."

The colonel leaned forward. "When did you see him last?"

"Christmas Day."

"Where is he now?"

"I do not know. Safe, I hope," Miriam answered.

"No letters? No word of where they are?"

"No, sir."

The colonel nodded. "Are you a truthful woman?"

Miriam's face hardened. "Indeed, sir, on my soul I am."

Annie couldn't help herself. "My mother never lies, ever. Even when it would make her life easier."

"Ah. And do you, miss?"

Annie hesitated just long enough for the colonel to straighten up with interest.

"I hope not to, sir" was her meager answer.

"And would you lie to protect someone you love?"

This was turning into a game of words, a dangerous one. Even knowing that, Annie could not curb herself into caution. "I might because I know what it means to be loyal, sir. Do you?"

"Annie." Miriam spoke sharply. "I've raised you to be polite, child, no matter what is said to you."

"Or by what kind of ruffian?" the colonel asked her.

Miriam didn't answer.

He laughed and crossed his arms. "I've heard you people are violently secessionist in your thinking. It will be the ruin of you, madam. Now, miss." He turned his attention back to Annie. "Have you heard from your brother, or a suitor, perhaps?"

"No, sir."

"Come now, a fiery, handsome girl such as you. Perhaps a Confederate officer let slip some important plans to impress you, press his suit? I hear this Stuart is quite the ladies' man and that his staff follows his lead."

Annie could feel herself begin to blush and took a deep breath to suppress the flush of pink that always gave her away. As she did, she instinctively touched her skirt. She often tucked Stuart's poem inside a pocket to read when she was in private. This night, she was extremely grateful she had. Instinct told her that the poem might be used against her and the people of Hickory Heights.

Miriam interrupted before Annie could answer.

"My daughter has many admirers, Colonel. But she is young and thus far unattached. In fact"—Miriam pulled out a letter of her own—"she received a truly moving thank-you note from a Massachusetts lady whose son we helped at the Manassas battlefield. If a boy is wounded, it doesn't matter to me, sir, whether he is from the North or South. I will help him." She handed him the letter.

Annie looked at her mother with admiration. Oh, she was clever.

Miriam waited until the colonel finished reading. "Now, about my boy, Colonel, my son Jamie. He's only a child. If he did something wrong, he didn't know the consequences of it. Fault me, a doting mother, for not teaching him better, Colonel. I lost three sons. My boys are precious to me."

Annie felt the sting of being excluded, but said nothing.

"I hear he is addlebrained?"

Miriam didn't move, simply glanced at Annie and then back to the colonel.

"I told them about the accident, Mother," Annie jumped in.

The colonel watched Miriam's reaction, like a cat tracking a bird, Annie thought. Miriam cast her eyes down to her plate, and Annie saw her set her jaw. "I don't like to talk about it, Colonel. I feel responsible for his behavior."

Silence dropped over them as the colonel thought. He reread the letter.

Suddenly, he stood up. His voice had softened: "I have already sent him to Alexandria, Mrs. Sinclair, along with two men we arrested. To our prison there. I have to make an example of him. I have orders to collect all the firearms in this county. We cannot be fighting the citizens as well. Children can't be pointing guns at us from trees. I'm sorry. I do have my orders."

Miriam looked up at him, her face pinched with worry. "He's just a boy, Colonel," she said urgently.

The colonel shuffled his feet and looked away from Miriam. "I can't imagine he'll be kept long, madam. I'll send a message that he's to be treated well and released quickly, given his youth." Then he fled the room.

Miriam sat staring at the tablecloth for a long time. Then she stood up. "Let us go upstairs, darling. I do not think I could be civil to these people a moment longer. I will plead Jamie's case with this Yankee again tomorrow morning." Her voice quavered and she hooked her arm around Annie's. Miriam leaned heavily on Annie as they went. "My fault," Miriam whispered. "Thaddeus would be so disappointed in me."

Annie listened and wondered. She didn't remember much about her father, just a large laugh, huge feet, and occasionally being tossed high in the air and barely caught on the way down. Miriam often sounded slightly afraid of him, or at least terrified of disappointing him. Annie helped her mother to lie down on her bed. The two of them were sharing Annie's room that night. Union officers had taken Miriam's, Jamie's, and Laurence's rooms.

She propped several feather pillows behind Miriam's head and shoulders. "There was nothing to be done, Mother. But I think the colonel will be true to his word." Still, Annie did feel horrible about it. "I . . . I'm sorry, Mother, that I didn't get Jamie down faster. He's just so . . . so . . . headstrong sometimes."

At that, Miriam smiled. "Yes, child, it runs in the family." She patted Annie's face. "Look at you, taking care of me. You'll be a fine mother someday, darling. You are already a lady."

Annie smiled back. Those were sweet words to hear.

Checking the water pitcher, Annie found it empty. There'd been no time for regular chores that night, clearly. "Mother, I'm going to go down and draw us some water. I'll be back."

"I'd best come with you, Annie." Miriam raised herself. "There are so many strangers about."

Annie gently pushed her back in the bed. She liked the idea of Miriam depending on her for once, as she always did with Laurence. "I'll go to the kitchen and get Aunt May or Rachel to go with me. It'll be fine. Rest, Mother." Annie slipped out the door before Miriam could insist.

In the kitchen, Annie found more soldiers, asking for eggs, milk, and bread. One was very sweetly thanking Aunt May for feeding him. "Our Millie always fixed me warm milk before bed," he was telling her. "I sure miss her." Looking at his soft face, Annie reckoned him to be only slightly older than Jamie.

Annie took Rachel's hand as they walked through the gloom to the well. It was only a hundred yards from the house, and the moonlight was bright, but the surrounding campfires made Annie nervous. She could hear a fiddle playing up the hill, and the sound of rough voices arguing about a card game. Light shone out from the windows. The major's wife was playing their piano, using Miriam's sheet music for Stephen Foster's "My Old Kentucky Home."

Several officers surrounded her as they listened.

"The world seems turned in on itself, Rachel," Annie said.

"Sam told me that this would happen," Rachel answered. "Told me to be careful when it did."

"Sam knew that our troops would withdraw?"

Rachel hesitated a moment. "Annie, he doesn't know anything except what he can see with his own eyes. Mr. Laurence and his friends are brave, for sure, but look at your fields." She nodded in their direction. "Look at those campfires. There'll be more and more of them coming. More and more."

Holding the bucket of clear water between them, the two girls had walked back into a pool of light from the house's back door. There was pity on Rachel's face. Annie didn't like anyone feeling sorry for her. And why should Rachel feel pity? Annie was about to tell Rachel not to look at her like that when a man stepped out of the shadows. It was the sergeant who had arrested Jamie. The girls stopped abruptly, sloshing water on their skirts.

"Sergeant," Annie said shakily. "You startled us."

"Yes," he answered coldly. He moved forward, into the light, and Annie saw that he was staring at Rachel. "Yes," he said again. "Evenin', girl."

Rachel nodded. The bucket handle began to tremble, and Annie realized that Rachel wasn't just startled; she was afraid.

Annie looked back to the sergeant. He was holding a small paper sack.

"I have peppermints, girl. Ever taste one?" He held the bag toward Rachel.

Rachel shook her head.

"Take one." He stepped closer.

Rachel looked to Annie.

"You don't need to ask your mistress."

Rachel found her voice. "No, thank you, sir," she answered. "I don't care for any."

The sergeant frowned. "Fancy words." He looked at Rachel and a nasty smile grew on his face, a smirk like the one he'd had for Gabriel. "Fancy looks, too." He squinted.

Annie felt sick to her stomach. She wasn't sure why. "Excuse us, Sergeant. We need to take this water inside."

The sergeant stepped directly into their path. "Not so fast." His eyes were still on Rachel. "Some of us are pulling out tomorrow, heading down to take and repair the railroad. Want to come?"

Rachel frowned. "No, sir," she said emphatically.

He stepped so close to Rachel that she leaned

backward to keep his face from touching her hair. "I'd look after you. Got money. Can buy you lots of fancy dresses and petticoats with Union pay."

"Now see here, Sergeant," Annie began, but a hand on her shoulder stopped her.

It was Gabriel. Gabriel, again, praise God. "Let me take that water for you, Miss Annie. Rachel, Aunt May was calling for you. Best hurry in now."

Annie grabbed Rachel's hand once again and pulled her inside, Gabriel behind them. Almost as quickly as he appeared, Gabriel slipped back into the night.

The next morning, the troops left, heading for Middleburg and points south. Annie went to the stable to thank Gabriel for all he'd done to protect them. He wasn't there. She checked the corncrib, the granary, the paddocks, the smokehouse, the potato cellar, the dairy, the icehouse, even the henhouse. Gabriel was gone. So was Rachel's older brother, Jacob, Hickory Heights' farmhand. When Isaac checked their cottages, he came back to say that their clothes were missing, too. All Annie could suppose was that they had followed the Union army.

The recognition sliced her cold to the bone. Could Thomas Walker, that Massachusetts officer, be right? Could Gabriel and Jacob have been *that* unhappy they'd cut themselves off from their family and disappear? Gabriel had never seemed that discontented at Hickory Heights. He'd always appeared so at peace, so affectionate with the horses. Gabriel and Jacob had been well fed and clothed, taught to read just as Rachel had been, although they'd never loved it as she did.

Certainly the life of a contraband—as that odious sergeant called runaway servants who followed Union troops—didn't sound like a step up in life—cooking, polishing shoes, and mucking up after horses for Yankees. Seemed as if they were simply exchanging one servitude for another. Poor Gabriel. Poor Jacob. They'd been seduced with false promises, sure, thought Annie, just like that sergeant had tried to trick Rachel with peppermints and petticoats into coming with him.

But then Annie thought again. Perhaps she hadn't seen things clearly herself. She thought back to Rachel and her book, the reverential way in which she held it; her hesitancy in taking it from Annie. No, kindness obviously wasn't enough, after all. The only thing that was enough was freedom. Freedom for each individual to follow his own path. How could she have been so blind?

CHAPTER ELEVEN

March 15, 1862
Hickory Heights

"What are we going to do, Missus Miriam?" Isaac asked. He'd just given her the sum of their losses: ten sheep, fifteen calves, half their store of the horses' feed corn, and most of the chickens. The soldiers had made a fine game of chasing the birds before cooking them for dinner. The only ones left were the rooster and a few hens, belonging to the servants, that he'd put in a burlap sack and hung down the well, where the darkness kept them quiet.

A lot of their tack was gone, too, harnesses and bridles. Out of pure spite, someone had taken a knife to the leather seats of their Sunday carriage. But the Yankees had left the milk cows and the seed for planting alone. According to Isaac, one of their officers had stopped them from stealing those.

Miriam reached over and patted his hand. "It's all right, Isaac. The Lord will provide. You were clever enough to save those hogs and horses. That will make all the difference."

"Angel?" Annie asked, worried. Riding in with the sergeant dogging her, Annie hadn't been able to hide her mare.

Isaac nodded. "Don't fret, Miss Annie. I took good care of her. I hid her down to the creek. She's in her stall now, enjoying her dinner." He glanced over at Miriam. "Missus, I can handle the horses and cows until Mr. Laurence come home. But I don't think I can help Bob plow those fields. My back done broke down now."

Miriam nodded. Without Gabriel and Jacob, planting would be hard. Isaac had retired from field labor long ago. Mostly he just helped around the house, bringing in firewood, following Aunt May's orders. "I appreciate all you've done, Isaac. I'll look to hiring a hand somehow. Although Lord knows where I'll find anyone or the money to pay him. Perhaps Jamie can help. It might be good for him to . . ." Miriam's voice trailed off.

Annie knew what she was thinking. Would Jamie even be home by planting next month? They had no idea where he was. Was he frightened? Most importantly, was he holding his tongue and for once not bragging about what he'd meant to do with that gun?

"Jamie will be all right, Mother." Annie sat down next to Miriam on the settee and put her arm around her waist. She tried to joke. "No one is going to want to keep Jamie for long. Once he starts in on them with his wild ideas and that mouth of his, they'll probably order the best horse-drawn carriage in Alexandria to bring him home lickety-split."

Miriam shook her head. "Don't use slang, Annie. Besides, child, it's no laughing matter. It's your baby brother they have."

Annie thought and then tried again. "We're lucky, Mother, truly, that they didn't shoot him right then and there. He was aiming at the road and bragging on shooting the first Yankee who came into view. That sergeant heard every word of it, I think. He was a cold man. If it hadn't been for Gabriel—" Annie stopped. She couldn't help feeling stung and saddened by Gabriel and Jacob's running off. She'd miss Gabriel, so would Angel, that was for sure. She hoped he'd be safe. Lord knows what the Yankees might try to convince him to do.

For a moment, Annie thought of Thomas Walker. Despite his rudeness, he seemed a gentleman.

Would Walker have allowed all this stealing around their farm? Did that colonel know what his soldiers were up to during the night, feasting on their hens? He had seemed ashamed of arresting Jamie, though, after talking with Miriam. There was some decency there. "You know, Mother, I think we can trust that colonel to send his message about treating Jamie well and releasing him soon. Surely."

"Do you think so, Annie?"

But before she could answer, Aunt May came bustling into the room, mad and loud. "That hussy done took your dress, Miss Annie. Your music box is missing, too, and I can't find three silver spoons. Those Yankees are like a swarm of locusts, Missus Miriam, no better than beetles. I won't cook for them again, I tell you. Good thing they took off like the cowards they are or I'd be telling them exactly what they could do with their sorry selves."

Annie and Miriam glanced at each other. How could they really trust any Federal at this point? Annie hated the thought of it, but they might have to contact Cousin Eleanor's husband to intercede for Jamie. She asked Miriam.

"Eleanor and Francis always thought me an unsuitable wife and an unfit mother, and here is proof." Miriam sighed. "But that's a small price to pay for Jamie's well-being. I'll write a letter right now." She stood and swept toward her desk.

But Miriam's letter could never be posted. Federal troops remained in the area, completely disrupting everyday life and terrifying the natives. Cannons fired along the western mountains every few days. Smoke rose on the horizon from fires and skirmishes. Annie often heard dogs barking and the sound of hooves thundering by somewhere close. Wagons rattled along the roads, and axes felled trees. Federal cavalry routinely dashed through the streets of Middleburg, Upperville, Paris, and Aldie. To go in and out of town required a pass. At night, picket fires dotted the turnpike. During the day, stragglers often appeared at Hickory Heights' doorway, demanding food.

"Here comes another one of those varmints," Aunt May grumbled one morning while Annie was in the kitchen, scrounging for a midmorning treat herself. Breakfast had been sparse and would be for a while—until the hens had enough chicks raised to lay eggs of their own and the new crop of corn had come in for cornmeal to make bread.

Shaking her head and muttering to herself, Aunt May filled a tin cup with some of their scant milk.

She handed it to Rachel and said, "Don't let him into the house. They're all covered with lice."

Annie glanced out the window at the figure coming up their lane. Something about the sullen way he moved, the way the hat was yanked down low on his head, the good quality of his clothes made her look harder. "That's no Union infantry, Aunt May. That's a gentleman's coat on him. And see how small he is."

Rachel joined Annie at the window. "Look, there goes Missus Miriam."

Through the window, Annie saw her mother running down the slope, out their white picket gate and into the lane. "Why's she doing that?" Annie wondered aloud. Then she realized. It was Jamie.

She rushed out the house and into the lane. "Jamie!" she cried. "Oh, Jamie!"

Miriam was holding him tight and trying to rock him back and forth as she had when he was an infant. Jamie did not return her embrace. His arms were down tight by his sides, his hands balled into fists.

"Jamie?" Annie reached out to touch his shoulder. "I'm so relieved to see you. Are you all right?" She looked him over. He'd been gone only ten days, praise God. He didn't look gaunt or hurt. But when

Jamie turned to face her, his look hit her like a slap.

"The next time you stand between me and a good aim at a Yankee, I'll shoot right through you," he said.

"James!" gasped Miriam.

He didn't even glance at his mother. "I mean it, Annie. Remember. You've been warned." Jamie stalked into the house.

It wasn't until late May that the Pennsylvania troops withdrew from Upperville and Fauquier County, marching west toward the mountains to confront General Stonewall Jackson and his die-hard Rebel infantry.

Where Jackson commanded and fought along the Shenandoah Valley, the Confederates won. In March, his infantry had pushed Union forces back across the Potomac River to reclaim Charlestown and Martinsburg. At the end of May, he retook Front Royal and Winchester. But things were not going well in Central Virginia, where General Johnston led in the Tidewater region. There, gray troops gave up the port of Yorktown at the mouth of the James River on May 4th. Now the Federals were only five miles from Richmond.

The South had also lost more than ten thousand

killed, wounded, and missing men in a place called Shiloh, Tennessee. They'd given up New Orleans and lost control of the Mississippi River. It was a fearful time.

Jamie had remained tight-lipped in his conversation. All he'd tell them about his arrest was that the Federals had taken him into Alexandria and held him in the old slave pens on the wharfs. Several of the older businessmen of Middleburg and Leesburg had also been arrested and jailed with him. They'd been incarcerated with a smuggler, a man who'd had an ear sliced off during a saloon fight, and a Union deserter. They'd wanted Jamie to take a loyalty oath to the Union.

"Did you, son?" Miriam asked.

Jamie wouldn't answer.

He had been unusually cooperative, though, in working with Isaac and Bob in planting the fields. They'd gotten in corn, wheat, potatoes, and timothy hay. Not as much as they had in the past, but enough. They'd just have to pray for good, easy weather that summer.

The physical labor seemed good for Jamie. The sun had tanned his face, hiding some of those freckles and somehow erasing the babyish pout that had been so unattractive. He held himself more erect and looked taller as a result. And although he talked far less than he used to, Jamie was more agreeable to Miriam's requests for help.

The one thing he did refuse to do, though, was continue his studies. Miriam did not push him to. Annie did only once.

"Jamie," she said as gently as she could, "your education is too important to let it go."

"And what good would it do me now?" Jamie asked.

"Why, all the good in the world, Jamie. Poetry, plays, novels, music, they are the cry of the human spirit trying to understand itself and make sense of our world. Without understanding, without expression, we are merely animals, eating, breathing, dying. We're the only species God gave the gift of speech and thought. Think of it. We're the only creatures who can paint, who can write down our thoughts, who can make music." She paused. "Well, I suppose you'd have to include a mockingbird in that, since he makes up the order of his songs." She shook her head at getting off track. "Remember your Socrates, Jamie. He said there is only one good, knowledge, and one evil, ignorance. Education gives us solace in times like these."

"Solace?" Jamie exploded. "I don't want solace.

I want the Yankees out of my homeland. I want revenge for their humiliating me, riding me through the streets of Alexandria for people to shout at. What are you going to do? Lie down and let them run over us, take everything we have, and then read a good book to make yourself feel better? Not me! Ignorance the only evil? Stop being so naïve, Annie. You and your books. There is all sorts of evil in the world, and a lot of it is wearing blue coats and pillaging our country."

CHAPTER TWELVE

July 30, 1862
Hickory Heights

Annie and Miriam sat huddled together, reading two letters that had miraculously made their way through all the upheaval and all the blue and gray troops to Hickory Heights.

The first was from Laurence. He was safe and full of stories of Stuart and a miraculous ride they'd made around McClellan's army near Richmond.

Dearest Mother,
I was saddened and worried to learn of the recent Union incursion into Fauquier, and hope to hear from you soon that all there are well. Please tell Annie to stay safely indoors when such happens—she will understand and I pray heed my instructions. Tell Jamie

that I am counting on him to stand by and shield you sensibly. I am sure that the Union officers will not allow civilians to be harmed or starved. Always appeal to those in charge, Mother. The captured officers I meet seem to be scrupulous men.

Most importantly, be assured that we are doing everything we can here to relieve the pressure on you at home. I cannot help but believe that we will indeed win this war when I ride with Stuart. You may hear of his daring ere this letter reaches you, but I'd like to tell you of it myself, so that you do not worry so much.

You may have heard that General Johnston was gravely injured in the Battle of Fair Oaks, in the marshes east of Richmond. General Robert E. Lee has replaced him. I do not know the man, but his reputation is one of steadiness and courage. His nephew, Fitz Lee, leads my regiment under Stuart, and a finer horseman and colonel you'd be hard-pressed to find. General Lee asked Stuart and our men to scout out McClellan's army, to ascertain the condition of the roads and the size of the Union forces facing us. Well, we certainly did that!

General Stuart chose his best scouts—John Mosby, Redmond Burke, William Farley (a Shakespeare scholar I'd much like to introduce to Annie)—and 1,200 riders, plus a twelve-pound howitzer. Around 2 A.M. on the twelfth of June, we were awakened and given orders to ride, we knew not where. Within ten minutes we were in our saddles, ready to go. We departed, guided only by moonlight. We rode all night and most of the next day. When we finally stopped and camped, no talking and no fires were allowed. We'd cooked three days of rations before we left on our scout, and we ate in silence—surprise being one of our weapons against the nearby Federals. We left before dawn the next day, and by midmorning we reached Hanover Courthouse. (Remember your history, Annie; this is where Patrick Henry first spoke out against the British to begin the Revolution. He once cried: "Give me liberty or give me death." I know we Confederates believe the same. If only Lincoln could have understood our desire to govern ourselves and respected it and the

Constitution's guarantee of it, all this bloodshed could have been avoided.)

Here we had our first skirmish. Just beyond the courthouse, in a field of young corn, we spotted bluebirds. "Form fours! Draw sabers! Charge!" Stuart yelled, and we complied, pounding down the road and easily capturing most of the Union pickets and destroying a camp of the 5th United States Cavalry.

Strangest thing, Mother—there is so much of this in this war—we paused a long time to chat with our prisoners, as the unit was Fitz Lee's old one, from his days in the Union army. He'd been a junior officer with them, and our prisoners laughed and greeted him quite happily. Fitz asked after all of them—who was the new sergeant, if particular men were still alive and well. The Union men cheered him as we finally rode off, wishing him Godspeed!

By that point we could see a huge encampment in the far distance, probably where McClellan himself sat. Our presence was no longer secret. Stuart had found McClellan, knew his strength and location, and could return to report all to General Lee. But rather than take that safe course, Stuart decided to press on to confuse the enemy, to return to Richmond by circling around the back side of the entire Union army.

He took us, Mother, right into the jaws of the enemy, 100,000 strong! I know you will think me insane when I tell you it was one of the most marvelous rides of my life. I was not out of my saddle from Thursday morning until Saturday noon, riding more than 100 miles. We burned two hundred Federal wagons, captured three hundred much-needed horses and mules, felled Union telegraph wires and bridges, attacked a Union troop train, and even managed to sink a large Federal transport.

All this while being chased by the Union cavalry!

We were all falling asleep in our saddles by the time we reached the final barrier to safety, the Chickahominy River, all swollen and raging from rains, rising like a wall to prevent our escape. The Federals were close behind us. There was no way to swim the river. We tried felling trees along its banks, but they did not extend to the other side. We were trapped against the river like a fox surrounded by hounds.

Our only chance was to quick build a footbridge to cross. Oh, Mother, if you could have seen how such tired men sprang to action. We found a skiff on the bank and floated it to the middle of the river and moored it with ropes. Then we stripped boards from an abandoned warehouse, placing the ends of the planks on the embankment and stretching them to the skiff, using it like a pontoon. We did the same from the skiff to the opposite shore. We crossed unsteadily, walking along the planks, carrying our saddles, sabers, guns, and bags in one hand and the reins of our horses in the other, steadying our poor steeds as they struggled to swim the currents. My horse, Merlin, was magnificent!

We could hear the enemy galloping along the road toward us as Fitz Lee was the very last to cross. As we set fire to our bridge, thousands of Federal cavalry thundered to the bank. We escaped by moments!

Despite the hail of their shots across the

river, we all made it home to Richmond safely, Mother, except for one poor rider. But isn't that something! Right around the enemy and back again with only one casualty. I swear, I think Stuart could somehow take on the Devil himself and either charm him or fool him!

"Saints preserve us," Miriam muttered, and crossed herself superstitiously. "God forbid that Laurence becomes reckless. What could that General Stuart have been thinking about?"

Annie smiled and wondered. Stuart's exploits only made her admire him the more. What dash!

"And what was the other letter, child?" Miriam asked.

It was an invitation to visit her school friend Charlotte in Warrenton. With all the fighting and with all the eligible young men off to war, Charlotte's parents had decided to postpone Charlotte's debutante ball. But they were gathering together a few friends to celebrate her eighteenth birthday. Charlotte had not been the cleverest of students at the seminary, but she was certainly the most prestigious socially, living in the county seat of Fauquier. She was two years older than Annie and always wore the latest fashions, twisting and curling her dark hair into the most amazing coifs, studded with silver combs. Annie was flattered by her friendship and had been uncertain of her hold on Charlotte until Charlotte had laid eyes on Laurence. Annie knew that this invitation came mostly because she was Laurence's sister, not because she was an especially great friend of Charlotte's. But that was all right with Annie.

"Please, please, Mother, may I go?"

"Certainly not, child. Think of the dangers between here and there."

"Oh, but Mother, the Pennsylvania troops have retreated all the way to Snicker's Ferry. Most of the Union army is down toward Culpeper, way south of Warrenton. The roads will be clear. It would be such a lovely thing for me. I'm so tired and bored of—" Annie stopped short. She didn't mean to hurt Miriam's feelings.

"I know, my darling. Life hasn't been very entertaining here of late. But I cannot let you ride into potential danger for the sake of a birthday party."

Annie thought for a moment. Clearly, she needed another reason to convince Miriam. "You know, Mother, Jamie could escort me. It might be good for him to do some business in Warrenton. We do need more supplies. Our salt is low, and we'll need much more when it comes time to slaughter the hogs for winter and preserve the meat. And I heard Isaac and Bob talking about how our remaining sheep are suffering for not having salt at all in this dry heat. No merchant in Middleburg has salt to sell now. Someone in Warrenton will, certainly. And Jamie really ought to sell that one horse that's kicking at Angel. She'd be a good brood mare. She has beautiful conformation, just a horrible temperament for riding; even Gabriel said so. She'd get a much better price at Warrenton. Maybe as much as a hundred fifty dollars. And in gold maybe rather than Confederate paper."

Inflation was becoming a horrible problem. Already a barrel of flour cost as much as forty dollars, when just last year the price was six dollars. In her common-sense way, Miriam wanted to use gold or even Federal greenbacks rather than Confederate paper money. And she had indeed been worrying about their salt supply. "We are going to need that salt if we're to preserve meat for the winter," she said more to herself than Annie. "I don't know what we'll do if we can't buy some."

But it was the thought of Jamie's attitude that

made her consider Annie's proposal. "Maybe if Jamie realizes how much he's needed to conduct the business of the farm, he will settle down and stop thinking of running off to fight. As a lady, I certainly can't negotiate the sale of that horse at market; nor can you, dear. . . ." Miriam's voice trailed off and she rubbed her forehead. "Let me think on it, Annie."

Annie could only stand to wait until dinner to ask again and again. By bedtime, she'd pestered Miriam into agreeing.

CHAPTER THIRTEEN

August 19, 1862
Warrenton, Virginia

Annie stopped to gaze up at the grand Greek revival pillars and the tall spire of Warrenton's courthouse. My, it was an inspiring sight. Even though she had visited it before, the town never stopped awing her. With *three* hotels, *two* newspapers, and an iron foundry, plus the court and law offices, the Fauquier county seat bustled with twelve hundred residents and a sophistication that made Upperville—for all its beauty—seem a dull, countrified mud pit. Warrenton even had wooden sidewalks and stores with ready-made dresses and hats displayed in their windows.

Letting her parasol slip back so she could see the courthouse's full height, Annie stared at the handful of men in top hats and tailed coats charging up its tall marble steps. She thought about all the lives that had changed upon entering those massive, ornate doors—innocent and guilty making their pleas and being judged, people claiming property and others disputing it, families recording their marriages, births, and deaths. That was the way of it, men scurrying and arguing, laying claim and throwing away, defining the world. Annie sighed. Men's lives seemed so much more vibrant and interesting than women's.

"She's gawking again," Eliza whispered to Charlotte, nudging her. The three girls had been strolling along Main Street together.

"Annie"—Charlotte took her arm— "you really mustn't stop in the middle of the sidewalk, dear." She straightened Annie's cream-colored parasol to shade her against the hot August sun and pulled her gently back to walking. "The sun is way too bright. You'll ruin that beautiful creamy complexion of yours, besides making us look like country bumpkins." She laughed gently as she said this, keeping the reprimand light.

"I'm sorry, Charlotte," Annie apologized. "But I just can't help wondering about all that might go on inside that courthouse. Don't you?"

That brought Charlotte and Eliza to a standstill.

"Land's sake, no," said Eliza. "Mama says you see the inside of a courthouse only if you're a vagabond or a ruffian or worse." She rolled her eyes and whispered, "Like a fallen woman."

"You mustn't mind Annie," Charlotte told Eliza. "She's full of ideas. It comes from all those books she reads. At school, she neglected her deportment and needlepoint dreadfully because of them. Miss Williams told her it would be the ruination of her, but Mr. Burton encouraged it." She smiled at Annie. "Eliza and I will just have to corrupt you a bit while you're here, Annie. Get you away from those books. Let's peep into the shops. I hear that some lovely new fabrics actually made it past the blockades into town. You might see something you like. This dress, I'm sorry to say, Annie, is a bit old-fashioned." She plucked at the skirt of Annie's fawn-colored walking dress, with its carefully stitched rows of flounces and crimson piping. "You know, the Zouave dresses with their little bolero jackets are all the rage now. You could carry those bell sleeves well, you're so slight of figure. I'm afraid I look rather round in them."

But Annie couldn't be distracted that easily. "Charlotte, really, don't you ever want to be a man, just for a day, to see what goes on in places like that? To argue a case in front of a judge? Or pass laws? Or ride in a cavalry charge?"

"Goodness!" Eliza gasped. "Next thing you'll tell us is that you are a suffragist."

Annie was about to answer that indeed, yes, she thought women ought to have the right to vote and to own property, but Charlotte's pretty face stopped her. There was a silent plea all over it. Eliza, with her ruffled silk dresses and dainty ways, was clearly important to Charlotte. Annie smiled stiffly at Eliza and answered, "I wouldn't presume such."

Charlotte changed the subject. "Any word from Laurence, Annie?"

As they crossed the street to look in shop windows, Annie told her about Laurence's letter and Stuart's ride around McClellan.

Charlotte's brown eyes shone and her face flushed a little as Annie talked. She was smitten, all right. Annie wondered if Laurence felt the same. He'd never said so, but then again, Laurence rarely talked about how he felt. Charlotte had a storybook face: heart shaped with pronounced cheekbones and large, thick-lashed eyes, all framed by shining black hair that held the ringlets her maid created with hot curling irons. She certainly was attractive enough to catch his attention.

"Do you suppose I could send a note to him

through you?" Charlotte asked, and then added hurriedly, "Just to wish him Godspeed."

"I'm sure he'd be happy to receive it, Charlotte. I was planning to write him about my visit with you and to re-assure him that Jamie is doing well with the farm business."

"You two better be careful about writing letters to soldiers in the Confederate army. Don't you remember what happened to those ladies last month, Charlotte?"

The trio had reached the front of a dressmaker's shop, the window a rainbow of fabrics, plumes, ribbons, and laces. They stood looking in but not really seeing, so intent they were on what Eliza had mentioned.

"Yes." Charlotte nodded her head and lost her smile and blush.

"What happened?" asked Annie.

Eliza looked around before pulling Annie close, their three parasols shielding them from the street.

"They were arrested. Rumor has it for corresponding with their relatives who are serving in our armies. That wicked Federal, General John Pope, encamped three divisions around Warrenton at the end of July, and he accused the ladies of spying."

"No!"

"Indeed." Eliza raised an eyebrow and grew angry. "But what can you expect from a person who authored the conscription bill and has ordered the arrest of any man he deems disloyal to the Union."

"Conscription?" Annie asked. She knew the word meant forcing men into military service. The British had done that to American sailors, and that had been one of the causes of the War of 1812. But clearly it also applied to food and supplies. "We lost many of our hens and livestock when the Union army came through Upperville this spring," said Annie. "They simply helped themselves. But an officer stopped them from taking everything."

"Well, if Pope has his way, officers will be ordering it."

"What?"

Charlotte again took Annie's arm. "Come read these Federal orders. They posted them on the window of the newspaper office. Pope lost no time in becoming a dictator. Within two weeks of Lincoln making him head of their Army of Virginia—such a name, honestly, for our foe to use—anyway, within two weeks, Pope issued this." She pointed.

With concern but no real surprise, Annie read Pope's General Order No. 5—which stated that the Union army would live off occupied territory, taking from Virginia citizens whatever it needed to feed its soldiers, horses, and oxen, giving nothing in return but a voucher, supposedly payable at the end of the war *if* the owners could prove themselves loyal citizens of the U.S. government.

General Orders Nos. 7 and 11, however, frightened her greatly.

No. 7: " . . . If a soldier or legitimate follower of the army be fired upon from any house, the house shall be razed to the ground, and the inhabitants sent prisoners to the headquarters of the army. . . . Any persons detected in such outrages, either during the act or at any time afterward, shall be shot, without awaiting civil process."

No. 11: "Commanders . . . will proceed immediately to arrest all disloyal male citizens within their lines. . . . Such as are willing to take the oath of allegiance to the United States . . . shall be permitted to remain at their homes and pursue in good faith their accustomed avocations. Those who refuse shall be conducted south beyond the extreme pickets of this army, and . . . if found again anywhere within our lines . . . they will be considered spies, and subjected to the extreme rigor of military law.

"If any person, having taken the oath of allegiance as above specified, be found to have violated it, he shall be shot, and his property seized and applied to the public use."

Good God.

"Jamie!" Annie exclaimed. "I have to find Jamie."

She grabbed Charlotte's hand and turned to hurry to the market square, where she knew Jamie would be with Isaac, haggling over a sale price for their mare. But her parasol blocked her view as she turned, and she bumped into a tall, thick-shouldered man. As she drew back her sun shield, she gasped. She'd stumbled right into a Union officer, neat and trim in his blue uniform.

"Afternoon, miss. Best look before you turn," he said pleasantly. "Are you all right?"

Speechless, Annie nodded.

The officer smiled and tipped the brim of his hat. "Afternoon, Miss Eliza, Miss Charlotte."

"Good afternoon, Major Goulding," Charlotte and Eliza sang out together, polite, schoolgirlish.

"I'm afraid I won't be seeing you ladies for a while. I'm leaving town today. But I very much enjoyed escorting you both to the outdoor theater our army hosted last month. Please take care of yourselves." He tipped his hat again and started to stride off.

"Oh, we will miss *your* company mightily, Major, but certainly not that of your army." Eliza smiled as she gave her insult. She cocked her head to one side, so that she looked at the major from the corner of her violet-blue eyes, veiled by her long lashes. She even fluttered them slightly as she spoke. It was the perfect coquette look.

Annie was aghast. Was Eliza actually flirting with this Yankee?

"Oh, now, Miss Eliza, you better accustom yourself to our company. General Pope is moving south, quite rapidly right now. I wager we'll be in Richmond within a month. And then the war will be over."

Annie saw Eliza's mouth tighten momentarily, but then she smiled again, dazzlingy. Her bonnet of white unfinished silk, edged with lavender flowers, perfectly framed her delicate face and highlighted those eyes. "Why, Major, you can't believe that," she said smoothly.

"Can't I? We're about to take Gordonsville and the Virginia Central Railroad Junction there. When that happens, Bobbie Lee will be completely cut off from his supplies in the Shenandoah Valley. You'll see. We'll be in Richmond in no time." He crossed his arms and grinned at her. "In fact, Miss Eliza, I'll wager you a bottle of champagne on it. In a month, I'll be dining in Richmond. And I hope to meet ladies there as gracious as you."

"I accept your wager, sir, with pleasure. You Federals have consumed all my father's wine. He will be glad to receive your champagne as payment for your lost bet when you fail." Eliza's voice was playful.

The major laughed good-naturedly and tipped his hat once more.

After he passed, Annie looked at Eliza with wide eyes. "You know that Yankee?"

"Of course." Eliza sighed, growing impatient with explaining everything to Annie. "The town has been flooded with them most of the summer. They attended our church services. They constantly paraded along our streets. They hosted balls. Out of politeness, we had to pretend to go along with them. But I always covered my ears when their bands played their horrible Union tunes. And I'd step into the gutter before walking under the Union flags they hung on our buildings.

"But, you see, Annie"—Eliza grew intense as she spoke—"they do fall over themselves to impress a pretty girl. They let slip all sorts of details of their plans just as the major did a moment ago. You never know when that might prove useful to our boys."

Charlotte chimed in. "They are quite the braggarts, Annie. Eliza's right." She turned to Eliza. "I had wondered where they'd all vanished to this week."

"They've been skirmishing up and down the Rapidan and Rappahannock rivers, south of here, following that battle outside Culpeper, at Cedar Mountain," said Eliza matter-of-factly.

How did she know that? Annie wondered. With their newspapers shut down by the Federal troops, Fauquier County residents had to deal mostly with wild and anxious rumors. But Eliza seemed quite confident in her information.

Eliza looked away from her companions for a moment, thinking. "I wish I had someone trustworthy to give this information. But I suppose General Stuart already knows Pope's plans. The man is so bombastic, he's sure to have bragged publicly and alerted our boys already. Did you hear what he told his troops? That he plans to keep his headquarters in the saddle. His own soldiers joke that he doesn't know his headquarters from his hindquarters.

"But I do wish I could just ride out and tell General Stuart myself." Eliza turned to Annie. "Perhaps I *would* like to be a man, just this once."

Annie couldn't help it. Maybe she and Jamie were more alike than she cared to admit. She blurted out the story of her own ride to warn Stuart the previous September. She failed to include the fact that Stuart had had no need of Annie's urgent information. Annie didn't exactly say that she saved Stuart's men from disaster, but her omission that they already knew the Federals were coming and were riding out to meet them definitely left the impression that her ride had been critical. Certainly it was daring, no matter what the outcome.

Charlotte gaped at her, her brown eyes the size of eggs. But Eliza smiled, eyebrow raised. From that moment, they were friends. For the first time in her life, Annie felt admired and coveted as a companion in a way she'd seen other girls bond at school but she herself had never known. It felt good.

Annie had no inkling how much she would come to regret having shared the story of her ride with others.

Three days later, Annie was packing to return home. It was early morning and she was trying to dress without waking her friend. The two of them had shared Charlotte's bedroom during Annie's visit, and Charlotte was still curled up in the massive canopy bed, her dark curls sweeping out across the crisp white linens.

It had been a wonderful visit. Annie had come to appreciate Charlotte's gentle nature and could see her affection for Laurence was genuine, not just one of many conquests. Annie had watched other girls gather marriage proposals by the handful, and although Virginia society fully accepted the light-hearted courtships, Annie had always thought it shallow. One either loves or doesn't. It shouldn't be played at.

But then again, how did one know that the queasiness, the heart flutters, meant love, true love? Annie sat down by the window and pulled out the poem from Stuart, rereading it for probably the five hundredth time. Most of it she had memorized. *I saw thy beauteous image bending o'er . . .*

"What are you reading, Annie?" Charlotte stretched and rubbed her eyes.

"Oh, nothing important." Annie fumbled with the letter, sticking it into the middle of the Byron poetry collection she had brought along to read during her trip. The very book she'd received from Thomas Walker, the cavalryman from Massachusetts. She noted the irony of hiding Stuart's letter within a Yankee's book. Still, Annie knew well that in another day, a day before the war, she could have seen Walker as a possible sweetheart. She stood up and faced Charlotte.

"I've had such a lovely time, Charlotte. Thank you for asking me and for tolerating Jamie!"

"Ah, yes." Charlotte grinned and sat up. "The red-headed rapscallion. How can he be Laurence's brother? And yours?" she hastily added.

Annie didn't mind the barb at Jamie. He had been a handful in Warrenton. After their encounter with the Federal major, Annie had hurried to find Jamie, worried by Pope's orders to arrest men disloyal to the Union. With the slightest encouragement, Jamie was all too ready to rant about the Yankees. He might even brag on his plans to shoot at Federal troops from that tree. Given Pope's orders, their house could be burned down for Jamie's exploits. Annie had another fear brewing, too: that Jamie had taken the oath of allegiance in the Alexandria jail while clearly having no intention of keeping it—something for which Pope's men could now legally shoot him, no trial needed.

They'd found Jamie in the market square, Isaac trying to get him into their supply-laden wagon. He had indeed sold the troublesome mare for a good price—$125 in Union greenbacks—to a Yankee officer. As horse-trading tradition dictated, they'd begun the bargaining with a drink of whiskey. They ended it with one as well. Jamie had never tasted spirits before. They didn't sit well with him. First he shouted across the green at Annie about how smart he'd been to sell a wild horse to a stupid bluecoat who'd surely be thrown and hopefully killed by her. Then he demanded to know where in the blazes they'd been. Poor Isaac was doing all he could to quiet the boy, and Jamie lashed out at him, pushing him over.

When they finally convinced Jamie to get into the wagon, he fell all over the supplies he'd managed to purchase from the sale of the mare—including the salt that was so vitally important to Hickory Heights. When Annie told him to hush and sit and not destroy the salt, he turned purple with rage. Then, rather suddenly, he threw up.

All this Charlotte witnessed and somehow thought funny.

"You know, Charlotte, I can't account for Jamie." Annie laughed. "Believe me, Laurence has tried with him." She grew serious. "But I do worry so about him and what he might—"

The door flew open, as if on cue, and in dashed Jamie.

Charlotte shrieked and slid under the covers.

Jamie didn't even notice her.

"Annie, Annie, finish dressing, for the love of God, and come downstairs. They say General Stuart is riding into town!"

CHAPTER FOURTEEN

August 22, 1862
Warrenton, Virginia

"Oh, listen, listen, can you hear?" Eliza called out. "They're singing! Hush, ladies, listen."

Annie strained to hear male voices, now just barely audible from the western edge of Warrenton. She stood among a crowd of people—old men, boys, women, schoolgirls, children. All were anxious, breathless. Some held hands. The women clutched whatever flowers they'd been able to pluck from their gardens, which were withering under the August glare.

It started as a whisper but then grew loud along with the clear clip-clop of horses—"The Bonnie Blue Flag":

"Then here's to our Confederacy, strong we are and brave,
Like patriots of old we'll fight, our heritage to save;

And rather than submit to shame, to die we would prefer,
So cheer for the Bonnie Blue Flag that bears a single star."

The crowd was absolutely still, mesmerized, until suddenly Eliza picked up the chorus in a murmur, followed by Charlotte, the elderly couple beside her, Jamie, and a knot of other teenage boys, one after another. The song rippled through the crowd, until hundreds of voices sang out:

"Hurrah! Hurrah!
For Southern rights, hurrah!
Hurrah for the Bonnie Blue Flag that bears a single star."

"Here they come!" Jamie shouted.

Around a bend in the street came Stuart and more than a thousand horsemen at a trot, somehow far more gallant in their drab gray uniforms and rowdy entrance than any spit-and-polish Federals with their bright navy-blue uniforms, brass buttons, flashy gold epaulets, and formal parades. Annie felt tears on her face as she and dozens of others pushed forward to greet them.

"Hurrah for Stuart! Hurrah for Virginia!"

A people starved for the sight of their champions rushed to surround the horsemen, swallowing them up. Ladies threw rose petals and daisies.

Others offered cider and biscuits. Men reached to touch the riders' boots. Citizens who recognized loved ones in the ranks cried out with joy. Riders leaned over to hug them. One man pulled two children up onto his horse and buried his face in the curls of the littlest girl, who clung to his neck.

Above it all, Stuart was laughing, and shouting, "Good day, citizens of Warrenton! Here we are to liberate you!" He was surrounded by the town leaders, their top hats reaching his hip. They gave way, however, to an elderly woman, who croaked, "General, may I kiss you?"

Stuart swept off his hat and immediately bent down. "But, of course, dear madam." Everyone cheered.

Annie watched it all from the edge, jostled by people pushing past her. The sight of him stopped her there, suddenly shy, trembling all over, hot from the blush on her face. What could she say to him, above all this? Why would he be interested in talking with her when an entire town was adoring him? Would he even remember her? Annie watched his every move, tried to will him to look her way.

And then suddenly he did. Was she imagining the look of recognition on that bearded face? Stuart's horse pranced and pawed the ground, uncomfortable with all the hands petting her, shoving flowers into her bridle. He looked down for a moment to steady her, but then he looked up toward Annie. She smiled and lifted her gloved hand to wave, then dropped it, feeling foolish. After all, it had been nearly a year since he'd seen her. While she remembered every angle of his figure, how startlingly blue his eyes were when the sun hit them, there was no need for him to recall anything about her. She was no one. He was the quintessential Virginia cavalier, a leader on whom the state, a whole new country, was hanging its hopes.

Sighing, Annie put her hand on her throbbing heart. Oh, if only she'd be able to speak to him. She looked down at the golden black-eyed Susans she held, then back up at Stuart, noting how the wildflowers matched his golden sash. She wondered absently what had happened to the gorgeous plume that typically festooned his hat.

"Annie?" Charlotte was beside her. "Do you see Laurence?"

Annie broke out of her daydreaming. No, she hadn't seen her brother. She was ashamed to admit that she hadn't yet looked for him. She took Charlotte's hand and began walking back down the line of riders.

It took a good fifteen minutes to locate

Laurence, way in the back. He and his group had dismounted and were letting their horses graze and drink water from the town's troughs.

Jamie had already found him. As Annie and Charlotte approached, Laurence put his hand on Jamie's shoulder. Jamie was talking excitedly, waving his hands around as he typically did when he was telling a story. Annie pulled Charlotte to a stop about fifty yards away. "Wait a moment," she told her friend. "Let them finish, please."

Jamie stopped, and Laurence smiled and patted his shoulder in a "well-done" gesture.

"Oh, good," Annie breathed. "That will make a world of difference for Jamie." She stepped forward, still holding Charlotte's hand. But Charlotte was rooted.

"Do I look all right?" she whispered to Annie.

For a split second Annie felt impatient, because now she'd forgotten Stuart and wanted to embrace her big brother. But she softened, seeing Charlotte's fluster. "Beautiful," Annie whispered back with a reassuring squeeze to Charlotte's hand. "I wish I were as pretty as you."

"Annie!" Laurence called out, and jogged a few steps. But when he recognized Charlotte, he stopped to straighten his collar, nervously fastening the top three buttons he'd undone in the heat.

So! Annie thought. *Good.*

After a kiss and a hard hug for Annie, and an embarrassed, formal handshake with Charlotte, the four of them sat under a shade tree. They talked about the campaign, Hickory Heights, and horses. Laurence said he'd be home on furlough soon to gather new, fresh horses. As a rider with the Virginia cavalry, he had to supply his own mounts. He reminded Jamie that the wheat would need to be harvested within the month, the hay cut, to tell Bob to be sure to watch the corn carefully. If it didn't rain soon, he'd have to go ahead and gather what was there, even if green. How were the potato fields? Any new foals? Jamie answered it all with pride.

Annie watched in surprise, Charlotte in awe. Laurence was having a tremendously positive affect on Jamie. Slowly, Annie recognized the reason for it. It was the first time Laurence had spoken to Jamie as if he were an equal, at least in terms of working Hickory Heights. She decided not to tell Laurence of some of the foolish, dangerous things Jamie had done in the past months. If only Jamie could take this new attitude home with him.

But the mood shifted abruptly.

"Why are you riding in the back, Laurence?"

Jamie asked. "If I were you, I'd be up there with old Stuart himself. When I join up, I'll be a captain in no time."

Laurence stiffened. "That so, little brother?"

Jamie started his swagger. "You can bet. Why, I almost took down a whole line of Pennsylvania yokels myself."

Laurence looked sharply at Annie. "That so? Aren't you watching him, Annie?"

The implication that she'd failed somehow smarted. She lashed out, "Oh, Jamie, for shame. We haven't seen Laurence since Christmas. Don't do this today. He doesn't need to be weighed down with your conceit and nonsense."

Jamie jumped up. "You'll all be sorry someday for treating me this way." He stormed down the road, kicking stones as he went.

Annie hung her head, mortified that Laurence thought she hadn't controlled Jamie—as if she could—and that they'd made a scene in front of Charlotte. She plucked at the grass.

After a few awkward moments of silence, Laurence, as usual, was the one to restore polite conversation. "Actually, ladies, you might not want to be sitting with the rear guard here, because we are, for the moment, in disgrace."

"What?" Annie and Charlotte cried out together.

"Oh, Laurence," Charlotte added, "how could anyone possibly question your honor and bravery?" It was one of the few things Charlotte had said during the past half hour, and there was a tremor in her voice. It touched Laurence. It took him a few moments to respond, and in that time they gazed at each other. Annie had to suppress a smile; they looked so silly.

Perhaps Laurence felt her amusement, for he adopted a lighthearted banter and joked. "Why, because, Miss Charlotte, General Stuart blames us for the loss of his best hat!"

"Oh, Laurence, do tell," said Charlotte.

With a grin, Laurence told the story of a rich felt hat with a monstrous plume that had arrived for Stuart along with a copy of the *New York Herald*.

When a truce had been called to collect the wounded and dead from the battlefield at Cedar Mountain—the very battle Eliza had mentioned to Annie and Charlotte—Stuart had overseen the Confederate gathering. He met up with an old U.S. army friend, General Samuel Crawford, who was on the field for the Union.

"Well," continued Laurence, "while their soldiers loaded wagons with corpses and bleeding men, the opposing generals shared a picnic lunch, remembering old battles fought together out west against the Indians. At their parting, Crawford congratulated Stuart on the Confederate victory at Cedar Mountain. Stuart countered that the Northern papers would surely call it a Union win. 'The Yankee papers claim every battle a Yankee victory, however it turns out,' one of our staff officers said.

"Crawford denied it. And then Stuart bet Crawford a hat that the Northern papers would do that very thing.

"Crawford took up the wager, saying, 'Not even the *New York Herald* would have the audacity to claim this.' It had been a terrible defeat for the Yankees. They lost close to three thousand men in one afternoon. But can you believe, ladies, the New York paper did, indeed, tout it as a resounding Yankee victory. So to pay off his lost bet, Crawford sent the hat, which General Stuart put on with great ceremony. It was good for our boys' morale."

Laurence's smile faded. "But Stuart lost that hat, he says, because our unit was late for a rendezvous the other night. He'd sent Fitz Lee a confusing order by courier, so we stopped to gather supplies and rest our horses, not realizing he wanted us to come immediately. It's bad because we lost the opportunity to trap Pope between the Rappahannock and the Rapidan rivers.

"But I think the thing that annoyed General Stuart most was the fact some of Pope's cavalry surprised him in the night. He heard horses and thought it was us coming. It's so hard to know who's riding up the road in the dark. Stuart had to make a rather sudden escape, jumping upon his horse and vaulting a fence. He left behind his hat, cloak, and haversack. He's had to wear a handkerchief on his head to protect himself from the scalding sun for several days. He is not pleased. So . . . " Laurence leaned back against the tree. "We ride in back!"

Annie didn't know whether to be angry with Stuart or to defend him. She couldn't help blurting out, "Don't you men have anything better to do than be bragging and making bets? Why just a few days ago—" Annie felt a sharp nudge against her foot through her skirt. She and Charlotte were sitting close to each other, their skirts great pools of blue linen and lace on the green grass. She turned to look at her friend. Once again, Charlotte's open, pretty face was awash in a silent plea.

Of course! Annie realized. *Charlotte doesn't want Laurence to know she's been talking to Yankees!* Annie's mouth snapped shut, and she smiled dumbly at her brother.

"Just a few days ago what?" Laurence asked. He laughed. "Did you forget what you were going to say?"

"Oh, no, it's not important." Annie shifted topics. "Where are you off to now?"

"I can't tell you, Annie, but you shouldn't worry," Laurence said quietly. "Although I must say this war is different from what I thought it was going to be. Different from what most people expected, I'm sure. I think General Stuart hoped that a few rousing cavalry charges would frighten them home—that our disagreements would be resolved easily and quickly through a set of chivalrous duels. Many of our Confederate commanders have a deep respect for the Union forces. Our officers and their officers went to school together and fought together out west, for pity's sake.

"Others don't have that kind of restraint. General Stonewall Jackson, for instance, is completely different in outlook, a prickly, eccentric, hellfire-and-brimstone, Old Testament type of warrior. After Cedar Mountain, there was a group of his infantry soldiers mourning a fallen Union officer. He had been so brave, leading his men in charge after charge, our boys felt badly for having shot him. But

Jackson reprimanded them for their regret and told them to shoot the brave ones because they lead the others."

Laurence shook his head. "It's becoming a different kind of fight, all right."

CHAPTER FIFTEEN

August 23, 1862
Warrenton, Virginia

It rained that night, great torrents, as if God had looked down, been shocked to see the parched earth, and ordered entire rivers of rain to make up for weeks of dry heat. Annie watched it through Charlotte's window. She and Jamie had stayed because of the uproar in town over Stuart's appearance. By the time the Confederate cavalry had ridden out, heading southeast, and everyone had calmed down, it was far too late to begin the long journey home. Given the mud that would surely result from the downpour, she'd probably be with Charlotte for a few more days.

Lightning flashed bright and lit up the room for an instant like midday. Charlotte had finally fallen asleep around midnight out of exhaustion from her flutter. Besides the thrill of seeing Laurence, she had met General Stuart and just about swooned from the excitement of it. But Annie was wide awake, plagued by a jumble of thoughts. The convulsing thunderstorm gave her a good excuse to get out of bed and pace the room to think through the day's events.

Stuart had not sought out Annie. Why should he?

But Eliza had. She wanted to speak with the handsome and daring cavalry leader. And who better to introduce her to him than Annie, who'd once, for sure, saved Stuart's life. Eliza was all sugar and deference.

In the blackness, Annie pressed her face against the cool windowpane and relived the mortifying experience.

"Oh, it wasn't like that, really." Annie had hastened to modify her boast and dissuade Eliza of her plans.

"You mustn't be so modest," Eliza answered. "You are an inspiration to me, for one. I would have given anything to see you—like Joan of Arc in a knight's armor, leading the English to destroy France."

"Actually, she led the French against the . . . oh, never mind." Annie bit her tongue to keep from correcting Eliza's muddied history. She'd seen that look before, on classmates' faces when they'd heard a romantic story and had no interest in its grittier, more factual details.

Annie had kicked herself. See where boasting gets you? What if Eliza said something to the general about Annie's supposed lifesaving warning to him in Lewinsville! She'd die of shame right then and there. Annie demurred, saying that the general would be far too busy with important tactical planning to take time for three girls. Then she said his staff wouldn't let them through. Finally, she said she didn't feel well.

"You mustn't keep the general to yourself, Annie Sinclair." Eliza tried tarring Annie with guilt. "He belongs to the nation, you know. Think how I'll feel if I had the chance to meet our champion and didn't. I want to be able to tell my children that I once shook hands with the famous Jeb Stuart himself."

All the while, arm in arm, Eliza had been walking Annie and Charlotte closer to the Warren Green Hotel. On the hotel porch, Stuart was drinking tea and amusing the crowd with his stories. While he entertained his admirers, his staff gathered information about the roads to Catlett Station.

As they approached, several townspeople turned from Stuart to look at the three girls. Fleetingly, Annie recognized that they did make a colorful appearance. She and Charlotte had both hurried into their best walking dresses—Charlotte's pale blue and Annie's deep royal. Eliza was in a pink frock, festooned with small crimson bows along the skirt and waist, plus a bonnet to match. (Annie was beginning to wonder how many bonnets Eliza owned! She herself made do with two.)

The crowd stepped back to make way as General Stuart stood up, beaming his greeting. "Ladies." He bowed. "To what do I owe the delight of a visitation by three such enchanting Southern muses?"

Eliza pushed Annie forward. Annie still clutched her black-eyed Susans, and weakly, she whispered, "General, I'd be proud if you'd wear this bouquet in your sash."

A wide grin broke open that mask of beard, and his blue eyes brightened with pleasure. "Why, of course. I'm sure it will bring me luck in battle, miss"—he paused. "Miss . . . ?"

Annie's heart sank with the realization that he didn't recognize her. He was trying to prompt her to provide him her first name. How would she explain this to Eliza and Charlotte? But just as she was about to murmur her name, Stuart put his hands on his hips and threw his head back to laugh. "Why, to be sure, it's Lady Liberty!" He took her hand and with great show leaned over to kiss it, bowing gracefully. As he straightened he caught her eyes. "You are even more beautiful today, Miss Annie, than when last I saw you. I was so completely enraptured with your loveliness that for a moment I was dumbfounded. Forgive me." He stepped back and added, "You have grown up into a breathtaking lady." He looked to Eliza and Charlotte. "And may I have the pleasure of meeting your fair companions?"

At their introduction, Charlotte was speechless. But Eliza spoke boldly. She told Stuart of the Yankee major, his boast about the Union army taking Richmond within a month, and his bet of champagne. "General," she finished with playful drama, "if you will capture that major, he will win his bet with me, since he will be on his way to Richmond—as your prisoner! If you will bring him by here, I will gladly pay him his bottle of champagne. Won't that be amusing?"

Stuart roared with laughter. "A lady after my own heart! Indeed, yes, Miss Eliza, we will look out for this unfortunate major and bring him straight back here to you." He turned to his staff and shouted: "Gentlemen, to horse. If God wills it, tonight we'll have captured Pope." He winked at Annie and lifted himself onto his thoroughbred.

"I'm going after my hat!" was his final jubilant shout before he rode off, trailed by fifteen hundred followers, kicking up dirt as they passed.

He had left Annie's flowers behind, as well as Annie, seething with uncertainty. Grown up? Had he thought her a child before? Oh, if only she hadn't been so lily-livered when she'd seen him, so tongue-tied. Why couldn't she have been forthright and poised like Eliza?

As thunder rumbled, matching her predawn mood, Annie flung herself down in front of Charlotte's dressing table and buried her head in her arms on top of it. General Stuart certainly had been all eyes for that Eliza. Miserable, Annie cried herself to sleep.

At daybreak, there was a pounding on the door and the shouting of male voices. Annie's head jerked up from the dressing table, where she'd slept. Terrified, she listened. Could it be Federals come back into town? Did someone want to arrest Jamie? Throwing on a dressing gown, she scampered to the landing of the stairs. Five men crowded into the front hall, their cloaks dripping water onto the gleaming hardwood floors. At the sound of her running bare feet, they looked up and took off their hats, letting a stream of rainwater fall from the brims. Their hair matted and soaked, their faces drawn with fatigue, it was hard to make out who they were.

"Do you think Charlotte's mother might have some real coffee for us, Annie?"

It was Laurence!

Charlotte's house burst into hospitality, laying out a mammoth breakfast, even offering up some sausage—nearly impossible to procure—for the cavalrymen. Laurence had arrived with one of Stuart's favorite scouts, William Farley. As Annie passed by him, pouring coffee, Laurence motioned for her to lean down. He whispered into her ear, "This is the gentleman scholar I wrote you about, Annie. Of all the men I've met, he's the one who most shares your love of books. You'll like him." Annie glanced over at the self-contained South Carolinian. He had a high, wide forehead; soft, dark hair; large, far-set eyes; and a thick set of whiskers outlining his mouth and jawbone. He had a quiet handsomeness about him, none of the charming liveliness, the bodaciousness of his commanding general.

Laurence clearly had no idea of Annie's foolish notions about Jeb Stuart. And they were silly, overly romantic, she knew. She smiled down at her brother and repeated from *Romeo and Juliet*, " 'I'll look to like, if looking liking move.' " She'd always loved the alliteration of that line, and marveled at how dutiful Juliet had been in promising to look favorably at a suitor of her parents' picking. If only Annie could make herself be that agreeable.

"What did you say?" Laurence asked. "You see, you prove my point." He teased, "You two should get married and *he* can try to keep you from jumping fences with crazy horses."

Annie swatted his arm and whispered back, "You mind your own romantic interests, brother. I don't suppose you chose this house for coffee by accident, did you?"

Laurence held up his cup, silently asking for a refill. Only his dimpled smile gave him away.

Despite the pelting thunderstorm, Stuart's raid had gone well, Laurence said. The aim had been to cut the telegraph wires linking Pope to Washington and to burn a railroad bridge over Cedar Run near Catlett Station along the Orange & Alexandria line. Without the bridge, reinforcements and supplies could not make it south from Federally occupied Alexandria to Pope's army. Robert E. Lee's plan was to isolate Pope, back him up against the rivers, and then attack him full force with the massed Confederate armies led by Jackson, Longstreet, and Lee himself.

Unfortunately, the downpour had so saturated the bridge that it wouldn't torch. Laurence and his brigade had even tried to chop it to ruin, but they were under severe gunfire from Federals across the stream, dug in on a cliff. They had managed, though, to slip through all the pickets in the black, stormy night and found themselves right in the middle of Pope's headquarters. As jagged lightning crackled through the heavens and lit their way, Stuart's men stampeded through dozens of tents.

There they discovered a treasure trove—a money chest containing thousands upon thousands of Federal greenbacks plus Pope's dispatch book. The book revealed Pope's fear of being attacked before Federal reinforcements arrived. The Confederates also captured a herd of well-fed, rested horses; wagons full of bacon, medicine, and Havana cigars; plus almost three hundred prisoners, many of them officers. To their disappointment, they found Pope was not in camp to capture.

"Oh, yes." Laurence sat up suddenly after relating all their success. "That field quartermaster, that Yankee major your friend was so interested in. We did catch him. General Stuart is going to present him to Miss Eliza so that she can honor her bet with him—since this very day he will be off to Richmond as he boasted. Of course, he is going as our *prisoner*, not a conquering invader—not exactly the way he hoped to win his bet, I'm sure!" He and his companions laughed. "Would you like to see the fun?"

Charlotte and Annie certainly would!

They arrived at the courthouse just in time to see the Federal major, still good-humored, still pleasant, accept his bottle of champagne from Eliza. "I shall be happy to drink the health of so charming a person," he said.

Eliza was dressed in her finest lavender silk. She curtsied prettily to the throng of Stuart's men, who cheered and laughed and wished the major a happy journey and stay in Richmond!

Eliza would be famous. Someone will probably write a song about her, thought Annie with a jealousy she couldn't squelch.

After that, Stuart announced that he held another honored guest as prisoner—General Pope's full dress blue uniform! Laurence's brigade leader, Fitz Lee, had found it in Pope's tent.

Stuart unfurled the long blue coat with delight and shouted to his assembled men: "I think I'll send a dispatch to General Pope asking for a fair exchange of prisoners—his best coat for my plumed hat.

"What do you think, boys? Shall I do it?"

His men laughed and laughed. It was like a game, the whole thing, a glorious cat-and-mouse chase, with ennobling salutes across the tournament fields from an impressed and amused enemy. Annie looked at the men, so enraptured by Stuart, so energized by his theatrical wit and sweeping charisma, which made the war seem a grand adventure. No wonder they followed so willingly behind him and his banjo picker, fiddler, and bones player. Annie glanced at Laurence, whose actions and conversation had always been tempered by his sensible and responsible nature. Her brother glowed. Annie felt swept up in it all, too, the feeling of invincibility, patriotism, and legend being made.

"*We few, we happy few, we band of brothers . . .*" a voice behind her recited.

It was the scout, William Farley. His face didn't have the same luminous excitement that his compatriots' did. It was more a studious recognition of the stirring scene before him—a scholarly spectator.

Annie knew the line from Shakespeare's *Henry V.* It was one of the playwright's most rousing, heart-stopping speeches, the words steeling a small force of peasants to go into a battle that by all odds would crush them.

Instinctively, the next phrase came out of Annie: "*For he today that sheds his blood with me / Shall be my brother.*"

Farley turned to Annie with a shocked and impressed look. She nodded at him and in her own mind continued: *And gentlemen in England now abed / Shall think themselves accursed they were not here / And hold their manhoods cheap. . . .*

Was that it? A sense of history, of being part of a tremendous, perhaps immortal moment of change that helped shore up these men, these boys, her brother? Was it the fear of being left out—abed in England, as Shakespeare put it—that pushed Jamie into such foolish brags? Is that what drove her to want to be part of it somehow?

Her thoughts were interrupted by the plea of one prisoner, who did not share the light-hearted jollity that Eliza's major had. It was a woman—a woman disguised in a Federal's private's uniform. She'd been posing as a man in Pope's infantry. Even the Union men who'd fought with her in her unit, who stood to the side under Confederate guard, seemed annoyed to learn her true identity.

The woman spoke: "General Stuart, sir, I insist that you release me." Although she stood tall and straight at attention, her voice was shrill, jittery. Her face was young, pretty, and frightened. "My gender should excuse me from going to a common Confederate prison. In all decency, please."

Stuart stared at her. Then he answered in words Annie would never forget: "If you're man enough to enlist, you ought to be man enough to go to prison."

Stuart's riders left immediately after that, a rush of hooves, huzzahs, and tearful good-byes, horses replenished by good feed, bucking a bit in exuberance. Warrenton seemed ghostly quiet afterward—the townspeople left behind to wait for news of the next battle, the next shift in the parameters of their lives and expectations, the next joy and the next sorrow.

Annie and Jamie left, too, after the roads dried a bit. All the way home, Jamie sang a new song written about Stuart, inspired by his raid on Catlett Station.

"Now each cavalier that loves Honor and Right
Let him follow the feather of Stuart tonight.

We are three thousand horses, and not one afraid;
We are three thousand sabres and not a dull blade.
Come tighten your girth and slacken your rein;
Come buckle your blanket and holster again;
Try the click of your trigger and balance your blade,
For he must ride sure that goes Riding a Raid!"

CHAPTER SIXTEEN

September 2, 1862
The town of Middleburg,
east of Hickory Heights

"*Yea, though I walk through the valley of the shadow of death, I will fear no evil: for thou art with me. . . .*"

The cherub-faced boy whispered his prayers and then looked at Miriam with huge, clear, blue eyes. They glistened with unshed tears, but his gaze was direct and steady and riveted on Miriam. She was smiling at him, that soothing, loving smile of hers.

"It's all right, ma'am," he said in a hushed calm. "You can let go now."

Miriam nodded, swallowed hard, kept her eyes on that young, beautiful face, and took her fingers away from his throat. Immediately, blood gushed along the boy's collar and onto his chest. Their eyes did not part until the boy's no longer had life in them.

Miriam reached out to close them. She folded his hands on his chest. Then she collapsed.

The doctor bundled her into Annie's arms. "When your mother comes to, take her outside for some fresh air," he said.

Numb with what she'd just witnessed, Annie fanned her mother with a towel.

Miriam had been plugging an artery in the boy's neck. He'd come in with the hundreds of wounded flooding Middleburg from the second Battle of Manassas and the Battle of Ox Hill. When they'd lifted him off the wagon, the wound, which had been bound with linen strips, suddenly burst open. Miriam had somehow known to staunch it with her fingers and had held herself there until the surgeons had determined there was nothing they could do to save the boy. He would bleed to death within moments from the sliced artery. Only her fingers—like a cork in a dike—kept him alive.

The boy listened to the surgeons explain. They were sorry, they said. The boy took a long, deep, wrenching breath and pressed his lips together to quell their quivering. Then he'd asked Miriam to write his parents and to tell them he had been as brave as he could. "You'll find the right words for me, won't you, ma'am? I never was good at letters."

When Miriam revived, she looked up at Annie with eyes that seemed a hundred years older.

She and Annie dragged themselves out of the church that had—like all the buildings in the town—been turned into a makeshift hospital. Although the air was clean and sweet from recent rains, being outside offered little relief to them as the wounded lay everywhere in the streets and under shade trees, awaiting help.

Women moved among them, offering them water and food. Wagons pulled up with meals hastily cooked by the residents of nearby farms. Aunt May was somewhere, ladling out stew they'd brought in from Hickory Heights. The Confederate army had dragged nearly eighteen hundred wounded men back from the battlefield but provided rations for only two hundred.

"Hmpf," Aunt May had grunted when she'd seen what meager biscuits, bacon, and beans the army offered. "Twenty hungry men could eat that for one meal."

At least the tide of bleeding bodies seemed to have stopped. The Confederates, led by Stonewall

Jackson, Lee, and old Pete Longstreet, had yet again pushed the Union forces back over Bull Run, back behind their line of fortifications ringing the city of Washington. All the talk was about Jackson's infantry, which had managed to march on foot fifty-four miles in two days to catch Pope by surprise. Jackson's soldiers were hailed as "the foot cavalry" for their remarkable speed and tenacity.

There was even speculation about Lee moving into Maryland, to circle up behind the city of Washington, isolate it, and perhaps then capture it from the north. The main hope was that Lee's maneuver would lure Federal troops out of Virginia and take some of the pressure off the state, which had been a constant battlefield and food store for both armies for the last year. Lee was adamant that this was not to be an occupation of Maryland but simply a march through the border state to feed his men and horses and to bring an end to the war. His purpose, he announced, was to defend the Southern homeland, not to invade or occupy as had "those people," his term for Yankees.

Annie watched the progress of the news through town. Whenever people huddled together and listeners closed their eyes and tipped their heads toward heaven, they were praying, "Please God, let it be so.

Let this end the war now."

Finding Aunt May and their wagon, Miriam crawled onto the driving bench. At the sight of her, Aunt May stopped serving stew and fussed, "Missus Miriam, you look all wrung out. We need to get you home now." When Miriam nodded feebly and said nothing, Annie knew something was wrong. But she assumed it was the tragedy of not being able to save that sweet young soldier. It wasn't until they reached Hickory Heights that she and Aunt May recognized how feverish Miriam was.

"It's diphtheria sure," said a local doctor that night. "Her throat is covered with the gray membrane. Several people are sick with it around here. The army must have brought it with them as they passed through on the way to fight at Manassas. Seems like wherever they go, they spread contagion. Last winter, when they encamped in Fredericksburg, more than two hundred children died of scarlet fever. I hear of regiments losing half their men from typhoid and dysentery. Army surgeons tell me they can hardly keep them well long enough to send them into battle to be shot down." He shook his head grimly.

Annie heard little of what the physician was

saying. She could only focus on the word: *diphtheria.* People typically died of diphtheria, suffocating because their throats were swollen shut.

The doctor was still talking, handing quinine to Aunt May and explaining that Miriam should take it and be bathed frequently. He wasn't going to use leeches unless he had to. He'd be back as soon as he could. There were so many wounded to tend to; he was trying to help out the army. If she survived the next seven days, she should live. Annie and Jamie, he finished, should not get near their mother.

In a daze, Annie watched Aunt May let the doctor out the front door. When she bustled back, she was as in command as if she were a general. "Annie, lamb, you listen to me good now. I can't let you back in the room with your mama. She'd rather die than you get sick. But you can help Isaac and Rachel gather up some things for me. I need spice bush for a tea, mashed garlic for a poultice for her chest. I need them to find some horehound and wild cherry bark, too. I need to mix it up with some honey and whiskey. Praise God we saved a little whiskey from those thieving Yankees." She pushed the quinine into Annie's hand. "Put that in the larder. It won't do Missus Miriam no good. All them surgeon quacks know are calomel and quinine and sawing off things. I seen them. Grandma Hettie taught me how to do for sick folk. I watched Missus Miriam, too. I know what to do, child." She patted Annie's face. "G'on, honey."

Annie staggered to do Aunt May's bidding, herself completely unprepared to nurse Miriam. Oh, if only she'd paid more attention to the things her mother had told her about tending the sick. She'd just always expected her mother to be there, the kind, nurturing, wise miracle worker. What would she do if Miriam died?

For two weeks, Hickory Heights hung in a gloom, waiting, as Miriam trembled with fever and chills, coughed and lurched for each breath. Aunt May emerged only to ask for clean linens, fresh water, and more of the syrups and teas she'd made. She ordered Isaac to burn the dampened cloths she'd used to cool Miriam.

Everyone tried to keep things running as Miriam would. Rachel took up Aunt May's cooking duties and Annie tried to help. Isaac, Bob, and Jamie separated the lambs from the ewes and counted a dozen males that could be slaughtered for meat for the winter, less than a third of what they'd had the year before. They cut and stacked twenty acres of timothy hay and began gathering wood to lay in for winter. But no one's mind was really on work. Everyone's thoughts were focused on Miriam's bedroom.

Once Annie found Jamie sitting outside Miriam's bedroom, his face hard against the door, trying to hear what was happening inside. Annie sat down with him and also pressed her ear to the thick, wooden door. All she could make out was Miriam's wrenching cough and the answering murmur of Aunt May's voice, gentle, soft, coaxing. The two of them remained huddled there. Instinctively, Annie put her arm around Jamie's shoulder, the way the two of them used to nestle together when they were little and Laurence read aloud by the fireside.

"Annie." Jamie looked at her with fearful eyes, naked of his usual defensive swagger. "Do you think Mother will die?"

"I'm praying not, Jamie. She's strong of heart. She'll fight to stay with us."

"Do you think she loves us that much?"

"Why, of course she does, Jamie." Annie squeezed him a little. He shrugged and looked down.

"Maybe she loves Laurence that much."

Annie sighed. She'd been thinking a lot about Miriam in the past few days, thinking about how devastated her mother had been when the boy soldier died despite her heroic attempt to save his life. It had stolen a little piece of her being. Annie had seen it.

"You know, Jamie," she said slowly, weighing her words as they came out for accuracy of what she meant, "I think Mother changed after our brothers and Father died. We were too little to remember what she was like beforehand. I imagine she was more carefree, more confident about life. I think her being with them when they died took away her ability to love without fear. I think she cares for us as dearly as she can while still worrying that someday we might get sick and die. I think she holds back just a little to protect herself."

Jamie mulled it over. Annie could tell he wanted to understand it. Of course, understanding and not being hurt were two different things. "She's not that way with Laurence," he finally mumbled.

No, she wasn't. Jamie was right about that. "Maybe it's because Laurence is of the old days for her. His childhood was mostly lived *before* Father and the boys got sick and died. Ours was just beginning afterward, after she was so changed by tragedy. Does that make sense?"

After a few moments, Jamie nodded.

Annie added, "And besides, Laurence *is* a good man, Jamie—you know that."

Jamie shuffled his feet around and nodded again, looking at the floor.

"Annie?"

"What?"

Jamie looked up at her, and there were tears in his eyes. "Do you remember the time Laurence got so torn up when his horse threw him?"

"Of course." Annie could still envision the uproar as Sam and Gabriel's father carried Laurence into the house, all covered with blood.

"Did he ever tell you how that happened?"

Suddenly suspicious, Annie drew back a little. "He said Merlin was just feeling his oats and spooked."

Jamie stuck out his lower lip and looked back down at his feet. "That isn't what happened. Laurence had given me a hard time about running through the stable—he can act so high and mighty, Annie, you know he can. It's not as if he's my father or something."

Annie said nothing.

"Well, I was good and mad at him for bossing me. So I hid in the bushes, and right before Laurence was about to take that fence, I threw a rock at Merlin and hit him on the flank. He reared, but Laurence stayed on. Then . . . I don't know what I was thinking, I was just so mad, Annie. I stood up—Laurence saw me—and I chucked another stone at Merlin and hit him smack in the chest. That's when he started going wild, bucking and running."

"Oh, Jamie," Annie gasped, "you could have killed Laurence!"

"I know that." Jamie jumped up and slammed his fists into his pockets. "It should have been all right. He would have just gotten a bruised backside, if his big foot hadn't caught in the stirrup and that crazy horse hadn't dragged him all over tarnation." Jamie glanced guiltily at Annie. "He never told you?"

"No."

"He never told Mother either," Jamie murmured. "Do you think she'd still love me if she knew?"

Annie reeled with the question. Her first instinct was to blurt out that no, Miriam would never forgive Jamie for doing such a mean-spirited thing. Yet Miriam was amazingly patient. How could Jamie be so jealous and ornery, just because Laurence tried to keep him safe? But then Annie thought about herself and hung her head. Hadn't she often plagued her big brother with her own defiance of his protective common sense? She felt a rush of guilt.

Lord, Laurence *was* a phenomenal person, even if he did take his role as big brother and replacement father a little too seriously. Annie would have tattled on Jamie the first chance she'd gotten. It was astounding that Laurence hadn't. But maybe it was Laurence's magnanimous, almost noble spirit that made Jamie so mad at him, so jealous all the time.

Annie dropped her head into her hands. These were too many confusing thoughts for one day. But then, it was as if Laurence were in her ear, telling her it was time for her to live up to her role as an older sister. She straightened herself and took Jamie's hand. "Of course she would, Jamie. You're her son, her youngest child, which I know is a very dear place to be." Annie smiled and added, "After all, you're her baby."

Wrong words.

"I'm not a baby, Annie!" Jamie ran away.

Would that boy ever end a conversation without darting away in a huff?

Toward the middle of the month, word came that the entire Army of Northern Virginia—all troops under Lee, Jackson, Longstreet, and Stuart—had indeed crossed the Potomac River at Point of Rocks, just north of Leesburg. For the first time in the year-and-a-half-long conflict, the Confederates were on the offensive. Lee's popularity, the country's faith in him, soared as some of his troops marched as far as Frederick, Maryland. Surely, Lee would be able to finish off the war soon with this maneuver. While Southerners turned their hopes northward, Miriam hung on to life.

In the midst of this hopeful news, the doctor returned to examine Miriam. He emerged from her room, very pleased with himself. "She's weak, Annie. She'll never be the same, that's certain. I can't tell how bad the damage to her heart is. Her pulse is quite erratic, skipping beats, fast as can be sometimes. But she's survived the diphtheria."

Annie grabbed the banister, dizzy from the intense rush of relief and joy. "May I see her, doctor? I haven't talked with her for almost three weeks now."

"Not yet. In a few days I think it would be safe."

As they reached the door, the doctor turned and grudgingly said, "That darkie of yours is a surprisingly good nurse. I hope she stays with you. All the other ungrateful wretches are running off."

Annie stiffened. How could this educated man

talk that way about Aunt May? Clearly it was she who had saved Miriam's life and not this pompous doctor with his paltry two visits and unused quinine. Ungrateful wretches? It seemed to Annie that the "ungrateful wretches" were the white families that Aunt May and so many of her race served so loyally despite their inherent bondage.

But all Annie could choke out was "Aunt May is a wonder, doctor. I don't know what we'd do without her."

The doctor raised an eyebrow quizzically before tipping his hat and strutting down the stairs.

Frustrated with herself for not saying more, not doing more to bring about the change she now knew was needed, Annie watched the doctor get on his spotless horse and trot down their lane. It was this kind of man who made all Southerners seem monsters; this kind of man who believed slavery to be right; this kind of man who probably did fight to keep people as property. Annie suddenly felt incredibly dirty. She turned toward the house, wanting to shut her door against the doctor and all he represented, all the things she didn't want to think about, and all the things she'd done wrong herself. As she did, she noticed a wagon overflowing with chairs and bags pull into their lane. One lone cow was dragging all that weight and stumbling as it came. She raised her hand to shade her eyes and tried to make out the figures walking alongside the cow. A white woman, an African woman, and three children. The children trotted behind five hogs they were herding along.

So many strangers had come up their driveway asking for food and overnight shelter since the war had begun. So many hungry people scattered onto roads, not knowing their future. But it took Annie only a moment to recognize this group even though one was a stranger to her. It was Aunt Molly and Annie's three little cousins.

CHAPTER SEVENTEEN

September 25, 1862
Hickory Heights

"After this round of warring right through my fields, I said to myself, 'Molly,' I said, 'get to Miriam. She'll know what to do for my babes.' This time when they squabbled over Manassas, the Yankees took everything, Annie. They cut down all my corn for their horses, chopped down my apple trees for their campfires. They took off with my gobblers, even though poor Will stood outside the pen and begged them not to take the turkeys he raised up from eggs he'd searched the woods for. Lord, have mercy."

She leaned across the teacup Annie had given her to whisper, "My boy isn't the same since he fished up that corpse in Bull Run this spring. Trying to catch some fish for supper for me and his baby sisters, and there he pulls up a soldier's skeleton, poor wee lamb." She leaned back and shook her head. "I don't know what will be left of the farm when we get back. John will be furious with me for leaving our land, but he's off with General Pickett. Husbands just have to go along sometime. I can't stay there with armies tramping over me."

Annie tried to listen, while calculating where she was going to put them all to sleep that night. "Who's the girl?" Annie nodded toward the young black woman Rachel was talking to out in the hall.

"That's one of the Robinson kin. Mr. Robinson is a freeman, works his own one-hundred-and-fifty-acre farm, one of my neighbors. He used to do carpenter jobs for your uncle John once and a while.

"Do you know, those Yankees camped all over *his* fields, took *his* house for a field hospital, and stole everything *he* had. I mean everything—even though he told them he was free and it was *his* land and hard work they were ruining. You got to figure they'd go after us white folk. But they're so mean, they wreck a man they brag on freeing. The Yankees tore down and burned a mile of fence rails—eight rails high!—around Mr. Robinson's place. They ate his two fat cows, and made off with eight hundred pounds of bacon and sixty barrels of good clean wheat he had ready for market. I was lucky to escape with my hogs, 'cause they took all his plus his two horses, one worth two hundred dollars. He told me they even stole his cooking utensils. And they didn't pay him one penny for it all.

"Now I ask you. Do you think those Yankees are going to treat the Negroes well if they free them?"

Annie didn't know what to answer to that. Her head was swimming. She'd forgotten how much her aunt could jabber. Aunt Molly was in good form again, healthy and plump in her calico, and able to talk the broad side off a barn. She hadn't yet answered Annie's question regarding the girl's name or why she was with them.

"Oh, land's sake." Aunt Molly laughed at herself. She was a jolly soul, Annie gave her that. "Her name is Lenah. Even though Mr. Robinson managed to buy his wife and some of his children out of slavery, a lot of his kin still is property of someone. Sad fact is, Lenah was about to be separated from her family and sold off. But Mr. Robinson talked one of the richer landowners around Manassas into purchasing her, to keep her in the area until he'd raised enough money to buy her out himself. Her owner then hired her out to Mr. Robinson. He saw me leaving and asked that Lenah come with us."

"Aunt Molly, we can't afford to hire her right

now. Our fields and livestock are way down. The bluecoats have robbed us, too. If we were going to hire someone, it'd be a field hand to help us keep food coming."

"Now, Annie, me dear, I know your ma can afford to take us in. Mr. Robinson said Lenah would work for free, for food and to be out of harm's way, until the fighting's over." She leaned back and looked around the room. "Yes, ma'am, a fine place to visit awhile. Thaddeus would never let us near the place after he made off with your ma. Where is Miriam, anyway?"

Annie felt a flare of anger. Aunt Molly had been eating and resting for more than an hour before she thought to ask about Miriam. When Annie told her how sick she'd been, Aunt Molly crossed herself and muttered, "Diphtheria. Sure now, that's bad. Can she swallow?"

Annie said she could.

Aunt Molly nodded. "Praise be." Then she looked at Annie with an odd expression. "That'll be making you lady of the manor. Would there be a room for me and my wee ones?"

"Of course, Aunt Molly. We're family." Annie stood up. But which room? She hated to put them in Laurence's bedroom, purely out of superstition.

She'd gladly give them hers and move in with Miriam, but clearly she couldn't sleep there safely for a while. If she moved Jamie into Laurence's room, he'd probably rail at being dislodged. No, there was nothing else to do but temporarily put them all in Laurence's room, save Will. He could sleep with Jamie.

And what about Lenah?

Rachel solved that one. "Lenah can stay with us," she said, putting her arm around her new friend. Like Rachel, Lenah had beautiful, large, black eyes and a chiseled, striking face.

Annie felt a strange pang of jealousy. She could see an instant bond forming between the servant girls. She foresaw many heartfelt chats between them in the two-room cottage that housed Rachel, Aunt May, and Isaac, and, until he ran off, Jacob, too. But Annie kept to her manners and said, "I hope your journey was not too arduous. Rachel will be sure to get you some food."

"Yes, miss," Lenah responded as she went outside to gather her bundle of belongings. She spoke in a clear, nonaccented voice, another similarity to Rachel.

Annie couldn't help wondering why Lenah hadn't lit out for Washington, as many slaves in

Fauquier County were doing. It made sense to Annie that a young woman whose family was part free, and who clearly had some education, would instinctively want to head for the Union capital. Annie's fear, of course, was that someday she'd wake up to find Rachel gone.

"Rachel?" Annie reached out and took her hand. "Why would Lenah come here and not . . . not . . . not stay with her family?" Annie couldn't bring herself to broach the subject of crossing the line to the North with Rachel.

"Do you remember that sergeant, the night all those Federal soldiers camped at Hickory Heights?" Rachel asked.

Annie did. He'd made her skin crawl, both when he'd threatened Jamie and when he'd appeared from the shadows to talk with the girls as they hauled water. It was clear he was after something from Rachel—Annie was still uncertain what exactly he'd wanted—but it just felt wrong, as if he were trying to lure Rachel into something.

"Lenah wanted to get away from where the Federals were camped around Manassas. The Yankees scared Lenah, too, the way they talked to her," Rachel continued. "I think the way the Federals will see Lenah or me will be a lot like it was for Rebecca in *Ivanhoe*, that book you lent me, Annie. Remember? She's a beautiful Jewess and one of the knights, that cruel one, falls in love with her, mostly because she's so different from him. He's never seen a healer, someone dark like her, before. Just like I bet a lot of Yankees have never seen a Negro woman. And even though that knight in *Ivanhoe* felt for Rebecca, he'd never marry her because she was a Jew. His commanders couldn't believe that a Christian could fall in love with a Jew of his own free will. So they accused her of witchcraft, saying she'd put a spell on him."

Rachel looked away and spoke almost to herself. "I think it's going to be like that for us with some Yankees for a while. Some of them are going to think of us in ways they'd never think of white women."

When Rachel turned back, she spoke matter-of-factly. "Anyway, I'm just staying here to wait for Sam. He loves Mr. Laurence and wants to see him safe through this conflict. But then . . ." She shrugged.

Rachel's coolness hurt Annie. She frowned and drew back.

Rachel picked up on her feelings. "Annie, Mama and Daddy won't ever leave you. You know they won't. They love you and Missus Miriam and Mr. Laurence as if you was—were, I mean—their own. You've always been good to us. You're good people. And this is my home. But you have to understand, I don't want to be seen as anyone's property anymore. I want to be my own person someday. I want my freedom. Wouldn't you?"

Slowly, Annie nodded. Of course she would. She took Rachel's hand again, and the look between them said more than they possibly could with words, given the strangeness of their relationship as defined by their surroundings. What if Laurence legally set Rachel and all their servants free as he'd planned? Could she and Rachel then truly be friends? She resolved to talk to him as soon as possible.

After a moment, Rachel spoke again in a hushed voice. "The end may be sooner than you think, Annie. Lenah told me there was just a terrible battle in Maryland, at Antietam Creek, in Sharpsburg. They heard the news on the road as they came here."

"Oh, Rachel, did the Confederates prevail?"

Rachel shook her head. "The Confederates have crossed back over into Virginia. I don't know what that means, except it sure doesn't sound like a victory for the South." Rachel paused. "Lenah said word was more than twenty thousand men were killed or wounded, all in one day, Annie, mostly in a narrow road they're calling 'Bloody Lane.' There were dead men piled on top of each other waist-high in that farm lane. Wasn't Mr. Laurence up there with General Stuart?"

Annie felt clammy. Indeed, Laurence was. And Sam with him.

It would be several anxious days before they heard that Laurence was safe, camped first at Winchester and then outside Martinsburg. Although Laurence joked about his experiences in a brief letter, written on a scrap of paper, Annie could tell that his surviving the fights and the harried retreat was nothing short of a miracle. Two horses had been shot out from under him, including his beloved Merlin. The last time, Laurence had been trapped under the horse as he hit the ground and was knocked unconscious. He was startled awake when a pair of hands yanked him up and out of the way of a racing supply wagon, just in time to avoid being crushed beneath the wheels.

The hands had belonged to Sam. Somehow, in the horrific frenzy of horses, men, and ambulances stampeding along the roadway home, Sam had found him. “I owe Sam my life,” Laurence had ended the scrawled note.

Annie didn’t read Miriam the entire note. She made up parts of it, trying to lessen the unnerving details. Her mother was so frail and gray as she lay propped up in bed, so unlike herself. She constantly put her hand over her heart and took in deep breaths, as if to quiet a beast inside. Annie didn’t want to frighten her. Miriam needed quiet and happy news; Annie and Aunt May were both adamant about it. Aunt May guarded the bedroom door still, refusing to let anyone other than Jamie or Annie in. “Too much fuss and nonsense,” Aunt May had grunted, eyeing Molly and her children.

In fact, Aunt May had quite a standoff with Annie’s blood aunt. Annie heard it as she carried soup up the stairs for Miriam’s dinner.

“Out of my way,” Aunt Molly had demanded. “That’s my sister in there.”

Annie sat down on the stairs to eavesdrop.

“You ain’t getting near Missus Miriam,” Aunt May had countered.

“How dare you talk to me that way? Miriam needs to remind you of your place in this house.”

“I don’t need no reminding. I raise up Miss Annie, Master Laurence, and Master Jamie from babes. I help bring up Mister Thaddeus, too, what you killed. I know where that scarlet fever come from that took him and those three boys. Missus Miriam brung it home on her from your house and your scroungy litter of Irish brothers and sisters."

Annie heard Molly gasp and felt herself suck in a sharp breath.

Aunt May kept on the attack. Annie knew from her own fights with her that Aunt May had her arms crossed and her feet planted, a formidable mountain of fury. "I had no use for Missus Miriam when Mister Thaddeus first brought her here. New Irish. Not much better than poor white trash, I told him, even though she was a beauty. But then I come to see her for herself. A gentle Christian woman. Her kindness all the breeding she need. She act a lady without no training for it. She was good to my children and me. It was easy to love her.

"I see the way Mister Thaddeus scare her sometime, even though he say the sun and moon set and rose on her. He could be harsh, certain. I see how she suffered after her babies and husband died. I couldn't do nothing to help her then. But I can now. She may have forgiven you infecting her—that's her way—but I ain't. And you ain't upsetting her now that her heart is weak. You lucky to have food and a roof. Now, git."

Aunt Molly didn't even stop to look at Annie as she hustled by her on the steps, scooting by like a dog whacked hard with a broom. Lines were being drawn at Hickory Heights as strong as picket defenses.

CHAPTER EIGHTEEN

November 2, 1862
Hickory Heights

He was down there, General Stuart, down among the tents that speckled their fields with campfires, as thick as fireflies on an August eve. Annie ached to talk with him. The Virginia cavalry had ridden into their farm in the late afternoon, regrouping after a stinging encounter with New York and Rhode Island cavalry in the nearby town of Union.

In fact, stinging was probably not strong enough a word. Laurence had come into their house, grim faced and limping, his leg bleeding badly from a rip in his calf where a bullet had passed through his boot. If it hadn't been for John Pelham, the tenacious boy major of Stuart's horse-drawn artillery, said Laurence, they might have all been captured or killed.

He and the Confederate riders had actually fought dismounted, behind stone fences. When Federal forces pulled back to reload their single-shot carbines, Pelham charged and scattered them with cannon fire. Even so, Stuart's cavalry had had to withdraw again and again under pressure from larger numbers. Fighting every step of the way, they'd given up only a mile of turf throughout it all. "We are obstinate, Annie, grant us that," Laurence muttered as she and Aunt May bandaged him. "It is a fact, however, and an alarming one, that the Union cavalry is much improved."

For the past several days, Stuart and his men had been within a few miles of Hickory Heights. On October twenty-sixth, McClellan's Federal army had crossed into Virginia and moved toward Loudoun and Fauquier counties. Trying to protect the Blue Ridge Mountains' gaps and passages into the Shenandoah Valley where Jackson and Longstreet were camped, Stuart had been sent out to attack. He'd skirmished up and down Snickersville Pike, once scattering the Yankees as far back as Aldie and the Bull Run Mountains. He'd also galloped into Middleburg and Upperville, sending the towns-folk into fits of joy akin to the greeting Annie had witnessed at Warrenton. She'd nearly burst with frustration, hearing about both visits *after* they'd occurred.

Now the poet-general was down in her pastures. And she wanted to talk to him. She'd seen him briefly, only long enough to offer him a huge shank of mutton for dinner. His staff had taken it to roast, while Stuart met with his officers to plan the next day's strategies. Laurence had wanted to offer the house to his commander, but hearing of Miriam's illness, Stuart had declined. Laurence was up with Miriam now. Surely it would be all right for Annie to approach Stuart's tent and speak with the general for just a moment. She bundled herself up and slipped out the back door.

It was a cold near-winter evening. The moon had an icy white sheen to it and the brown grass was laced with frost. Crickets were long dead or burrowed into the mudflats to wait for spring. There was no sound of owls or shriek of foxes out hunting, only the crackling of campfires and the murmuring of men hunkered down against the frigid air. There was no singing, no joking, no shouts of congratulations. She passed gaunt horses tethered together for the night. She fought off a surge of nausea when she saw one horse still saddled, with a bunch of severed hooves dangling from the pommel. Laurence had told her how desperate for horseshoes the Confederate cavalry was becoming. In the middle of a battle, they'd pause to cut the hooves off dead horses to keep the usable shoes and nails. Without shoes, the horses' hooves chipped and cracked. The horses quickly grew lame and unrideable. Without horses, there was no cavalry to scout out the Yankees or to shield the Confederate infantry.

Annie soon identified Stuart's tent by the mass of men swarming it. A courier ran in through the flap. Within a few moments a dozen captains and corporals exited and the tent became silent and still. Now, she thought, might be a good time. She approached the tent. Stepping into the light of the lanterns ringing the tent's entrance, she startled a young lieutenant, standing guard beside it.

"Evening, miss." He tipped his hat. "May I help you?"

"I was wondering if the general enjoyed the lamb," Annie asked.

The young man brightened. "Oh, yes, miss, he did very much. We all had a bit. Best meal in days. Thank you kindly."

"You are most kindly welcome," she answered, stalling to think of a way to ask to see Stuart without seeming forward. Since Miriam's illness, Annie had struggled to take on the behavior of being the head-mistress of her household. The niceties required of such a position were still new to her, but now she spotted an advantage in them. "I wanted to know if the general needed anything else for the night." There, that kept her from sounding like a lovesick schoolgirl.

"I'll ask, miss. Please, may I announce you?"

"Yes. Tell him it's Annie Sinclair."

The lieutenant stepped inside the white canvas. Annie heard low voices, and the young man came out again. "He asks that you wait just a moment, miss, and that you forgive his delay." He looked back at the tent and then moved closer to Annie. He whispered, "He's just received bad news, miss. His daughter is gravely ill."

Daughter? What daughter? Annie went as cold as the night. If he had a daughter, that meant he had a . . . a . . . wife.

Aghast, Annie took a step back. What a fool she'd been to read anything into that poem, his flirtatious banter. She thrust her hand into her pocket. There was the treasured letter she'd carried for more than a year now, hanging on each and every word. Her fingers wrapped around the crisp, thick paper and she crushed it, getting some satisfaction in the crunch it made.

"Is that Lady Liberty?" a familiar voice spoke, but it was husky and somber, lacking its usual merriment and theatrics. Stuart stood before her, pulling on his outer coat. No golden colors to him that night—no sash, no plume, no braided epaulets—just a tired, mud-splattered soldier. He brushed his eyes and pushed back his hair, and Annie realized that he'd been crying.

Stuart spoke. "I am sorry to hear of your mother's illness, Miss Annie. Please tell her how much I enjoyed the mutton she graciously shared with us." His voice was flat.

Annie had wanted to slap him, to shout her disappointment at him, to accuse him of leading her on. But suddenly, she just felt sorry for him; sorry for herself; sorry for them all in that cold, stark night.

She found her way in polite conversation. "Perhaps we could bundle Mother down in the morning, so she could meet you, General. I know that would mean a great deal to her. But"—Annie paused, then said—"you must forgive her if she is quiet, General. She is not herself just yet. The diphtheria has left her very weak."

Stuart looked toward Annie but was clearly not seeing her. "We must all bear the sadness that sickness brings us with Christian fortitude and resignation." He slowly shook his head in disbelief and mumbled, "My own little Flora, just barely five years of age . . . such a sweet nature, so devoted to her papa." He stopped and stared off into the night.

Annie didn't know what to say. This was not the raucous, charismatic Stuart she knew, the larger-than-life man who could embolden a thousand men by his speeches or reduce women to swoons by a glance. He looked small, hairy, dirty, unmoved by her presence.

She'd been so sure of his interest in her. But then again, she'd never been courted before. How would she know the difference? In the cool moonlight, Annie realized that Stuart's poetic tribute to her was just part of the fun, the game, the lore of the crusade, the precious Southern cause.

Flattering? Yes. Heartfelt? Probably at the moment of penning it. Serious affection? It couldn't be.

At least, Annie told herself, she had enough sense to not burden this critically important general with her infatuation while he was in the middle of a confrontation with the enemy. She also had absolutely no idea what to say, her sense of embarrassment ran so deep. She waited.

"Well." Stuart sighed. "There's sure to be a fight tomorrow. I cannot leave my men to see my daughter, as my wife asks. God's will be done. Flora will live or die whether I am with her or not. My place is here."

Stuart attempted a smile. "After all"—his voice swelled with a bit of his accustomed bravura—"I am the knight of the golden spurs." He lifted a foot to show Annie an elegant, long, gleaming spur. "They're gold, sent to me by a lady in Baltimore. Aren't they marvelous?"

There was something very childlike in the question. Annie looked at him with surprise, catching a glimmer of neediness akin to Jamie's. God forbid that his men, that Laurence, should see it, not this night, not when they'd need all their pluck and confidence come dawn.

"Indeed, General, they are very handsome." Annie smiled reassuringly, trying her best to imitate Miriam. Her mother had always known how to bolster someone. "They befit the man who will lead the Confederacy to victory."

Instantly, Stuart beamed and straightened up. "You see, Miss Annie, you do soothe the soldier."

Annie recognized the line from his poem to her. So he remembered. Or was it a line he used on women he hoped to inspire—or impress? Annie felt a new wariness, a new understanding of how words could have many meanings. And yet, on this night, this moment of changing history, did it matter whether she was one of many he so flattered? His honeyed words inspired, even romanced Southerners into patriotism. That's probably what should matter most, she told herself, and closed her mind to further questions.

Certainly there might be need for her, for all of them, even boys such as Jamie, to join in the defense of Virginia. The seemingly unconquerable knight of the golden spurs would not win his battles the next day, or the day after that. As bravely as they fought, Stuart and his riders were driven south by the 5th New York Cavalry. They scrambled back over the Hazel and Rappahannock rivers, burning bridges behind them. Stuart even buried two cannons that were slowing their withdrawal to keep the Yankees from having them.

Despite the Union cavalry victories, General McClellan slowed his pursuit of the Confederates, allowing them to regroup. By month's end, the gray forces were strongly fortified at Fredericksburg, Virginia. Frustrated, President Lincoln removed

McClellan from Federal command and appointed Ambrose Burnside to lead the Yankees. Burnside had commanded a brigade at the Battle of First Manassas and fought at Antietam, but how he'd be in command of the entire Union army was unknown. No one could guess what the Federals might try next.

But one thing was clear to Annie—Stuart was learning to retreat, and at speeds faster than a trot.

CHAPTER NINETEEN

December 30, 1862
Middleburg

It was the night before New Year's Eve, the dawn of 1863. Stuart and his men were celebrating. The cavalry had ridden up from their winter quarters near Fredericksburg, and for the past several days had been raiding Union outposts and telegraph stations just south of Alexandria, across the river from Washington, D.C. They completely surprised the Federals and captured dozens of Union officers, two hundred horses, mules, and sutler wagons filled with supplies—the most prized cache being three hundred pairs of boots!

They'd ridden through snow and sleet, catching every Yankee picket along the heavily fortified Telegraph Road without alarming the Federal camps sleeping nearby.

Stuart's final exploit had been at the railroad telegraph office at Burke Station. There he paused to send a mirthful, taunting message to the U.S. quartermaster general, complaining about the quality of mules Stuart had captured from the Yankees: "Quality of the mules lately furnished me very poor. Interferes seriously with the movement of captured wagons." Then he cut the wires, burned a bridge, and set off to look for more loot at Fairfax Courthouse, a Union garrison.

Stuart was back to his bodacious self.

Despite the death of his small daughter, Stuart was buoyed, as were many in the Confederacy, by their victory at Fredericksburg in mid-December. Theirs was a hushed satisfaction, however. It had been a terrible slaughter of the Federals. Forced by their generals to cross a wide-open field toward a thick line of Confederates safely dug in behind stone walls and atop a rim of hills, thousands of Union soldiers had been shot down. Surely, sent in to such certain death with such callousness by their leaders, the bluecoats would give up fighting and the war would end.

With such thoughts, Stuart pressed on toward Fairfax Courthouse. But this last raid was not to be. Stuart was ambushed by pickets just outside the town. Stuart and his men withdrew without firing, relieved to find only one man nicked by a bullet. Confused by their lack of return gunfire, the Federals sent out a flag of truce and called through the darkness to Stuart's men: "Friend or foe?"

"The flag will be answered in the morning," one of Stuart's men shouted back. Stuart had his men light enormous campfires as if a large force were settling down for the night. Then, silently, they rode west until they reached Middleburg, some twenty miles away.

There, they stopped to rest and to share with the citizens the bounty they'd captured.

From a house on the town's outskirts, Laurence sent for Annie. She and Jamie arrived, with several other locals, to celebrate the holidays with some of the canned meats, fruits, and cheese Stuart's men had found in the Union wagons.

While his men gathered around the fireplace to sing Christmas carols, Stuart approached the settee on which Annie sat. She was glad to be wearing a new dress made out of the Massachusetts velvet. Midnight blue, it was a grown-up gown. The bodice was high in the back, low and square in the front, modestly trimmed with an edge of lace. The fabric sent by the Yankee mother was so elegant, Miriam had left the skirt unadorned, save for a wreath of lace at the hem and at the elbows of the puffed, short sleeves. Annie even wore Miriam's choker of pearls. Thus dressed, she felt very self-assured.

Still, Annie's heart skipped at the sight of Stuart. She couldn't help admiring him, even though her schoolgirl infatuation had died that night in her fields. She fleetingly thought of what Stuart might say if he knew the fabric had come from a Union family. Given his enjoyment of needling the enemy, he might relish the idea. She planned to tell Stuart until she noted the attitude of the small, wiry man accompanying him. The stranger was definitely all business.

"Miss Annie, this is Lieutenant John Mosby, one of my best scouts," said Stuart. "We are heading back to the main army, back to Fredericksburg. But John wishes to stay behind to keep watch on the bluecoats, to harass the enemy's rear for me. I think it's a good idea. I'm giving him a contingent of nine men from the 1st Virginia.

"This lady"—Stuart turned to Mosby—"is Miss Annie Sinclair, a great friend to the cause. Don't let her size or beauty fool you. She is Lady Liberty to me. If you are in need, I am sure she will come to your aid."

Mosby turned to Annie. Unlike Stuart, who was dressed in all his finery, Mosby wore plain, unadorned gray. He was clean-shaven, with a long, sharp nose and fine, honey-colored hair. His eyes were piercing blue, lighter than Stuart's, and serious as they assessed her. There was something shrewd, even calculating, about him, despite his polite manners. Annie was surprised that Stuart would think so highly of someone so very different from him. But then again, Stuart adored Stonewall Jackson, a dour, humorless man.

"Lieutenant." She nodded at him.

"Miss Sinclair." He nodded back.

"Why stay here in Fauquier and Loudoun, Lieutenant? The enemy is currently farther east, isn't it? In Fairfax County—Centreville, Chantilly, Vienna, Occoquan?"

Mosby hesitated, perhaps assessing Annie's sincerity, perhaps surprised by the directness of her question and her awareness of enemy locations. "This is the perfect landscape for my operations," he answered matter-of-factly. "There are woods in which to hide, hills that offer long views, high fieldstone walls for me to use in ambush, and, hopefully, loyal inhabitants such as you to keep me apprised. I can hit the very places you describe and quickly return here to safety." He shifted his feet and added bluntly, "Besides, the enemy will come again into this area, miss. I am sure of it. This is the highway to the Shenandoah."

His words filled Annie with dread. Yankees again. They had plundered through the neighborhood during much of November. She was so sick of scurrying to hide things—Angel in the cellar, feed bags on her hooves to quiet her tread; the silver in the pigeon roost; wheat in pillowcases and mattresses; bacon up the chimneys; meat shanks carefully wrapped and buried. The thought brought an end to her holiday mood.

It also was the end of Mosby's conversation, beyond asking where Annie lived and making note of Hickory Heights' location. He excused himself.

"A lawyer," Stuart whispered to Annie. "Old Mose is not one for idle chatter. I gather he read the law while he was in prison. He shot a fellow student at the University of Virginia who had insulted and threatened him on a dark stairway. John is definitely not someone to tangle with. My kind of rogue!" Stuart laughed heartily and took Annie's hand. "Now, Miss Annie, do tell me all about yourself. You look exquisite this evening."

Annie felt her face flush and took a deep breath

to keep herself from silliness and reading too much into his banter. "Well, General, you know it is difficult these days to—"

But Annie never finished. Laurence stepped up, and behind him was a hot-faced, breathless Jamie. Laurence wore an amused look. "General Stuart, I need to introduce you to my brother, James." He winked at Annie, who couldn't help smiling. Jamie was about to split open from excitement. "I didn't have the chance to do so when last we were together at Hickory Heights. The general had other concerns." Laurence pointed the last words at Jamie.

Jamie sputtered his hellos, and Stuart bowed formally to the boy. "I am glad to make your acquaintance, James."

"I . . . I . . . I hope very much to join your ranks, soon, General. Laurence here"—he glanced sideways at his brother, who rolled his eyes—"won't let me."

Trying to hide his growing amusement, Stuart asked solemnly, "How old are you, son?"

"Fifteen come March." Jamie was wriggling all over, like a happy puppy.

"Well," drawled Stuart, "this is December, which still makes you fourteen. Am I correct?"

The wriggling stopped. Jamie blurted, "I have a

friend who's a drummer boy. He's only three weeks older than I."

"I have no need for drummer boys, James. A drum cadence would take away the cavalry's surprise, now wouldn't it? But if you are as good a rider, as cool a head as your brother, and wait a year, I would be glad to—"

A brusque voice from the corner interrupted. "I'll take him. He knows the area."

Laurence turned, and his eyes narrowed when he saw Mosby. "For what?"

"For my ranger operations."

Laurence looked to Stuart, who explained.

"I see. Guerilla tactics." Annie noticed that Laurence's jaw had set, his eyebrow had twitched then quieted—a look she knew well. Laurence was controlling his temper and his words. There was something about Mosby he didn't like. His next statement was careful. "I need James at home, for my mother's sake. This spring, for instance, in my absence, he will oversee the planting of crops that my family needs to live."

"If we don't rout the Yankees, there will be no need for crops, Sinclair," Mosby answered quietly. "Remember a statement of Napoleon's—an army marches on its stomach. If the Federals are here, they will strip the land. We need to stop them first. I will need the help of people like your brother, your sister, to trip them up."

Laurence's fair face began to tint pink. "My sister is no soldier, Mosby. And my brother is a boy."

Mosby said nothing. Jamie looked like thunder.

Sensing trouble, Stuart stepped in. "This is all temporary duty, in any case, Laurence. And here we are wasting the presence of a lovely lady to argue over soldiering. Miss Annie, do you play?" He gestured toward the piano.

Annie didn't play brilliantly, but well enough. There had been so little time of late to practice.

"Do you know 'The Dew Is on the Blossom'?" Stuart asked.

Dutifully, Annie played while Stuart and his companions sang:

"The dew is on the blossom,
And the young moon on the sea.
It is the twilight hour,
The hour for you and me. . . ."

When she was done, and most of the group had begun playing charades, Laurence requested a three-day furlough from Stuart. Sam had asked to marry Rachel. Laurence wanted to give him a wedding feast before they returned to Stuart's encampment near Fredericksburg. "Who knows when we will be back this way, General, and it is very important to Sam. I want to do this for him. He saved my life, after all, in Sharpsburg."

. . . to have and to hold, from this day forward, for better, for worse, for richer, for poorer, in sickness and in health, to love and to cherish . . .

Sam held Rachel's hands as he repeated the vows, steady, sure. Rachel smiled up at him. She looked ethereal in the candlelight. She wore a white muslin dress that Annie's grandmother had given Aunt May to wear when she married Isaac. Aunt May had had to take it in considerably to fit Rachel. Lenah and Annie stood beside Rachel, Laurence by Sam. Miriam was bundled into a chair by the fire, listening. Aunt May stood behind her, tears streaming down her face. Molly and her brood huddled beside Jamie. Isaac had played the wedding march on his fiddle as Rachel passed through the parlor door. He stayed there now, sniffing loudly.

"Those whom God hath joined together let no man put asunder. I now pronounce you man and wife, in the name of the Father, of the Son, and of the

Holy Ghost," said the traveling minister Laurence had found to perform the ceremony. Then, in an abruptly loud, resounding voice, the gangly, black-clad man added, "Obey your masters as you would the Lord."

Everyone froze. Annie felt sick to her stomach as she saw Rachel's face switch from happiness to defiance to nothing. Surely, this man didn't compare a master's authority to God's, even if he was a believer in slavery. She started to open her mouth to say something, to push away the despicable nastiness of the moment, but Laurence put his hand on Sam's shoulder and stepped in front of the minister.

"This is not the way I wanted to do this, but now seems the best time to speak. I have made a decision, and Mother agrees with me. Tomorrow is New Year's Day. Tomorrow is the day a statement from the Union president called the Emancipation Proclamation will go into effect, freeing slaves in areas Lincoln considers to be in rebellion. Officially, the Confederacy will ignore it. But I have long held the institution of slavery to be wrong. I had meant to do this myself last year when I turned twenty-one and legally was able to do so, but the war interrupted all my plans. Forgive me.

"Sam, Rachel, it is perhaps more fitting that you

be granted your freedom today, your wedding day. You and everyone else here at Hickory Heights who have for so long been part of our family and our concerns are free. Two weeks ago, I filed the papers to make it all legally binding. I cannot undo the way you came to be part of our lives, but I can change the way you remain in it. The choice to stay is yours."

Rachel caught her breath and Sam's arm. He beamed. But no one knew what exactly to say.

Laurence tried: "May I kiss the bride?"

Rachel nodded vehemently and held her cheek toward him. Laurence brushed her face with his lips and then turned back to everyone else. There was a stunned silence.

Laurence cocked his head, frowning slightly. He tried again. "Let us enjoy the feast." He held up his arm, gesturing toward the dinner room, where awaited an enormous dinner of fried chicken, sweet-potato custards, and apple pies. There were two tables, one for the servants and one for the family, both laid out with the best silver and china, drawn out from their hiding places and polished to shining.

No one moved.

"What's wrong?" Laurence finally asked.

It was Bob who stepped forward. "What that mean, Mister Laurence? Do we have to leave

Hickory Heights? Where we go?"

Laurence put his hand to his forehead. "Of course not, Bob. I'm sorry. I should have said that you are all welcome to stay here forever. This is your home. I have to be honest that I don't know how I'll pay you, but I will once the war is over. I'm thinking that maybe I could give each of you some land to work and then we'd share the profits. But each of you needs to think about what you want to do. All you need to know right now is that you are free to leave if you wish. I have legal papers that say you are free. Or you can stay. If you do, and I hope you will, we'll do the best we can to keep everyone fed and healthy until the war ends. Just as we always have."

Still puzzled, Bob nodded. Then he brightened. "Land of my own to work?"

"Yes."

"Well, I ain't going nowheres," announced Aunt May loudly, "except to eat that dinner we worked hard to make for my baby and her new husband." She grinned and wagged a finger at Sam. "Don't you forget who her mama is and what I'll do to you if you turns into a varmint on her!" She hugged Sam hard. Sam laughed.

"Aren't you going to have them jump the broomstick?" Lenah asked.

"Lord have mercy, no, child. That's a superstition for ignorant darkies," said Aunt May. "My children are book-learned, thanks to this family. But we will have some fiddling later on. That all right, Mister Laurence?"

Laurence nodded.

Miriam smiled at Aunt May. "Does Isaac know 'Star of the County Down'?" It was an old Irish song that Miriam had sung often at bedtime when Annie was little.

"If you hum it for him, missus, he can pick it out," Aunt May said gently as she helped Miriam to her feet and guided her to the dining room. Annie heard her whisper, "You ain't getting rid of me nohow, Missus Miriam, you remember that."

Annie stopped Laurence and let all the others pass. "I'm so glad you did that, brother. I've been worrying about . . . about . . . ," she stumbled, "about how happy our people are, even though we've tried hard to make their lives good, ever since Gabriel . . . well . . . left. I've been so troubled about my relationship with Rachel, too. I don't know how I didn't see it before. No matter how kind we were to them, no matter how good their lives might be here at Hickory Heights, the premise for it was so wrong. Nothing could make up for it except what you have just done. Do you suppose . . ." She tried to ask if he thought Sam and Rachel could now see them as true friends, but stopped again and shrugged. Laurence couldn't answer that for her. She simply ended with "Thank you, Laurence."

"I should have done it before, Annie. I meant to. Gabriel and Jacob running off hit me hard, too. I would have let them go if they'd asked. I guess they didn't realize I felt that way. So I wanted to make their choice legal, just as we say we have the right, the freedom, to choose whether we want to remain in the Union of states.

"Beginning of the month, General Lee filed papers in Spotsylvania Courthouse to free all his servants, according to the wishes set out in his father-in-law's will. Mrs. Lee had inherited them, you see. Her mother was evidently a big proponent of educating and freeing slaves and helping them colonize in Liberia. Two of their servants travel with General Lee in the Confederate army. He's freed them, too, and pays them the equivalent of a soldier's wage. I've heard that Lee feels slavery to be a moral and political evil. If the general can take time out to do what's right while he's planning the defense of our country, then surely a lowly lieutenant can as well."

He shook his head and added with bitterness in

his voice, "Lincoln's proclamation applies *only* to Confederate states, not to slave-holding Union states such as Maryland or to the Southern territory under Federal control. It's so hypocritical. There are still many Northern leaders who own slaves. General Grant—a rather ruthless leader who commanded at that slaughter in Shiloh—his wife evidently still owns slaves and has brought them with her when she visits Grant in camp.

"Truth is, some Yankees are as bigoted as some of our countrymen. I have seen and heard Confederate mistreatment of servants during my travels with the cavalry that I could never have imagined before, and it shames me, Annie. Our family just never thought of our people in such ways. And I hear about how some Federals treat the runaways they call 'contraband'—lots of demands for them to dance at gunpoint as evening entertainment for the troops. God forbid they do that to Gabriel or Jacob. We are all tainted by this. Slavery should have been outlawed in the Declaration of Independence or the original Constitution. And I wish to God that the South had not allowed itself to become a bastion of it. The reality is, if we do manage to win this accursed war, it will become even harder to try to abolish slavery in the South. But I can do right by our own people. And when this war is over, I plan to argue the point beyond Hickory Heights. I don't know how far I'll get with it, but I need to try. Right now, all I can focus on is protecting Virginia."

He stopped, thoughtful, and Annie's mind wandered to the long-ago words of Thomas Walker. Funny, thought Annie: In another day, another time, Laurence and he probably would have liked each other a great deal.

"Let's go in for dinner." Laurence interrupted her musings. He held up his arm to escort Annie into the dining room.

She took it and then paused. "Where's Jamie?" Their brother was nowhere to be seen. "I didn't see him leave the room."

"Oh, Lord," sighed Laurence. "I should have told that hothead about my decision beforehand. I just hadn't planned to announce it right after the service. That fool preacher. Oh, that reminds me, Annie; I need to pay him and send him on his way. I don't think he needs to join us for dinner, given his obvious sentiments. Could you find James and herd him into the dining room so they can begin, please?"

Annie went in search of Jamie. To her amazement, she found him in his bedroom, reading. She hated to interrupt; she'd tried so often to encourage any interest in literature. "Jamie, it's time for dinner."

Jamie looked up at her with the surprise of someone who'd been completely lost in his book.

"What are you reading?"

"Lieutenant Mosby told me his riders would be 'Tam O'Shanter' Rebels, or like Robert MacGregor in *Rob Roy*, snookering the English. He told me to read them both, and then in March, when I turn fifteen, to find him. I couldn't make any sense of Burns' poem." He pointed to a volume of Burns' poetry, lying discarded on the table. "But this MacGregor fellow." Jamie grinned. "Now there's a man!"

Indeed, thought Annie, recalling the Sir Walter Scott novel. The real-life Scottish rebel MacGregor whom Scott immortalized was quite the fighter—clever, idealistic, tenacious, and incredibly courageous in the face of better-armed, more numerous foes. But his actions also sparked horrendous acts of retribution by the English on Scottish villages, on women and children. Would Mosby bring about the same?

CHAPTER TWENTY

January 29, 1863
Middleburg

"They won't be hauling you off, will they, Annie?" Her little cousin Will looked up, his huge eyes agleam with worry.

"No, darling." Annie leaned down so that their faces were very close. "Even the Yankees haven't sunk to that level. I'm not going to leave you." She squeezed the little hand that lay in hers.

Annie had ridden into Middleburg, hoping to purchase medicine for her mother. Miriam was suffering terrible headaches that seemed to shove her heart into convulsions. Before dawn, Jamie had gone out deer hunting with Isaac. It had snowed recently. The animals' tracks would be easy to find and follow. They were running dangerously low on meat and had to keep the livestock alive somehow through the winter to breed babies in the spring. If Jamie could kill a deer, the venison would be a welcome relief for the twelve hungry people living at Hickory Heights.

Since Jamie couldn't accompany her to town, Annie had brought Will along, just for fun. The boy had been so quiet and skittish since arriving at her home. He'd begun to shadow Annie everywhere. One night she'd even awakened to find him curled up at the bottom of her bed. He told her he'd had a terrible nightmare, that Bull Run skeletons had him by the throat. Annie had thought coming into Middleburg might show him that life was still going on, was still safe even with the Union army ranging so close.

She couldn't have been more wrong.

Two hundred New Jersey cavalrymen had galloped into Middleburg under Colonel Percy Wyndham. They were hot after Mosby and anyone helping him.

Mosby had begun his midnight raids on Union encampments with a vengeance. In the past ten days, he'd snatched horses, food, ammunition, and officers from Herndon and Chantilly. These were picket posts along the chain of Union camps that stretched in a protective arc from the Potomac River west of Washington, D.C., south to the Potomac

River east of it. Along that line were 3,300 Union cavalry. Yet, with his minuscule band, Mosby had slipped through the night, struck, and then melted back into the darkness. Already he was being called the Gray Ghost.

But Union commander Wyndham was not going to be undone by this sneaking, upstart rebel. Wyndham was an English mercenary, knighted in Italy for his distinguished military service. Mosby was besmirching his honor, his reputation. He was going to harass the locals until they gave up Mosby.

"Search every building," the Englishman shouted.

The Federal cavalrymen dashed into houses, overturned beds, ripped clothes out of closets. They found no Mosby riders. Instead, they rounded up the twenty-one male civilians, mostly ancient, still in the village.

Unaware of the turmoil, Annie and Will had ridden up Ashby's Gap Turnpike toward the outskirts of Middleburg, loudly singing:

"In Dixie's Land where I was born in,
Early on one frosty morning,
Look away! Look away! Look away,
Dixie's Land!"

Two bluecoats posted on the town's perimeter cantered out to meet them and roughly ordered them into town. "Why are you coming into the village?" one asked.

"For medicine," Annie answered truthfully.

"Do you have knowledge of the whereabouts of Mosby or his men?"

"No, sir." Again, the truth. She hadn't seen Mosby since before the New Year.

From his horse, the man then loomed over Will, setting him atremble. "What about you, boy? Know anything? If you lie, we'll find out."

Will's eyes welled up with tears.

"Shame on you," Annie blurted out. Will was already broken up by what he'd seen at Manassas. Annie jumped off Angel and went to hold the reins of the small old mare Will sat atop. "Are you Federals so afraid that you must terrorize a child?"

The Union man sat back. "Stand over there," he grunted, and rode back to his position.

Annie and Will took their places beside the wives, sisters, daughters, and mothers of the arrested men as the Federals herded their prisoners to the middle of Washington Street.

Sitting erect in his saddle, Wyndham shouted at

the citizens. Mosby was a coward, a horse thief, he said, and would be treated as such. "If these raids continue," he warned, his horse pawing and pacing, "I will burn this village to the ground."

Then he left, carting off Middleburg's men. Women sank to their knees, crying, praying, asking dozens of unanswerable questions of one another.

Annie watched the Federals thunder past the row of brick houses, climb a hill, and then disappear on the other side. Anger and disgust welled up inside her until she felt as if she would vomit. She helped lift a few of the elderly women to their feet, dusted off their dresses, and then turned to Will. "Let's see if the doctor still has some powder left."

One of the ladies she had helped turned to her. "He's gone, honey, carried off." She nodded toward the east.

Annie fought off a most unladylike curse. No telling when the bluecoats would release the doctor. They would eventually, but how long would Miriam have to suffer before he'd be back? And would he even have anything left in his saddlebags then?

Annie felt a tug at her skirts. Will was looking up at her again, with those huge eyes of his. He looked more and more like a startled kitten. "Ma knows," he whispered.

"Aunt Molly knows what?"

"How to chase the Devil away from your head," Will said with a solemn nod.

Annie looked at him skeptically. "You mean she prays?"

"Naw." Will shook his head. "She mixes the bark of willow and dogwood trees into shrub."

Shrub was a drink of vinegar and fruit juice given to the sick. "Does it work?"

"Rightly so. Most times," he said.

"Why didn't she say so and save us this trip?" Annie asked with annoyance.

"She's afraid of the black witch," Will parroted his mother.

"Aunt May," Annie corrected him. She frowned. Her blood aunt was becoming a real nuisance.

"Well, let's go home then." As she started to get back on Angel, there was a popping sound.

Not again, she thought.

Pop-pop-pop. Pause. A riot of blasts sounded.

The Federals were fighting someone.

Evidently, Mosby had been at a nearby house. Alerted by a servant, he had managed to collect a handful of his riders and was charging after the Federals.

"Oh, he can't be that reckless," breathed Annie.

"He's got to be completely outnumbered."

Within moments of the crackling exchange of guns, Annie could hear the sound of a horse thundering up the road from the east.

Pop-pop-pop.

"Oh, hurrah, our boys are coming!" cried the women.

Yes, at a gallop, thought Annie, and running hard from something.

Pop-pop-pop.

Rifle fire sounded closer.

Annie grabbed Will's hand and the reins of both horses, setting Angel into a fit of whinnying and dancing. "This way. Hurry!" Annie shouted.

Just in time, she darted around the corner of a building.

In rode Mosby, barely controlling his frothing horse. He wheeled the horse around and shouted toward the east, shaking his fist. "I dare you to shoot at me!" he cursed the bluecoats.

They did, sending bullets winging down the village. Mosby turned again and fled west, out of town.

A few more gunshots. Then silence.

Finally, Annie emerged from her hiding spot, still keeping Will behind her.

Mosby had disappeared. Annie wasn't so certain

that this was the Confederate savior they'd hoped for.

Two weeks later, though, Annie wouldn't stop to question Mosby's methods or benefits to her community. She was again trying to find medicine for Miriam. Aunt Molly's home remedies had only twisted Miriam's stomach into spasms. She'd heard that a doctor who lived just south of Aldie might have supplies. She was thinking about begging him to come see her mother. In any case, it was going to be a long ride east from Middleburg. The roads were hard and icy in spots, crusted with mid-February snow that refused to melt. She'd stopped with Jamie at the mill in Aldie to warm up a bit. The miller had kindly given them a cup of hot coffee. It wasn't real coffee, of course, just ground-up chicory, but the hot liquid felt good going down.

"Hey," said Jamie, who'd been pacing at the window. "What's that coming?"

Annie and the miller joined him. On the road was a line of six covered wagons, slowly rumbling along the frozen dirt. Escorting it were eighteen Union cavalrymen.

"Supply train," said the miller, who'd gotten accustomed to the comings and goings of Union men in front of his mill. "Wonder where it's heading."

"Who's that in the lead?" Annie asked, pointing.

The miller rubbed the window glass clean with his shirt sleeve and squinted. "Humpf," he grunted. "That's Yankee Davis. A Union sympathizer who lives just up the road." The miller scowled. "I swear I'll never sell that man another grain of flour, even if he pays for it in gold."

Jamie was still glued to the window. He whistled. "Wouldn't that be a prize for old Mosby. Yes, sir. He'd swoop right down on that, I bet, like a hawk on a field mouse."

Annie looked at her brother and then back out at the train. Something about it bothered her. As she watched, the final wagon hit a huge hole in the road and swayed violently, rattling the canvas cover. For a split second, the barrels of two guns lurched out the back, and then, just as quickly, were pulled back in. Annie leaned forward, breathless, and studied the wagons hard. She saw nothing else poking out. But as the wagons struggled up the road, she noted how weighed down they seemed.

Then she thought about an ambush she'd heard Wyndham had set for Mosby several days before that the Confederate had thwarted. Annie swallowed hard. She recognized a Trojan horse when she saw one. And it made her furious.

She grabbed Jamie's arm. "Jamie," she blurted, "you finished the *Aeneid*, didn't you?"

"Aw, for pity's sake, Annie, don't be pestering me about books now."

She couldn't help shaking him slightly. "Think, Jamie. Think of how the Greeks got into Troy and destroyed it. Remember they built a huge wooden horse and stuffed it full of their warriors, who couldn't be seen from the outside. A wagon train like that looks mighty tempting to Mosby, just like that wooden horse looked like a tribute to the Trojans. That's a trap the Yankees are setting, for sure."

Jamie smirked. "You've been reading too much, Annie."

Annie huffed in frustration. "I saw rifles pop out the back when that wagon seesawed. Didn't you?"

The miller interrupted. "I thought it was just my old eyes playing tricks on me. I don't know anything about a Trojan horse, but I think you're right about it being a trap. And if old Davis is with them, there's something rotten about it."

"Do you know where Lieutenant Mosby is?" she asked.

The miller shook his head. "I know the rendezvous point for his men now is Rector's Crossroads.

And sometimes he stays at Lakeland or Rockburn or Heartland." All were manor homes near Hickory Heights. Annie knew and trusted the families. Getting to all three of them, though, would take a hard, fast ride. Rector's Crossroads was just on the western side of Middleburg. To cover every point, both she and Jamie would need to ride.

Annie turned to Jamie. "You need to ride to the houses and see if you can get word to Mosby. Be careful who you talk to, Jamie. I'm going to head straight to the crossroads, in case they've gotten wind of the train and are gathering to attack it."

Jamie's face lit up with joy. Without a word, he buttoned his coat and ran out the door.

The miller caught Annie's arm as she tried to follow. "That's not a job for you, missie."

There was no time for this. The wagon train was already down the road. "Do you have a horse?" Annie asked him urgently.

The heavyset man shook his head.

"Then let go of me, because Angel would never carry you."

The miller looked shocked by her bluntness. But he released her.

"Warn anyone else you can think of," Annie called as she dashed out the door.

This ride would be different from the helter-skelter one she'd made with Cousin Eleanor's old carthorse in Lewinsville. This was Angel. This was Annie's territory. She knew the way and she knew the horse and she knew *why* she was riding. It had nothing to do with politics or philosophies that now she wasn't even sure she agreed with. No, Annie was tired of the gunfire, tired of her county being ransacked and threatened. She might not admire Mosby or his methods the way she did Stuart. But Stuart and Laurence were across the Rappahannock River, far away. Lee's armies had abandoned them. Mosby was here.

Annie lit out across the fields. She'd have to avoid the turnpike, and she'd have to keep Angel at a slow canter, no faster, because of the slippery snow that dusted the rolling hills. Angel tossed her head, fighting the bit, wanting to stretch out in a run. She snorted, and white puffs of her breath wreathed them as they flew.

Over a fence. Down a slope, up again. Through a sleeping cornfield. Across a tiny sliver of stream, where the earth had opened itself up a crack to let water pass, bringing green, bringing life. Annie crossed one slippery lane, another, and another. She was close now.

Annie brought Angel down to a trot, prayed that the cold and the long exercise would not break her lungs. She patted Angel's neck, stroked her soft mane, and brought the panting mare to a walk, then to a stop atop a hill. From her vantage point she could plainly see Mosby's meeting point, where the Atoka Road crossed Ashby's Gap Turnpike. This was only a mile or so from Hickory Heights. She knew the terrain well. She scanned the horizon, first north, then west, where the Blue Ridge Mountains crested along the earth, disappearing here and there in the clouds, their hazy purple line like the parapets of a castle. She saw no riders.

Frustrated, Annie let Angel trot around in a circle to keep the mare's muscles warm. She'd need to take Angel home if she didn't spot Mosby soon. She'd pushed the horse hard to cover close to ten miles in an hour. As Angel turned, Annie continued to search.

"Are you looking for me?" a voice suddenly called along the cold air from a grove of trees.

Annie whirled, her heart thumping at the sound. Someone had been watching her. What should she answer? She started to reply that it depended on who he was. But then she realized if the voice belonged to a Federal picket, that would open her to the question of just whom was she seeking. No, better to use arrogance as a shield. At least she had learned something about tactics from all the stories Laurence had told her about Stuart bluffing the enemy.

"Show yourself, sir," she called back. "I'm not in the habit of shouting to bushes."

Three riders emerged. They were bundled in *Yankee blue*!

Annie sucked in her breath, the frigid air bracing her. *Think, Annie. Think. Why would you be out riding in such cold, in such a hurry? Think!*

The blue-clad riders sat waiting. Annie felt herself begin to tremble under her layers of wool. *Ride it out. Don't say anything until they do.*

The four sat silently, eyeing one another. It felt like an eternity. Annie steeled herself to stare at them defiantly, even haughtily, as if their presence was a mere annoyance to her. Then she began to look at the one in the middle more carefully. He was thin, almost frail, clean-shaven, familiar-looking. Could it be Mosby? Dressed in a Federal overcoat?

The horsemen clearly weren't going to speak—it was part of the game played across picket lines every day during the war. If she said the wrong thing, she'd set and spring her own trap.

Suddenly Annie thought of a safe way. "I'm Annie Sinclair," she said with as much disdain and superiority as she could manage. "And who, may I ask, are you?"

The middle rider clucked his horse forward. He nodded at her. It was he—Mosby.

Annie told the story of the wagon train hastily. She saw Mosby poke out his lower lip and nod approvingly when she described it as a Trojan horse.

"Obliged, Miss Sinclair." Mosby tipped his hat in thanks. "Gentlemen," he said to his companions as he turned his horse. Off they rode, with no other words.

Annie watched them disappear into the cover of a glade and then emerge on the other side with about a dozen riders. They headed east, toward Middleburg.

He's going right for it, thought Annie, shaking her head. Just like Stuart.

Well, she'd done her part. She'd warned them. She headed for home.

That night, Jamie returned afire with news. Just as the Trojan horse wagon train neared Middleburg, fourteen of Mosby's men charged it, attacking the cavalry bluecoats who were riding far in front. They had panicked and galloped back toward the wagons. The Federal soldiers hidden inside heard the frantic hoofbeats. Blinded by the wagons' covering, they assumed it was Mosby. The Yankees threw back the canvas and began shooting—at their own riders. Mosby captured most of them.

Jamie had a new prize, an advanced Spencer seven-shot repeating rifle that the "Trojan" soldiers had been carrying. He showed it to Annie and then danced around the room.

Annie waited for elation, the triumph she had expected to feel for successfully warning Mosby. This time she *had* made a difference. This time she had known exactly what to do and how to do it. And yet she felt no joy, just a cold, clammy sense of responsibility. She didn't ask Jamie if any of the men had died. She didn't want to know.

CHAPTER TWENTY-ONE

April 15, 1863
Hickory Heights

"Jamie, what in the world are you doing?" Annie grabbed her brother by the collar.

He looked up at her with a grin. "Making a trapdoor, silly. What do you think?" He shrugged her off and shoved the saw back down through the floorboards.

"Jamie!" Annie pushed him so hard that he fell over, the saw left standing and wobbling, making a strange metallic warbling. "Are you out of your mind? You're ruining the dining room!"

Jamie sat cross-legged on the carpet that he had rolled up. "You of all people should know, Annie. You're the Confederate spy, the friend of generals, the all-seeing rider who recognizes Trojan horses." He grinned up at her again.

Was the boy mad? "Jamie, don't ever call me that. What if someone heard you? I could get arrested, you know. Besides, I'm not a . . . a . . ." She choked on the word—it sounded so clandestine. "A spy. I just did my part."

"That's right, and I'm doing mine," Jamie said. He was absurdly happy and good-natured.

"By hacking up the dining room floor?" Annie nearly shouted.

Jamie made a face and spoke in a patronizing tone. "Underneath this flooring is a part of the cellar that was dug but was never completely finished. I discovered it this morning. It's a little cavern, about four feet wide and ten deep, right behind the jelly closet. I don't know why they didn't extend the cellar into it, but they didn't. I guess because it's not really square and they got tired of digging. Anyway, it's a perfect hiding spot. The wall of the jelly closet has lots of cracks and seams in it—I stuck my hand through it; that's how I found the hole—so there'll be air aplenty for two men."

"Air?" Annie couldn't understand this mischief of Jamie's at all. "Two men?"

"Me and Joseph Dickinson."

"Joseph Dickinson?"

"Another Mosby ranger. I promised Major

Mosby that we'd board him here."

Annie plopped down onto one of the dining room chairs as Jamie turned and went back to work. She had feared this—that Mosby would want them to house one of his men. It was a dangerous business. If one of the Union raiding parties came through and found the riders . . . well, the least they did was arrest everyone. One house had already been burned down as punishment and warning.

Still, most of their neighbors were keeping at least one rider, especially after Mosby's capture of the Union general Stoughton in March. That had been perhaps the most amazing feat of the war so far—one that reportedly had President Lincoln and other Washington officials so worried about Mosby that ten flooring planks on each side of the Chain Bridge were taken up each night to prevent him crossing the Potomac River into the city. It was a capture that had emboldened everyone in Fauquier and was drawing dozens of volunteers into Mosby's rangers. Mosby himself had jumped up two grades in rank from lieutenant to major in two weeks—General Lee was that pleased by his performance.

In the middle of the night of March ninth, Mosby and twenty-nine of his rangers had ridden straight into Federal headquarters at Fairfax

Courthouse. They slipped past miles of Yankee picket posts and the garrison's guards, going right into the general's bedroom and out again, without firing a shot and without waking anyone—anyone, that is, but the captured Union general, two captains, thirty soldiers, a telegraph operator, and fifty-eight horses.

Such joy there'd been among Annie's friends and neighbors as they retold the story of Mosby pulling back the bedsheets on the snoring general and asking him if he knew of Mosby.

"Yes," the general had replied sleepily, evidently groggy from too much champagne before bedtime. "Have you caught the devil?"

"No, sir," came the reply of the Gray Ghost. "He has captured you!"

It was already legend.

Annie watched Jamie saw. She understood why Mosby wanted his riders spread out among the hills. He had camped as a group only once—seventy of them together in a barnyard—and it had been a disaster. A local woman had betrayed them, reporting them to a nearby Union cavalry post. The Federals had brought double Mosby's numbers and charged down the farm's narrow lane. Mosby's rangers were trapped, hemmed in by fences and hedgerows and the tight driveway. They escaped through pure pluck, jumping the tall fences with their horses and shooting wildly. The Federal commander had also made a stupid error—ordering a saber charge. Their swords were no match for Mosby's revolvers.

And so from now on, Mosby's men would vaporize into the night, like the mists of the Blue Ridge breaking up and settling into different pockets of the mountains, remaining hidden and secret, alone or in pairs, until he sent word for them. It would certainly build up Mosby's mystery, enhancing his partisans' allure to Southerners and their threatening unpredictability to Union troops.

Sighing, Annie made a decision. She was having to make so many these days, and this was definitely not something to bother Miriam with. Hickory Heights would take on this Mosby partisan, feed him, and protect him. She stood up and was about to ask Jamie what he would need to finish the trapdoor when Jamie's words came back to her. *Another*. Annie's heart began to beat quick-time. "Jamie," she whispered hoarsely, "you said 'another ranger.' Who's the other?"

Jamie pulled back a plank. "Why, me, of course. I joined up last week. There's a hundred of us now."

"Oh, Jamie," Annie gasped.

Jamie stood up and faced her. "I turned fifteen two weeks ago, Annie. You know the major said I could join when I turned fifteen." He was matter-of-fact. "Now, see if Isaac can find two hinges for me. They need to be flat, so that there isn't a bump in the carpet when we cover it up." He turned and squatted, back to work.

Already he was different.

Two weeks later, on April twenty-seventh, Annie was grateful for that trapdoor.

It was late afternoon. The world seemed a sweet-smelling pink haze as cherry and apple trees across the county opened their blooms to the warm air. Annie was standing in their hillside orchard, closing her eyes and just inhaling the delicate scent that promised fruit for the autumn. Her cousins Colleen and Sally were tossing hard green hickory balls back and forth. Annie wished she had enough money to buy them some real toys to play with. She leaned over to pluck some tiny violets that were growing in the tall, greening grasses. Some were deep purple, others white, even more a cross between. Those—white with purple stripes that looked almost gray—were being called Confederate violets. She thought she'd make a tiny bouquet for Miriam's bedside. Her mother had always loved to walk among the tree blossoms this time of year. Today she just hadn't the strength.

Annie meandered from violet clump to violet clump until she came to the last one, cast by itself against the split-rail fence. She almost missed it.

Full many a flower is born to blush unseen, / And waste its sweetness on the desert air. Annie leaned against the fence and tried to remember the rest of Thomas Gray's poem about a peaceful country churchyard. *And all the air a solemn stillness holds.* . . . That world of gentle poetry, her time of tearing up over love sonnets, seemed so long ago. That kind of quiet verse seemed naïve now. The world had become such a violent place.

Her mind shifted to some of the Byron poems she'd read. They certainly were more reflective of the anger, frustration, and restlessness she sensed around her. Byron wrote about brooding heroes with mysterious, perhaps criminal pasts. So many of his poems were filled with despair and unhappy lives, predetermined by a mean-spirited fate. Only a few, such as the one quoted by Thomas Walker, retained the hope, the idealism that Annie looked for in her reading.

One night Mosby had stopped at Hickory Heights to eat dinner with them. He'd noticed the Byron volume, lying on a table in the parlor. "My favorite poet," said Mosby, picking it up.

Annie had laughed and told him who had sent it to her.

"Really?" Mosby had said, turning to look at her carefully. "Have you had any more contact with this Yankee?"

"No, Major, and I wouldn't care for any either. He was quite rude," said Annie.

"But if he ever shows up in these parts, you will forget that, won't you, Miss Sinclair. It seems to me the man was quite taken with you."

Annie blushed. "I don't think so."

Mosby shook his head. "You want him to be, Miss Sinclair. He might tell you something useful to me. I'm sure you understand."

She understood all right. Mosby saw her as a useful tool, a lure. She had felt cold all over, assessed like a horse at an auction.

Full many a flower . . . Annie leaned over to pluck the last Confederate violet. Her life was not what she had thought it would be. Would she just waste away, unloved, a mere pawn that men would push across a chessboard of war?

A tug on her skirts stopped Annie's thoughts. There was little Will, his eyes ever wide and fearful. Annie reached out and put her hand on his thick, tousled hair. "What is it, Will?"

"Do you see the blue?" he whispered.

Annie looked up to the sky, awash in soft spring turquoise, not a cloud freckling it. It was a glorious day. "Yes, darling. It's beautiful, isn't it?" Was little Will a poet in the making? she wondered. Wouldn't that be lovely?

He frowned, tugged at her skirts, and pointed to the east. "The blue."

Annie followed his point. In the distance was a growing sea of blue uniforms, as if a hunk of sky had fallen down across the valley. Toward them, out of the mass, came a thin stream of riders.

"Good Lord! Girls, get to the house! Tell Aunt May that Yankees are coming. She needs to hide the hens." She grabbed Will by the shoulders. "Find Isaac and Bob. Get them to run off the livestock. Hurry!" She pushed him ahead of her as she gathered up her skirts to run.

Will darted silently. The girls squealed, "Yankees coming, Yankees coming," almost like a nursery rhyme. Annie glanced back at the blue swarm. They were coming at a trot. They had maybe twenty minutes. "Curse these skirts," she muttered as she tripped and almost fell.

Hickory Heights was suddenly abuzz with frantic action. Isaac burst out of the house's back door carrying a broom, shouting at Bob to "Git them horses loose." He thundered after the hogs, swatting them and shouting, herding them toward the woods. Aunt May ran for the smokehouse to retrieve the bacon hanging there and stuff it up the chimney. Rachel and Lenah scrambled after the hens and chicks, grabbing them by the necks and thrusting them into their aprons. Bob opened the paddock gates and whistled, waving his arms, stampeding their few remaining horses into the fields. With a lump in her throat, Annie watched Angel, tail high, take off toward the hills. "Fly, girl, fly far away. Come back to me tomorrow."

Annie could already hear the sound of banging canteens and jingling stirrups and sabers. It would be only a few moments before the Union cavalry was in their yard. She looked back again and gasped. There were so many of them.

Hurling herself up the front porch steps, Annie flung open the door and called into the house. "Jamie! Jamie!"

"I'm here." Jamie stepped out of the parlor. A

Colt revolver was thrust into his belt. But what horrified Annie most was his clothes. He had on a private's uniform, Confederate butternut.

"What are you doing? You've got to hide."

Clattering down the stairs came Joseph Dickinson. He was a grown man from Prince William County with two small children, and a true marksman. He was wrestling himself into his coat as he came. Two pistols gleamed at his belt as well.

"Let's head out the back, and shoot our way clear if we have to," Joseph said to Jamie.

Jamie nodded.

"Don't be ridiculous!" Annie cried. "There are too many of them. Maybe hundreds. Use your cellar, Jamie."

The front-hall door swung open with a long, groaning squeak. Little Will, solemn, stood in it. "They're here."

Behind him came a racket of hooves skidding along gravel.

"Rein in!" came a shout.

"Hurry!" Annie shoved Jamie, then shoved Joseph Dickinson.

"Dismount!"

Annie careened into the dining room, slipping across the floor to the carpet. The three of them grabbed the corner of the rug, tearing at the tasseled ends, yanking it up. Jamie snatched the trapdoor handle and pulled.

"Surround the house!"

"You first." Joseph pushed Jamie toward the hole.

The front door creaked open. *"Where's your mother, boy?"*

Jamie disappeared into the hole like a diver into water.

"In here?" Heavy, slow footsteps.

Joseph looked over his shoulder and cursed. "No time," he whispered to Annie. He let go of the trapdoor so that it closed with a *thunk* and scrambled toward the kitchen, dropping one of his pistols.

"What's that?" Running feet slapped the hall floor.

Annie flung the carpet corner in place, batted the pistol under her skirt with her feet, and shook her petticoats so that they flounced open like a balloon to cover the trapdoor and the gun just as three Union officers rushed into the room.

One stood eyeing her as the other two officers ran past, jostling her dangerously. Annie noticed their tread made a hollow echo as they crossed the trapdoor. She inched herself completely over it, nudging the pistol with her toes until it lay between her feet. She took a deep breath and tried to make her feet take root there, like an oak, to hide her brother.

Will appeared at the dining room door and ran to her side. He took her hand and planted himself on the trapdoor as well. He was a clever boy, that Will. Annie smiled down at him and felt courage. She looked back up at the officer and waited.

"We are searching for Mosby and his men by order of . . ."

BANG! Out back, a rifle shot reverberated.

"*Here's one.*"

"*Stop or I'll shoot again!*"

More shots. Silence. Then a scuffle of feet as Joseph Dickinson was dragged in front of the Union officer.

"Well, you caught me, boys," Joseph said agreeably. "I hope you have some good grub. I'd just come to ask this lady for some food. I haven't eaten for two days."

The Union officer snorted. "Where there's one, there's sure to be more. Unless he's a deserter."

Joseph laughed. "I'm no deserter, Captain. I'm just taking a break from rousting your camps to look for some dinner. Thought this house looked promising. That's all. My ma used to say I must have a hollow leg, I'm so hungry all the time. And with you boys ranging around the country, it's been right hard to get a decent meal."

He was a cool one, thought Annie with admiration and relief, to think up such a good charade so fast.

The captain hesitated a moment, weighing Joseph Dickinson's story, then changed his mind. "Search the house." He snapped his fingers.

Two dozen Yankees crowded through Hickory Heights like ants over a picnic, yanking open doors, stabbing suspect walls with their sabers. They even pulled open drawers, saying with sarcasm that Mosby was cowardly enough to shrink to that size to hide.

All the while, the officer stood watching Annie. She glared back at him.

From upstairs came a booming voice. "*Git away from that door, you varmint. Missus Miriam's in there.*"

Annie couldn't help a smile. "Heaven help your soldiers, sir, if they take on Aunt May. She's fiercely loyal to my mother."

There was a yelp of pain.

"Git, I say."

A young corporal appeared at the dining room door. His face was red with embarrassment. "Sir, there is a lady upstairs. She's ill, sir. I . . . I . . . I think we should leave her room alone, sir."

"Dangerous up there, sonny?" Joseph asked with a grin.

The young man nodded sheepishly and rubbed his backside.

The Federal officer's lip curled in disdain. Curtly he ordered, "Look under the woman's bed, soldier. Feigning illness is the perfect ploy."

The young man nodded. A few minutes later there was another sound of scuffling and a *thwack.*

"Ain't you got no respect? Lord have mercy on your soul for disturbing a kind lady. . . ."

Feet raced down the stairs and the corporal reappeared, breathing hard. "Nothing there, sir."

The officer nodded and the boy disappeared.

Another soldier appeared carrying some of Jamie's clothes.

"My brother's," Annie said quickly. "He's off with Stuart."

Voices from outside: "*Here's a cellar. Bring candles.*"

Annie squeezed Will's hand as he stiffened to the sound of muffled voices below their feet. Her heart pounded in her ears and she fought hard the urge to call out a warning to Jamie.

Joseph started complaining, "If you're going to

take all this time, could I ask the miss here for some milk?"

The Union officer looked at him with contempt. "We'll be leaving soon enough, Reb. I wouldn't be in such an all-fired hurry. Some of us feel you Mosby riders should be hanged as horse thieves. I, for one, would love to carry out that sentence."

Crash. Annie heard the sounds of metal pushing through wood, glass breaking. She couldn't stand it. What if they stabbed Jamie through the wall? Arrogance was fast becoming her ready weapon. She said icily, "Really, sir, surely you have better things to do than to break our jelly jars? Or are those and sick women the only foes you're brave enough to attack?"

Joseph whistled. "We do grow them sassy down here." He grinned. "What say you, Captain?"

The officer grunted, stuck out his jaw, and stomped the floor. The sounds below stopped. Within a few moments, soldiers dusty with cellar dirt appeared. "Yes, sir?" They saluted.

"Confiscate whatever horses and feed you find so that they cannot supply Mosby." He turned to Annie. "Harboring Mosby raiders is a crime, miss, to be punished severely. I am within my rights to order this house torched. I spare it because of the sick woman. If we come here again, though, it will be a different story."

He turned and left. As Joseph Dickinson was led away, he tipped his hat to Annie. "Good luck, miss." At the door, she heard him say, "Now, what have you boys got to eat?" playing his part of a hungry, wandering soldier to the last. She was grateful to him. He'd definitely distracted the Union officer.

It took another thirty minutes of searching to satisfy the Union troops that they'd found all they could take—four horses that had wandered back home and all the feed corn in the barn. They rode off, their noise fading away like thunder disappearing over the mountains.

Not until then did she move off the trapdoor and release Jamie.

He popped up, red-faced, furious, sputtering. "They nearly stabbed me. I should have shot them through the wall!"

Annie flopped into a chair, suddenly exhausted from all the tension. "Thank God you did no such foolishness, Jamie. See what Mosby's raids bring on us? I hope he waits awhile before trying anything else."

"Wait? What for? We've been called to rally tomorrow."

CHAPTER TWENTY-TWO

May 30, 1863
Hickory Heights

A Confederate rider arrived carrying a letter from Laurence. He was delivering many messages throughout the county for Stuart men. The cavalry was now 9,500 strong and General Stuart planned to host a fancy parade review, the likes of which had not before "been seen on this continent," Stuart proclaimed. He wanted ladies to attend. Lots of them. There would be a ball and parties that needed their presence—especially that of "Lady Liberty."

Besides that bit of flattery from Stuart, Laurence's letter contained much news, some to mourn and some to celebrate.

My dearest sister, I write with invitations, news, and requests. First let me tell you of our current situation, for it is far happier than some of the news I must share. We are currently camped at Fleetwood Hill, just above Brandy Station and Culpeper. Many recruits have joined us, and our number is strong and impressive. We are resting right now. The horses are getting fat on tender spring grass that grows thick as it does at home. They have been so starved the past few months. It is a much-needed rest and rebuilding of our spirits, for the month of May was hard and costly.

I'm sure that news has reached you of the death of General Stonewall Jackson. It is a tragedy that is hard to bear or comprehend. He had been out in the night, scouting the route for the next day's attack against Hooker's men in the dense thickets near Chancellorsville. He was mistaken by our own pickets as being the enemy. Our men shot him. His fortitude, his cunning in battle cannot be replaced. General Lee is said to be disconsolate. He called Stonewall his right arm. The gallant Pelham is also dead, killed near here in a battle at Kelly's Ford. With his death, it seems as if our horse artillery has lost its soul.

I have been promoted to captain; we are losing our officers so quickly. I am a horseman, Annie, no real soldier. But I am trying to learn the tactics of war—how to plan and command—as quickly as possible. I am reading an infantry guide called Hardee's Tactics, and a captured Union cavalry manual, as so many of us do when we are pushed into the line of command by the death of our superiors. But I fear if the war goes on much longer, we will run out of officers who know what they are doing. We are brave—that's certain; no one rides into the jaws of death with more grit and determination than we. But there are only so many of us. We lost almost 13,000 at Chancellorsville alone. And the bluebirds only seem to grow in number.

But these are fearful thoughts that I really should not voice. It's just that you, dear sister, of all our family, are the one person I can be completely honest with. I would not worry Mother for the world. And Jamie should not be thinking of war yet.

Annie sighed. If he only knew. What should she tell Laurence of both her and Jamie's deepening involvement in the war's intrigues?
The letter continued:

> *My real reason for writing is to make sure that you come to the grand cavalry review that General Stuart is organizing for June fifth. Riders have been sent to a dozen counties to invite Virginia's loveliest daughters. A special train may even be commissioned to bring dignitaries up the O & A line from Richmond, as the railroad runs close to the proposed review grounds. General Stuart has insisted that you come. "'Twould not be the same without Lady Liberty," he said. So I am sure to be in some trouble with the general if you do not come.*
>
> *I must add that the Shakespeare scholar, the scout William Farley, has asked after you as well. He tells me he saw you in Warrenton and was awed by your beauty and your command of poetry. You see, sister? I knew you two would have much in common, and so you will forgive my trying to play Cupid. You will dance away the*

night with many suitors, for there is to be a ball the night before in the town of Culpeper. I know how little gaiety there has been for you of late, Annie, and I am sorry that there have been few real parties for you to enjoy as you should in your youth. So come, dear sister. Just promise me you do not break too many hearts. I've spoken to Mrs. Crawford—do you remember her? She was an old friend of our family, and she said she would be happy to play hostess to you. Indeed, the whole town will be overflowing with visitors.

She has also offered to entertain one other guest, and here, Annie, I must ask your sincere help. No teasing me about it, as I am far more fearful of this than of a saber in battle. I have been in correspondence with our mutual friend Charlotte. I must admit to being struck down by Cupid's bow myself. I have asked her to attend this review as well, saying that you would come and fetch her as you passed through Warrenton on your way to Culpeper. The two of you could then travel together.

And I have yet another request about Charlotte. There is a box buried deep in my mattress. It contains a watch and other trinkets from Father. I hid them there, not knowing what the war might bring. Inside it is a ring that belonged to his mother, that Father told me I should give to the woman I ask to marry me. Could you bring that ring to me, Annie? But keep the fact of it to yourself? Please don't tell Mother or Jamie. Or Charlotte, obviously! I want her to enjoy the ball and the review and come to her own decisions about me, before I ask her. If you tell her before, I fear she might not come.

Annie caught her breath and smiled. Not come? Why, Charlotte would probably sprout wings and fly down to Culpeper like a songbird if she knew Laurence's intentions. "Oh, brother Laurence," Annie whispered with amusement, "how blind you are."

There was one more paragraph.

I have a last request of you, Annie. I need you to bring me two good horses from Hickory Heights. I don't know how many are left. We have heard that the Feds have been confiscating every horse that they find in the attempt to cut off Mosby's supplies. By the way, I saw Mosby when he delivered that captured Federal, General Stoughton, to Fitz Lee. Stoughton and Fitz Lee had been classmates at West Point, and the Yankee popinjay asked to be turned over to Fitz. Mosby is a cold, calculating man, Annie. Fitz hates him and despises the hit-and-run tactics he uses in the night, no matter how much favor General Stuart lavishes on him. Beware the man. And do not let Mosby coerce Jamie into riding with him.

Annie's eyes blurred with tears. What could she say to Laurence? He clearly didn't understand that Mosby seemed their only protection against the Union buzzards. Stuart and Lee had moved south, deep into the heart of Virginia, and left them unguarded, completely open to Federals. Mosby's daring raids brought hope to them, inspired them to keep up their defiance of the Yankees. And yet she knew that much of what Laurence said was true. There was nothing warm or reassuring about Major Mosby. And although his raids did disrupt the Federals, they didn't win real battles.

She blinked to clear her vision and kept reading:

When you pick out the horses, remember

that I need a fast, brave horse, one that will jump anything and outrun a gunshot. And then I need a replacement of the same ilk in case that one is shot down. Think of Merlin—he was fearless, willing to charge down anything. I can't count the number of times he carried me out of harm's way, jumping huge fences and fallen trees. I must admit that I wept for him more than for some of my fallen comrades when he died. On Merlin I felt invincible. I need another Merlin. Do we have any such horses, Annie?

Annie dropped the paper. Hickory Heights had seven horses left of the sixty they had at the beginning of the war. These remaining few were brood mares and youngsters, not really trained for riding yet. Jamie rode their one remaining well-trained gelding. And given his activities with Mosby, Jamie needed a fast, strong horse as badly as Laurence. There was only one horse left that matched Laurence's needs: Angel.

Annie stroked the shining black mane as she rode. Angel's ears pricked up, and her head lifted high in response. How could Annie send this beautiful, affectionate horse into the gore of a battle? She let the jaunty clip-clop of Angel's prancing walk reverberate up through her own bones, memorizing the feel of it. Angel had such joy in her gait, a thrill to be moving. Annie could sense that Angel took in everything she passed, reveling in the smells, the sounds, the winds that rippled along her body. Every ride with Angel was a celebration of life.

Annie shifted in her saddle and fought back tears. There was nothing else to be done. She glanced back at Isaac, who was accompanying her to Warrenton. Jamie had announced that he was too busy for dances and that he might be needed for a raid. So Isaac drove their carriage, to which their next-best horse was tied. He was a three-year-old, fast and sleek and muscled. But he was barely broken to saddle and was a silly thing, spooking at everything and yanking against his halter. God forbid that Laurence would actually have to count on that horse in danger. No, he must have Angel. Angel would keep him safe. No matter how headstrong Angel was, she was fleet, and she could jump the moon.

"You be good to Laurence, my beautiful girl," Annie whispered, and she patted Angel. The mare snorted and shook her head, jingling the bridle.

Even though she felt like crying, Annie smiled and nodded. Sometimes she truly believed that Angel read her thoughts.

Annie put one gloved hand to her throat to check for the feel of a ribbon tied round her neck, tucked underneath her clothes. Slipped through the ribbon was the ring Laurence had requested she bring. She'd hidden it under her clothes for fear of running into stragglers on the road. Isaac carried an old musket with him, but Annie wasn't sure he'd know what to do with it if they were attacked. The county was plagued with deserters from both armies, and even the Southern ones were bad. They were hungrier and bitter.

That was one thing, at least, in which Mosby, the one-time lawyer, was unquestionably a Godsend: policing the area and establishing some sense of law among the citizens. Mosby's rangers hunted down thieves and looters as avidly as they did Union supply trains. Horse and cattle thieves were often executed by Mosby's orders. His justice was feared. Most troublemakers avoided what was known as "Mosby's Confederacy," a large wedge of valleys in Loudoun and Fauquier counties. It stretched from Snicker's Gap in the Blue Ridge Mountains, east along Snickersville Turnpike to Aldie, south down the edge of the Bull Run Mountains, and then west again, along the Manassas Gap Railroad back to the Blue Ridge, which then drew the long, back spine of Mosby's territory.

As Annie left the heart of Mosby's terrain and rode south toward Warrenton, she felt intensely vulnerable. Although Mosby often raided Union camps around it, his presence was not pervasive in lower Fauquier. Warrenton itself was forever changing hands. She wasn't even sure which side currently controlled the town.

When she finally saw Warrenton's church spires in the hills before her without having run into any Union picket posts, Annie was hugely relieved. The ride had been a bleak one. She'd passed farm after farm whose fences were broken down and houses and barns were deserted. Some of the mills along the way had been burned and looted. The giant mill wheels stood still, the grinding stones silent. Fields that should have been neatly plowed and lush with new growth of wheat or corn instead lay barren, pimpled by weedlike cedar trees trying to retake the land. Miles of her homeland were deserted and ghostlike.

Warrenton, too, lacked its usual busy bustle. As she rode through the streets, she noticed two women bartering with a seedy-looking sutler. From the eaves of his covered wagon hung shoes, hams, and bags of sugar. Inside she could see bolts of material, sacks of flour, canned fruit—rare, coveted items.

Angel danced past and Annie heard one of the women gasp, "Thirty dollars for a pair of shoes? Eight dollars for a turkey?" Then the woman held up a bracelet and asked the traveling merchant if he would take that instead of cash. Sickened, Annie goosed Angel into a trot. She wondered if the bracelet was a beloved heirloom or something given to the lady by a sweetheart. How many treasured things—like her beautiful Angel—would they all be forced to give up before this fight was over?

"Annie! Annie!" Charlotte was on the stoop of her house, waving her handkerchief.

Annie smiled and wondered how long she'd been watching the road. And Laurence was afraid that Charlotte might not come!

Charlotte skittered down the steps and onto the street to catch hold of Annie as she dismounted. Like a child, she swung Annie around in a circle, hand to hand. "Oh, Annie! I'm so excited. Do we really have to wait until tomorrow to leave?" She giggled and chattered on. "How silly I am! Of course, you must be exhausted. Come in, come in. We'll have tea this afternoon with Eliza. Is that all right? She is so interested in all the news from you. She wants to learn if you know the legendary Mosby. She'll be pea green with envy if you do!"

Charlotte dragged Annie up the stairs and into their house. Annie noted that the elegant home didn't have any saber marks along its walls or obviously missing items. Perhaps there was an advantage to being in a town that mostly had been occupied by an enemy that wanted to enjoy it and use it. Still, she noticed that Charlotte's pretty face was not as round as it used to be and her waist was thinner. And tea that afternoon was a meager offering, a few ham biscuits and a bitter brew of raspberry leaves.

Eliza, however, remained her coquettish self. One of her sisters was engaged to a Mosby ranger, and she was full of gossip about the Gray Ghost. Did Annie know him personally? What was he like? Was he part man, part spirit, the way everyone described him? If Eliza were to hear of troop movements or the like, how would she get information to him?

Annie answered all her questions, again flattered and seduced by the girlish friendship she was so unused to enjoying. Isolated as she was at

Hickory Heights, with so many grown-up worries, she was rejuvenated by the teasing, gossipy conversation.

Their banter had become quite bubbly when Eliza leaned back in her chair and said, "Oh, Annie Sinclair, I do believe you are the luckiest girl in the world. Not only to know General Jeb Stuart, but Major John Mosby, too."

"Why, you don't know the half of it, Eliza," blurted out Charlotte, caught up in the vivaciousness. "General Stuart actually wrote a poem to Annie."

Annie gasped.

Eliza's face changed from mirth to dead serious. "Really? Oh, let me see!"

Annie was speechless. She'd never shown that poem to Charlotte. She felt completely naked and violated. She glared at Charlotte.

Charlotte's mouth popped open. "Oh, Annie. I'm so sorry. I . . . I . . ." Her cheeks turned red and she looked down at her hands. "I noticed you reading something one night that made you sigh . . . and . . . I . . . I . . . found it after you went to sleep and read it. I didn't mean to, Annie. And I didn't mean to say anything. . . . I . . ." She stopped.

Annie was furious. How could Charlotte invade

her privacy like that and then blab it to Eliza? Annie had another horrible thought. "Charlotte, have you told anyone else?"

Charlotte stammered and her voice became almost inaudible, like a guilty child's: "Well, I might have mentioned it to one or two other friends, right after General Stuart was here."

"Charlotte! How could you?"

"Oh, Annie, it was just so exciting when he came through, and everybody was talking about him and how dashing, how princely he was, and I said, 'You'll never guess the half of it. The man's a poet as well!' And then they said, 'How do you know?' and I couldn't not tell them, don't you see, Annie? It was a matter of honor then, and I—"

Eliza interrupted her. "Well, Charlotte, I can't believe you didn't tell *me*! I thought we were like sisters—how can you keep confidences from me?"

Charlotte looked as if she were going to cry.

Annie couldn't believe any of it—first Charlotte's betrayal, and now Eliza's irritation at not being in on it.

Eliza turned to Annie, who was still staring at Charlotte in disbelief. "Annie, I want to see that poem. Please, oh please," she wheedled. "It must be simply awe-inspiring. Don't you be denying a poor girl that joy. Belief in our leaders is what keeps us going. Unless, of course, there's something in it that . . . well . . . might embarrass you."

Annie wanted to scream at Eliza that she'd never share something so personal. Who did she think she was to ask for it to begin with, or to imply that there might be something improper in it? She wanted to slap Charlotte and tell her that Laurence had planned to marry her, but that Annie was going to tell him what a simpering idiot she was and put a stop to it. She balled up her fists and imagined how splendid spitting out those words would be.

But instead, Annie stood up and lied. "I don't have it with me, Eliza. I'm tired, Charlotte. I'd like to rest for a bit upstairs." She swept from the room.

As she reached the stairs, Annie heard, "Well, Charlotte, that one is certainly stuck-up."

Charlotte burst into sobs.

CHAPTER TWENTY-THREE

June 4, 1863
Culpeper Courthouse, Virginia

Annie stood among a grove of ferns that had been dragged in to decorate the courthouse for the ball. It was a warm night, and she was flushed from dancing a spirited polka with a rather fat lieutenant who stomped on her toes. She flipped her carved ivory fan in front of her face, for the moment glad to watch the dancing parade before her and to ease her bruised toes out of her tight shoes. Honestly, she wished propriety didn't insist that she accept all dance requests. That lieutenant was a horrible dancer! She smiled in understanding at his new partner as he turned her awkwardly past Annie. She recognized the sudden look of pain on the girl's face. Yes, the lieutenant had found her toes as well!

Although the hall was dim from lack of candles, the faces before Annie were clearly visible, lit up from a joy within. There was a grand festivity to it all, a swell of hope-filled giddiness. Hundreds of handsome cavalry officers strode through the hall picking out Virginia beauties to squire. The dance floor itself was a swirl of bright colors—pink, yellow, turquoise, silver—as men waltzed their breathless partners around and around and around, hoopskirts swinging in unison, the rustling a backdrop to the band's music.

Hanging from the high ceiling were Confederate flags and long banners of blue and white. Culpeper gardens had been completely emptied of their flowers, and the hall was filled with the strong scent of full-bloom roses, lilies, and peonies, competing with the spicy perfumes worn by the ladies—and some dandified gentlemen.

Enraptured, Annie took it all in, recognizing that she might not see the like again. As her eyes scanned the room, pausing at each satin dress, each golden sash and saber, they came to rest on the waltzing figures of Laurence and Charlotte. For a moment her happiness was dampened. She still was very angry at Charlotte, even though her friend had apologized, often in tears, at least a dozen times on their trip to Culpeper. She cocked her head and watched them. They did make a beautiful couple—Laurence so fair and lithe, Charlotte so dark and soft. Their eyes did not leave each other's, even as other, less graceful couples bumped into them. Charlotte was clearly hanging on his every word and look. Annie had watched her duck behind the flower arrangements when other young gallants approached her to ask for a dance. She was saving herself for Laurence.

Annie sighed. She had burned to tell Laurence all about Charlotte's foolish indiscretion when he'd asked for the engagement ring Annie had brought along. Did he really want to spend his life with someone who was so nosey and gossipy? But his boyish excitement had been too great to spoil. And how could she explain that poem to her big brother anyway? Instincts told her that Laurence would not approve of it, and that it could make him frosty toward his commanding general.

Besides, hadn't Annie herself made mistakes before? There had been nothing malicious about Charlotte's blunder. She knew that. Still, she would love to be able to just throw a real tantrum once in a while. All this ladylike self-containment and patient understanding was infuriating!

She looked at the dais at the front of the hall. There sat General Stuart with the town's mayor and other Confederate army dignitaries. At the last moment General Robert E. Lee's frantic schedule had kept him from the festivities. Annie knew Stuart was terribly disappointed. She had spoken to him briefly. The flash of genuine gladness that had come into his eyes at seeing her was buoying her through the night. She smoothed her skirt and touched her hair to make sure it was still held back by its wreath of flowers. She wore one of her mother's dresses—thin white muslin atop an underdress of sky blue silk, with off-the-shoulders puffed sleeves, all trimmed with black velvet ribbon. She knew she looked pretty. But it was unlikely that Stuart would ask her to dance. And besides, Annie reminded herself harshly, he's married.

"Will you give me the pleasure of a dance, Miss Sinclair?"

Annie jumped at the sound of a soft, lilting voice in her ear. She hadn't heard anyone approach her from behind. She turned and faced William Farley.

Farley smiled at her shyly. "I am sorry if I startled you."

"Oh, no, Captain Farley, not at all." Annie blushed. He had large, light gray eyes, with long, dark lashes, and an open, pleasant face. "It must be your ability as a scout that allows you to move so silently."

Farley held out his right hand, and she took it. There was something almost elegant about him as he led her toward the floor.

"Form lines for the Virginia reel!" shouted the caller from the band platform.

"Yeehaw!" yipped a few of the more exuberant youths as they grabbed girls and whirled them to the floor.

"Oh, dear." Farley laughed. "This dance is not my forte."

Annie happened to love the capering and swinging of the Virginia reel, the frothiness of the hornpipe music. She'd brightened instantly at the call. But she tried to respect Farley's reticence. "Well, if you'd rather wait," she demurely said.

"Oh, no, Miss Sinclair. Just forgive me if I falter!" They took their place as the second couple in the line of dancers.

As the jaunty Irish jig began, the women and men took four quick steps forward, curtsied and bowed, and skipped back into place. A lady and man diagonally across from each other skimmed forward, joined left hands, and made a complete swirling turn. They do-si-doed, passing each other right shoulder to right shoulder. And as the head couple joined hands and chasséd, skip-sliding, down the line, the others clapped to the music, until it was their turn to pass through the line, turning it inside out on itself.

Annie laughed and gasped and smiled and flirted as she chasséd and twirled. This is what she had been missing and longing for—a night of being young and happy, like a foal feeling her oats and kicking up her heels. It was the first of many dances with Captain Farley, who actually turned out to be a deft dancer, supporting her with his arms but never drawing her too close for modesty and never ever stepping on her toes.

Over glasses of punch and moments out in the cooling night air, they talked about school and poetry. Even though he was from South Carolina, Farley had attended the University of Virginia, studying Shakespeare and the early English poets. Once, as they came out of the night into the music-filled hall, he smiled down at her and sheepishly quoted the playwright: *"If music be the food of love . . ."*

Annie glanced up into his eyes, blushed, and whispered back the line's ending: *"Play on."*

Farley smiled and took her hand for the waltz.

Annie liked him. She liked his self-effacing manner, which made him so different from the many hot-headed bucks frolicking about her that night. So different from General Stuart.

As Captain Farley swept her around and around, making them one of a hundred pirouetting couples, perfectly in sync with one another, as if everyone in that room had the same heartbeat, the same glorious, swirling fate, Annie noticed Laurence and Charlotte stepping into the room. Her arm was hooked around his and he pressed his gloved hand atop hers. They beamed.

Annie knew. Laurence had asked. Charlotte had accepted. And it was all right. Tonight, for the first time in a long time, everything felt right.

"There he is! There!" Charlotte tugged on Annie's arm and pointed. It was the next morning and time for the grand review, a military tradition that allowed commanding officers to assess the strength and readiness of the troops, but also served as a spectacular entertainment for civilians. Of course, some of the excitement was dampened by the fact that General Lee had been detained at his headquarters with pressing war plans. But Stuart planned to make up for Lee's absence in show.

Below them, on a long vast hill, Stuart was surrounded by his staff. Their horses were spotless. Their gray uniforms were brushed clean, with brass so polished that it seemed the sun would reflect off their buttons. Bugles sounded to herald the fact that Stuart was about to begin his formal inspection of all his cavalry. This was really why all were gathered in Culpeper, although the dancing had been delightful, ending only a few hours before. Stuart wanted to show off his cavalry—their beauty, their prowess, their discipline, their superior horsemanship. Their number alone awed. The line Stuart would inspect stretched a mile. As he trotted his high-spirited mare along the ranks, other horses stamped in place. Bright flags snapped and billowed in the winds. Three bands played. The cavalry looked invincible.

Charlotte and Annie sat together in Annie's carriage, surrounded by wagons and other townsfolk. Behind them a special train from Richmond had stopped on the tracks, and the passengers crammed themselves out through the open windows to watch. Charlotte had been holding Annie's hand all morning, and now Annie broke loose to lift field glasses to her eyes.

She was thrilled to watch Stuart, of course, and interested in locating Captain Farley and Laurence among the thousands of spit-and-polish men before them, but what she looked for now was her horse. She wanted to make sure Angel was holding steady in all this crowd and fuss.

She ran the glasses up and down that long, long line, looking for glistening black and graceful white stockings. There! No. What about that one? No, again. She checked twenty black horses until suddenly she was sure she spotted Angel. She recognized the tall thin figure of her brother atop an elegant horse with raised tail and impatient, prancing hooves. There! There she was. She looked magnificent. Annie smiled. It was the greatest—and the hardest—gift she had ever made.

Annie turned her glasses back to Stuart. His inspection of the troops took more than two hours. Finally, he climbed a knoll near them. He seemed like a king looking down upon his realm. He sat still and erect; his black ostrich plume ruffled with the wind as his men broke themselves into squadrons and began to parade in review before him.

As Laurence trotted her past their carriage, Angel snorted and tossed her head happily. He waved at the girls. Charlotte gushed, "Oh, Annie, I cannot believe that your brother has chosen me. You must teach me to be as brave and well-read as you are, darling, so that I am worthier of being your sister."

It was said with such sincerity, Annie softened and let go of her grudge. "You'll be fine, Charlotte. He is quite smitten, you know. What Laurence has always appreciated is kindness." Then Annie repeated a line from Shakespeare that she had often used as a guide for herself: *"Beauty lives with kindness."* She smiled. Charlotte smiled back.

"Oh, look, Annie, isn't that Captain Farley?"

Annie turned in enough time to see the gentle South Carolinian scout ride by, his horse, like himself, dignified and graceful. She blushed slightly.

"Aha, Annie, I see the beginning of something." Charlotte wagged her finger. "Do tell!"

Annie's smile faded. It would be a while before she completely trusted Charlotte again. She said nothing and simply put the field glasses back to her eyes, but she noticed Charlotte's hurt expression.

Boom-boom-boom-boom.

Suddenly, as part of the show, twenty-four artillery guns exploded. Acrid smoke billowed across the valley and the nearly ten thousand riders took up the Rebel caterwaul. They drew their sabers with a resounding scrape of metal, and with bellows of "Charge!" spurred their horses into a gallop to show the gathered civilians what a battle would be like. Swords gleamed, dirt clods flew, horses reared and whinnied, the earth trembled with the thundering of forty thousand hooves suddenly tearing along the earth.

Charlotte gasped and clutched Annie, holding her handkerchief to her mouth. Annie frantically searched the mayhem of horses for Angel. Don't let her be stampeded by some larger horse, Lord. Don't let her get kicked. Don't let Laurence fall under all those racing hooves, prayed Annie. Finally she found Angel, pulling ahead of dozens, her tail arched like a battle flag. Laurence's hat was gone, his hair flying like her mane. Annie focused on his face. He was laughing.

Annie followed with the glasses. See, brother. See how wonderful my horse is, she thought. See why you always had trouble stopping me from galloping her!

The mock charge went on and on. Annie shook her head, disapproving of pushing the horses like that purely for show. And yet—she couldn't help it—her heart raced at the exciting pageant before her.

Boom-boom-boom.

The guns exploded again. By now the thick

smoke from the cannons was drifting toward the crowd. Annie heard a thud to the left of her and another to the right. Ladies were swooning. Now this was getting silly. The vanity of it was foolish; Stuart could break the horses running them like that. And why waste all that ammunition just to show off to a crowd that already worshiped him?

Boom-boom-boom.

Another two ladies standing in front of the carriage fell over—perfectly—into the arms of their escorts. Annie checked Charlotte, who was fanning herself frantically, her eyes wide and frightened. "Oh, Annie, I never imagined how terrible a battle could be before. I . . . I . . . I feel sick." She leaned up against Annie.

Well, thought Annie, at least she didn't faint.

That night, there was yet another ball. Again, Annie spent the evening mostly with Captain Farley. They danced outside under the stars. For Annie, it matched the romance of any book.

The next morning Farley arrived at Mrs. Crawford's house and asked for Annie. Mrs. Crawford, as was proper, stayed in the parlor with them as they talked.

"I am not sure with whom to entrust this," he

said, holding out his carefully folded dress uniform. General Stuart had insisted that all his officers buy new uniforms for the review. Laurence had had to as well. "It is a fine material and meant for formal events; it's rather expensive, I'm afraid. If I take it with me, it's sure to be ruined in my haversack." He looked hopefully at Annie.

Before she could respond, Mrs. Crawford stepped forward. "I'll keep it for you, son. It will be here waiting for you when next you come to Culpeper, or when the war is over."

Captain Farley looked slightly disappointed, but he smiled graciously at the plump old matron. "Thank you, ma'am. I am grateful to you. We are to move again within days. General Lee is planning a campaign north. If anything befalls me, please wrap me in this and send me to my mother."

It was such a simple, sweet request. Annie hardly knew this man, really, but he had already won a spot in her heart that was growing. This time she stepped up. "There will be no need, Captain," said Annie. "You must promise to visit me at Hickory Heights very soon. My brother will show you the way."

"Gladly, Miss . . ." He paused and then shyly said her first name for the first time. "Miss Annie."

CHAPTER TWENTY-FOUR

June 17, 1863
Hickory Heights

"It was terrible, Annie," Laurence said quietly, describing a surprise attack by the Union cavalry four days after Stuart's grand review. "They came from all directions. They caught us completely unawares. We were exhausted from the pomp and fuss of Stuart's review and that fool saber charge he had ordered. Plus we had to repeat the review for Lee when the general was finally able to come. That one, at least, we held at a walk. But we were tuckered out, so we'd stretched out across four miles of hills to let our horses graze and recuperate. My men were snoring like bullfrogs, when around three A.M. a picket cries out: 'Yankees! Great God! Millions of them!'

"Ten thousand of their riders were on top of us

before we could collect ourselves or protect our guns. The fighting went on till nightfall."

Annie was listening only so well. She was circling Angel, running her hand along her flanks, fighting off tears from the sight of the gashes across her beautiful coat, from the way the horse flinched when Annie's light touch neared one of the cuts. Angel would carry those scars forever.

"She's all right, honey," Laurence reassured her.

He sat atop Angel, at the gate of Hickory Heights' lane. His division was moving east along the turnpike from Upperville toward Aldie, to hide the infantry's march up the Shenandoah Valley on the other side of the Blue Ridge Mountains. Once again, Lee was crossing into Maryland to find food for the hungry horses and men and to pull the Union armies away from Richmond. At all costs, Stuart was to keep the Federals from getting to the mountain passes at Ashby's or Snicker's gaps and seeing the Confederate army on the move. Stuart had ordered pickets to be established up and down Loudoun and Fauquier counties to watch for and fight any Union cavalry trying to find Lee.

"Angel saved my life, Annie," Laurence continued. "You saved my life by giving her to me. There was one charge from the bluecoats that cut down every rider within twenty feet of me. Six men, Annie, blasted from their saddles within a few seconds of one another. I was the only one to survive. Angel moved so fast, they just couldn't fix their sights on her."

For a moment he was silent, watching the Virginia cavalry pass by. "I have to rejoin them, Annie. But I'll try to come back to visit Mother once we've camped for the night." He shifted in his saddle uncomfortably. "Annie, I need to tell you something." He paused and cleared his throat. "William Farley was killed."

Annie looked up at him in surprise. Her stomach lurched. She'd seen death in Manassas and in the Middleburg hospitals, but miraculously no one she'd known well before had died. Farley's gentle, aristocratic face came back to her. She shook her head. How could it be? He'd been so alive, so promising, the last time she'd seen him, just two weeks before.

"A shell exploded right beside him, Annie. There was nothing anyone could do." Laurence reached out and took her hand. "He was his gracious self even at the end. As we tried to get him to an ambulance, he said, 'Good-bye, gentlemen, and forever. I know my condition, and we will not meet again. I thank you for your kindness.' "

Angrily, Laurence pulled his hand away and straightened up. "There was no need for it," he said huskily. "Vanity brought that battle on. The blue-coats were alerted to our whereabouts by all the noise we'd made—guns booming, our shouting—during that review."

Annie felt numb. She'd read the scathing condemnation of Stuart in the Richmond papers. They'd called him negligent, self-aggrandizing, more interested in ladies (rollicking, frolicking, and running after girls, said his critics) than in protecting the country or knowing the whereabouts of the enemy. She'd not known what to think. And now this? A man of poetry and grace, cut down. She thought of William Farley trying to give her his dress coat. It was as if he had had a premonition.

"I'm sorry, Annie. You should know that William was very taken with you."

Suddenly, Annie was furious. "Is that supposed to make me feel better?" she shot back. "That this dead man might have come to love me? I think I could have loved him, Laurence; you were right about that. The fact that there was a wondrous possibility there only makes the loss sting harder. It is no comfort."

"I only thought you'd like to know." Laurence sighed. "But I understand what you say."

"This war costs too much." Annie choked out the words. For the first time, the tragic waste of it all revolted her.

Laurence nodded, pulled his dusty slouch hat back on, and tried to cluck Angel into a walk. The mare nuzzled Annie and refused to move. Laurence let the reins fall. "I haven't the heart to pull her away from you. I know she's been looking for you."

Tears fell down Annie's face unchecked. For a moment, she put her cheek against Angel's forehead. Then she took her by the reins, led her into the lane, and pushed her on. Swishing her tail and looking back over her shoulder, Angel complied unhappily. Laurence slouched in the saddle.

Annie watched them go until they disappeared into the crowd of slowly moving horses and riders. It was hard to recognize them as the swashbucklers who'd charged up and down the hills of Brandy Station and made ladies swoon.

That afternoon some of Stuart's riders clashed with Union cavalry just outside Aldie. These Yankees were new regiments, from New York, Massachusetts, Ohio, and Maine. They were fresh, emboldened by what had happened at Brandy Station, and they fought hard, finally struggling hand to hand in a hayfield. The Confederates lost a hundred men.

Stuart himself rode into Middleburg. As always, the town's ladies surrounded him with joy and flowers. But the celebration lasted only a few moments, until Rhode Island Federals rushed in, firing their guns. As darkness fell, blue and gray cavalrymen dashed up and down the village streets, shooting at one another, jumping barricades each side put up to trip the other.

That's when the call came to Jamie. Mosby wanted to join Stuart's forces for this scrap, which was turning uglier by the moment. Annie followed Jamie, carrying a candle to light his way in the stable as he tacked up his horse. She didn't want anyone else at Hickory Heights to see him get ready. It wasn't that she didn't trust them. She just didn't want them to have knowledge that could endanger the household if the Yankees came asking questions.

It was a damp, misty night. "Jamie, be careful. Promise me," she said. "This is a real battle, not just a surprise raid on a sleeping camp."

Jamie whirled around to face her. "I know that!" He grinned. "Isn't it grand?"

He cantered away down the road, the ground

barely visible through the fog, the moonlight only so much of a guide. For the first time in a long time, Annie knelt and prayed.

At dawn on the nineteenth, as light filtered through her bedroom windows, Annie stretched and listened for the usual sound of morning singing. The birds were silent. She sat up quickly. There was a distant rumbling. She looked at the soft beam of light creeping across the floor. It was a bright day coming. That wasn't thunder. It was artillery, sure.

"Annie?" Through her bedroom wall Annie heard her mother's call.

"Coming," she answered. When she opened the door, she found Miriam leaning against the wall, holding back the curtains, looking out.

Annie joined her. There on the hills were two small armies—bluecoats to the east, gray to the west. Tiny puffs of smoke dappled the hills as carbines and rifles shot at one another. Punctuating it all were rumbling booms and large bursts of red and smoke—cannons. First there was a swell of blue riders moving forward, a crescent moon shape that surged, then wavered, then broke into bits as gray swarmed to meet it. Then the gray line wavered, broke, and fell back.

One by one, Will, Colleen, and Sally tiptoed in and knelt by the other window, peering out at the fighting, their noses on the sill. Even Aunt Molly braved Aunt May to join them. "Just like Manassas," she muttered. "They'll run over us again, Miriam. What are we to do?"

Miriam ignored her sister. "Where's Jamie?" she asked Annie.

Annie caught her breath. Somehow they had managed to avoid telling Miriam that Jamie had joined Mosby. She started to lie, to tell her mother he was probably up a tree watching himself. But Miriam's light green eyes were fixed on Annie's. Annie hesitated.

Miriam reached out and patted Annie's face. "He's out there, isn't he? My baby?"

Biting her lip, Annie nodded her head.

"Both my boys." Miriam pulled in a long, shuddering breath, and then looked back out the window to the tiny waves of cavalrymen, careening back and forth across the distant hills. "It's like a fever, Annie darling. There's nothing to be done but to wait it out."

The cannons thundered off and on. Not until midnight could Annie and Aunt May convince Miriam to get into bed.

"Wait until I see that rapscallion and give him a piece of my mind, plaguing Missus Miriam all day long, charging up and down hills playing soldier," Aunt May muttered as she covered Miriam.

Miriam smiled. "May," she said, as she closed her eyes, "you'd be the same if Jacob were fighting."

It was the first time anyone had brought up Jacob since he and Gabriel had run off. Annie froze. But the conversation remained one of mother to mother.

Aunt May straightened up and sighed. "I wonder where that boy be."

"I'm sure he is fine, May. I feel it here that he is." Miriam touched her heart.

Before Aunt May could answer, there was a loud rapping on the front door.

Trembling, Annie ran down to open it.

The first of the wounded had arrived.

"Saints preserve us," Aunt Molly whined as she poured water for a young man who was stretched out on the settee.

This time, though, they had only a handful of wounded men, not badly hurt, whom the Confederate cavalry left as they withdrew a few miles down the road. They needed water, minor bandaging, and a few hours' peace to recoup.

Next day there was more hard fighting, this time south and west of them. Stuart was definitely falling back. The wounded at Hickory Heights recovered enough to get up on their horses and make their way to the front line to rejoin their companies. Stragglers kept trotting down the road. There was the occasional *pop-pop-pop* of a pistol and then nothing.

Miriam stayed by the window, although now there was nothing to be seen on the back fields or the hills behind them. They waited, waited for the armies of horsemen to disappear, leaving Fauquier, or to suddenly ride through their fields again.

When news finally came, it careened up the front lane. A wagon rattled up the lane, mules braying at being pushed to work so hard and so fast. Horsemen cantered up behind it, filling the air with gravel dust. Among them was Laurence.

"Annie!" he bellowed at the house. "Annie! Come here at once!"

Annie burst through the front door. "Oh, Laurence, is it Jamie?" she gasped.

"Jamie!" Laurence exploded. "Why would it be Jamie?"

Annie couldn't speak.

He jumped off Angel and grabbed Annie's arm.

"Why might it be Jamie? What has that fool boy done?"

"He . . . he . . . he is with Mosby."

"What? I told you, Annie, not to let—"

"Captain, we've got to hurry." The driver interrupted Laurence. "They're right behind us."

Laurence rubbed his forehead to control himself. "I've got to leave Major Heros von Borcke with you. He's one of General Stuart's closest aides and friends. He was shot through the throat yesterday. No one expected him to live through the night, but he has. General Stuart wants all attention paid to him. We're regrouping a mile west. Hickory Heights is the closest house. We'll carry him up to the attic. If bluebirds search the house, you'll have to try to trick them into not going there, somehow. Can you manage that, Annie?"

Stung by the implication that she hadn't kept Jamie safe, she shot back, "I've done it before, brother. It hasn't exactly been a tea party here at home."

For a moment, she thought about suggesting they put him in Jamie's cellar hideaway, but seeing the size and condition of the man, she knew that wouldn't work. It took all four men to haul von Borcke up the stairs. He was a huge man, a

Prussian, one of the Europeans who had attached themselves to the Confederate army. At the landing, Aunt May met them.

"Where you going with that man?"

Laurence told her.

"You think them Yankees ain't going to see that pull-down door in the ceiling?"

Laurence hesitated.

Aunt May turned to Annie. The two of them thought hard, looking at each other for some guidance.

"We could push the wardrobe up under it," Annie finally suggested.

"They'll see them marks on the floor," Aunt May countered, sticking out her lower lip.

"Not if I sit there knitting, they won't."

Aunt May snorted. "P'shaw, Miss Annie. Since when you knit?"

"Since now," laughed Annie.

Laurence gaped at them. "You sound as if you've done this before."

Annie humpf-laughed, a most unladylike sound. "Move along, brother Laurence. The Yankees are behind you, aren't they?"

Von Borcke was laid carefully on a blanket in the attic, with a pistol and his saber across his chest.

The Prussian was wheezing horribly. Annie couldn't believe he'd live. And after all this trouble, she thought, as she watched the cavalrymen push the attic ladder up and close the door.

They shoved the wide, heavy wardrobe into place. Its crown molding reached within a hair's breadth of the ceiling door. Annie quickly moved a chair across the floor to the telltale outline left from the heavy wooden cabinet that had been sitting on the same spot for years. Her skirts would hide it.

She hugged Laurence. "Go on now. We'll be all right."

Laurence shook his head. "Lady Liberty." He bowed. There was respect in his teasing. He took several quick steps toward the door and then turned. "You tell James that he and I are due a talk."

Then he was gone.

Within twenty minutes, Yankees arrived. As soon as they rode up the lane, Annie slipped upstairs and took her position in the chair. She'd given up on the idea of knitting. Aunt May was right; she didn't know how to, and it'd be obvious. She grabbed a book instead. She'd use her new defense of arrogance. She would remain reading in her chair. The Yankees simply didn't warrant her interrupting herself. She sat, straightened her spine, and tipped up her nose, making herself the picture of feminine disdain.

This group of Union cavalry at least was polite. They were from Massachusetts. They went about their business quickly and quietly—no stabbing the walls, no running helter-skelter, no prying into drawers. Annie heard the front door open and several more step inside. Someone thumped across the hallway to them. She could imagine a salute from the junior officer. She was beginning to know the drill well.

She heard: *"We've searched every house in Upperville. There's some big Rebel officer wounded. We saw him fall from his horse. He wore a plumed hat and fancy uniform. We think it might be Stuart."*

"Keep looking" was the reply.

Annie heard footsteps on the stairs.

She perfected her aura of haughty disinterest and waited. She forced herself to look down at the text on the page before her, although she read no words.

A Union officer walked into the room.

Annie didn't look up. She turned a page and pretended to keep reading.

"Well, I'll be. Is that Lord Byron?"

Annie hadn't even noticed what book she held. What is it with these Yankees and Byron? she wondered. She didn't answer.

The officer stepped closer. "I believe it is."

Annie slowly turned another page. She held herself even more upright. She sniffed slightly and made a face as if something near her smelled horrid. Still, she did not take her eyes off the pages.

Softly, the officer recited: *"She walks in beauty, like the night . . ."*

She couldn't help it. Annie looked up with surprise.

Before her stood Thomas Walker.

CHAPTER TWENTY-FIVE

June 20, 1863
Hickory Heights

"I hoped that our paths would cross again, Miss Sinclair." Thomas bowed his head and removed his hat.

Annie felt a ripple of gladness in seeing this young man who loved poetry. She opened her mouth to say something welcoming, but then her mind played back parts of the Manassas battle during which they'd met—trees exploding, men crumpling up in agony before her, she and her mother surrounded by men running in terror. Sickened, she swayed in her chair.

Immediately Thomas knelt beside her. "Are you all right?"

Blinking hard to push back the nightmare memories, she focused on his face. It was a kind face, still lean and handsome, although now there was a small, trim, moustache on it. He had large dark brown eyes, almost black they were so dark, very intense in their look of concern. For a moment, Annie steadied herself by his sympathy. But then anger took over. Yankees such as this man were to blame for that Battle of First Manassas—they and their self-righteous, meddling politicians! If only they had let the Confederates go in peace, then all this bloodshed, this invasion of her home, this slow starvation of her family never would have happened. And William Farley would be alive.

Annie leaned away from him. "I can't say, sir, that I had the same wish."

Thomas sat back on his heels. He frowned, then stood. He put his hat back on and became official. "I'm afraid that I must invade your family's home and ask your help. We are looking for a Confederate officer who was wounded and presumed to be hiding in the vicinity. There is the thought he might be General Stuart. Do you know of his whereabouts?"

Annie took a deep breath. As of yet, she had not had to lie to a direct question from a Union soldier. If she wanted to be nitpicking, the way he phrased things, it sounded as if he were asking if she knew where General Stuart was. She had no idea where

General Stuart was at the moment. "No," she answered truthfully.

A colonel and a lieutenant entered the room.

"Anything, Major?"

"No, sir," Thomas answered.

"Well, keep looking."

More soldiers came upstairs. They began tapping the walls, listening for a hollow ring that would betray a hidden compartment. No one had yet looked up at the ceiling.

"Major Walker." Annie spoke to distract. Politeness dictated she stand at this point, but Annie remained rooted to her chair, her skirts spread wide over the telltale marks on the floor.

The colonel raised an eyebrow. "You know the lady?"

"Yes, sir. She and her mother bandaged me during the First Battle of Bull Run. I think they saved my life."

"Ah. They are Unionists, then?"

With some amusement, Thomas answered. "No, sir, I think not."

The colonel turned to assess Annie. His look was not unkind, but confused.

"My mother believes a hurt boy is a hurt boy," explained Annie. "In its retreat, your army left many of your soldiers in great need. They were lucky my mother is so skilled as a nurse." From the corner of her eye, she saw one of the soldiers approaching the wardrobe. She rushed on, "My mother is in the next room, and actually quite ill. If you must disturb her, I prefer Major Walker be the one to question her. For some reason"—she pulled out the words with sarcasm—"Mother liked him." She added icily, "Surely your men will not do me the insult of fishing through my clothes?"

Walker grinned at the colonel. "Definitely not a Unionist, sir." He snapped his finger at the private peering into the wardrobe. "That's enough. This room is clear." He stepped out of the room himself, waiting for Annie to follow.

This was a terrible moment. She would have to move swiftly and keep their attention on her. Annie fairly bolted out of her chair, crossed the room, and closed the door behind her. In her haste, she snagged her skirts in the door.

As he leaned over to tug the skirt free for her, Thomas spoke. "I am grieved to hear your mother is sick. Is there anything we can do? We have a surgeon at camp. I could—"

The colonel interrupted. "I can't be carrying our sawbones all the way here without good cause,

Thomas. Why don't you speak with the woman just to clear her room? I will wait downstairs. Otherwise, I don't see anything suspicious here. Miss." He tipped his hat to Annie. "Thank you."

Annie opened the door to Miriam's room. Despite all the noise, Miriam was asleep. She seemed to sleep most of the time now, or drift between wakefulness and what looked like sleep. Aunt May sat in her usual chair, in the corner of the room, keeping watch.

Seeing the scene, Thomas whispered, "What is wrong with Mrs. Sinclair?"

"She had diphtheria last summer. Her heart has just gotten weaker and weaker."

"I am deeply grieved to hear it," he murmured. "She is a very kind lady." He thought a moment. "Please, would you tell her I asked after her? Perhaps I can procure some meat or medicine for her."

Foolishly, Annie let her pride answer. "We don't need Yankee charity."

Thomas's face tightened. "I see that the war has changed you. I am sorry to see it. I had been much impressed by your prior graciousness in the face of an invading army. I spoke often of it when I was home and people expressed opinions of what renegades Southerners must be." He bowed to leave.

Stung, Annie held out her hand. "Here. Take this book. I don't want it. Byron is a self-infatuated poet. Much like the Northerners I have been forced to meet."

Thomas looked down at the book and shook his head. "There are moments of beauty in the verse, though, you must admit, Miss Sinclair." He smiled at her. "Please keep the volume. Surely poetry can be neutral territory for us."

He jogged down the stairs.

The next day Stuart's cavalry skirmished repeatedly with Union riders along Goose Creek and Ashby's Gap Turnpike between Upperville and Middleburg. That evening General Stuart stopped at Hickory Heights to see his friend von Borcke. He could stay only a few moments. His cavalry needed to parallel Robert E. Lee's infantry as it marched north along the western side of the Blue Ridge, using the mountains as a curtain. To the east, on the other side of the Bull Run Mountains, the Yankee army was lurking, waiting, trying to foresee Lee's next move. Stuart was between the two. Even though he'd fallen back during the fighting of the previous three days, he'd held the mountain gaps and kept Union cavalry from discovering Lee's movements. The general's plan for northward invasion remained hidden.

It was a momentous plan. Dick Ewell and his troops were already in Maryland close to the Pennsylvania border, waiting for Lee's command. Longstreet's army was crossing the Potomac River. The Confederates were massing for a huge strike. If only, only they could continue to move undetected and catch the Union army by surprise. That was Stuart's responsibility—to shield them from Union scouts, to distract the Yankees with his raids, to keep a sharp eye on the Federal enemy's movements.

Stuart and his staff cantered up Hickory Heights' lane with their usual showmanship. The general jumped off his horse and ran up the porch steps two at a time, excited, off on an adventure. But he slowed and lost his glamour when he saw his friend.

Isaac, Bob, and Jamie had carried von Borcke out of the attic and brought him onto the front porch for some fresh air. The Prussian had managed to down some soup and sit up. It was a miracle that he had survived at all. A bullet had cut part of his windpipe. Annie could see that he'd never ride with Stuart again. He'd be lucky to be able to speak and walk.

Stuart's long gait shortened as he crossed the porch. His face changed to a mask of careful cheeriness. "Von, old fellow," he said heartily, "you are looking marvelously well." Stuart sat down beside him and took his hand in his.

Von Borcke tried to answer, but only a whistling sound came out. Stuart patted his arm. "Don't try to speak, Von. Rest. Mend quickly. Our camp will not be the same until you return. I will miss you."

Fighting his emotions, Stuart stood and went to his horse.

"Miss Annie," he called to her. He was quiet, serious. "Thank you for taking in Von. Poor fellow. He was sitting right beside me when he was hit. Just before he was struck down, another close bullet had torn off some gold braid from his uniform trousers. Von did love to dress smartly. I think they thought he was me. Von said . . . he said . . ." Stuart swallowed hard and continued hoarsely, "He said, 'Those Yankees are giving it to me rather hotly on your account.' And then he was hit."

Stuart looked down and kicked some dirt. After a moment, he reached into his pocket. "I had hoped that I might see you. I began another verse in December. I was going to give it to you at the Culpeper ball, but you were occupied with William

Farley." He paused again to control his voice. "Poor William. So many bright stars fallen." He shook his head slowly and handed Annie a folded paper. "You have become a beautiful woman, Miss Annie. I hope that life gives you great happiness."

For a moment their hands touched. But it was a solemn exchange. Stuart was saying good-bye. Annie could feel it. He expected never to see her again.

Without another word, Stuart heaved himself into his saddle and rode off, silent.

Later, she read the snippet of poetry:

When music's soft enrapt'ring swell
delights thy list'ning ear,
When zephyrs whisper all is well
and all thou lov'st are near,
When skies are bright and thou art all
that thou couldst wish to be,
I dare not ask, for 'twould be vain,
that thou couldst think of me.

There were more good-byes in the next days. Laurence rode to the house to see Miriam. As he left, walking down the stairs, weary, saddened with worry for his mother, he ran into Jamie. It was like two stallions meeting each other over a herd of mares.

Annie was standing by the hall door. She couldn't believe the violent change in Laurence's face. He hurled himself at Jamie and grabbed him by the collar. "Where have you been, boy?"

Jamie's face turned its rage-purple. But he held his ground and answered stoutly, "I've been out with Major Mosby, scouting a ford for you boys to cross the Potomac." He tried to shove Laurence away from him. Jamie was quite tall and thickset for his age, but the older brother was stronger.

Laurence held fast to his collar and shook him. "Why aren't you watching out for Mother? Don't you realize your shenanigans weaken her further and imperil this family? Why aren't you here protecting the house?"

"Because I'm fighting for my country. I'm doing my duty."

"Duty?" Laurence spat out. "All Mosby's done is steal from supply wagons and keep the loot for himself. There is no honor in that, Jamie. Choose honorable service, if you must fight. In the end, when this war is over, that's all we're going to have left to us. Ride with me instead."

"And be bossed around by you wherever I go? No, thank you, brother. Mosby not honorable? Shows what you know. We've kidnaped a Union general right out of his bed. We've cut railroad lines and disrupted supply trains, even when we were outnumbered ten to one. So what if we keep the spoils? The Confederate army sure doesn't supply us with anything. Had a decent meal recently, brother? I have. I've brought food home for everyone here, too. All you've done is take our horses.

"I've also had the satisfaction of watching Yankees turn tail and run like the dogs they are. You're so all-fired high-and-mighty—Stuart and his fancy parading cavalry. From what I've seen in the last few days of fighting, you boys could use our help. I saw your riders turn and run plenty."

Laurence drew back and struck Jamie's jaw. The blow made a horrible cracking noise. Jamie staggered, then flung himself at Laurence, knocking him down. They rolled on the floor, until Laurence surfaced on top of Jamie. Jamie kicked at him from underneath. They came up with their hands wrapped around each other's throats.

"Laurence! Jamie! For shame," shrieked Annie, wading into the fray. "Take your hands away!" She tugged on Laurence, who let go instantly, shock and shame registering on his face.

Jamie held fast.

Laurence held his hands down by his side, doing nothing to get his brother off him.

Jamie tightened his grip.

"Jamie!" Annie began pulling at his fingers.

Laurence's breath began to come in fits, but he didn't say a word. Didn't make a move.

"Jamie! Jamie. Let go! You're choking him." Annie was sobbing. She tore at his hands.

Suddenly, a little body flung itself on Jamie's back and began beating him. It was Will.

The surprise of it stopped Jamie. Finally, he let go. Laurence fell back to the floor, coughing. Jamie shoved Will away and stood.

"I am a Mosby ranger, Laurence," Jamie gasped. "You do not own me. I don't care what you think of me any longer. And I'm going to do whatever I must to stop the Yankees." He stormed out the front door, slamming it hard.

It took a long time for Laurence to catch his breath, a long time for Annie to stop shaking. Meanwhile, Will disappeared as silently as he had appeared.

Finally, Annie voiced a question she'd had for years: "Laurence, what is the matter with you? Why are you so hard on Jamie?"

"Hard? You consider that hard? You should have seen Father with me."

Laurence looked down and changed his tone. "I don't know, Annie. Mother always told me I was responsible for making a man of him. I don't know how to do it. How do you be a brother and a father both?" He looked at Annie, but she had no answer for him.

"Really, I just don't want him to get hurt. I don't understand why he doesn't see that and listen to me. I don't understand why he's so angry with me all the time. All I'm trying to do is help. Do you know that once he . . . ?" Laurence stopped short.

Annie waited for him to tell the story about Jamie throwing rocks at his horse while Laurence was riding. But he didn't. He muttered to himself, "My other brothers wouldn't have done that."

He shook his head as if trying to shake off an annoying bee. He finished aloud with, "I simply don't understand the boy."

But Annie had heard the comment about their other brothers. She recognized something new about Laurence. And felt like a fool for not seeing it before. Laurence missed those dead brothers! Jamie was not a replacement for them, not by a long shot. Spoiled, hotheaded, jealous, he didn't even compare. She suddenly felt immense pity for both of them. Neither one had what he really wanted—Laurence those long-gone brothers, or

Jamie his real father.

But how could Annie speak to that big of an empty space in them? Clearly they loved each other as much as resented each other, or they wouldn't fight so much. All she knew was that Laurence was going to have to let Jamie make his own mistakes from now on, no matter how painful it was. That was the sad truth. Jamie wasn't going to listen to advice from either Laurence or Annie. In fact, anything they told him right now, he'd be sure to do the opposite.

"He's not a child any longer, Laurence," said Annie. "Nor am I. And if you listen, you may actually learn something from us."

Laurence thought a minute. "I can see that in you, Annie. I was amazed by your calm resolve and cleverness about hiding von Borcke. Very different from the girl who was so afraid at Manassas. But Jamie . . . Jamie is too young to die for the cause, Annie."

He looked away from her. "The cause . . . the accursed cause . . . I was fighting for Hickory Heights. To save Hickory Heights. To take care of you and Jamie and Mother and everyone else. And I can see that it will probably be for nothing. I don't know what will be left after all this killing. Look at how Jamie and I instinctively grabbed each other's throats. That's what the war has taught us."

He dropped his head in his hands and wept.

For a long time, he cried. Annie sat paralyzed.

Finally something told her to put her arm around his shoulders. "I'm here, Laurence," she whispered to the top of his fair-haired head. "I'll do the best I can to keep home safe." She turned to teasing, their old way of relating. "If the Yankees come, why, I'll get one of Jamie's precious guns, and Aunt May will get her broom, and between the two of us, we can take on all the whole Union army. I promise."

Laurence laughed. "I imagine you two could," he said into his hands. He lifted his head and wiped his eyes. "Forgive me, Annie."

Annie's heart swelled. *Oh, dear brother.*

There was a light tap on the door. It was Sam. Rachel stood a few feet behind him. "They're waiting for us at the end of the lane, Captain."

Laurence nodded and picked up the saddlebag that Aunt May had stuffed with biscuits and bacon.

He hugged Annie. "You are worth twelve brothers, Lady Liberty. Don't forget to take care of yourself now."

He handed her an envelope to post to Charlotte

and then pulled himself onto Angel. Sam got onto his horse.

Annie couldn't help a final embrace for Angel. "Do you know where you're going, Laurence?"

"North somewhere. Word is General Lee plans for this campaign to break the war. We can only hope."

There was a gallant sadness, a stoic determination about Laurence as he turned Angel and cantered away. Annie squared her shoulders and tried to adopt the straightforward, no-nonsense courage of her brother. She took Rachel's hand. "You all right?" she asked.

Rachel shrugged, then nodded. As all right as she could be, watching her husband ride off into another battle, purely out of love and loyalty to a man, a friend, who had once owned him. Laurence had a deep sense of honor, but Sam did, too—both of which outsiders could probably never understand. Together, Annie and Rachel went back into the house, back to their work of tending the sick, stretching their food, and waiting.

CHAPTER TWENTY-SIX

July 11, 1863
Hickory Heights

Robert E. Lee's northern campaign did seem to break the war. But not the way the Confederate leader had hoped. In a tiny town in Pennsylvania called Gettysburg, Lee turned his army and stumbled onto the Federals who'd been shadowing him without his knowing it. In the stifling July heat, the two armies lunged at each other. Gorged on cherries they had plucked from trees as they marched, the half-starved Confederates suffered horrible dysentery after eating the fruit. They had no clear-cut strategy because Stuart had not arrived to scout the area. Without his cavalry to ride out and back to report what they saw, Lee was blind. As he began the battle, he had no idea what he was facing. He flung his men at the enemy that he could spot through his field glasses and prayed that thousands more weren't behind them.

But there were.

Stuart and his cavalry had been delayed at the Potomac River by horrendous summer thunderstorms and misjudgments. When they finally crossed the flooded waters, they found themselves stuck *behind* the Union army as it pursued the Confederates northward. By that point, Stuart had no idea where Lee was. He simply continued north. Trying to redeem himself for the Union's devastating surprise attack on him at Brandy Station, Stuart insisted on capturing and then carting along 125 Union wagons full of oats, boots, medicine, and whiskey. The much-needed supplies simply delayed him further.

By the time Stuart and his cavalry arrived in Gettysburg, eight thousand soldiers—blue and gray—already lay dead or wounded on the ground. It was only the first of three days of brutal killing.

Stuart's captured supply wagons now only got in the way of an army frantically trying to maneuver. Reprimanded by Lee, condemned by Longstreet for worrying more about his own ego and standing than the lives of the army's infantry soldiers, Stuart joined the fight with a burning need to rebuild his reputation. On the final day of battle, Stuart ordered a daring saber charge against Michigan cavalry. There was charge and countercharge, until finally the Federals regrouped. The two sides hurled themselves at each other, the lines breaking into mass chaos as riders slashed at one another, demanding surrender. At the end of it, neither side had gained advantage. But hundreds of riders and horses were cut down, crippled and bleeding on the ground, crying, praying, dying.

The next day, before dawn, the Confederates withdrew and staggered toward home. Lee and his Army of Northern Virginia had lost twenty thousand men—one out of every three of its fighters. Those left standing were desperate to cross back into Virginia, or they'd be surrounded, trapped against the Potomac River, and beaten for good. The Confederacy would die. Lee had no choice. He left his wounded stranded on the fields, in a torrential rain.

Laurence was among the abandoned.

An anxious gloom settled on Hickory Heights as the inhabitants waited to learn if Laurence had survived. But news of Aunt Molly's husband came swiftly. Uncle John had been killed. He had fought under General George Pickett. On that last frantic day of slaughter, Lee ordered Pickett's division of foot soldiers to charge across a mile-wide open field against a thick line of Federals, dug in and waiting behind a stone wall. The place was called Cemetery Ridge. Fifteen thousand gray-clad soldiers obeyed. Ten thousand of them died or were wounded. Pickett's officers fell, too. Of his thirteen colonels, seven died, six were wounded.

Annie's little girl cousins didn't seem to understand what the news meant. It had been so long since they'd seen their father—almost half of Colleen's short life—that he seemed long gone anyway. But Will understood. And Aunt Molly set up a wail that could have been heard a mile. Miriam had somehow dragged herself down to the parlor to comfort her sister. Annie was embarrassed that her first thought was to worry about how she would continue to feed them all now that they wouldn't be going home. Perhaps ever. Widows had a hard time running a farm.

Annie didn't let herself think on what could have befallen Laurence. Or Angel. Annie would wait. She took all her fears, all her *what if?*s, and shoved them into a cellar in her brain and locked it. If she didn't, she couldn't function, couldn't keep

Hickory Heights going, couldn't look after Miriam. She'd just be hanging, swaying in misery, watching, hoping, agonizing.

The Union army, led by a General Meade, eventually followed Lee into Virginia and took possession of Fauquier and Loudoun counties once more. Meade settled into Warrenton.

Ever defiant, Mosby called for more raids. He captured merchant wagons, hit a Union wagon train out foraging for supplies, and made off with a number of mules from a Federal encampment. Ever more men were joining his ranks.

Thanks to Jamie, Hickory Heights had a new boarder, a Charles Murdock. Annie did not care for him. There was something sly about the angular man. She was glad that von Borcke had been moved out of their home and taken to Richmond. Annie was sure that Mosby's bold raids would bring them trouble, and she didn't want to be worrying over hiding the seriously injured Prussian.

On the morning of the eleventh, trouble came.

Again, it was Thomas Walker and the Massachusetts cavalry that arrived to search their home. As much as Annie tried to detest the man, she was relieved that he was there. His unit was respectful; his colonel, by the name of Lowell, was clearly an educated man.

The search lasted only half an hour. Murdock and Jamie were out of the house, catching bullfrogs and fishing for dinner. They had evaporated into the hillside when they heard the horses coming. Just the night before, Isaac had tethered in the woods the Union army mules Mosby had been stabling at Hickory Heights. There was nothing for the blue-coats to find.

It was a different story that evening.

They were all gathered in the dining room—Annie, Aunt Molly, Sally, Colleen, Will, Jamie, and Murdock—enjoying the fat fish Jamie had caught at the creek, when the sound of horses came up the lane.

Murdock and Jamie jumped up. Annie ran to the window. "Thank God," she called out quietly. "It's only two riders." They might even be Mosby men. She strained to see and went cold all over. It was Thomas Walker again.

"Quick, into the cellar," she hissed at Murdock. "Jamie, you sit at the table. You live here. You're minding the farm."

Everyone scrambled into place.

Annie went to the door. Emotions she didn't understand took possession of her again. This

Walker was a kind, polite man. Yet she responded to him with rage. He represented the force that was destroying her life, plundering her house, killing people she cared for, forcing a multitude of hungry cousins on her, robbing her of her youth and her hope in life. Perhaps it was because she instinctively liked Thomas Walker that his part in crushing her homeland infuriated her more.

Annie opened the door and her mouth. Out came rudeness that normally would have shamed her: "Have you come to take the meager dinner I could manage tonight away from our children, Major Walker?"

Thomas had just dismounted his horse. He stiffened, but didn't take the bait this time. "No, Miss Sinclair. I've brought a surgeon to see your mother."

Annie caught her breath, embarrassed, grateful, ashamed.

"May we come in?"

She nodded, for once at a loss for words.

Annie showed the surgeon upstairs. *Oh, what she'd do, Lord, if this doctor had something to help her mother.* For the past month a terrible fear had festered in Annie that she didn't want to voice or consider, a fear that Miriam was slowly slipping away as Annie and Aunt May kept watch, helpless.

Even though Annie had been running the household for almost a year now, Miriam was still upstairs. Annie half expected her mother to just get up one day and again take up her duties. Miriam was strength. Miriam was hope. Miriam would somehow return Hickory Heights to normalcy. If she died, it meant the life Annie once knew could never be retrieved. Annie would become the linchpin, the one who would have to fix everything, the one who would have to comfort everyone else. And she was only seventeen. She'd fail; she knew it. And now that Laurence might be . . . Annie shook her head with the thought. No, she wouldn't even think on it.

Annie opened Miriam's door for the doctor. He was a large but fit man, younger than Middleburg's doctor, and the saddlebag he carried seemed to actually have supplies in it. "Please, sir," Annie whispered. "Please help my mother."

"I'll do the best I can, miss," he said. "Major Walker told me how she saved his life. He went through quite a lot to bring me here. He pushed Colonel Lowell about as hard as he could without being cited for insubordination. You should know that."

Annie sighed at the surgeon's relatively subtle

reprimand. She owed Thomas an apology, certainly her thanks.

"Mother?" Annie gently held Miriam's hand to rouse her.

Miriam opened her eyes slowly and a smile spread across her face. "Hello, darling," she answered. "I was remembering a day when Jamie was a baby and you were just a slip of a thing. We were out in the garden with all my boys. They were playing tag and carousing, and you so wanted to play with them." She feebly reached out to touch Annie's face. "My little firebrand. As brave as any boy, God help you."

Annie smiled back. "Mother, there's a doctor here."

Miriam looked alarmed. "Is someone sick, darling?"

In the corner, Aunt May buried her face in her apron. Annie heard her cry.

Annie swallowed hard. "You're the one sick, Mother. And we want you to get well. That Thomas Walker from Massachusetts, remember the man wounded at Manassas? The man whose mother sent that beautiful cloth for Christmas? He's brought a Union doctor for you. A Federal doctor has medicine that we can't get. May he look at you, please, Mother?"

Tenderly, Miriam spoke, "Annie, my darling, you can't be doing much for me now. You must know that. It's all right. Don't be grieving for me. I've lived to see you grow into such a good lady. I marvel at you. I just wish I could see you married and happy and have headstrong babies of your own."

The doctor spoke up. "Ma'am, why don't you let me be the judge of your condition?" He snapped open his bag.

Annie stepped back to give him room. *If this doctor helps, I promise to be a better person, Lord. I promise to be polite to Thomas Walker no matter how many times he searches this house.*

Oh my God! Annie had a sudden, terrible realization. Thomas is downstairs with Jamie!

Hastily, Annie excused herself and fled down the staircase. She tried to glide into the dining room without seeming flustered. The scene she found sent her heart racing.

Jamie sat glowering at Thomas. Her little cousins were frozen in their seats as well, not eating. Only Aunt Molly was consuming her food. Normally, Annie might have been mightily annoyed that her plump aunt was happily eating in such a tense situation, but next to Molly was something of far greater concern. Next to her was Charles Murdock's plate, still full of food! No one had thought to remove the extra setting.

Alarmed, Annie looked at Thomas. He was leaning up against the wall. He smiled at her.

Had he noticed? He must have. It was so clear that someone should be sitting in that empty seat, eating that dinner. What should she do? Should she try to concoct some story? Should she say something before he asked about it? What explanation could she give for an extra place setting except the obvious—that a person sitting there had left in a hurry, afraid of being seen.

All eyes were on her. No one uttered a word, except Thomas.

"Is the doctor with Mrs. Sinclair?" He looked at her encouragingly, as if he were trying to help her start a casual conversation.

"Yes . . . yes, he is," Annie stammered, regaining her balance. "I must thank you, Major Walker, for bringing him. I . . . I . . ." Oh, the words of apology stuck in her throat. "I am sorry for my rudeness earlier."

Thomas bowed slightly. "Think no more of it, Miss Sinclair. Your brother, here, has explained to me how often your home has been—what was the word you used, James? Ransacked? I can understand your dislike of our troops."

Annie ground her teeth. What else had Jamie been saying? Hadn't he learned to hold his tongue?

"He also told me how mistreated he was in Alexandria, and I am sorry to hear it. I was actually quite well cared for by your officials while at Libby Prison before I was exchanged. I am relieved to hear that your brother has returned to take care of your farm. I'm sure he is a great comfort to you."

Annie assessed Thomas' face as he spoke. Was this a trap somehow, this recitation of everything Jamie had said? In some ways, it had the opposite feel, as if he was making sure that Annie knew of Jamie's ramblings so that she would not contradict anything he had said by mistake. Which was it?

Thomas waited a moment—making sure Annie had taken it all in?—then continued. "I was telling James about our purposes in this area. Colonel Lowell was actually a schoolmate of mine when we were quite small. I went to the Point and he went to Harvard, but we remained close. I went home to Massachusetts after my prisoner exchange, and Colonel Lowell was there mustering a new cavalry regiment. He asked me to join him. Now we are here to police Mosby's rangers. Washington is quite afraid of them."

Thomas began to walk around the edge of the

table. He paused a moment to pat Jamie's shoulder—Jamie turned purple—and kept walking. He stopped beside Murdock's empty place and actually laid his hands on the chair to lean on it nonchalantly. But his words were calculated and slow: "Most of our people do not respect Mosby. Colonel Lowell feels differently. He thinks him a worthy adversary, certainly a clever one. We've been ordered to burn down any house that we find harboring his riders, but Colonel Lowell says he will avoid following that order when he can. However," Thomas continued as he walked toward Annie, "we will have to arrest any ranger we find."

He closed the gap between them and reached Annie's side. "May we sit in the parlor until the doctor is finished, Miss Sinclair? Perhaps you could tell me more of the poets you enjoy, since Lord Byron offends you."

He offered her his arm. Mesmerized, Annie took it. She had understood that little speech in the dining room. He was telling her he did indeed see the plate, that he understood its implications, and that he was going to ignore it. At the same time, he was warning her. Next time, she wouldn't be so lucky. Next time, Thomas Walker himself might have to make the arrest.

In the parlor, Annie sat and Thomas awkwardly paced in front of the bookshelves. Amazed, she wondered at the generosity of what he had just done. She suddenly felt very shy.

Thomas attempted a few beginnings of conversations. But they all fell flat.

"The doctor is taking a long time," she murmured.

"He is very thorough, Miss Sinclair. If there is something that can be done to heal your mother, he will find it."

She nodded. The carved wooden clock on the mantelpiece ticked loudly. Thomas cleared his throat. Annie smoothed her skirt.

"Now, about Lord Byron," Thomas tried. "You know, he really isn't my favorite, although his narrative poems—*Childe Harold's Pilgrimage* and the like—are quite impressive. I generally prefer . . ."

Annie brightened. She remembered. "Keats," she interrupted him. "Keats saved your life!"

Thomas beamed. "I am flattered that you recall that, Miss Sinclair. I'm afraid I haven't had the time to replace that volume after the bullet destroyed it."

Annie rose and swept toward the bookshelf. "Let me give you one." She pulled out a book and turned to him. "In thanks for bringing the surgeon."

"I will *borrow* it, Miss Sinclair, while we are in Virginia."

Their eyes met.

"Annie," she said softly, unbelieving. "You may call me Annie."

Embarrassed, she fled to her chair.

Thomas looked down at the book, suddenly nervous himself, and flipped through it. "Ah," he said after a few moments, "now here's a poem I've thought of a great deal recently."

"Yes?" Annie reached for safe dialogue. "Which one?"

" 'La Belle Dame Sans Merci.' " He grinned and hesitantly added, "I hope after tonight it will not seem so fitting to my life."

Annie laughed in spite of herself. He was witty, this Thomas Walker. Keats' poem, "The Beautiful Woman Without Mercy," was about a knight suffering unrequited love.

"Would you like me to read?" he asked.

It had been months and months since her family had sat in the parlor to read aloud together. It used to be a favorite evening pastime before the war. That and charades and singing together round the piano. She missed those happy hours dreadfully. She nodded.

He read:

"I met a lady in the meads,
Full beautiful—a faery's child,
Her hair was long, her foot was light,
And her eyes were wild."

He looked up at her hopefully, and Annie felt herself blush horribly. What was happening?

"Ever since I saw you," he whispered, "I've been haunted. I . . ."

"Miss Sinclair?" The doctor entered the parlor.

Annie nearly knocked over the chair as she stood, she was so flustered.

"I'm afraid I have bad news."

CHAPTER TWENTY-SEVEN

August 1, 1863
Hickory Heights

It had been the worst possible news.

"Her heart is failing," the doctor said quietly. "In fact, I am stunned that she is still alive. She can't last much longer. I am terribly sorry. I can tell she is a great lady. She was quite worried that I might be disappointed in myself that I could not mend her."

Annie had tried to smile in thanks. But she couldn't. She did manage to say: "That is very like Mother. She always worries about everyone else first. Her heart may be failing, but it is probably the largest heart in Virginia."

That had been three weeks ago. Thomas had visited many times since then, bringing fresh foods, medicine for Miriam's headaches, lemons to prevent rickets and strengthen her body. He seemed to refuse to believe the doctor's diagnosis. Several times, Miriam had asked to be taken downstairs to the porch to sit in the sunshine. There, she could see the hills and breathe in the breezes. Mercifully, the July weather was unusually mild. Twice she had been outside when he arrived, so Thomas could politely sit and talk with her.

Miriam had remembered him instantly, even though she drifted in and out of wakefulness. She wanted to hear of his mother—what she was like, what he liked best about her. She wanted to hear the story of his mother's joy at his homecoming.

Thomas told her. He described his home, his school, his town, and his friends. Annie heard as he told, and came to know who he was and how he could be so kind. She began to trust that he was as he seemed. The war stayed away for those weeks, and she could forget that he was the enemy. His concern opened her soul.

One morning before dawn, Aunt May called softly to her. "Miss Annie, honey, your mother is asking for you and Jamie."

No. Not today. Annie shot up from bed and woke her brother.

He was with Miriam for a long time. When he left, he was crying. Annie reached out to touch him, but he shrugged her off.

"Annie, darling?" a weak voice called.

Annie settled herself in the chair next to Miriam's bed. She took her hand, so cool, so pale, so thin now, that hand that had held up Annie so often when she was little. Her own hand was hot and sweaty, showing her panic.

Miriam squeezed it. "Don't be afraid for me, darling. I saw the angels this morning, calling me. I saw your brothers. I know it's time now."

Annie's head dropped to their hands. "Don't leave me, Mother, please don't."

"Oh, darling," Miriam murmured. "I can't fight any longer. I am sorry." She stopped talking to breathe, each intake of air a short gasp and struggle.

Annie lifted her head and waited.

"Annie, I need you to take care of Jamie. He asked me such questions this morning." Miriam's eyes filled with tears. "I didn't know that I had failed him so. How could he not know I love him?"

Annie fought off her own questions about past favoritisms and hurts. Miriam was dying in front of her. She couldn't burden her mother with her own insecurities now. It was time for her to help her mother as Miriam had helped Annie throughout her life. "Jamie knows, Mother. He's just a hothead sometimes. And whatever you give him, he seems to need more. He'll . . . he'll grow out of it, Mother."

Miriam nodded. "I love you, Annie, dearly. You know that, don't you? You're my only daughter. You're precious." Her eyes drifted closed.

Annie held fast to that hand. *Don't say good-bye yet, Mother. Not yet. I'm not ready.*

Miriam's eyes shot open. Annie could tell Miriam was using all her strength now. "Annie, darling. I know that Laurence was hurt. But I didn't see him with his brothers this morning in my dream. I know he lives, somewhere. I know it. Take faith in that, Annie. He'll come home. Tell Laurence . . . tell him to find a happy life after this war. Tell him for me?"

Annie nodded. "Yes, Mother," she said, a sob slipping out with it.

"There, there, my darling," Miriam whispered. "You, too, Annie. I'm so glad that we never completely tamed you. You'll need that now. Take all that courage and fire, and that beautiful rebellious heart of yours, and be happy. For me?"

Annie nodded again.

"Remember . . . " Miriam trailed off, forced herself awake, to breathe, and then finished:

"Remember that it doesn't matter where someone comes from, but where that person is going. Your father knew that about me."

Her eyes drifted shut. "Annie?"

"Yes, Mother?"

"Help me say the Lord's Prayer." Her voice was distant, tiny.

Annie stammered, "Our Father, who art in heaven, hallowed be thy name. . . ."

Before she finished, Miriam was gone.

A mockingbird sang throughout Miriam's burial. Annie tried to focus on the minister and his prayers, but the bird distracted her. It was a hot, wilting August day. No other birds sang. No bees flew or buzzed. They were all hiding in the trees and bushes from the sweltering sun. And yet this mockingbird sat in the cherry tree beside the family cemetery and warbled song after song, as if it were April and he were showing off to find a mate, joyous in the new life spring was bringing.

Inwardly, a bittersweet belief grew in Annie. If any soul could do it, Miriam could send a bird to tell Annie that she was all right, even happy where she was. Annie made herself believe that it was a final embrace, a final reassurance from her mother. If she could believe that bird and his concert was indeed a sign from Miriam, Annie could somehow make it through the rest of that mournful day. She believed and survived.

The comfort the mockingbird had somehow provided her helped Annie withstand the next week, too, when a letter arrived. It was from Laurence, but written by Sam. It was addressed to Miriam, for, of course, Laurence did not know that she was gone.

Annie held it in her hands a long time before she could open it. She looked at the handwriting, simple, clean, childlike. Miriam had taught Sam to read and write. She wondered briefly how Sam would react to the news of Miriam's death. He was always so quiet and brief in his speech. And yet, she knew his loyalty ran deep. The letter would bring that fact home hard.

What was inside it? It couldn't be good if Sam had had to write it for Laurence. Why couldn't he write himself? The cellar inside her head where she had trapped all her fears about her brother's safety flew open, and terror seized her. Hands shaking, she undid the stiff envelope.

Dearest Mother, I trust you are resting and recuperating. I have thought often in recent weeks of your well-being and of your care for all of us when we were sick. I hope you know how grateful I have always been for it. I know, too, my sweet mother, how devastated you were when scarlet fever took Father and my brothers. I have been watching many surgeons and nurses work. They lose many patients, perhaps because they can't wrap them in the gentle love in which you always blanketed us. You must forgive yourself, Mother, for not being able to save them. If you could not, no one could. God wanted them back and that was all. I have tried to say this to you before, but you must believe it. I know this for a fact now. My eyes have shown me.

Annie had to stop reading and wipe her tears. Laurence had realized, then, when he left for Gettysburg, that Miriam was dying. He was saying his good-byes to her. Oh, if only Mother had been able to see this letter before dying. Annie took a deep breath and kept reading.

I know because I am in a hospital now. Sam is penning this for me. I don't want you to worry. I am fine. I am just a little unsteady as of yet. Sam keeps a close watch on me and insists I am given the best of everything. He is quite the guardian.

I don't want to relate much about the Battle of Gettysburg, Mother. It was a terrible thing. So much death. I was hurt in the final battle of the final day. Bad luck. Afterward, General Lee had to withdraw or surrender. He could not give up and render the sacrifice of all those boys worthless. So he left those of us who were hurt and could not walk or ride. I know he made that decision with regret. But he had no choice.

I was captured by a very agreeable set of bluecoats and taken to a Union field hospital. They have treated me very well. Right now I am at a place called Camp Letterman. I am told that I will soon be transferred to a permanent hospital, perhaps in Washington, which would be a wonderful thing, not too far from home. From there I am not sure what will happen. I hope to be paroled. In any case, my dearest Mother, please do not worry. I am safe. I am no longer in danger's way. I am grateful to be alive. Your devoted son.

Annie worried about the terseness of the wording. It was unlike Laurence. But perhaps he was tailoring it to suit Sam's writing and spelling abilities. She turned the final page, and as she did a small folded paper dropped out.

It was from Sam to her.

Miss Annie:

I best let you know how it is with Mister Laurence. He don't want Missus Miriam to know, but you needs to before he get home. They will parole him because he is bad hurt. He lost his arm, Miss Annie. It was all broken up during that saber charge. The doctors said they couldn't fix it, it was busted so bad. They said something called gang-grene would poison him if they didn't take it off. They tried to run me off, Miss Annie, but I would not leave him. I stayed with him in the rain, him in so much pain, I thought sure he die. Mister Laurence is a brave man, Miss Annie. Men were screaming and throwing fits all around him. He did not say a word. But I could tell from his eyes it hurt something fierce. He didn't say a word, neither, when they put him on the table to saw into him.

The Federals are fixing to send Mister

Laurence on a train to Washington now. They say I can't go with him. They say their military trains ain't for darkies. They say I am free so go on now and make my own way. I told them I was already free and I wanted to stay with Mister Laurence to make sure he all right. They still say I can't. Then they jabbed their bayonets at me and yelled, "Git."

So I fix to come home, Miss Annie. Please tell Rachel. I have to walk through Pennsylvania and Maryland, so it may take time. That's how it is.

Miss Annie, I know you set a store on that horse of yours. She was hurt, cut up pretty good. But she stayed right beside Mister Laurence after he fell. That's how I find him in all those bodies. I saw her. When they carried Mister Laurence to the hospital, the Feds took her. I will try to find out what happened to her before I set off walking.

Sincerely, Sam.

Annie dropped the letter. She could hardly breathe. It felt as if her ribs might crack open from the heaviness of her heart.

CHAPTER TWENTY-EIGHT

September 30, 1863
Hickory Heights

"I thought the children would like her."

Annie held up a china baby doll. Its eyes closed when she laid it flat, opened when she held it upright. It wore a little yellow bonnet and dress. "It's darling, Major," said Annie. "You are too kind."

"Thomas," he corrected her.

"Thomas," Annie repeated shyly. She called to Colleen and Sally.

Colleen squealed at the sight of it. She'd never had a doll made of anything other than cornhusks or rags.

Sally looked at it solemnly and asked, "Is she real?"

"No, child," Thomas answered with a laugh. "But you can pretend."

Sally cocked her head. "Is she a Rebel baby or a Yankee baby?"

"Sally!" Annie gasped.

"It's all right. I don't mind. Which do you think, Sally?"

"Well . . . " The little girl thought, looking at the doll hard. "She's pretty, so she must be a Rebel. No Yankee is pretty, 'cepting you." She grabbed the doll, clutched it to her chest, and ran away.

Colleen darted after, screeching, "Mine, mine." Neither had said thank you.

"Oh, I'm sorry," said Annie. "I wish Mother were here to teach them some manners. I'm failing miserably at it."

"Oh, I can't imagine that," Thomas said pleasantly. Then he held out a gift for Annie: a handful of chocolate candies wrapped in tissue. Annie almost drooled. She hadn't seen chocolates for two years.

She reached out, but then dropped her hands. "I can't accept that, Major. The doll was gift enough. I know that it was costly." A sutler had passed through the lines recently, and Annie knew full well that doll had cost as much as twenty dollars—nearly a month's wages for Thomas.

Disappointed, Thomas pulled back his outstretched hand. But then he had an idea; Annie could see it. He grinned impishly. "You won't mind if we sit on the porch a moment?"

Annie eyed him with amused suspicion. He was up to something. But it was a pleasantly cool autumn afternoon, and she was happy to sit down for a while. She had been out with Rachel and Lenah, picking apples to dry for winter. She was unused to such back-straining, tedious work. Her arms and shoulders ached. She nodded and sat.

Thomas seated himself across from her and opened the tissue. "Do you mind if I have a chocolate, since I cannot convince you to have one?"

It wasn't exactly a polite request, but Annie could already see what he was up to. "Mmmm-mmm," he mumbled as he chewed. "This is mighty fine." He held the chocolates toward her again.

Annie laughed. "I do believe you are the devil incarnate," she teased, "tempting a poor girl with such things." She hesitated, then reached for a small dark rectangle. She nibbled the end demurely. Lord, did that sweetness melt in her mouth. She couldn't help it. That was lovely. She took another small, delicious bite, savoring the treat.

In truth, she had recently enjoyed what now seemed tremendous delicacies. A few days before, some of Mosby's men had raided the outskirts of

Warrenton and found sutler wagons stuffed with sardines, pickled onions, oysters, figs, and cakes. Jamie and Charles Murdock had brought home raisins and cheese, and she and the children had feasted on them. These days they lived on what they had in their own fields and woods—rabbits, fish, wild onions, dandelion greens, root vegetables that hadn't been trampled by cavalry. It was lean, plain food. The occasional taste of the fancier life she used to know was wonderful.

The bad part of the raid, though, was that Murdock had also brought home claret and champagne. He'd drunk himself silly and staggered about the house, bragging, swaggering, swearing. Annie had had to herd the children upstairs and Rachel and Lenah out of the house to their cottage. She didn't like the way he talked to them. Jamie had done nothing to help. In fact, Annie worried that once she'd gone upstairs, the boy had sampled some of the claret himself.

But she shoved those thoughts away. This was the first time Thomas had visited since right after Miriam's death almost a month earlier. Annie had to admit that she was sorely glad to see him. He had not come to the funeral, perhaps knowing that many of those attending would not have welcomed his presence in the least. Instead, he had ridden up the next day to tell Annie how sorry he was. He had been unable to stay and had handed her a letter, in which he reminded her that Miriam was now out of pain, away from *"The weariness, the fever, and the fret / Here, where men sit and hear each other groan,"* once more quoting Keats.

Perhaps they could read a bit of poetry this afternoon. They hadn't since that night the doctor came to see Miriam and Thomas had started to say something, well, something wonderful. Annie took a final bite of the chocolate. Jamie and Murdock were off somewhere. They'd see Thomas' horse and not ride up until he was gone. It was safe to linger a moment. Thomas was her first real gentleman caller. And she was almost eighteen years old now—practically an old maid.

She smiled over at Thomas. He smiled back.

"Can you stay a bit?" she asked.

"I'd like to," he said, "but I'm afraid I'll need to return to my detail soon. I—"

Annie's expression stopped him. Over his head she had suddenly noticed something alarming: a plume of smoke in the distance. Then she realized she saw another one, farther off to the east.

Thomas turned and looked where she did. He

sighed. "That is where I must head," he said, and stood. He took her hand and lifted Annie to her feet. "You must forgive us, Annie. We only follow our orders."

Annie looked up at him in horror. "What orders?"

Thomas kept his eyes on hers, even though his face flushed. "Do you remember a month ago, Mosby attacked a thirty-man detail of ours that was escorting a hundred horses?"

Annie played dumb, although she knew well of it. Murdock and Jamie each rode one of those Federal army horses now, keeping their old ones as reserves. Mosby had also been shot through the thigh and groin on that raid. He'd been recuperating until recently.

"Well," Thomas continued, growing uncomfortable, "that raid really ruffled headquarters, because healthy horses are scarce right now. There's been a terrible outbreak of hoof-and-mouth among our mounts. Even so, we've skirmished back and forth with Mosby's company on what horses we have."

Annie knew that, too. Just a few days ago, in fact, the 2nd Massachusetts and Mosby had clashed at Rector's Crossroads, just about a mile south. Annie had half hoped to see Thomas then when

Jamie and Murdock and several other rangers had scampered through their fields into hiding.

"Headquarters is pressing its orders to burn down houses that harbor Mosby's men. Colonel Lowell refuses to obey the directive for men who simply belong to Mosby's command. But he has agreed to destroy known rendezvous points. If he doesn't, Annie, they'll replace him with someone who has no compunction about destroying homes and chasing off women and children."

Annie recoiled from him. "Whose homes?"

"I don't know to whom they belonged. Two mills and a farmhouse."

Annie felt sick. She'd been a fool to think that she could be friends with this man who rode with an army determined to starve and burn her people into submission. She took several steps back, shaking her head. "You have to go," she said hoarsely.

"Annie, please." He moved forward.

"No," she choked. "You have to go."

Thomas stopped, gazing at her sadly. "I'll be back."

"No," she said, shaking her head again. "Please, don't."

"But I will, Annie," he answered quietly as he backed down the stairs. "I have to. Now that I have found you again, I must. I retreat today. But I do not surrender."

The first weeks of October brought quiet to Hickory Heights. Thomas Walker had not come back; his regiment was staying close to its Vienna camp. Annie busied herself and everyone else at Hickory Heights with harvesting all they could from the hills around them. They picked up black walnuts, hickory nuts, and chestnuts from the ground beneath the trees. They picked pawpaws for jelly, and persimmons. They ensured they had found every last apple. Wood was cut and hauled and stacked to heat the old, drafty house.

The world was beginning to paint itself. Orange, gold, and red flashed up in little flares of color amid the fading greens. Armies of migrating birds gathered, flicking up into the air in a dance of wings at the slightest movement along the ground. The air was crisp and invigorating. The world moved her, and the ache of sadness in Annie began to lift a little each day. The wariness war had taught her, though, never left. Her eyes constantly scanned the horizon for sudden armies, checked the lane for potentially dangerous riders. So much trouble had dashed up that tiny dirt road, one that before the war had always promised the arrival of invited guests or happy news.

When she first spotted the pair of slow riders, one morning in mid-October, her heart jumped happily with the hope it was Thomas. Then she slapped it down with reprimands. There was to be none of that. He was a good, kind man, certainly, but not one she should allow to romance her. That would be even worse than having feelings for the married General Stuart. People would have understood and forgiven her being infatuated with Stuart—half of all Southern women were. But falling in love with a Yankee? No one would understand that.

She watched the riders for a moment, steeling herself to be polite but firm. She'd have to turn Thomas away. Why are they moving so slowly, she wondered? One of them looked to be leading the other's horse, and the led one slumped in the saddle. Oh, Lord, is Thomas hurt? She rushed to the top of the lane.

There she could see the riders' distant faces. She gasped. "Aunt May! Isaac! Come quickly! It's Laurence!"

He was bone thin and pasty faced, as gray as his faded, frayed uniform. Annie fought off tears as she and Aunt May fussed over getting him into the house and settled by the fire. He mustn't see that his condition worries me, Annie told herself, mustn't see that I'm frightened. She could have kicked herself for flinching when she tried to help him into the chair, grabbing to steady him by an arm that was no longer there.

Laurence had seen it and smiled at her wanly. "It's all right, Annie. I do that myself all the time."

Then he'd asked that terrible question: "Where's Mother?"

Annie broke the news as gently as she could. But no matter the delivery, of course, the news was the same.

He didn't cry, though, until Annie shared Miriam's last words, that she'd known he was alive because Laurence was not with their dead brothers in a dream she'd had. That's when Laurence began to cry, and then sob, breaking into wrenching coughs and shudders. Annie only made it worse by trying to quiet him with Miriam's last request for him to find a happy life.

"A happy life?" he choked out. "Look at me, Annie. Look at all of us. Hickory Heights is on its knees; so is the Confederacy. I'm not capable of pulling us back up. Mother was the one who knew how to do that."

"Oh, Laurence, you're wrong," Annie tried. "It's you who've always kept us strong."

"No, Annie. It was Mother—Mother telling me I could do it." Laurence looked so lost. "I will be nothing but a burden to you now. I need . . . we needed Mother." Then he turned away. "Please, leave me, Annie. Leave me alone."

Annie tiptoed out and went to find Aunt May. She collapsed into the wide, strong arms of the old woman.

"Miss Annie, you've had time to get used to Missus Miriam being gone," Aunt May consoled Annie. "Poor Mister Laurence. All anybody as hurt as him would want right now is his mama. Give him a few days. He'll find himself. He always has."

The man who had brought Laurence home continued on his way. He, too, had been captured at Gettysburg and paroled. He, too, was gaunt and sickly, but his body was whole, the wound to his leg mostly healed. The long, circuitous trip had been less hard on him. Both he and Laurence had been taken from the Washington hospital to a Federal prison at Point Lookout on the edge of Chesapeake Bay. From there they'd been taken by barge to Aquia Creek in Virginia for prisoner exchange. When

Confederate authorities had seen their condition, they'd discharged them from the army and told them to go home. It was up to Laurence and the man to make their way there.

"It's only a few more miles to my home, Miss Annie. Don't you recognize me?" the man said.

Annie nearly fell over when he told her who he was. She had known him somewhat, an excellent foxhunter. He couldn't be older than twenty-five, but he looked twice that age.

"Give your parents my hellos," she called after him, as he rode away. "Thank you for bringing Laurence."

All day, Annie did her best to make Laurence comfortable. But she could tell he was in pain. The surgeons had just recently removed the final strings from his severed arteries, and there were tiny pin-pricks of blood stains on the shoulder of his jacket. She tried to ease it off him but bumped him about as she did, clumsy from nervousness. Finally, right before dinner, he dropped off to sleep in his chair.

That's when Jamie crashed into the house with Murdock. They were laughing and hooting. Annie rushed to silence them.

"Laurence?" Jamie asked excitedly, then stopped himself and adopted an unimpressed bluster. "Big brother's home now, Murdock. Better go upstairs and stay out of trouble."

Murdock smirked and started up the stairs. He was carrying a bottle of whiskey.

Annie was appalled by Jamie's attitude. Even at his most impudent, Jamie would never have spoken so callously before. Murdock was a bad influence. Annie made a quick decision. "Best go upstairs and pack your things, Mr. Murdock. We can no longer house you. With my brother so ill, you'll have to leave. I'm sorry. If the Federals come again, I can explain Jamie. But I cannot explain you. I cannot risk their arresting Laurence, given his current condition. I am sure you understand."

"Don't listen to her, Charlie," Jamie fairly shouted. "I'm not about to take orders from her now, too. You stay. I say so."

"Jamie!" Annie moved closer to speak so only he could hear. She didn't like Murdock. He frightened her somehow. The last thing Laurence needed right now was to be disturbed by some renegade ranger. Murdock's presence certainly wouldn't benefit the already volatile trouble between Jamie and Laurence. But when she drew near to Jamie, she smelled the distinct sticky-sweet scent of whiskey. She gasped, "Have you been drinking?"

Jamie grinned at her, like a schoolboy caught in stealing a pie.

"Have you?" came a clear, commanding voice.

Annie and Jamie turned. Laurence stood in the doorway, steady, tall. Annie knew just how much it cost him in pain to look so normal and strong.

Jamie turned his usual shade of red. He said nothing, nothing about Laurence's condition, nothing to welcome him home.

Laurence studied his younger brother. Then he turned to Murdock. "I must ask you to leave—Mr. Murdock, is it? My sister requests it."

It was Murdock's turn to color red. "It's nightfall. I've nowhere to go."

Laurence's answer dripped with contempt. "I am sure a seasoned soldier such as you is accustomed to bivouacking for the night. Please help yourself to a blanket if you have none and leave. And be sure to take that whiskey bottle with you. We do not drink in this house."

Murdock scowled and stomped his way upstairs.

Laurence turned to Jamie. Annie held her breath. Oh, please, Laurence, please, Jamie, she thought, I can't bear a fight between you now. She thought of their horrible fist-fight the last time they'd been together, right before Laurence had left to ride into Pennsylvania, into disaster.

"James," Laurence began with thunder, then stopped. He reached up to wipe his forehead, and Annie started for him. Laurence held up his one hand. "No need, Annie. I'm all right; the rest did me good. You'll see that I remember what we talked about before I left for Gettysburg. There is enough warfare outside our home. We needn't have it here between brothers," he added quietly and sadly, "especially when one is now only half a man."

He began again, carefully, with a weary voice, the spark all gone. "James, I know if you had thought through that, you would have thought better of your answer. A good Southern soldier . . . like yourself . . . always supports a lady's decision." Laurence fell back to lean against the wall, slumping. "Come. Give me your arm to lean on."

Jamie at first looked suspicious, as if there had to be a rebuke or disapproval hidden somewhere in Laurence's words.

Laurence held up his hand. "I need your help now, Jamie."

Jamie looked about ten feet tall as he helped his brother to his chair.

CHAPTER TWENTY-NINE

November 1, 1863
Hickory Heights

"Miss Annie! Miss Annie! Come quick! Lord have mercy! Miss Annie!"

Annie nearly fell out of bed, scrambling to answer. It was just past midnight. With shaking hands, she lit her candle and stumbled to the top of the stairs.

Below in the front hall were Aunt May and Isaac, in their nightclothes. Aunt May had sunk to the floor and was rocking back and forth, crying.

"Good God, what is it?" cried Annie, frozen to where she stood. She knew it had to be awful since Aunt May was so upset.

"That Murdock man. He came to our cottage. He and another man," Isaac began.

"He done took my baby," wailed Aunt May.

"They took Rachel and Lenah and said they was going to sell them to a trader 'cross the river. My baby!"

"What?" Annie gasped. Behind her came the running feet of the entire household, followed by the slow, unsteady tread of Laurence. Annie skittered down the stairs to free herself of the frightened clutch around her knees of her little cousins. Jamie followed.

"Aunt May." She crouched and held the shaking body. "How long ago?"

"Just now. They tied the girls onto a mule. Murdock held a pistol to my baby's head so I wouldn't do nothing. If he'd held it to mine, it wouldn't have stopped me. He could've put a bullet in my head and I'd still have kicked that varmint to death."

"Jamie!" Annie turned to scream for her brother, but he was already beside her.

"Who was with him? Do you know?" Jamie asked.

"No."

"Describe him to me."

She did.

"I know who it is." Jamie turned to Annie. His calm stunned her. "I think I know where they'll go, too. Murdock muttered something about this. His friend was furious with Mosby because the major didn't give him a share of some money we found last raid. Major Mosby said the Confederate army needed it instead. So he and Murdock started concocting a plan to steal some slaves and sell them."

"Jamie, why didn't you say something to me!"

"He was drinking. I didn't believe him."

"Miss Annie," Isaac asked in a quavering voice, "what about that e-man-sup-ta-tion proclaim Mister Laurence told us about? Ain't we free now?" Tears were streaming down the old man's face.

"Not in Maryland, Isaac," Annie answered as gently as she could. "The Emancipation Proclamation only applies in states that seceded from the Union, those states in rebellion. Maryland stayed with the Union, and so slavery is still condoned there. If he makes it across the Potomac River, he might be able to sell Rachel and Lenah back into slavery."

"We'll get them back," Jamie spoke. No swagger, no yipping in his voice—just calm confidence.

"And how will you do that?" It was Laurence.

Jamie looked at him, looked at Annie, thought for an instant. "I've got to ride out now."

"You can't do that. You're only a . . . " Laurence stopped himself, swallowed, recalibrated. "You can't do it alone, Jamie."

"That's right, you can't," said Annie. "I'll go too."

"No," said Laurence. "I forbid it. I'll go."

The three siblings looked at one another, there in the light of a few candles, held in shaking hands. Annie had the sense to wait, wait for Laurence to remember. But Jamie blurted, "Look at you, Laurence. You can't ride."

"I can!" Laurence shouted, a desperate rage in his voice. "I can ride!"

"Maybe you can ride, but you can't hold a gun, too," Jamie countered.

The agony of being helpless, no longer able to defend those he cared about, overwhelmed Laurence. He pounded the wall with his good hand. "I can!" His head fell against the wall and he cried out, "What will I tell Sam? Sam saved me. What will I tell him if his wife is lost and I did nothing?"

Annie ached for Laurence. But his anguish was wasting precious minutes. A strange calm settled on her as well. She took Laurence's face and held it in her hands so that he looked at her. "Brother, there is no time. With every moment Murdock gets farther away. You tell Sam this. You had the sense to send Jamie and me to find her." Laurence stared at her. She went on. "They're drunk. We'll surprise them and get Rachel and Lenah back. It'll be easy. There's no other choice, Laurence. You know it. Jamie can't do this alone."

Slowly, Laurence's eyes cleared. A look he must have worn in battle came over him. He nodded.

Annie kissed his cheek. "It will be all right."

"We'd better hurry," said Jamie. He turned to Isaac. "I've got only one Colt loaded. You need to help me. Annie's going to need two revolvers as well."

"I need some breeches, Jamie," said Annie. "For this I need to play a man's part."

"Lord preserve us," muttered Aunt May. "Missus Miriam, forgive me."

"Where are we going?" Annie called through the moonlit darkness. Jamie was in front. Although Annie was the better rider, Jamie had been traversing these paths in the night for the past year. He knew his way better than she. At a canter, through the woods, that knowledge was crucial to their safety.

"To Seneca Fords," he called back.

"But that's near Dranesville. There'll be Federal pickets everywhere. Why would they ride that way?"

"Easier crossing," said Jamie. "And Murdock

knows that Mosby will be furious about this scheme and likely send out riders to stop him. Major Mosby goes by the law, you know, no matter what people say about his tactics."

Annie fell silent. She knew they'd better not talk much if they wanted to catch Murdock by surprise. Jamie hadn't even allowed them to take canteens of water that might clink against the saddle and give them away. She was already panting from thirst.

Annie shifted the two Union-made revolvers that were shoved into her belt. Lord, they were heavy, horrible things. She'd watched Isaac load them as Jamie prepared more for himself. The revolver was loaded through its six-shot cylinder. To fill a cylinder, Isaac inserted a skin-gut cartridge containing powder and a conical bullet, which he rammed in with the loading lever from under the barrel. He repeated the process six times. Finally, he put a copper percussion cap, which would ignite when struck by the pistol's hammer, into the notch of each chamber. It seemed to take forever. No wonder Jamie always went off on his raids with at least two guns already loaded and ready. And at that, he'd have only twelve shots. That's all she'd have tonight if, God forbid, she needed to defend herself. She'd never even fired a gun before.

"The Colt tends to shoot high," Laurence had told her before she left. "Aim for the stomach to hit the heart."

She shuddered at the thought. *Please, God, help me tonight.*

They rode on. They'd been out almost an hour now, riding at a good clip. She shifted in her saddle and smiled for a moment about the pants she wore. They certainly made riding easier. They'd made running to the stable a lot easier, as well. She couldn't help wishing that she could wear them all the time. Her hair was yanked back and shoved into a hat, too, no fuss with braids and combs. With their clothes, at least, boys sure had it easy.

Ahead of her, Jamie waved his hand and slowed his horse. She brought hers down to a trot and then a walk. She tried to shorten its stride to make it quieter. For a moment, she choked on the thought of Angel and how silently she'd glide through the night.

She pulled next to Jamie and stopped. He pointed to his ear and then ahead. She listened. In the distance, she heard cussing.

"Someone's fallen off his horse," Jamie breathed. "Probably Charlie. Can't ride worth a lick when he drinks." He eased a pistol out of his belt. "We've got to charge in. If they have time to pull their guns, we're lost. Stay right behind me. Let me talk. Ready?"

Annie nodded, her heart pounding.

"Take out your gun, then, Annie." Jamie grinned and booted his horse into a gallop.

It all happened in a blur. Rushing through the trees, holding up the heavy gun, Annie was way off balance as they crashed out of the woods into a clearing.

"Stop right there!" shouted Jamie.

Annie fumbled to aim her pistol at the man accompanying Murdock. He pointed his at her at the very moment she lined up on him. When she heard him cock the hammer of his gun, she did the same. They were in a standoff, gun pointed at gun. *Aim for his stomach, aim for his stomach*, she repeated to herself, trembling.

Murdock had indeed been thrown and was on the ground. Jamie had his revolver inches from his head and was circling him with his horse, preventing Murdock from reaching his own. "Tell your friend to drop the gun or I'll fill you full of lead, Murdock."

Murdock said nothing.

"I mean it, Murdock. Andy there can shoot a squirrel off a tree a hundred yards away. Your friend may get off one shot, but he won't live to talk about it."

Andy, who in the world is Andy? thought Annie. Then she realized. It was she! Annie tried to look mean and was grateful that the half moon could shed only so much light on her face.

"All right," snarled Murdock. He told his friend to back off. The pistol facing Annie was lowered. She kept hers aimed.

"Now cut Rachel and Lenah loose," Jamie ordered.

Murdock did it.

"I'm going to have to take you boys back to Mosby, you know. This kind of rascality doesn't sit with the major. Give me your gun, Charlie."

Murdock did.

"And the other two in your coat."

Cursing, Murdock complied again.

Annie marveled at it all. Jamie thought of everything. He instructed Murdock onto the mule. He had Rachel tie his hands and tether the mule to Jamie's horse. Lenah dealt with Murdock's friend. Jamie obviously was practiced in securing prisoners. Rachel and Lenah were not, however, tying the hands of Murdock and his friend loosely, in front of them, instead of behind their backs. Still, nothing went wrong until Lenah and Rachel were on Murdock's horse, Murdock and his partner on the mule, and they were ready to go.

That's when Rachel got a good look at Annie. "Annie?" she gasped.

"Annie?" snarled Murdock. He shouted at his companion, "She's nothing but a girl!" He kicked the mule, making it rear and ram into Jamie's horse. While Murdock grabbed at Jamie, his friend slid off the mule and ran toward Annie. She saw him reach to his belt and pull something out that gleamed momentarily before the rope fell away from his hands. A knife!

Aim for the stomach, aim for the stomach! Annie cocked the hammer and squeezed the trigger. It seemed to take forever to fire.

BLAM! The kick from the revolver felt like a lightning bolt going up her arm. Annie reeled from it, the horse bucked and lunged, but somehow she stuck to the saddle.

The bullet seemed to ricochet off the ground and clip the man's leg. Cussing, he stumbled, dropped his knife, and grabbed his ankle, falling to the ground.

"Jamie!"

Murdock had scrambled onto Jamie's horse and

was trying to choke Jamie from behind with his rope-bound hands.

"Get off him," Annie shouted. Somehow, her anger and terror turned into a cold-blooded force. She kicked her horse over to him and got the revolver right up beside the nape of his neck before Murdock could pull his hands up over Jamie's head to attack her.

"Don't move. Not an inch. I may be just a girl, but this is my brother and you're not going to harm him."

Murdock stiffened and sat still.

This time it was Annie's turn. "Rachel, come here."

"Annie, I'm so sorry," Rachel stammered when she reached the horse's neck. "I shouldn't have said—"

"It's all right," Annie interrupted her. "Pull that other gun out of my belt. Aim it at him. At his stomach," she added.

Soon, positions were corrected. Murdock again sat on the mule. His partner sat behind him. This time Jamie did the tying.

But the night still didn't end correctly. They weren't the only ones who had heard the shot that Annie had fired.

CHAPTER THIRTY

November 2, 1863
Hickory Heights

"How bad is it, Laurence?" Annie hovered behind her brother as he tried to pull the blanket up over Jamie.

"Confound it," Laurence mumbled. "I never realized how dependent I was on my right hand."

"Oh, Laurence, forgive me." Annie felt like a fool for standing there watching an amputated man struggle with the covers. She arranged the bed, all the while watching Jamie breathe, in-out, in-out, peaceful. Like this, he looked just as he had when he was five years old and Annie tucked him in for the night. A person would never know to look at him that there was a huge gash in his side.

"It's not bad, Annie. He'll be all right. The bullet basically glanced off him, just left a slice as it flew by. We got it sewn up just fine. You did all the right things. Mother taught you well, you see?"

Annie could feel her eyes grow as big as walnuts as he spoke. Tears built up and fell, tears of relief. It was then, and only then, that instinct and its surge of strength gave way and she fell into a chair. Suddenly, she felt as if her feet weighed three hundred pounds apiece.

Laurence collapsed into a chair beside her. "Laurence," she whispered. "I'm so sorry he got hurt. I didn't mean for it to happen. It just got so confused . . ."

"Honey"—Laurence took her hand—"don't apologize. I've been in enough skirmishes to know how hellish, how confusing it all is. I'm ashamed you had to do my work for me. I should have been there, not you, such a slip of a girl, even with all your courage." He paused and then said bitterly, "I'm nothing now, nothing but a worthless scrap of a man. . . ." His voice trailed off. He sighed heavily. "I've been thinking, Annie, that I should release Charlotte from our engagement. She shouldn't be saddled with me now. Tonight really showed me that."

"Laurence, hush. You let Charlotte decide for herself whether she wants this magnificent hero, a man who gave everything for his country, as her husband. I think she'll say yes."

Laurence stared into the distance for a long time. Then he shook himself. "See, here I am worrying about myself. I'm sorry. Hospitals and prisons do things to your ability to think straight. Tell me again what happened."

Annie took a deep breath and began—what she could remember about it, anyway. It had been such a nightmare; while parts of it were crystal clear, others were murky and blurred. "We were going back into the woods. Everything seemed fine. You would have been so proud of Jamie. He was amazing, Laurence, truly—in command, knew exactly what to do. But we had had a little trouble in the clearing. I'd fired a shot. And I guess pickets heard us. Just as we slipped back into the trees and I was thinking all was well, I heard this voice telling me to halt and identify myself. Jamie pretended we were Federals and answered that we were on patrol for Colonel Lowell. For a moment they seemed to believe him, but then Murdock's friend called out: 'They're Mosby men and there are more coming up right behind us.'

"Well, they opened fire on us, Laurence. Shows how scared they are of Mosby, I suppose. They hit Jamie right away. The mule went down, too.

Murdock got up and ran, even as trussed up as we had him. But his partner was killed. He didn't move afterward, not a twist. Jamie somehow sat up and started firing back, so I did too, into the underbrush. It's so overgrown right there, a tangle of blackberry bushes and wild roses, Laurence; I couldn't see anything, until . . . until . . ." This was the part she recalled precisely, every inch, every sound, every horror of it. "Until this boy stood straight up out of the bushes and aimed his musket at me. He was maybe twenty feet away, Laurence. I saw the end of the gun, like a cavern it seemed, and I pulled the trigger on my pistol. It sounded *click*, *click*. I knew I was dead; but the boy seemed to be having trouble with his gun, too. So I squeezed one last time and it fired. That boy, Laurence, that boy just seemed to explode in front of me. I . . . I . . . oh God." Annie leaned over and retched. She felt she might cough up her heart, she was so sick.

"It's all right, honey, all right." Laurence held her as best he could. "I know how you feel. I do. The first time I shot a man, I felt like shooting myself, too. But you were defending yourself, Annie. Praise God, you're safe. I don't know how you managed to get everyone home, but you did, honey. My brave little sister—you're the hero today."

*

Even Mosby, when he visited Jamie two days later, complimented her valor. It was terse, but noteworthy, as Mosby was not one for compliments. All the same, it meant little to Annie. All she could see was that boy crumpling up before her. *We few, we happy few*? Annie no longer agreed with that concept of war's glory. She simply felt like a murderer.

"What is it General Stuart calls you?" Mosby asked. "Lady Liberty? I think the general is right." The major bowed formally and then sat across from her in the parlor to begin amassing evidence against Murdock. While some northern Virginia residents adored Mosby, and others grumbled about how they suffered retaliations and constant searches because of him, none doubted the benefit to the area in terms of policing. Because Mosby, ever the lawyer, was tenacious in his pursuit and prosecution of horse and cattle thieves, deserters who typically did the stealing and plagued the South did not stay long in Fauquier or Loudoun. Mosby also didn't want grain wasted in the production of whiskey, and he kept the area sober by having his men search out and destroy stills. He settled disputes over property. His word had become law, returning some semblance of order to the war-torn area.

"What did Murdock say he was up to?" Mosby asked.

Annie told him.

"And the women in question were previously freed by your brother?"

"Rachel was, Major. I'm not sure of Lenah's status." Annie explained how Lenah had come to live with them, hired from her owner by her father and sent west to them for safety.

"But Murdock does not own her?"

"No."

"Has no claim to her in any way?"

"No."

Mosby nodded. "Then he is akin to a horse thief and will be hanged when we catch him."

Annie cringed at Mosby's likening Lenah to a horse. Mosby had a reputation for being blunt, cantankerous, harsh in sentencing. Annie could see why.

As often as Mosby had passed through their home—dropping off captured horses for stabling, instructing Jamie to gather the men, devouring hasty meals—Annie had never really had a long talk with him. She hadn't noticed before how truly tiny he was, only a few inches taller than she.

After his questioning, he tried to be conversational. "You remind me of my wife when she was young," Mosby said. He stared at Annie a moment. She knew of Mosby's wife, a beautiful, extremely well-educated woman with a great deal of pluck. She'd come to visit Mosby that summer, and one night had held Union soldiers searching for him at bay purely by her witticisms as Mosby hid in a tree outside their bedroom window.

Mosby continued, "She's Catholic, too, you know, as I assume your Irish ancestors were. Her father was a U.S. congressman and a diplomat, but he lost his run for governor of Kentucky because his wife is Catholic. My friends worried what Pauline's religion might do to my law career. Religious prejudices are so unyielding, aren't they? But I told them she knew all about the Crusades, Henry VIII and the Tudors, Rob Roy, Robin Hood. Her mind captivated me. I had to marry her."

He stood abruptly. Annie did the same.

"I've sent men out to apprehend Murdock," he said. "But I fear he may have made it into Colonel Lowell's camp."

Annie went cold all over. "Colonel Lowell?"

"Yes, of the 2nd Massachusetts. One of the few worthy opponents I've had." Mosby nodded his head and said as he left: "Tell James to mend. I have need of him in a few days."

Annie sank back into her chair. In Colonel Lowell's camp? What would Murdock tell them? What would Lowell do with the information? Would he come with his cavalry to arrest her and Jamie? And what would Thomas think?

It wouldn't take long for Annie to find out.

Three weeks later, in a bone-chilling rain, on the night of November twenty-second, Lowell arrived in Middleburg with 250 cavalry. Following Murdock's information, the Union riders dispersed, heading for homes the Confederate traitor had identified as Mosby safe houses. Their searches were swift and successful, capturing twenty Mosby rangers, thirty-some horses, bridles, and two dozen Colt revolvers. They would have caught more had Mosby not taken seventy-five of his riders that very night on a raid on the Orange & Alexandria railroad. Jamie was with them.

Annie was not so lucky.

Thirty Massachusetts horsemen rode up the lane to Hickory Heights. Murdock was with them. Thomas Walker was in command.

Annie heard the horses; heard the shouts of "Surround the house!"; heard Laurence demand, "What is the meaning of this?"; heard Thomas' polite reply: "I am sorry to disturb you, Captain Sinclair, but I have orders. I must see your sister at once, please."

She dressed quickly, strangely calm. She couldn't think of any way to deny her actions—disguising herself as a boy, riding a raid, and shooting a picket. All she could think of was what Stuart had said in Warrenton to the woman the Confederates had caught posing as a Union soldier the night of their raid on Pope's camp.

"If you're man enough to enlist," Stuart had said, "you ought to be man enough to go to prison."

CHAPTER THIRTY-ONE

January 3, 1864
Carrol Prison,
Washington, D.C.

Annie snuffed out her short candle and watched the smoke drift up to the festoon of thick spiderwebs draping her prison window. Pale moonlight illuminated her. Behind her the prison room was filled with blackness, a fearful place.

"Come away from the window, Annie," Millie called from the darkness. Millie was another young prisoner, sharing the room. "You'll catch pneumonia. Come lie down next to me, won't you? It's so very cold tonight. We can share the blanket."

"In a minute," Annie answered through teeth that were beginning to chatter. She pulled her heavy winter cape closer around her. There was half a pane missing in the dirty window, and only one thick log in their fireplace to heat the room. It did nothing against the wind that poured through the opening as the sea would a break in a dam.

Annie twisted around and craned her head so that she could see the cold crescent moon that glowed in a yet starless night. It was too early to climb into the torture of that bed and her nightmares of the picket she'd shot. Annie blew on her hands to warm them and settled herself in to watch for the stars to come out, one at a time, building the outline of a constellation or two in the small square of sky she could see between the tall walls of the prison yard. She thought longingly of home, where the sky seemed to stretch for the entire universe. Home, where it was easy to see heaven move slowly across the earth's face, tickling it with its flooring of clouds.

"Please, Annie." Millie's voice was small and scared.

Annie sighed. She couldn't bear the thought of lying down yet on that dirty straw mattress with its bedbugs and smells. The other night a rat had run across her foot as she lay there. She shuddered, remembering.

She knew that's why Millie wanted her to come. Two against the army of vermin that infested their room made their presence somewhat less terrifying.

Of course, poor Millie was terrified by everything—the soldiers, the nightly prisoner checks, the fishlike eye of the guard who peeked through the hole in the door at them, the fitful coughing that echoed through the building all night long, announcing that consumption and typhoid stalked the halls.

Millie was new to it all, brought to Carrol Prison only a few days before. Her crime? Trying to carry vials of quinine out of Washington into Virginia. She'd stolen them from her uncle, who worked in the Federal hospital. She was heading for her Confederate sweetheart in Richmond. When Union soldiers stopped her at a checkpoint, forewarning travelers of an outbreak of smallpox ahead, her skirt gave a telltale clinking sound. She'd sewn the vials into her dress. They arrested her for smuggling.

"How long have you been here?" Millie had asked in a trembling voice when first the guards shoved her into Annie's room and bolted the door as they left.

"A month," Annie had answered quietly, wondering if the petite Millie was a Yankee spy sent in to eke some sort of confession out of Annie through friendship. They did that sort of thing, she knew. One of the other prisoners had told her so in a quick, dangerous whisper when passing her in the hall.

"Beware others who wish to chat," the woman had breathed.

A month. The worst month of Annie's life.

It wasn't as bad as the dungeons of Chateau d'If in *The Count of Monte Cristo*, she'd told herself. Carrol Prison was just an old boardinghouse, three stories of dingy brick, right behind the new Capitol building that President Lincoln was completing. Adjacent to it was the Old Capitol prison, another ancient tavern and boardinghouse that had briefly been used by Congress for its sessions after the British burned down the original Capitol building in 1814. That building housed Confederate soldiers, blockade runners, and prisoners of war. Carrol was used for women.

There's even wallpaper on the wall, Annie had tried to console herself the first night she'd been thrust into the dark, dank room. Of course, it was peeling off, and where it didn't hang in sheets, there were nasty large grease spots. Dust and cobwebs covered the few pieces of furniture—an iron bedstead, a table with a tin cup and a jug containing water, and a rickety chair.

She'd sunk down in the chair and been crawled over by a startled mouse. That was when Annie had started hoarding the small candles they gave the prisoners each day. The nights were so frightening, she wanted extras to light in case one night she simply couldn't stave off the nightmares through sheer willpower. By now she'd gathered and hidden in her bonnet a dozen stubs of candles and about five matches. Occasionally, she'd walk over and shake the bonnet to remind herself that they were in there. It wasn't as if she needed to wear that bonnet to go anywhere anytime soon. She was awaiting trial. And it was clear to Annie that it wasn't going to occur quickly. She had briefly been housed with a woman who'd been at Carrol for a year with no trial, accused of carrying Confederate messages across the border to Southern sympathizers in Canada.

Annie had been interviewed repeatedly by the prison superintendent and a man from the Bureau of Military Affairs. But his questions were less about Annie and her so-called crimes than about other potential "spies" in Fauquier. Who harbored Mosby rangers? Who supplied them? Who kept informing them of Union supply wagons and whereabouts?

"Major Mosby has his own scouts, sir," she'd answered, "very effective ones who slip in and out of your lines all the time."

"It wasn't scouts. It was spies, like you."

"I am not a spy," Annie said firmly.

The superintendent had rattled his papers and scowled at her. "It says here that you warned that pirate Mosby of a raid and caused the death of several Federal soldiers with that information."

Annie held her head high. Murdock would have told them that, because Jamie would have bragged of it to him.

He shuffled through more papers and squinted at one. "Also, that you were a confidante of General Stuart. We had another young woman here recently who had a commission as an honorary member of his staff. Found lots of letters on her. Perhaps you have some, too."

Annie forced herself to sit quietly, to reveal nothing beyond: "My brother rode with Stuart's cavalry. I did know the general, as any family member of his officers would."

As far as she knew, the Federals had no paper to prove her friendship with Stuart. The night she was arrested, Will, that clever, silent child, had slowly inched his way toward the table in the parlor, where sat that volume of Lord Byron. Annie had noticed him doing it out of the corner of her eye, as Laurence argued and pleaded with the Union cavalry not to arrest her. It was only then she remembered that she'd left Stuart's two poems stuffed inside. How Will knew, she could only guess, but she was grateful to the boy. The poems didn't say she did anything in terms of spying or war work, but Stuart's bold signature was on them, and she knew the kind of insinuations the Federals might make of that. She'd suffered many such off-color remarks already from the guards.

They hadn't been as wrenching, though, as the look Thomas had given her when Murdock pointed at her and said: "That's her, Major Walker. That's the one that shot the picket. That's the one warned Mosby of the raid in Middleburg so he could set a trap of his own for your boys. Mosby's been in and out of this house plenty. She's kept mules and weapons for him, too. Her and her freckle-faced, loud-mouthed brother. I spent a couple weeks here, so I know. There's a hidey hole right over there. Check it out for yourself."

Walker nodded at his men, who quickly located Jamie's hidden cellar.

"Check the rest of the house," Thomas ordered. "See if the brother is here." His voice was hollow. He turned to Annie, those dark beautiful eyes of his anguished. "What can you say to this, Miss Sinclair?"

What could she say? She pursed her lips and said nothing.

Thomas sighed deeply. "You'd best collect some warm clothes. It's cold out tonight. The rain is hard. You'll have to ride. I have no other transport."

"What about him?" a round, red-faced lieutenant asked, talking about Laurence. "We're supposed to arrest every male we find in these houses."

Thomas shook his head.

"You can't leave him, Major. He may be one of them."

"No," said Thomas.

"I ain't gonna get in trouble for not arresting this man," the lieutenant snapped. "It's already rumored you're soft on these cursed Rebels. I hear tell it might even be this very gal got you cowardly." He jerked his thumb toward Annie.

"That's enough," Thomas roared, stepping forward so he towered over the fat subordinate.

The lieutenant sputtered, "I'm gonna report it."

"Fine. Do so," snapped Thomas. "Report this, too. I refuse to torch this house or its barns. This man"—he gestured toward Laurence—"fought an honorable fight under the command of General Stuart. He lost his arm at Gettysburg, a bloodbath only the bravest dared enter. Such an adversary is to be respected. He's done his part. He's been paroled by our army and discharged by his because of his wound. He's not to be bothered. Do you understand me?"

The lieutenant blew out his cheeks like a toad, then stalked away.

Thomas turned to Laurence and asked quietly, "Do you have your parole papers?"

Laurence held himself up tall. "Yes, upstairs. Do you wish to see them?"

"No, not I, Captain," said Thomas. "But make sure you have them available if someone else comes. I am sorry for this . . . this arrest."

He turned to Annie and with a husky voice asked, "Why?"

Why? Annie wasn't sure. Why did Laurence fight a war even after he saw that surely there was no winning it? Because it was their home. He was defending it.

Why had she? At first she'd been smitten with and motivated by Stuart, she had to admit it. She'd wanted to be part of the glory of the brave, part of the songs, part of the ennobling speeches, part of the legend in establishing a new country. She was an idealistic, poetry-loving patriot. But then the fight became more of a stubborn hanging on, a defiance of the armies that plundered her state, her home. It had nothing to do with philosophies and politics she had, in fact, grown to question. Now it was simply about her family, and protecting those who were trying to defend her family. She owed Mosby and his rangers—Jamie—her loyalty and her effort. She'd acted on instinct and on her heart. There was no ideology left in it. Could Thomas ever understand that?

Her heart ached at the look on Thomas' face, so conflicted, so baffled, so disgusted, so hurt, so guilt ridden for what he must do. Her pain told her that she loved him. It was a surprising, wondrous, and horrible recognition.

She tried to speak, but nothing came out of her mouth. Stupidly, she smiled at Thomas, the love she now recognized inside her making her forget how desperate her situation was. Thomas stared at her in confusion.

In their gaze, Laurence saw the chance for mercy. "Do you know why she was out in the night?" he asked.

"Don't believe anything this cripple tells you," Murdock sneered.

Maimed as he was, Laurence had Murdock pinned against the staircase within seconds, crushing his throat with his good hand.

Three Yankee soldiers pulled their guns on him.

"Oh, Laurence, don't." Annie threw herself on him to shield him.

"Hold your fire!" shouted Thomas.

Everyone froze. For a moment all was silenced save the clock, the heavy breathing of the soldiers, and Murdock's choking.

"Tell them, Murdock, tell them about kidnaping two defenseless women and trying to sell them for slaves, you sack of garbage. Tell them how my little sister and baby brother rode out to stop you. Go on!"

"Captain Sinclair, let go of that man."

"Laurence, please," Annie cried, tugging on his arm. "Please don't do this. Don't get yourself killed over this snake of a turncoat, after all you've survived."

Laurence hesitated and then threw Murdock from him, releasing his throat with a shove. "You're the kind of trash who will finish this war up," Laurence hissed. "You're nothing but a buzzard feeding on a dying people."

"Annie." Thomas began, then corrected himself. "Miss Sinclair, please, explain this to me."

Annie thought of the first time they had met and he had condemned her and her family for having slaves on the very evening Miriam bandaged his wounds. Would her riding out to save Rachel and

Lenah make him understand once and for all that she and Laurence were different from the stereotypes he had expected to find? She had learned that there were good and bad on both sides, kind and cruel on both sides, thieving, lechery, and mercy on both sides, according to the morals and personality of the individual. Had Thomas?

Lonely enemy pickets shared meals together at night, traded tobacco for coffee, asked each other about their homes and families, and then shot at each other the next day of battle. She had felt destined to fall in love with someone like William Farley, one of her own kind, and yet her heart had attached itself to a Yankee, a man who might have killed her brothers in battle. If she and Thomas had faced each other in the dark in that skirmish with the pickets, would they have aimed and fired?

No, there was nothing clear-cut in this war. Not by a long shot.

"This man"—Annie pointed to Murdock—"and his partner were angry about not receiving some money from Major Mosby. They took Rachel and Lenah from their cottage here at Hickory Heights and were carrying them to a slave dealer. Rachel is a free woman. Laurence freed all our people last winter. Her husband, Sam, rides with Laurence and has kept him alive. He's saved Laurence's life at least twice. Rachel and I have played together, read together, since we were children. We couldn't let Murdock take Rachel."

Thomas started pacing, looking down at the floor, shaking his head. Annie could only guess at his morass of questions and confusion.

"Major, you ain't going to believe what this—" Murdock began.

"Get this scum out of my sight," Thomas ordered.

As Murdock was pushed out the door, Thomas straightened himself up. "God help me, Annie. My orders are to arrest you, for spying, shooting at our pickets, and harboring Mosby rangers. I can't not do it. If I don't, they'll simply send someone else. Get your things." His voice was heavy and thick with anger and frustration.

He looked at Laurence. "I will do everything I can to win her release promptly." Then he turned back to Annie and said slowly, with overwhelming tenderness and sadness, "You absolutely confound me."

In her prison room, Annie looked back up through the spiderwebs, blocking her view now of the moon that had traveled part of its nightly orbit. *"Oh, what a tangled web we weave / When first we practice to deceive,"* Annie muttered. She hadn't meant to deceive Thomas Walker. Of course, she hadn't meant to care a fig about what any Yankee thought, either.

Thomas had been kind on that long ride to jail, so kind. Taking off his own oil poncho to protect her from the rain. Stopping frequently to let her rest. At the Union camp, he'd argued with Colonel Lowell. He'd argued with the Federal detective who came to escort her to Washington. There were tears in his eyes as he bade her Godspeed. "I don't understand you, Annie," he repeated. But he added in a whisper, so the soldiers standing nearby couldn't rob them of their privacy, "But I believe I love you even more after this night, Lord help me."

Lord help you, indeed, thought Annie.

"Annie, please, come lie down," Millie's frightened voice wailed again. She was younger than Annie and very childlike sometimes.

Annie finally took pity on her. She stood, wrapped her cloak tight around her like armor, and went to the bed to lie down for the night. She steeled herself to withstand mice crawling over her body and dreams of the boy picket crumpling up from her shot.

"It's all right, Millie," she said to reassure herself as much as the other teenager. "Morning will come soon."

CHAPTER THIRTY-TWO

January 4, 1864
Carrol Prison,
Washington, D.C.

With morning came a visitor.

Hope filled Annie as she was led to what once must have been a parlor and now was a long barren room with heavy wooden gates, desks, and chairs. Sitting on one of them was a spindly, dour, black-clad matron—Cousin Eleanor.

Annie tried to hide her disappointment. If only it could have been Laurence or Charlotte or . . . or . . . She shook off the hope of Thomas. He would completely ruin his career in the army if he associated with her now. She knew that. But, oh, she wasn't sure she could withstand a lecture about her mistakes from this stern Unionist lady, who had never respected Annie's mother or her parents' marriage.

She hadn't even come to Miriam's funeral. And was it possible that she knew about Annie's ride to warn Stuart of Federal troops passing by Cousin Eleanor's house in Lewinsville when she and Miriam were visiting? That had been almost two and a half years ago, in September 1861. So very long ago—a whole other person ago, thought Annie, who knew how very different she now was, how different the world was. Could Cousin Eleanor be an agent for the U.S. government, trying to trick Annie into revealing that ride as well as the one that helped Mosby? Well, come what might, a visitor would at least break up the monotony of anxiety.

Cousin Eleanor stood up, a stiff statue of disapproval.

Annie swallowed hard and readied herself.

For a moment the old woman gazed sternly at Annie. But her face gave way and softened. "Oh, child, look at you." She reached out and took Annie's hand and drew her to a chair next to her own.

Embarrassed, Annie tried to smooth her hair and realized it was a mass of stray, dirty strands. She had not been permitted a bath. Indeed, she would have feared taking one, knowing she would be observed through that peephole in the door. She had packed a comb and toothbrush the night she was arrested, but she'd lost the energy, or the desire, to worry about them a day or two ago. Or was it a week? She waited for Eleanor to speak.

Eleanor turned to the junior officer who sat at a desk behind them, writing down their conversation. "Guard, this is unconscionable. This child needs fresh water and soap in her room."

The clerk shrugged and wrote it down. He answered in heavily accented English that he had no authority for that.

"Who does?" Cousin Eleanor asked imperiously.

"The superintendent."

"My husband, Francis, will contact the man tomorrow. He is a lawyer, mind you, and this girl has rights."

"She's suspected of treason, ma'am."

"We'll see about that." Eleanor turned back to Annie. "Are you all right, child?"

Annie was fighting back tears. Treason? She was a citizen of the Confederacy, not the United States, and therefore couldn't betray it in treason. Could she? She didn't answer.

"Annie." Eleanor squeezed her hand. "I've brought you a basket of food and a few clean clothes.

Did you receive the other two baskets I brought?"

Annie thought of the potted potatoes, stale bread, and porridge she'd been given and mostly refused to eat. No, she hadn't received any fresh food baskets.

She shook her head.

Eleanor pursed her lips. "No cheese? No apples? No cake? Not even on Christmas Day?"

Annie shook her head again.

Eleanor turned on the clerk. "And what would have happened to that food?"

"Must have had contraband items in't," he mumbled.

"Contraband items? A little cake?" thundered Eleanor. The clerk began to cower as she continued, "Is this how you plan to win a war, starving a poor young girl who did nothing more than stand up for her family? No matter how erroneous it was?" Cousin Eleanor grew sarcastic. "Take a good look at her, sirrah. Lord knows she looks a monster, able to knock down whole armies with a flick of her finger. I'm stunned you don't have her chained to the wall to prevent her laying waste to the entire city of Washington." Eleanor stopped and was breathing hard against her corset. "This child will be allowed this basket. Today is her birthday, of all things. If I come back and find out that she has been denied these gifts, I will find you, sirrah, and bring down the wrath of your superiors upon you."

Annie guessed the clerk didn't know half the words Cousin Eleanor used, but he certainly understood the tone. He dropped his eyes to his paper and scribbled furiously.

Cousin Eleanor turned back to Annie and calmed down by straightening her black skirt and neatly folding her shaking hands in her lap. "Happy birthday, child," she finally said.

Birthday? Annie had lost track of time. Was it January fourth already? Then she'd be eighteen years old today. She felt one hundred.

Eleanor pulled a cloth from the basket and revealed a small teacake, a loaf of bread, canned peaches, and a few dried apples. "Make sure you eat these, Annie." She pulled out a clean towel, petticoat, nightshirt, and shawl. "Clean yourself. You are the daughter of Thaddeus Sinclair. Do not let yourself go like this."

She'd also brought a copy of *Harper's Weekly*, the *New York Herald*, and a beautiful bound book, *The Scarlet Letter.* "I remembered that you had started reading this book at my house," she said. "I hesitated to bring it, Annie, given your current circumstances, but perhaps the fortitude of the character Hester will help you bear your own imprisonment. I know how much joy you garner from reading. Your mother told me."

Reviving a bit, Annie reached for *The Scarlet Letter*. Yes, she remembered reading a passage about Hester standing poised and silent on the steps of the Puritan prison, withstanding the jeers and taunts and questions of the crowd before her. It was not the same as, but not unlike, Annie's own predicament.

"How did you come to know I was here?" asked Annie hesitantly. "They promised I could write letters—only eight lines a note, they said—but they would never provide me paper and pencil."

"Laurence sent a Major Walker to see us, thinking Francis would be able to plead your cause with the authorities. Laurence could not procure papers to travel, since he has been paroled but has not taken the oath of loyalty." Cousin Eleanor paused and added, "I am sorry to hear of Laurence's condition, Annie. But we must thank the Lord that it was only his arm that was lost."

"No oath?" the clerk behind them interrupted. "Why, no oath?"

Eleanor turned even paler. "The U.S. army did not deem it necessary. He is a Confederate officer who has promised not to take up arms against us again. That is enough."

The clerk scribbled down the information.

Eleanor frowned. "God forbid I've made matters worse with that," she mumbled.

"Annie, Francis has spoken to the authorities. He is doing his best. He hopes you will have a hearing soon, and he will be there when you do. This Major Walker has also written and contacted commanding officers about you. He has somehow gotten a message through the lines to Mosby, asking that Mosby send a letter stating you were never involved in any plots against officers."

She paused and they both listened to the clerk scribble.

The sense of hopelessness that had kept Annie so downcast and lethargic was lifting. Thomas was helping? How did he dare risk his reputation with his own people? She started to ask, but then silenced herself. Any more talking about him would simply be recorded and perhaps endanger him.

"Thank you, Cousin Eleanor," she said meekly. She suddenly felt ashamed for tricking the older lady by riding out to Stuart on one of her carriage horses.

Eleanor cleared her throat. "Of course, child. I

do not condone or understand your"—she glanced over at the clerk and finished—"what happened to you. But we are family. The greatest tragedy of this war is what it has done to families."

That night, Annie and Millie devoured the fresh bread and one dried apple. Annie carefully tied up the rest in the towel and hung it on a peg next to her bonnet. Like that, the mice couldn't get to it. Annie could only hope the roaches wouldn't find it.

A few days later, Millie was released. Annie was alone again.

That first night of solitude was unbearable. Annie used up six candle stubs to make it through the hours of darkness. By the quavering, tiny beam of comfort she read and read and read.

But *The Scarlet Letter*'s tale of a woman branded as a sinner by the letter *A* on her clothes brought Annie little comfort. She came to a passage describing Hester and her daughter walking through the woods, a symbolic "moral wilderness" in which Hester could never come out of the shadows into a sunbeam:

> **. . . A gleam of flickering sunshine might now and then be seen at its solitary play along the**

path. This flitting cheerfulness was always at the farther extremity of some long vista through the forest. The sportive sunlight . . . withdrew itself as they came nigh, and left the spots where it had danced the drearier, because they had hoped to find them bright.

"Mother," said little Pearl, "the sunshine does not love you. It runs away and hides itself, because it is afraid of something on your bosom."

Without thinking, Annie raised her hand to her own chest, over her heart. Like Hester, she felt she had committed a crime against God and humanity by shooting that picket—a boy with a mother, a sister, a betrothed perhaps, who would mourn dreadfully all their lives. Like Hester, Annie would carry the stain of it on her forever.

Annie tried to shake off the thoughts. She slammed the book shut and closed her eyes for a moment. But the picket boy's face loomed huge in front of her, his mouth open, screaming, his eyes wild in fear.

She snapped her own eyes open and sat, like a sentry against her own thoughts.

Finally, when dawn came, she laid her head on

the windowsill. Feeling the warmth of the sun on her hair, she fell asleep.

She awoke when the door to her room was flung open again. She raised her head and blinked.

"Visitor," the guard announced.

Another?

This time it was Charlotte. The detective who had escorted Annie to prison loafed beside the clerk's desk.

Seeing him, Annie began to tremble. She knew it was no accident that he was there. This was far too dangerous for Charlotte. She might be implicated somehow by coming and what she might say. Or, God forbid, she might blurt out something that could only make things worse for Annie.

Annie roused her wits and rushed to embrace Charlotte. "Charlotte, my dear, you shouldn't have come all this way," she said. She kissed Charlotte quickly, caught her eye, looked urgently at the clerk and the detective and back again to Charlotte. Annie raised her eyebrows. *Please understand me*, she prayed silently.

Charlotte looked puzzled. Annie repeated the glance so that Charlotte looked sideways as well. To her great relief, Charlotte nodded.

"Oh, darling, I couldn't not come while I was in town," Charlotte prattled, playing the Southern belle. "Those delightful Union soldiers currently occupying us gave me a pass to come to Washington to buy dress material. There's absolutely none to be had in Warrenton. And there are so many lovely parties to be going to. I do wish this silly war would end so that the shops could open again. Honestly, Annie, you could certainly use some new clothes yourself." Charlotte's eyes were filling with tears, but she kept her voice merry.

Annie smiled encouragingly at Charlotte. That's right, she thought, you're doing well. She reached over and squeezed Charlotte's hand.

"Eh-hem," the detective cleared his throat.

Annie flushed but held her empty hand up and open so that he could see that Charlotte had not passed her anything.

The detective nodded and then sauntered into the next room. Annie sighed in relief, although she knew the clerk still would record everything.

She winked at Charlotte. "How is dear Eliza? I've so missed her." Annie, of course, detested Eliza now, but one of her greatest fears was that somehow Eliza would compromise Annie concerning Stuart.

Charlotte again appeared baffled but then a

slow smile spread across her pretty face. She understood. Her answer told Annie that Eliza was precisely the reason Charlotte had braved the trip to come. Eliza had betrayed her—whether she had meant to or not.

"Well," Charlotte began with that voice of schoolgirl gossip, "don't tell her I said this, but my goodness, that girl is a flirt. She has all sorts of Federal officers falling all over her. I wouldn't be surprised if she didn't marry one of them, and then she'll never be received in society again!"

Annie winced at the condemnation of a Yankee-Southerner marriage, but continued the jolly tone. "Oh, do tell."

Charlotte drew closer, her face quite serious and intent, even while her voice retained its party tinkle: "She loves to bedevil them. I heard her tell one of them that if he didn't come back with an engagement ring for her, and right fast, she was going to ride out to Stuart's cavalry and find herself a husband there. *Said she knew a girl who rode out like that once to find Stuart.*" Charlotte spoke the last words slowly and loudly, capable of only so much subtlety. Then she forced a giggle. "Can you imagine such brashness? I think Eliza has three or four rings already, from Yankees and Confederates both."

Annie's heart plummeted. She'd gotten the message. Somehow, perhaps merely in a slip of silly chatter, or in a careless maneuver to garner information about Union troops, Eliza had told Federals in Warrenton that Annie had warned Stuart of an impending attack. The Washington prison officials would see it as further proof of her spying, sure. If Eliza had blabbed about the poems, they might search Hickory Heights to stack up evidence against her.

She needed Charlotte to go to Hickory Heights and make sure those poems were destroyed or hidden where no one would ever find them. Annie forced herself to join in Charlotte's throaty laughter. "Speaking of engagements, when do you and Laurence wed?"

Charlotte blushed and glanced over at the clerk. He seemed not to have connected that Laurence was Annie's brother. No longer able to keep up the pretense of merriment, Charlotte spoke haltingly. "Laurence is much changed, Annie. He himself seems to doubt we are suited for each other, and I . . . I . . . well . . . he is much changed."

Annie felt herself pull away from Charlotte. You can't be that shallow, Annie thought. You can't destroy Laurence that way!

Charlotte saw Annie freeze up. "Oh, Annie, I'm not as good, as brave as you. . . ."

The scribbling of the clerk picked up. Charlotte broke off.

"Nonsense," Annie chirped. "He is changed because of not seeing you. You go to him and tell him to tear up that silly letter he wrote you. Tell him *his sad poetry will do you no good right now.*"

Charlotte shook her head. She didn't understand.

Annie felt as if she would scream. After all, it was Charlotte's snooping and gossiping about Annie that had given Eliza the information that might hang Annie. She forced herself to keep playing the game and to adopt a girlish whisper of confidential advice: "Don't be afraid to be honest with the man you love, Charlotte. We ladies spend too much time worrying and waiting for them to make up their own minds. The war has brought a new urgency to life." She leaned forward to say pointedly, "Tell him *to tear up those ridiculous poems.*"

She sat back and waited a moment for her underlying meaning to sink in. Finally, Charlotte drew in her breath, as if fresh cold air had just hit her, and nodded.

Annie felt her heart begin to beat normally

again. She finished quietly, "And then marry him, Charlotte, for he loves you dearly. He needs you."

A few minutes later, the detective reappeared and announced that their visiting time was up.

The friends stood and hugged. Annie wanted to warn Charlotte to flee the city at once before she was accused of something, to hurry to Hickory Heights. But she knew anything she said at that moment could bring terrible danger to Charlotte. She had been incredibly good to come. Now, if she could only be strong enough to go to Laurence. And then steady enough to marry him. How could she not marry him, just because Laurence was missing his arm?

"I know you'll find some beautiful material, Charlotte. Have a happy journey home," Annie said as casually as she could.

She turned and waited for the guard to shadow her back to her prison room.

CHAPTER THIRTY-THREE

February 10, 1864
Carrol Prison,
Washington, D.C.

"Room change. Come this way."

Annie gathered her few belongings and followed the guard upstairs. To her amazement, women were out in the hallway talking to one another. They greeted her with smiles as she passed.

"In here." The guard ushered Annie into a tiny but far more inviting room. The coarse unbleached sheets on the bed were actually clean. The barred window had all its panes. When Annie looked out it, she caught her breath with joy. Before, in the oppressive room she had occupied for six weeks, her view had been of the whitewashed courtyard of the prison, where male prisoners were allowed to walk and stretch during the day in a yard of dust and filth.

Here she could see out to the Capitol grounds, to trees and sky and lawn. She put her cheek against the cool glass and looked and looked.

It had snowed. It had been a mercilessly cold winter, she knew. She hoped that Isaac and Bob had remembered to cut ice from the creek for the ice-house. Poor Laurence. He'd only be able to watch such work now. She tried to envision the twists and turns of Goose Creek, the stretch that was wide and still enough to freeze for ice skating. The few winters it had frozen solid, she, Laurence, and Jamie had slid about, laughing hysterically. She could hear them; remember the happy sting of her frozen nose; Laurence catching her when Jamie tackled her; great, stomach-hurting, gasping guffaws. In her current lonely sadness, the thought of such carefree happiness was too much to bear.

Annie shut off the memory and turned. She jumped to see the door open and a woman standing in it.

"They'll lock the door at night," the stranger said gently, introducing herself as a Mrs. Jackson. She was the widow of a diplomat, a North Carolina native but longtime resident of Washington, who'd gathered much information about Union troops and generals at parties she'd hosted. She'd been caught passing the valuable tidbits on south to Confederate president Jefferson Davis. He'd been her friend and neighbor when he'd served in the U.S. Senate.

"I've been a boarder of Uncle Sam's for a while now," she joked, referring to the prison. "Come have a cup of tea with me."

Mrs. Jackson's room seemed a small home. She had china, glasses, books, and a clean quilt upon her iron bedstead. Half a dozen dresses hung on the wall pegs. An African servant woman brought in the tea and left. Annie looked after her wonderingly.

"Runaway," explained Mrs. Jackson. "The U.S. government doesn't know what to do with the female ones, so they house some of them here and put them to work cleaning the prison."

Annie frowned. That certainly didn't sound like the freedom that this girl obviously had hoped for. Good thing Lenah had come to Hickory Heights, thought Annie. She asked, "Will they let her go on her own way soon?"

"Goodness, you are an innocent, Miss Sinclair. You're not a closet abolitionist, are you?" Mrs. Jackson asked, only so jokingly. "Some Yankees may want to free the slaves, but even fewer wish them assimilated into our society afterward. Most don't want to have anything to do with them. There is a movement to send all the darkies off to Liberia once the war is settled. I remember hearing President Lincoln speak of the African recolonization plan himself when he was to dinner at my home. He seemed for it at the time."

She smiled at Annie and changed the subject. "Those visits by the Lincolns were extremely useful, you know. His wife would dither on about all his plans quite openly—silly, extravagant woman. They say she's purchased four hundred pairs of gloves while the United States taxes its citizens to pay for the invasion of the South. Drink your tea now."

Annie took a sip and went wide-eyed. "It's real!"

"Yes, honey, it is. I still have a few influential friends."

Mrs. Jackson did not ask about Annie's plight or background, and over the hour, Annie began to relax. She remained bewildered, however, about her sudden change in circumstances.

"I believe you have some powerful friends yourself," said Mrs. Jackson. "Or at least persistent ones. Don't you know the romance about you?"

Shocked, Annie shook her head.

"Oh, it's all over the prison that the Yankee who arrested you is completely besotted with you. He's evidently been here several times."

Annie looked blankly at her in disbelief.

"Oh, my," said Mrs. Jackson. "I can see you didn't know." She walked to the door and called, "Bettie?"

In a few minutes the servant girl was back. "Yes'm?"

"Bettie knows everything," Mrs. Jackson told Annie. "Didn't you tell me that there was a Union officer fussing about Miss Sinclair's housing?"

"Yes'm. Was yesterday. I was cleaning out the cinders and cigar butts from the fireplace when he come in. I seen him before, talking with the superintendent. He make a fuss that the lady should be out of confinement. Then he hand over a letter. He asked she gets it."

"Have you received any letters?" Mrs. Jackson asked.

"No, not any."

"A pity. Honestly, the transgressions these jailers get away with. I hear there is a closet downstairs crammed full with cakes turning green with age that they've refused to deliver to the prisoners. Thank you, Bettie." Mrs. Jackson dismissed the girl. "Perhaps we can dislodge those letters for you. Things will get better, now that you're upstairs with us. You'll see."

Annie didn't know what to say. It had been so long since anyone had been the least bit kind to her, save Cousin Eleanor, and her visit had been a month ago. Her eyes filled with grateful tears.

Mrs. Jackson patted her hand. "Drink your tea, honey."

Things did get better. That afternoon Bettie brought up a large pitcher of warm water and soap. Annie closed her door and, finding no peephole in it, thoroughly washed herself for the first time in weeks. It was heaven. Later, her dinner gruel arrived and there was actually a bit of meat in it. When her door was closed and locked, Annie blew out her candle and fell asleep. For once, the picket stayed away from her dreams.

But there was a reason behind the changes, reasons beyond Thomas' appeals. The next day Annie was taken to court, to a military commission of six U.S. army officers. Her cousin Francis was there, waiting for her. She had not seen him for years, but she instantly recognized the wizened, bespectacled, balding man.

He pulled her away from her guards and spoke hurriedly. "I am not sure why you are here, Annie, whether to serve as a witness or to be tried yourself.

Listen to me carefully, for although they allow me to serve as your attorney, I am not sure that they will permit me to speak during the proceedings."

He went on to explain that the Lincoln administration was trying to find a way to convict Mosby rangers quickly and easily. "It all hinges on the interpretation of the military nature of Mosby's command. The secretary of war and the judge advocate general say Mosby's men are *not* commissioned soldiers, that they are instead felons, not entitled to the rights accorded prisoners of war. That means burning bridges, stealing horses, destroying Federal property, *attacking pickets*," he drew out the last pointedly since it applied to Annie, "those kinds of activities are not viewed as military maneuvers. They are seen as civilian crimes punishable by hanging or firing squad." He paused a moment to make sure Annie understood. She didn't quite.

He tried again: "They have a witness, a deserter who's going to say that Mosby is not a member of the Confederate army, that he leads a gang of robbers who come together only for the purpose of plunder. If the commission believes his testimony, it will bring a death sentence to every Mosby rider they prosecute."

Annie understood now. Her throat had gone

completely dry. "Do you know the name of the deserter?"

Cousin Francis checked his notes. "Charles Murdock."

Annie first went cold and faint, then hot and furious. Why did people like Murdock exist?

At that moment, the defendant, a baby-faced, twenty-two-year-old private named Philip Trammell, was marched past them and into the courtroom.

Annie was ushered in as well, but she was told to sit in the back. A few minutes later, Murdock entered. Oh, how Annie wanted to kick the man.

The charges were read. Trammell was accused of robbing and being in "violation of the laws of war in carrying on guerilla warfare." The prosecutor then read General Order No. 100, which said that men not enrolled in the army, or who took off their uniforms and returned to their homes between raids, "shall be treated summarily as highway robbers or pirates."

Then Murdock had his say. He testified that during his time with Mosby he had not formally enrolled in the Confederate army, that he drew no pay, only part of the spoils gathered from the raids. He explained that when the raids were over, Mosby dispersed the men. The accused, Philip Trammell, said Murdock, always went home to his father's house in Loudoun County. None of the riders were required to answer Mosby's call for a raid.

Annie seethed. She knew Mosby's men were indeed officially enlisted in the Confederate army as the 43rd Battalion of Virginia Cavalry. Jamie had showed her a card that said so. They were eligible for the same salary as regular Confederate cavalry—*when* the government had the money. And if they did not report regularly for raids, Mosby sent them off to serve in the Confederate infantry, something Jamie and his cohorts recognized as a near death sentence after the slaughter of Gettysburg.

She'd heard repeatedly from Mosby and Jamie that their purposes were to rattle and disrupt the Union troops, to scout out their movements for Stuart and Lee, and to take their supplies to slow them down. Why didn't someone try the Yankees for taking all her livestock and feed corn? She didn't see any specific military tactics in that either—just harassment.

She was twitching in her seat to talk. Cousin Francis laid a firm hand on hers to quiet her. He leaned over and hissed, "Do you want to be next?"

Annie quieted as Trammell rose to defend himself. To her dismay, the young man did not cross-examine Murdock, nor reply to his charges. He merely quarreled with the court's definition of armed robbery.

The prosecutor rose to give his final statement. "It is clear," he boomed, "that Trammel rode with Mosby, and that the band is not a regularly organized military group. It forms purely to steal, rob, and maraud through the country."

The six-man tribunal was unanimous in its decision: Trammel was guilty and sentenced to be shot to death.

"Get me out of here." Annie caught hold of Cousin Francis' arm. "I'm going to be sick."

"Guard." Francis snapped his fingers. "Help me get the lady some fresh air."

They half dragged Annie down the hall to a long bench, where she desperately fanned herself.

"Dear, oh dear," tut-tutted Cousin Francis, "this is not good at all."

Annie's nightmares that long black night were endless. The picket lurched and bled; the prison clerk wrote in an enormous book, pointed at her, and laughed; she felt rope around her throat. At daybreak, she stoically rose and dressed herself, brushed her hair, washed her face, and sat in the corner, waiting. Waiting for the soldiers to come and escort her to court and to her doom.

They didn't come. They didn't come the next day either, or the following weeks.

Winter turned to a cold, wet spring. Still Annie waited to know her fate.

A basket from Cousin Eleanor arrived. In it was a book of poetry by Henry Wadsworth Longfellow. Tucked inside the book was a note from Thomas.

The note was purposefully anonymous in its tone, perhaps to trick the guards into thinking it was from Cousin Eleanor. But the thought contained in it, the immense loyalty and concern it represented, the promise of a future, thrilled Annie. It read:

> *I do not know if you have ever read this poet, as he is from New England and a former professor at Harvard. But he follows the tradition of British poets you do enjoy. He has a great love of nature, as you do, and his simple, melodious poems carry great solace. See "The Day Is Done." Signed: T.W.*

Turning to the poem, Annie understood that Thomas was trying to remind her of the few times they had been able to share bits of poetry, free of the world around them; that things other than prison bars, fear, and self-recriminations did exist. She soon memorized stanzas to repeat to herself in the night:

Come, read to me some poem,
Some simple and heartfelt lay,
That shall soothe this restless feeling,
And banish the thoughts of day.

. . . .

Read from some humbler poet,
Whose songs gushed from his heart,
As showers from the clouds of summer,
Or tears from the eyelids start;

Who, through long days of labor,
And nights devoid of ease,
Still heard in his soul the music
Of wonderful melodies.

. . . .

Then read from the treasured volume
The poem of thy choice,
And lend to the rhyme of the poet
The beauty of thy voice.

During the days, terrible news of the war filtered into Mrs. Jackson's room with local newspapers. Union general William Tecumseh Sherman, a pitiless man, was burning every Georgia farm he saw as he marched swiftly toward Atlanta. Closer to home, Union soldiers, under General David Hunter, were laying waste to the Shenandoah Valley. Trying to defend the area, cadets as young as fifteen from the Virginia Military Institute were slaughtered just outside New Market in a muddy cornfield.

But for Annie the most heartbreaking news came out of a small crossroads, just north of Richmond, called Yellow Tavern.

Stuart was slain.

Riding along the battlefield, alone, whistling, Stuart had joined a bedraggled line of sharpshooters—boys and old men—trying to hold off an attack by Federal cavalry. "Bully for Old K," Stuart had called out to Company K, Marylanders from the Eastern Shore, riding for his 1st Virginia Cavalry. "Give it to 'em, boys!" He fired his own silver-chased pistol.

Rallied by Stuart's presence, the handful of gray gunners held their line. As the Federals retreated, and Stuart called, "Steady, men, steady," a Union private trotting back to the Federal position passed just across the fence from Stuart. On the run, the Yankee took one last shot. His bullet ripped into Stuart's side, under his ribs.

Stuart suffered for a day. In between spasms of pain and bleeding, he thought to give his two remaining horses to his closest aides, carefully designating the larger horse to the heavier man. He asked that a little Confederate flag sent to him by a lady admirer from South Carolina, which he'd tucked in the sweatband of his plumed hat, be returned to her. He left his golden spurs to Lily Lee, the widow of a close friend. His sword was to go to his son.

His friend Heros von Borcke, the big Prussian Annie had sheltered, managed to make it to his side in time to say good-bye. His wife, delayed by the battle raging in her way, arrived three hours too late. Stuart died May twelfth at the age of thirty-one.

His funeral was a quiet, quick ceremony in Richmond's Hollywood Cemetery. There was no music, no military escort, no parade of carriages. Richmond was under siege.

Mrs. Jackson told all this to Annie. Dry-eyed, Annie excused herself and retired to her room to mourn. Annie felt cold and empty, cheated, as Stuart had been cheated of his final heroic moment. He hadn't perished as he would have chosen, in one last glorious, legendary, tide-turning charge. He'd died as they all would die now, in a stubborn death grip, where the end would come not in brilliant stratagems or in inspiring, crusading acts of courage, but in blunt, brutal, even cowardly harshness, like the burning of homes, and the hanging of boys following orders their conquerors would rule as being nothing more than highway robbery.

The brave, eloquent, witty Stuart killed by a man running *away* from battle. The injustice of it. The sickening symbolism of it. The chivalry, the idealistic poetry, the infectious esprit that had started the war was being replaced by a simple, murderous blood thirst. Stuart's death was a harbinger of all to come, Annie just knew it.

And for what? What had it been for? Had their cause been a justifiable one? Could anything justify this much carnage?

Lord, she'd give anything for it to be over.

CHAPTER THIRTY-FOUR

July 12, 1864
Carrol Prison,
Washington, D.C.

"What's all the excitement?" Annie stood looking out the window onto the Capitol grounds. A huge mass of bluecoat soldiers were rushing into ranks.

"Well, my dear," Mrs. Jackson said, drawing her near, "Old Jubilee has liberated parts of the Shenandoah Valley and moved into Maryland. He's firing on Fort Stevens, just north of Washington. Rumor has it that Lincoln himself went out to watch and now is trapped there. The Feds are massing everyone they can to march out and resist." Her eyes were shining. "We may have our long-awaited invasion of the capital yet. Wouldn't it make our incarceration worth it, if we were here to watch the city of Washington and Lincoln fall?"

Annie felt no thrill at all. She knew a little about General Jubal Early because Mosby had often spoken ill of him. Early was yet another West Pointer who disapproved of Mosby's methods. Robert E. Lee had called him "my bad old man," this cantankerous Virginia lawyer, who'd once battled Indians for the U.S. army. Annie sighed. He'd keep the fighting going until every single soul was dead.

There was a knock on the door. Two guards stood there. Annie and Mrs. Jackson exchanged nervous glances, worrying they'd overhead Mrs. Jackson gloating.

"Ann Sinclair?"

Annie nodded.

"You're wanted downstairs."

Had her hearing finally come, then? "What for?" she asked.

"Ain't been told that. Please come with us, miss."

She was shown into an anteroom off the large receiving room. Waiting there were a judge from the Bureau of Military Affairs, the superintendent of the prison, the very detective who had delivered her to Carrol, the same odious clerk who'd recorded her conversations, Cousin Francis, and—Annie began to tremble—Thomas Walker.

He seemed taller, thinner, and even graver than the last time she'd seen him. There was a new, nasty, red, barely healed scar running along the side of his handsome face and his neck, disappearing into his blue uniform's stiff collar. She looked to him to speak, but all he did was smile slightly. She couldn't read his dark, intense eyes. "Stand tall," they seemed to say, but that's foolishness, she told herself. He's probably been called in to give testimony *against* me.

"I wish some information from you," the superintendent said harshly.

Annie clasped her hands together in front of her skirt, a stance she'd taken a thousand times as a dutiful schoolgirl. But what came out of her mouth was still saucy: "I will gladly give you information that I honestly know."

Cousin Francis rolled his eyes. "Be polite," he mouthed at her.

"There is fighting just outside the city. You probably are privy to that information?" the superintendent continued.

Don't answer that, Annie. You could compromise Mrs. Jackson. She waited.

The flabby-faced superintendent eyed her.

"Well, there is. Jubal Early has invaded Maryland and threatens the capital. Does that make you happy?"

Again, Annie said nothing.

Cousin Francis interrupted: "I believe this line of questioning is off the subject and badgering Miss Sinclair. If I hear that she has been questioned in this manner before, I will protest it as well as this."

Her interrogator scowled. He continued, "Mosby has ridden into Maryland, presumably to join forces. The Union commander of the defense of Washington wishes to know his number and who there among the citizens would help him."

Surprised, Annie answered truthfully, "I would not know, sir. I think that Major Walker and the Union cavalry could better answer that."

"Surely you would know who his informants are."

"No, sir, I would not."

"Perhaps, you simply don't know those located in Maryland."

Yet another potential trap. "No, sir, I would not know any informants of his anywhere."

"But you know that informants exist then?" The bulbous superintendent sat up as if he had caught her in something.

Was this to be another endless cat-and-mouse game of words? Annie felt a twinge of fury and said obstinately, "Only because you have told me so and I assume an officer of the United States government to be nothing other than honest and knowledgeable."

She heard Thomas cough and saw a smile twitch across his face briefly before he suppressed it.

The superintendent rattled his papers. "I suggest you adopt an air of cooperation, Miss Sinclair. How you answer may determine what charges we bring against you. We know that you have alerted both Mosby and Stuart of our troop movements, twice that we can prove with witnesses. That constitutes spying. We know from our own operatives in Warrenton that Stuart was quite impressed by your loyalty and espionage abilities and communicated with you frequently."

Cousin Francis stepped in again. "There has been no proof of that. You have thoroughly searched Miss Sinclair's home and found absolutely nothing to support your egregious insinuations."

Thank you, God, for little Will. Annie hadn't known what had happened about those poems. She had heard nothing further from Charlotte. Either Will had hidden them completely or Charlotte had told Laurence to destroy them. Oh, she hoped

Charlotte had found her compassion and married Laurence, too. She longed to know.

Her questioner noticed the change in Annie's face. "You needn't look so relieved, Miss Sinclair. We also know that you shot a picket. You are lucky that the soldier lived—otherwise we might see fit to charge you with murder."

Annie couldn't help herself. A wave of joy overcame her. "He lived? He did? Oh, praise God!"

"Annie," shushed Francis.

"Aha!" The superintendent said triumphantly. He slapped his papers onto his desk and wrote furiously.

Annie didn't care. The boy had lived. She hadn't killed him. She knew she had shot in self-defense, but oh, the guilt of thinking she had taken another life had imprisoned her as surely as the walls of Carrol Prison had. Now she was free of it. She felt life flood through her. Beaming, she looked over at Thomas. He was watching her so carefully; she felt that his eyes burned through to her soul. She looked at Cousin Francis, who had lowered his head and was shaking it back and forth, his bald scalp shining. There was no sound save for the scribbling of prison officials.

Annie laughed out loud, clapped her hands

together, and repeated happily: "He lived!" She wanted to dance!

Suddenly Thomas burst out laughing as well. "God help me, Annie," he said, "I just knew it had to be an accident. I just knew you couldn't have planned to do it."

"Major Walker," Cousin Francis fairly shouted. "You're making things worse."

Thomas sobered quickly. "No. I'm going to fix them."

He stepped forward, pulling a letter from his breast pocket. "I have a letter here that was delivered under a flag of truce from Colonel Mosby."

The superintendent's head shot up.

A letter from Mosby? wondered Annie, still too pleased by the news of the picket's survival to grasp her peril—that this military tribunal was aiming to prosecute, try, and sentence her all at once.

"And how did you come by a communiqué from Mosby?" the superintendent sneered.

"Through proper channels of war," replied Thomas. "Colonel Mosby is a lawyer; he knows the law. And he writes:

"Miss Ann Sinclair comes from a family of Southern patriots, serving their country with

bravery. Her brother James is an enlisted member of the Confederate cavalry, assigned to my command, the 43rd battalion of Virginia. Upon occasion our soldiers have been billeted at the Sinclair home, which is in accordance with the practice of lawful warfare. Miss Sinclair has never engaged in subterfuge, coercion, stealing of information, crossing borders illegally, carrying of official Confederate documents, or deceit. Her shooting of the Union picket, who had fired upon her and her companions from the cover of bushes, was entirely in self-defense. As such, she should be acquitted of all charges immediately. Lieutenant Colonel John S. Mosby, Esquire."

Thomas pulled another letter out of his pocket and held it up high for emphasis. "This is a letter I have written but not yet delivered to Mrs. Lincoln at the White House. It is well known that she is a devoted abolitionist. I'm sure if she is informed of the purpose of Miss Sinclair's ride out into the night, in which Miss Sinclair fired in self-defense, the first lady would surely persuade her husband to grant her clemency. Miss Sinclair was out to defend the life and freedom of a freed slave, her servant, her friend. I wouldn't be surprised if President Lincoln didn't decide to oust *you*, given the length of Miss Sinclair's imprisonment and oft-improper denial of visitors and food. I know that he plans to commute the sentence of Private Trammel from death to ten years of hard labor. President Lincoln wishes to show clemency once this war is over. He wants the country reunited. Persecution of persons such as Miss Sinclair will only prolong the hatred between North and South."

He lowered the letter and stood in a kind of spread-legged swagger she'd seen Laurence adopt sometimes, a king-of-the-hill kind of posture. "In fact, I suggest you release Miss Sinclair today, before a heap of trouble befalls you."

The superintendent had been gaping at Thomas all this time. He blinked his froglike eyes. "Are you daft?"

"No, quite sane. You've jailed her long enough."

The superintendent sputtered. "The only way I would release this woman would be if she swore allegiance to the United States by taking the loyalty oath, and even then I would have serious doubts that she would hold to it."

"How dare you, man." Thomas stepped closer,

his chest heaving. "This lady has done nothing but act with integrity and the deepest of loyalty to humanity. She and her mother nursed Union wounded at Manassas even as our troops trampled their crops and stole—oh, excuse me—*appropriated* their horses. She risked her life to save the freedom and well-being of her servant. If she signs an oath of loyalty to the United States, she will keep it, probably more strongly than any man."

Thomas' words rang in Annie's ears. They were the most heartfelt words of love and admiration he'd ever spoken, even though he had not said the specific word.

Cousin Francis broke into her thoughts: "Will you sign an oath of loyalty, Annie? If you do, they will release you. This very day."

Would they? Today? Annie's heart raced at the thought of being free. Still, she couldn't sign those papers. She would be betraying all she'd fought for, suffered for, if she did.

Slowly, Annie shook her head. "I do not plan to ever engage in this war again. I will pray for it to end soon. No matter the outcome. But, no, I cannot sign a paper to be loyal to a government that seems obsessed with degrading my people, or to a country to which I no longer belong."

The superintendent smirked. "So much for your speech, Walker. I am going to see that you are written up for insubordination and consorting with the enemy and . . . "

Thomas held up his hand to stop the superintendent's prattle. He was so unafraid, Annie marveled. Thomas approached her and took her hand. His smile radiated confidence and entreaties both. "Could you promise loyalty to your husband's country?"

Annie caught her breath. What a place for a marriage proposal! If she accepted, would it later feel she had done so simply as a way out? How could she give up so many things for this man—her homeland, her family, some would say her honor—after fighting so hard to save them? He was the enemy. And yet, he was all she had ever wanted to have in a husband, a true soul mate.

Thomas saw her wavering and whispered fervently, "Come read me a poem, Annie, a poem of *your* choice, and lend it the beauty of your voice."

Oh, it was so tempting. Flustered, Annie looked at the floor to think. If she kept his gaze, that passionate, imploring gaze, she'd say yes automatically, completely beguiled. What should she do? Annie felt complete with him, protected and challenged at the same moment, coveted for the right reasons—her mind and her heart. Now she knew what love felt like—not some breathless infatuation based on unfulfilled hints, but a heart-pounding trust and respect and desire to be with someone, no matter how different the two people were.

Still, Annie lingered in confusion. Then, quietly, magically, Miriam's gentle voice came to her, steady and reassuring as in life, repeating something she'd said as she died: "Remember that it doesn't matter where someone comes from, but where that person is going."

Did it matter where either of them had come from, as long as they moved forward together? But it had to be a new world of their combined voice. Annie looked up and saw fear on Thomas' face. Tenderly, she reached out to the jagged welt that ran along his face. *Their own voice.*

Her answer came. "Yes, Thomas, I could, if you could promise never again to raise arms against my homeland."

Now Thomas hesitated.

Annie knew what she asked him to sacrifice: a distinguished military career he had worked for since his youth. Thomas was an honorable soldier, one who believed in the Union he fought to preserve.

If he said yes, they would both be emigrants, cut off from all past alliances, roots, beliefs, and dreams. But they'd have each other.

She waited.

It took Thomas only a moment. "Done," he said. "I'll resign my commission from the army. We will make our own peace treaty between us."

"Done," said Annie.

And so it was.

CHAPTER THIRTY-FIVE

September 24, 1864
Hickory Heights

There it was—home. But no longer *her* home. Annie pulled up her horse. Thomas halted his, waiting for her to be ready. Ready to say good-bye.

They paused at the bottom of the lane. Autumn gold was beginning to seep into the leaves of the vaulting hickory trees surrounding the house. The dogwood underneath them blazed red, and Annie remembered how, come spring, their white flowers would look like a constellation of stars strung through the green sky of taller, larger trees. She felt a hard lump growing in her throat. "Do you have dogwood in Massachusetts, Thomas?"

"Not as many as here," he answered quietly. "We do have mountain laurel the size of elephants that grows thick through the forests."

"Does April come gradually, with misty rains that wash the earth in soft green and bring the scent of lilacs and apple blossoms? Do Carolina wrens nest in the crooks of houses and bring luck with their warbling? And are there valleys wide and open enough that you can watch the shadow of a red-tailed hawk drift across its entirety?"

"Not where I—where *we* will live, my dear," said Thomas. "But there's a brook that runs through our property that laughs as it goes, and wisteria that climbs along the porch, inviting the same humming-birds you have here. The winters are long but filled with books and reading and music in fire-lit rooms. There are hills, and there is the ocean—a coastline of waves and the promise of worlds beyond. There is beauty there, too."

Annie nodded. She was excited by the idea of new landscapes. She'd never seen the ocean. And yet, this good-bye would be so very hard. Not even the difficulties of the past two months had prepared her for how much her heart was aching at the thought of it now that it had come.

She and Thomas had left Carrol Prison the evening of her hearing, after she'd signed her oath of allegiance. It would take several days before Thomas could complete his resignation. They decided to remain in the city until that was done. Besides, it wasn't safe to leave Washington after dark and try to cross the Potomac or pass through lines of Federal pickets to the home of Cousin Eleanor and Francis. So the three of them walked to a hotel near the White House.

"It's a delightful place. They'll have a fine dinner, too. I certainly could use a decent meal," said Cousin Francis, who'd been congratulating himself for Annie's release all afternoon. He suddenly realized, however, that it was Annie who could really use a filling supper. "It will do you a world of good, Annie. I'll see if they can provide you a bath as well. Major Walker and I will share a room."

Annie hardly heard him. She was overwhelmed at the feel of fresh, twilight air on her face, the push and bustle of the street, the seemingly acres of white columns and marble staircases of the government buildings and imposing town homes near them. She tucked her hand around Thomas' arm and tugged him toward her as a shield.

"It's all right, Annie," Thomas soothed her. "I know it is a hard adjustment after being locked up for so long. We'll get you into a quiet place quickly. Here we are." He nodded toward the wide steps of a grand old building.

They climbed the stairs and walked into an elegant foyer. Annie took in the huge, gleaming chandelier, the wide, colorful Oriental rugs, the potted ferns, and red velveteen sofas with their claw feet. Her head began to swim a bit from the sudden change to her circumstances. Thomas gently guided her to a chair that was as puffed up as a pincushion. Cousin Francis approached the official-looking man behind a polished brass cage and mahogany desk.

"We need two rooms for the night, please," said Francis. "One for the gentleman and myself, and another for the lady."

The man eyed him and then peered around him at Annie. "We'll be glad to serve the gentlemen, but I'm afraid we cannot accommodate the . . . red-headed girl," he said coldly. He pointed to a small sign in the window beside the door.

It read "No Dogs or Irish Allowed."

It had taken several hours after that to find a boardinghouse with rooms available. Before sinking into a bed that was only slightly cleaner than what she'd suffered at Carrol Prison, Annie remembered horror stories that Aunt Molly had told about her maternal grandparents' arrival in the United States, how much prejudice they had encountered in New York City. "It was even worse in places like Boston, dearie," she'd said. "You'd think them English be running the new world. That's how it was the family came to Virginia, to build railroads. 'Tis better for us in the country."

"Thomas," she asked the next day, "you don't live in Boston, do you?"

"No," he answered. "But not too far away from there, outside a small hamlet. Why do you ask that now, Annie? You won't change your mind and break my heart, will you?" His smile was so disarming, she almost forgot the question. And when he kissed her, it no longer mattered.

Still, there were more difficulties. Thomas faced a great deal of inquiry regarding his resignation. He then became as suspect as Annie in terms of travel. They couldn't leave Washington until Cousin Francis had convinced the judge advocate of the War Department to grant them passports and to hold Francis responsible if they caused any trouble.

They traveled to Francis and Eleanor's home then. There, they were married in early September. Cousin Eleanor read from the Song of Solomon, "*Rise up, my love, my fair one, and come away. For, lo, the winter is past, the rain is over and gone; the flowers appear on the earth; the time of the singing of birds is come. . . .*"

Amazed by the choice of such lush biblical verse, Annie wondered about Cousin Francis and Eleanor's youth. The old lady certainly wasn't as crusty as Annie had once thought. But then, so much about the world was different from what Annie had believed it to be. She felt a glimmer of a strong affection for Eleanor. Her indignant wrath at the clerk and her baskets had kept Annie breathing, hoping.

Gaining passes to travel to Hickory Heights had been an enormous task as well. But in that instance, Thomas' past service with Colonel Lowell helped. Lowell was now riding with General Sheridan, and Sheridan had retaken Winchester and again occupied most of northern Virginia. Atlanta had fallen. The Yankees felt confident enough to be magnanimous. Thomas was issued a pass through.

And so they had arrived. What reaction would Laurence and Jamie have to her marriage? Annie drew in a deep breath.

"Let's find Laurence," she said, and clucked the horse into a trot up the lane to Hickory Heights.

"Mrs. Walker, I presume?" Laurence asked happily as Annie dismounted the horse.

She smiled and nodded shyly.

He caught her up with his good arm and swung her around. Oh, he felt strong and whole again. Annie was so glad. So grateful for his understanding.

"How did you know?" she asked, gasping a little from his tight embrace.

"Oh, I just knew, honey," Laurence said, suddenly sober. "Any bluebird who could be that distressed at arresting such a hardheaded Confederate as you . . . well, it was clear to me that he loved you. I knew he would do all he could to win your release when I had no power to do it. The only thing I was uncertain of was if he could win your heart—that proud, brave, rebellious heart. I'm glad he did." Laurence turned to Thomas and extended his left hand. "I thank you for my sister's safety . . . brother."

Thomas extended his left hand as well and the two former adversaries, now kin, shook hands.

That's when everyone else, who'd been waiting quietly in the hall, rushed forward to surround Annie.

"Look at you, Miss Annie, all growed up. Why, you is the spitting image of Missus Miriam when I first laid eyes on her." Aunt May had to put her apron to her face and cry.

Colleen and Sally joined hands and danced

around her, singing a nursery rhyme: *"The King of Spain's daughter kissed me wild and free / And all for the sake of my little nut tree."*

Annie blushed and shooed them off.

"Congratulations, Miss Annie, I . . . I . . . ," Isaac began, but he choked up as well.

"What Daddy's trying to tell you, Annie, is thank you." There stood Rachel, safe, beautiful, and . . . round!

"Rachel!" Annie gasped, holding Rachel out at arm's length. "Are you?"

Rachel nodded. "If it's a girl, I'd like to name her Anna. If it's a boy, Andrew. In honor of the lady who made the baby's life possible. Would that be all right with you?"

"I cannot think of a greater honor for me," Annie whispered with emotion. What kind of world, what kind of acceptance awaits this baby beyond Hickory Heights, Annie worried silently. What she had seen in Washington did not reassure her in terms of their prospects. And some Southerners, no matter how much she hated to admit it, would only become more bigoted and resentful if—*when*—they lost the war. She shook her head. This was not the time to think on such worrisome matters. Now was time for jubilation. She turned to congratulate Sam on becoming a father, but a sudden recognition changed her words. "Sam! You made it home."

Rachel and Sam nodded, perplexed by the obviousness of Annie's statement.

"Did . . . did . . ." Annie couldn't even hope enough to ask the question.

Seeing Annie's fluster, everyone stopped jumping and crying and dancing, wondering what she wanted.

But Laurence knew. He took her hand and motioned to Thomas to follow. "I have a surprise for you." He led Annie to the stable paddock, and there she was—thin, her coat dull and gone in patches, her front legs lumpy and bowed, long jagged scars across her flanks, but alive. Angel.

"I've got to warn you, honey, she's skittish these days. It's taking her a while to trust anybody."

Slowly, tears falling fast, Annie held out her hands and inched toward her horse. "Angel, come here, girl, pretty girl."

Angel reared her head back and rolled her eyes wildly so mostly white showed.

Annie stopped. "Angel, girl. It's me. Come here, girl," she coaxed.

Uncertainly, Angel lowered her head. Her nostrils flared and she sucked in great whiffs of smells.

She took one shaky step forward. Annie did likewise. Another and another, until Angel's muzzle rested on Annie's shoulders. She began to nibble Annie's hair, the way she'd always greeted her in the field when she was ready to give up her pasture freedom and grant Annie a ride.

Annie reached up and wrapped her arms around the gaunt black neck.

"She's broken up pretty badly, Annie. I don't think she can ever be ridden again," said Laurence. "She can barely trot, she limps so badly. It was Sam who saved her. They were about to put her down for meat when he found her. Took a lot for him to barter—everything he had almost—to get her. Then he had to walk her home. That's what took him so long to reach Hickory Heights."

Annie kept her face against Angel's. Lord, the price they'd all paid.

"But she can bear foals," Laurence continued. "They'd be beautiful, too. If it's all right by you, Annie, I'd like to keep her here and let her be a brood mare. She's the only horse I've got," he said with a laugh, "but maybe, after the fighting's over, I can find a stallion for her and we can rebuild the legendary herd of Hickory Heights."

He stroked Angel's head.

Annie stepped back and let Angel jostle Laurence, looking for treats. He pulled a carrot stub out of his pocket that he'd obviously been saving for her, and let her take it.

Gladness filled Annie as she watched Laurence. The war hadn't broken his core. But could he be happy? Where was Charlotte?

"Laurence," Annie dared to begin, "what happened with you and—"

But she was interrupted by a rider hurtling up the drive in a tornado of dust and gravel. The man jumped off his sweat-lathered horse and dragged it, its chest heaving, toward the stable. When he pulled off his slouch hat, Annie recognized Jamie's flaming hair.

Worried, protective of Jamie, Laurence shot a sharp, aggressive look toward Thomas.

Annie did, too. She couldn't help it.

Hurt, Thomas shook his head at Annie. She blushed in shame at her instinctive distrust of her own husband.

To Laurence, Thomas said, "I resigned my commission, Laurence, to marry your sister. Like you, I am now an avowed bystander of the war. That is, of course," he added, stepping forward, "what I hope you are doing. If you are harboring a Mosby ranger in your house, there will be nothing I can do to help you."

"He does not stay here any longer," Laurence answered. "All Mosby's men are staying in shebangs now. It was too easy for Union cavalry to find them in their homes."

"Shebangs?"

"Shanties and lean-tos they've built in the woods. I have not seen my brother for several weeks. I honestly do not know why he is here. I just hope he is not injured."

Laurence walked ahead to meet Jamie. Annie stiffened. Although she had been unsure of what Laurence would think of her marriage, she knew at least that he would be reasonable about it. Jamie was a different story. She'd tried to convince herself that it wouldn't matter to her what her impetuous little brother might say. But it was a lie. She cared.

"Laurence!" Jamie was shouting. "I need another horse."

"I haven't got one."

"I'll take Angel."

"She can barely walk, Jamie. You can't ride her."

Jamie was beside himself, frantically pacing and waving his arms about. "I need another horse! Now! I must avenge Henry! Those murderers, those dogs!"

"James, what has happened?"

Jamie kept pacing until finally he seemed to wear himself out. "Yesterday, the Yankees dragged him, lashed to two horses, into a field and shot him down. Right in front of his mother." He covered his face as if to block the sight of it.

"Who?"

"Henry! A schoolmate of mine. We were riding near Front Royal after a train of supply wagons and ambulances and we passed Henry's farm. Henry'd stayed home all this time to take care of his widowed mother. When he saw me, I told him to grab a horse and come on along, that we'd have some fun. His mother ran after us, begging him not to do it. . . . Well, we hit some bad fire and we had to hoof it out of there double-quick, toward Chester Gap. But Henry's horse collapsed and the Feds got him.

"The Yankees went crazy, claiming we'd shot one of their officers after he surrendered. So they tied Henry's arms to the saddles of two Yankee cavalrymen and they dragged him along, between them, through the town. When his poor old mother saw him, she hung on to him and begged for his life. The Yankees threatened to behead her with their sabers unless she got out of their way. She followed, weeping, as they pulled Henry to a farm outside of town, untied him, and then shot him as he fell to his knees and prayed for mercy."

Jamie pulled his hands away from his face. It was twisted with hatred.

"They stood two more of our riders, who'd surrendered, up against a church wall and riddled them with bullets. One of them, Lucien, was only seventeen, just like Henry. They hanged two others for refusing to tell where Mosby was. One I swear they shot just for fun. I'm going to kill every last Yankee I set my eyes on."

They all stood silent, shocked at the barbarity of what Jamie related.

It was Thomas who spoke first, outraged. "Who did this?"

Jamie had covered his face again and didn't notice who asked. "Michiganders."

"Under Custer?" Thomas asked.

"Yes, that cur in his black velvet uniform and perfect curls."

"Who's that?" Annie whispered.

"A man I went to West Point with. Thank God, it wasn't the 2nd Massachusetts," breathed Thomas. "I swear Custer is going to meet a bloody end someday."

Jamie's head shot out of his hands. He turned to

glare at Annie and Thomas as if he had just then noticed them. Perhaps he had.

Without hesitating, Jamie pulled out his revolver and pointed it at Thomas.

"No!" shrieked Annie, stumbling to shield her husband.

"James!" shouted Laurence, hurling himself at his brother.

The two fell to the ground. The revolver fired, the bullet going wide, rebounding off the stable wall. Wrestling, Laurence somehow managed to kick the gun free of Jamie's flailing grabs. Annie snatched it up.

"Stop it! Stop it!" she cried.

All the while, Thomas had stood stock-still.

Laurence picked himself up. Looking down at Jamie, he said, "This man managed to win the release of Annie from prison. They've married. He's our brother now."

Jamie sat on the ground, panting. He looked from one to the other, and his eyes narrowed to slits. "He's no brother of mine." He stood, dusting himself off, and turned to Annie. "So, you sold yourself for freedom?" He spat on the ground at her feet.

"That's enough!" Laurence roared.

"Enough? Maybe you've had enough. But I

haven't. I'll never give up. I don't care if Lee himself surrenders; I never will."

Annie was quaking, unable to speak. The scene, Jamie's rage and contempt for her, were all too horrible.

"James." Thomas spoke, controlling his anger. "There is something you ought to know. While I was petitioning the War Department and the prison for your sister, I learned that you once signed the loyalty oath. They just executed a twenty-one-year-old boy at Old Capitol Prison—not for spying, not for his activities with Mosby, but because he had violated that oath. If they catch you in a skirmish, they can hang you immediately. You must honor the oath you took if you wish to survive this war.

"The South will not win," Thomas continued. "You cannot. The Union is too strong, too determined now. From now on, there'll just be more irrational blood revenges like this one. You know the Union men executed those boys in retaliation for all the pickets and train guards Mosby's men have surprised and killed in the night."

Jamie stared right through Thomas. He picked up his hat and held his hand out for his revolver. Laurence took it from Annie, emptied its cylinder of percussion caps to disable it, and handed it to Jamie.

Jamie remounted his horse, which trembled with tiredness, and kicked him to walk down the lane. "If the war ends and we haven't won," Jamie shouted over his shoulder, "I'm heading out west. I won't live in a country ruled by Yankees or turncoat cowards and traitors."

CHAPTER THIRTY-SIX

The road leading away from Hickory Heights

Jamie's bitterness and his base condemnation of her haunted Annie and everyone else at Hickory Heights. It was a meager, quiet dinner that she and Thomas shared with Laurence and her cousins. At dawn, she'd have to pack what belongings she could carry on horseback to begin the long journey to her new home. Most of her clothes she was giving to Rachel, with the exception of her emerald green princess gown and the elegant dinner gown her mother had made of the midnight blue velvet Thomas' mother had sent. Annie slept little. She and Thomas were in Miriam's room, and Annie kept waking to look about, remembering. Finally, she arose and tiptoed downstairs. She was going to leave all the books for Laurence. She knew Thomas had plenty. She just wanted to sit in the parlor and people it with all she loved, before war had broken them apart.

She paused at Miriam's desk, remembering the arc of her mother's slender neck, the crispness of her lace collar as she bent over her letters or accounting. She heard the sound of her own laughter, when as a child Annie snuck up behind Miriam and threw her hands in front of her eyes, and Miriam's fond chuckle as she laid down her papers and reached behind to catch Annie up in her arms. A tiny patch of silver gleamed in the moonlight drifting through the windows. Annie reached for it and found one of Miriam's thimbles. She slipped it onto her thumb, thinking of all the gorgeous needlework Miriam had made, and kissed it. That she would take with her for luck.

Annie eased herself into the window seat, imagining Laurence reading a book aloud to them, so vital, so handsome; Miriam by the fire, sewing, looking up occasionally to smile at Laurence; Jamie, youthful, impish, darting to the piano to bang out marches and camp songs.

It had been a loving, pretty place.

"Annie?"

Annie startled, thinking sure a ghost was speaking to her. But it was Will.

She held her arms open for him and he cuddled against her. "I'm going to miss you," she whispered. "Will you be all right here, with Laurence? He'll take good care of you. Or maybe I should ask you to take care of him, the same way you helped me, especially when the soldiers came."

He nodded solemnly. Then he handed her tightly folded papers—Stuart's poems.

Annie gasped. "Where did you have them?"

"In my shoe," he answered quietly.

"That was very brave of you, Will. Promise me that you'll always be brave enough to be kind, just as you are now," said Annie.

He nodded again.

Annie weighed the cherished poems. They would only endanger the family now. She went to the fireplace, threw them in, and struck a flint to set them on fire. *Forget not him you met by chance.* She'd remember.

The next morning, early, as dawn seeped crimson along the sky, Annie waded through heavy dew to the family cemetery. She didn't know what to say to her father and brothers buried there, but Miriam she told about prison, about Thomas, about Laurence, and finally about Jamie. "I'm so sorry, Mother. I can't keep my promise about Jamie. He's disowned me. He called me a coward and a traitor. He thinks I sold myself in marriage to Thomas for my freedom. It wasn't like that." She ached to hear an answer, some reassurance, but there was none save the wind and a whirling cascade of falling leaves. Annie picked up some of the tiny, wild purple asters dappling Miriam's grave.

Anne turned back slowly. When she reached the house, she put her hand on its wall, dragging her fingertips along the fieldstone as she walked around to the front door. She memorized the stubbly feeling, the smell of the morning-damp stone, the occasional prickle of the horsehair mixed in the mortar, the touch of cool ivy that grew up it here and there. Her hand dislodged a tiny sliver of the stone. She bent and picked it up, lovingly stuffing it into her pocket along with the thimble and the asters. Silly, little bits of her childhood home, but she needed them for strength. She knew that most likely she'd never see Hickory Heights again. She closed her eyes and etched its picture in her mind. Then, each footstep feeling so final, she made her way to the front gate, where the people she'd loved all her life waited to send her away.

Everything was packed; the horses were saddled and ready. She said her good-byes to everyone but Laurence. That was the hardest.

As much as she was suffering to leave her home, she knew she would be all right with Thomas. They had a promising life, their own frontier, ahead of them, away from the ashes of the war. Jamie was lost. The war had ruined him, perhaps forever. Annie would mourn him as surely as if he had died. But Laurence, dear Laurence, he had the chance to begin again. As he'd said himself, he'd fought a good fight. He could honor a truce, knowing he had fought his battles with bravery and honesty and respect for his enemy. His body was sound now. He seemed committed to living, breathing in, breathing out. But Laurence wasn't yet healed enough to be capable of looking for happiness; she could sense it. He was simply strong enough to be stoic.

Oh, how Annie wished Miriam could tell her what to say to Laurence at this parting. Instinctively she knew Laurence would read but ultimately dismiss any worry or advice she expressed in a letter. The time to help him was now, before she left.

Annie braced herself. "Laurence, what happened with Charlotte?"

"We needn't discuss it," Laurence growled.

Annie ignored the warning in his tone. "Yes, brother, we do need to. I have to leave in a moment, and it is important to me to know." She tugged on his sleeve. "Please, Laurence." She smiled up at him.

"Well," Laurence began grudgingly, "she came back here after seeing you, to tell me about those . . ." He looked over at Thomas, who was talking to the children, and lowered his voice. "About those fool poems General Stuart wrote you."

"It wouldn't matter now to Thomas," Annie reassured him. "He's remarkable that way. Go on about Charlotte. It was incredibly courageous and loyal of her to come to the prison, you know."

Laurence's face clouded and his hand balled into a fist. "I know that! That's why I couldn't . . . I can't shackle her with someone like me."

"And what did *she* say about it, Laurence?"

He shuffled his feet and didn't answer.

"What did she say?" Annie prodded.

"She said she didn't care and that she loved me all the same, perhaps more," he mumbled.

"Why aren't you married then?"

"I'm missing my arm, Annie! Can't you see? I don't want to be married for pity. I can't even dance with the girl anymore." His voice caught and he turned his head, ashamed.

"Laurence." Annie shook her head. She thought of the radiant couple he and Charlotte had been that night of the Culpeper ball—the gallant officer and the breathtaking girl circling the dance floor. It was tragic that that picture could be no more. But there could be bits of it for them.

Annie had an idea. Gently, she took her brother's left hand in her right and held them up at shoulder's height. Then she put her left hand on his right shoulder, steadily, not flinching from the lump of scar tissue she could feel underneath the fabric of his coat.

She began singing an old Stephen Foster tune they'd sung together in those earlier, easy times: "*Open thy lattice, love, listen to me! / While the moon's in the sky and the breeze on the sea!*"

It was a perfect slow waltz melody. Up on her toes, slowly she turned, pulling Laurence with her. At first he scowled and tried to pull away, but she refused to let go of his hand. "Sing with me, Laurence. Remember what music sounds like?"

He shook his head. His hazel eyes grew foggy with unshed tears and a storm of conflicted, raging thoughts.

"Yes, you can, Laurence. You can remember.

You see, you can still lead Charlotte in a dance. You can still look in her eyes and sweep her across the floor. The only thing she might need to do is hold you tight with her arm. She can do that, Laurence. Give her that credit. Give her that chance."

Annie continued singing and turning. *"The moon like a queen, roams her realms of blue, / And the stars keep their vigils in heaven for you. . . ."*

All the while Laurence struggled with his pride, his embarrassment, his anger at Annie's insistence. Annie could see it. But she refused to stop. It was like riding Angel to jump a stone wall. If she faltered, they'd turn away, never to try the fence again. She sang on, pulling his rigid body along in the dance: "*Or skim like a bird o'er the waters away . . .*"

Finally, finally, Laurence's body began to relax. He started to follow her. Then—miraculously, like the Laurence of old—he burst out laughing, flashing that amused, dimpled, disarming grin of his. "I never have been able to say no to you, little sister. God help your husband. Does he know what he's in for?"

"Let us hope not," Annie teased back. "Or he might abandon me."

"Oh, I think not, Annie. I think not. Lord, I'm going to miss you, honey."

Laurence picked up the waltz lead himself, turning her round and round, her skirts flying, and brought her back to her husband and the crowd of Hickory Heights, waiting at the front steps.

"Is this a Virginian custom I need learn? Dancing a good-bye?" Thomas asked in his good-natured way.

"Perhaps so," Annie said. But before she let go of Laurence's hand, she looked at him with great earnestness. "You'll write her, today?"

Laurence nodded, but his grin broke as he looked down at his left hand, and he hesitated. He'd always been right-handed.

"I'll scribe his words for him, Miss Annie," Sam said quietly. Rachel nodded.

Annie knew it would be done.

It was time to leave. As she and Thomas rode down the lane, Annie refused to turn back. She couldn't have borne doing so. Instead, she thought of the foals Angel would have someday. She tried to imagine what they'd look like. Ebony like their mother, she hoped, with lightning blazes of white down their legs and faces. They'd be beauties, for sure.

"Thomas." She turned to her husband. "Do you think we could manage to have one of Angel's foals brought to us, way up north?" Her voice shook a bit as she asked.

Thomas blessed her with one of those calming, self-assured smiles of his. "Of course," he promised.

Of course, Annie thought. Of course. If they could manage to fall in love, to still care about poetry, to respect and admire each other across enemy lines amid all this bloodshed, they could manage to bring a little bit of Angel into their lives.

Annie rode on. As they slipped onto the turnpike, completely out of sight of Hickory Heights now, Annie tried to save herself from a searing sadness. Leaving her home, her family, was an amputation of sorts. Like Laurence, she'd have to learn to do without, and, like Laurence, she could be happy as long as she *made* herself look for joy.

Annie knew that Jamie's bitterness foretold how many of her fellow Southerners would be—they wouldn't give up the fight. Or if they survived the war, they'd never give up their grief and disappointment, their anger and hatred, inflamed by the outrages the Union had inflicted on civilians—their wives, children, and aging parents. While men like Laurence would work to restitch the country, men like Jamie would try to unravel it.

She glanced at Thomas again. He was humming

to himself the Stephen Foster melody, giving her time to sort out her feelings.

How would she fit in with Northerners in a Northern land? Annie worried. Would they ridicule the way she talked or her Irish looks? Would they ostracize Thomas for marrying her, and would he come to hate her for it? Would they demean the Virginian people she so loved, the terrible fight they had fought, their sacrifices? Undoubtedly, as Thomas initially had, they would probably assume that her family had been advocates for slavery. They might even believe that she had been cruel to Rachel, Aunt May, and Isaac. How could she bear it? How could she hold her tongue if they did so?

Annie's head swam.

Then her mother's voice came to her again, a final good-bye from Hickory Heights. "Remember that it doesn't matter where someone comes from, but where that person is going."

Miriam had done it—she had stepped into a social world that disapproved of her and made it on her own. She had even managed to disprove a few prejudices about her countrymen and to carry a bit of her past into her new life. If Mother could do it, so can I, Annie reassured herself. Thomas would help her. Perhaps their union promised what America itself could become after the war, for the nation, too, North and South, would have to redefine itself.

Annie took a deep breath. Massachusetts. What would it be like? Cold, for sure. In heart as well as weather? The only thing she knew about it was the novel *The Scarlet Letter*—hardly reassuring. She thought of the character Hester Prynne, stepping out of a Puritan prison with the letter *A* embroidered so brazenly, so beautifully, on her dress. In Hawthorne's novel, the Massachusetts court had ordered Hester wear it to identify her crime of adultery to anyone she met. And yet, through her elaborate needlework, Hester had turned the letter into a statement of her own—part shame, part pride. Shame for her mistakes, pride in her courage in admitting them and in her devotion to making a new, better life for her baby.

Annie felt a sudden kinship with the book's heroine. Like Hester, she would be justly branded—not for adultery, but for the institution of slavery—because she was a Southerner. At least she could now speak for change, for abolishing the practice. And like Hester, she could still have pride in other aspects of her life—the bravery and compassion of men like Lawrence and Sam, her own dedication to Virginia and her Hickory Heights family.

Annie squared her shoulders. Besides, she thought with a spark of mischief, if I have a foal of Angel's, I can show those Yankees a thing or two about riding—the Virginia way.

Resolved, Annie started singing with her husband's humming: *"Open thy lattice, love, listen to me! / In the voyage of life, love our pilot will be!/ He will sit at the helm wherever we rove. . . ."*

Thomas joined in the words, nodding at their meaning for the two of them, his voice straining to keep the melody.

Annie smiled. Thomas sang quite off-key. Oh well, she thought. Far better to sing with the man she loved, even if he was not a very good singer. There was no way that their marriage would be completely harmonious or trouble free. But it would, she knew, be a remarkable journey, because they took it together, traveling a course of their own choice, their own voice.

AUTHOR'S NOTE

The tragic statistics of the Civil War are well-known: 3 million fought, 620,000 died, 420,000 were crippled or wounded. It caused 10,000 armed conflicts. Of those clashes, 384 were principal, strategically decisive battles.

One in three of those major battles took place in Virginia. The last state to leave the Union, and the state with the most residents voting against secession, Virginia ironically endured the overwhelming majority of the war's bloodshed. (The state with the second highest principal battle count was Tennessee, with 38 pivotal battles compared to Virginia's 123. South Carolina, which fired the war's opening shot, withstood 11.)

Serving as the main fighting ground of a four-year war meant constant upheaval for Virginians. The state was the feedbag, hospital, gateway, camp, stage, and burial ground for two armies that staggered back and forth across its lands, neither quite establishing a lasting dominance over the other. The town of Warrenton, where Annie visits Charlotte, changed hands sixty-seven times.

The title of this book, *Annie, Between the States,* carries many meanings. One of them has to do with this horrendous reality of perpetual invasion. Like so many Virginians during the Civil War, Annie and her family can look out almost any day to see an army marching through their fields. She has relatives who remain loyal to the Union. And, while opposed to secession, she is forced by circumstances and regional loyalty to choose Virginia over the Union.

Robert E. Lee wrote in a farewell letter to a Northern friend, "I cannot raise my hand against my birthplace, my home, my children. I should like, above all things, that our difficulties might be peaceably arranged. . . . Whatever may be the result of the contest I foresee that the country will have to pass through a terrible ordeal, a necessary expiation for our national sins. May God direct all for our good, and shield and preserve you and yours."

Annie's story is historical fiction, meaning the setting and details of day-to-day life are accurate. The plot, its conflicts, and its moral dilemmas grow out of the times. Therefore, every battle and date mentioned in this book is factual. Annie is not, although she is inspired by several northern Virginia women—among them Laura Ratcliffe, Roberta Pollock, Annie Lucas, Amanda Virginia "Tee" Edmonds, and Antonia Ford, who did, in fact, marry the Union officer who carried her to Federal prison. The details of Annie's life, from the Battle of First Manassas to her home and events in Fauquier County, are gleaned from firsthand accounts, war diaries, memoirs, biographies, local histories, and interviews with Civil War experts in the region.

The oft-asked question of any historical fiction is: What *really* happened? I will tell you.

Jeb Stuart, John Mosby, William Farley, Heros von Borcke, Major Goulding, Mr. Robinson, General Stoughton, Colonel Lowell, "Yankee" Davis, and Private Trammel are all true historic figures. Eliza is based on a "high-spirited girl" in Warrenton who did make a champagne bet with a Major Goulding about his making it to Richmond. Stuart did order a woman disguised as a Union soldier be sent to prison. (Records indicate someone released her before she arrived in Richmond.) Mr. Robinson, a free black, did have his farm destroyed by Union troops. (Details come from a petition he made after the war for reimbursement.) He did convince a sympathetic white man to purchase his enslaved daughter to keep her nearby until he could raise enough money to buy her out. William Farley did give his dress coat to a lady in Culpeper days before he died in the Union surprise at Brandy Station.

All skirmishes and troop movements are factual. The raids on Annie's house are timed to coincide with actual Union raids through Fauquier and Loudoun counties by the troops mentioned. While there is no evidence that a teenage girl warned Stuart at Lewinsville or Mosby of the Trojan horse, there are countless stories of women riding or walking through bad weather and picket lines to alert both leaders of oncoming Federal troops.

Stuart's poems to Annie are snippets of verse the cavalry general actually wrote to Laura Ratcliffe, a beautiful young woman whom he first saw nursing the wounded of Manassas and who later saved Mosby from a Union ambush set for him near the village of Herndon.

The brutal executions in Front Royal of Mosby's followers and two seventeen-year-olds, Henry Rhodes and Lucien Love, did occur as I describe them. Battlefield reports and memoirs written by Stuart's officers tell of white-flag conversations between Stuart and old Union army friends, the Cedar Mountain bet, the hat and coat "prisoner exchange," the Culpeper ball, and Mosby's capture of the sleeping Federal general. Charles Murdock is based on a Mosby rider named Charles Binns, who did desert and lead Union raids on homes hiding his former comrades. According to the records of Mosby's 43rd Battalion, Binns and another man abducted two slave women with the thought of selling them. Binns did give testimony against Mosby ranger Philip Trammell in a Federal trial.

The story of Annie and Jamie's ride into the night after a Mosby ranger who did indeed abduct two African-American women is my invention, but it is plausible. So, too, is Annie's presence when Stuart receives news of his daughter's fatal illness. (Stuart encamped near Upperville that night, enjoyed a large shank of mutton, and received bad news about little Flora.) Heros von Borcke was wounded and hidden from searching Federal troops by a Confederate family in the area. William Farley was as he is described, a soft-spoken Shakespeare scholar. It makes sense that he would admire a young woman such as Annie. His final words are what his companions recorded.

Everything else, while fictitious, is culled from accounts of the types of things that did happen during the war. The prisoners and their treatment at

Carrol Prison, for instance, are modeled on what is described in the memoir of an incarcerated woman. According to the letters of a Manassas resident, Union troops did run through her house as they retreated in the Battle of First Manassas. Rachel and Sam's wedding is similar to that described by some former slaves. Mosby's men did have secret closets. Unfortunately Union soldiers did vandalize homes frequently. One Fauquier memoir tells of troops pouring molasses into their family's piano and filling it with feathers from their pillows and mattresses. Epidemics, like the diphtheria that kills Miriam, were spawned by the poor sanitation of army camps and the lack of immunity soldiers from isolated rural areas had to contagious diseases. These illnesses decimated civilian populations.

The people most important to Annie—Laurence, Miriam, Jamie, Thomas, Charlotte, Aunt May, Isaac, Sam, and Rachel—are imaginary, but again are reflective of loved ones described by many of the region.

The poems, songs, and books mentioned were popular during the time. The nineteenth century's equivalent of television and movies, they were one of the few common links between Northern and Southern people, who were so separated by geography and culture. According to Mosby's biographers, Lord Byron was indeed his favorite poet.

One of the most perplexing aspects of the Civil War was the cordiality that existed amid such carnage. Pickets did cross lines to trade and talk with one another while on duty. One Manassas area resident told of Union soldiers asking her family to set up a meeting between them and Mosby raiders. The enemies talked long into the night in the family's parlor, and then shook hands before departing. There seemed to be a sense of curiosity as well as pity between them.

West Point classmates constantly opposed one another on the battlefield. They worried about one another's safety as they ordered murderous charges. Perhaps the best-known friendship was that of Confederate general Lewis Armistead and Union general Winfield Scott Hancock. At Gettysburg, Armistead longed to cross the field to talk with his old friend before the next day's battle. Both Hancock and Armistead were wounded that day—Armistead fatally. But before he died, Armistead asked that his personal Bible be sent to Hancock's wife as a remembrance of happier times their families had shared.

Stuart, the quintessential Virginia cavalier, also faced divided family loyalties during the war. His father-in-law, Federal general Philip St. George Cooke, remained with the Union and, by a twist of fate, was the commanding officer pursuing Stuart during his famous ride around McClellan's army in June 1862. Stuart's military star rose after the encounter; his father-in-law's sank. Cooke lost his field command and spent the war serving on court-martial duty and recruitment boards. Stuart showed little regret for his father-in-law's plight. Unable to forgive Cooke for remaining with the Union, Stuart changed the name of his son, which originally honored his father-in-law, from Philip to James Ewell Brown Stuart, Jr., calling him Jimmy.

Stuart is perhaps the most endearing and exasperating of all Confederate leaders. A true romantic, he collected wildflowers and bird feathers to press into scrapbooks alongside poems during his time in the West. He courted his wife on horseback rides for a mere two months before marrying her, saying, "I came, I saw, I was conquered."

Wherever he went, Stuart wanted to be liked. And typically he was, even by his opponents. As his cavalry rode through Urbana, Maryland, on their way to the ill-fated Battle of Sharpsburg by Antietam

Creek, Stuart was so beguiled by the young women of the town that he hosted a ball for them despite their Union loyalties. Girls from all around came. In the middle of the festivities, Federals attacked the Confederate camp outside the village. Stuart and his men donned the sabers they'd hung on the wall and rode off to meet them. After the skirmish, Stuart returned. He restarted the dancing, which went on until three A.M., when stretcher-bearers began bringing in wounded men. In their party gowns, the Union women helped tend them. One injured Confederate said he'd be hit any day to have such surgeons dress his wounds. Maryland did not join the cause as Lee had hoped, but Urbana, at least, was certainly captivated by Stuart.

Many historians and people of his time condemned Stuart for not arriving at Gettysburg in time to guide the floundering Confederates with cavalry reconnaissance. Some blamed the devastating loss on him and his sizable ego, which kept Stuart looking for spoils on his ride north and delayed his arrival. Still, it is hard not to like the effusive, flamboyant Stuart.

Mosby, on the other hand, is more complex and less accessible. A brilliant but prickly man who survived seven wounds, Mosby believed in eye-for-an-eye retribution. After the savage executions of his men at Front Royal, Mosby ordered that when they were captured, any Federals who belonged to the Michigan regiment responsible for the acts should be separated from other prisoners. When his rangers had collected twenty-seven Michigan cavalry riders, Mosby ordered a lottery. A hat with slips of paper was passed among them; seven bore an *X*—the death sentence. During the first round, a young drummer boy drew an *X*. Not previously knowing that a youth was among the captured, Mosby pardoned the sobbing boy. The hat was passed again and the painful drawing repeated. The condemned seven were taken out to be shot or hanged. But his men were reluctant to carry out Mosby's orders. Two of their prisoners easily escaped and were not pursued. Another two were only wounded when shot. They survived.

The escapes evidently did not anger Mosby. He called the lottery and executions a "judicial sentence, not revenge." Had he been seeking revenge, wrote Mosby, he "would have ordered others to be executed in their place." He did not. His purpose was to "prevent the war from degenerating into a massacre" by answering the Union's actions measure for measure. Mosby wrote to Federal general

Philip Sheridan, who commanded Union forces in the Shenandoah Valley: "Hereafter any prisoners falling into my hands will be treated with the kindness due to their condition, unless some new act of barbarity shall compel me reluctantly to adopt a course of policy repulsive to humanity."

The executions of Confederates stopped, but Sheridan's overall harshness did not. Ordered by Grant to "eat out Virginia clean and clear . . . so that crows flying over it for the balance of the season will have to carry their own provender," Sheridan began systematically destroying the Shenandoah Valley, a plunder begun by Union general David Hunter. For three days in October 1864, right after harvest time, Sheridan's troops scoured the valley, burning every barn, every mill, and all crops, farm equipment, and outbuildings they found. They killed or carried off livestock. A month later they did the same to Fauquier and Loudoun counties, even to Quaker villages that supported the Union, claiming Mosby might find provisions there. For decades, the residents remembered the famine-producing destruction as "the burning."

Interestingly, Mosby was one Confederate leader who embraced Reconstruction. Before the war, he had voted against secession and publicly campaigned for a Unionist candidate for president. Like Robert E. Lee, Mosby followed Virginia's final choice to join the Confederacy because: "Virginia is my mother, God bless her! I can't fight against my mother, can I?" When the war was over, he plunged back into his law practice and public life. Although Grant had once issued a death warrant for him, Mosby and the general became good friends during Grant's presidential administration. Mosby campaigned for his reelection.

His support of Grant cost Mosby. Many Virginians called him a traitor. His law practice dwindled. He further alienated his former admirers by criticizing Lee and defending Stuart's role in Gettysburg. He eventually embarked on what he called a self-imposed twenty-five-year exile from Virginia, serving in various Republican administrations, as consul to Hong Kong, as special agent in the Department of Interior, and as an assistant attorney for the Justice Department's antitrust division. Mosby personally knew four presidents: Grant, Rutherford Hayes, William McKinley, and Teddy Roosevelt. All but Roosevelt he had fought during the war. McKinley frequently joked that Mosby's men had made life miserable for him when he served in the Shenandoah Valley.

In 1916, Mosby died in Washington, D.C., at the age of eighty-two. By the end of his life, he had again become a popular folk hero, remembered as the "Gray Ghost" who bedeviled superior and sometimes cruel forces. He became the subject of three silent films, in one of which he actually appeared himself. And in 1957, CBS produced a weekly television series about him.

Writing about the Civil War is one of the hardest things I've ever done. Not because its stories weren't compelling. On the contrary, the courage, the bravura, the mercy shown by the combatants and civilians alike produced some of the most heart-wrenching, inspiring, and maddening anecdotes one will ever read. It was difficult because of the obvious and appalling moral issue involved—slavery—and the choice to feature a traditional Virginia family as protagonists.

Living almost one hundred and fifty years later, we see the cause of the Civil War as slavery. But for most Southerners it had as much to do with regionalism; people at that time identified their citizenship primarily according to their state, not the country. Most never traveled beyond a few dozen miles from their home. They interpreted the Constitution as setting up an alliance predicated on a state's desire to be in the Union, and therefore breakable. By that point, the United States had become two very divergent entities—the agricultural South and the industrialized North—with very different needs. The North, however, had twice the population and dominated Congress, passing high tariffs that impeded Southern imports and exports and in essence chained the South to Northern factories and their high-priced finished goods. The South wanted out of what it increasingly saw as a lopsided marriage.

An overwhelming majority of Confederate soldiers did not come from slave-holding families. Most Africans held in this abhorrent bondage labored on Deep South plantations that produced single crops such as cotton or rice and where the percentage of slave-holders climbed to slightly over one out of three whites. (In Mississippi and South Carolina, that number neared one-half. It was on these plantations, which often held more than twenty slaves, that the "capital value" of slaves exceeded the value of the land, making the reprehensible institution a highly profitable one.)

In Virginia, by comparison, three out of four whites did *not* own slaves, and of those who did, forty-one percent held three or fewer "servants" (a euphemism they used in their memoirs). Some—such as Stonewall Jackson, who set up a Sunday school for one hundred slaves and freemen in Lexington, Virginia—ignored public disapproval and laws to teach blacks to read and write. Others, such as Robert E. Lee, freed their slaves before the Emancipation Proclamation or did so when the edict took effect. And surprisingly, records show that free blacks voluntarily joined the Confederate army as wagon drivers, cooks, blacksmiths, and musicians, some even serving as pickets. One Tennessee regiment asked a black man to serve as its chaplain.

Said one Civil War battlefield historian: "It is impossible for us to understand that mindset today. Certainly the cruel Hollywood stereotypes existed, but there were different breeds of slave-owners, some more progressive than others. There were those who were quite charitable, and slaves quite devoted to their masters who actually followed them into battle." North Carolina's Department of Cultural Resources, for example, tells the story of a slave named George Mills who discovered his master dead at Antietam. He could have fled to freedom easily, but instead carried the body through three war-torn states back to Hendersonville, North Carolina, so that his master would not be buried in a ditch with the thousands of other soldiers who died there.

Such stories are in sharp contrast to the better-known, horrifying, and tragic ones—of abuse; of African-American families standing on the auction block being sold separately and broken apart; of runaways being chased by dogs and whipped or shackled when caught; of slaves sent in to build Confederate fortifications at gunpoint or under Union fire during battles. But they do exist.

The uncomfortable fact is that racism permeated the entire country. For all its noble, inspiring, devoted abolitionists and the thousands of women who traveled south to teach freed slaves, there were indeed four states in the Union that practiced slavery throughout the Civil War: Maryland, Delaware, Missouri, and Kentucky.

Kentucky, in fact, continued to buy and sell human beings until the thirteenth amendment was ratified—eight months *after* the war ended. Officials in that Union state actually seized several hundred runaway slaves who had fled the Confederate states of Tennessee and Alabama and followed the Union army to what they thought would be safety. The refugees were put in prison and then sold back into bondage.

Abraham Lincoln's "paramount" objective was

to save the Union. He said, "If I could save the Union without freeing *any* slave, I would do it; and if I could save it by freeing *all* the slaves, I would do it; and if I could do it by freeing some and leaving others alone, I would also do that." When support for the war began to wane in the North in 1862, Lincoln issued his Emancipation Proclamation, elevating the fight to a nobler crusade. However, his Proclamation applied only to areas that remained in rebellion. It left slavery intact in the Union and in Southern territories already under Federal control to appease slave owners there. After announcing it, Lincoln even proposed an amendment to the Constitution that would have postponed the final elimination of slavery until the year 1900. Fortunately, Congress voted it down. It was also Congress in 1862 that abolished slavery in Washington, D.C., and the Western territories and passed an act forbidding Union soldiers to return fugitive slaves to owners.

It is interesting to note two waves of desertions, one in each army. On the Confederate side, the first large desertion occurred as Lee crossed into Maryland in September 1862. Soldiers left because they had signed up to protect their states, their homeland, not to invade others. One Confederate general's wife would write her husband that she could no longer pray for him because of their offensive move into Union territory. On the Union side, large numbers deserted during the very same month, when Lincoln announced his Emancipation Proclamation. One Illinois regiment lost a majority of its men, who disapproved of Lincoln's policy. Mosby's most trusted guide, "Big Yankee" Ames, joined his ranks in that way.

Northern enthusiasm for the war continued to fluctuate, so much so that in the spring of 1863, Lincoln instigated the first federal draft to ensure that the Union army had enough soldiers to fight. All men between the ages of twenty and forty-five were required to register. Any man whose name was drawn had to serve for three years.

This did not sit well with many Northerners, who were further alienated by the fact that rich men could buy their way out of service with $300—a fortune to most. (Future presidents Grover Cleveland and Chester A. Arthur paid their way out, as did the fathers of Theodore and Franklin Roosevelt.)

In New York City, the names of the first draftees were posted at the same time that long lists of Gettysburg casualties were published. The city erupted in violence. For three long days, mobs carrying clubs and torches rampaged, breaking into buildings, smashing windows, and murdering several men—including two disabled veterans—who tried to stop them. The largely immigrant crowds from the city's slums not only targeted the homes of the wealthy, they specifically went after African Americans. They torched a black church, a black orphanage, and black boardinghouses. They lynched a black coachman, chanting "Hurrah for Jeff Davis," before setting his dead body on fire. It took troops arriving from Gettysburg to finally stop the madness.

When runaway slaves approached Union troops before January 1863, they were dubbed "contraband" and often put to work mucking stalls, cooking, cleaning, and digging latrines. Or they were run off at bayonet point by soldiers whose fight would ultimately free them but who didn't want much, if anything, to do with African Americans afterward. Colonization plans—sending African Americans to Liberia or to Central America—were widely promoted.

After the Emancipation Proclamation went into effect, however, "contraband" blacks and slaves in the Union states were allowed to enlist in "colored" regiments in the Federal army. Enlisting brought freedom to a slave's family as well. Some Union officers questioned it, such as General William Tecumseh Sherman, who said: "Can a negro do our skirmishing and picket duty? Can they improvise bridges, sorties, flank movement, etc., like the white man? I say no."

Grant, on the other hand, gave his "hearty support" to the idea of black soldiers. Ironically both the son of an abolitionist and the husband of a slaveholder, Grant wrote: "By arming the Negro we have added a powerful ally. They will make good soldiers and taking them from the enemy weakens him in the same proportion they strengthen us."

Even so, black privates serving the Union were paid three dollars less a month than whites. They were also denied the clothing allowance given whites. Their death rate from disease was double that of whites serving in the U.S. army, because of exposure to the cold and the fact that military doctors were reluctant to treat them.

Despite such outrageous inequities, 180,000 African Americans fought for the Union, braving execution or being sold into slavery by Confederates taking them as prisoners of war. They faced their own command sending them into sure slaughter in the forefront of battles such as Fort Wagner, South Carolina, and the siege of Petersburg, Virginia. The tenacity, resourcefulness, and dignity of these black soldiers probably did more to erase prejudice among those who witnessed them than any acts of Congress or orders from President Lincoln could. Twenty-three of them were awarded the Congressional Medal of Honor—many years after the war ended.

Ultimately, the Civil War *did* become about slavery and emancipation. It did put a stop to a sickening, incomprehensible cruelty that American leaders seemed unable to stop through a civilized vote. In the end, the best statistic to remember about the Civil War is that 3 million human beings were freed.

Michael Shaara concludes his Pulitzer Prize–winning book, *The Killer Angels*, with a quote from the British statesman Winston Churchill, who wrote that the American Civil War was "the noblest and least avoidable of all the great mass conflicts."

Perhaps. But let us hope that future generations remember the Civil War and its tragic bloodbath when we need to find the courage to stop injustice, eliminate prejudices, and reconcile our differences.

ACKNOWLEDGMENTS

A book such as this cannot be written without doing massive amounts of research, as the following bibliography attests. When I speak to student groups about writing historical fiction, I always try to reassure them that research truly can be fun, like a treasure hunt. Certainly, the reading and interviewing I did yielded up many gems of details to make Annie's story come alive. I am indebted to the many scholars who have written factual histories of the Civil War, which I read in preparation and used as reference while building this book and its characters.

I owe a large thank-you to Jim Burgess, museum specialist at Manassas National Battlefield Park, who patiently allowed me to interview him for hours, dug out unpublished and little-known memoirs, and then read my manuscript for accuracy. I cannot thank him enough for his generosity, good humor, meticulousness, advice, and knowledge.

Budd Reitnauer of Sky Meadows State Park graciously opened its historic Mount Bleak House for the jacket photograph and educated me more on the life of Fauquier residents during the Civil War. Historians at the Lee Mansion in Arlington, Virginia; the Gettysburg battlefield; and the Fauquier Heritage Society also fielded questions with grace and a wealth of information.

I must say a special thanks to Dr. Edwin Wilson, of Wake Forest University, who long ago instilled in me a love of the English Romantic poets and who made sure my references to literature were correct.

To my editor, Katherine Tegen, I owe my beginnings and existence as a fiction writer, after many years as a magazine journalist. Katherine has encouraged, nurtured, guided, and championed me. What more could a writer ask? Illustrator Henry Cole first introduced me to Katherine. His enthusiastic generosity is equaled only by his artistic talent.

And finally, to my husband, John, and my children, Megan and Peter, who inspire me, hug me when I'm tired and discouraged, and bless me with sincere excitement about my books. Their insightful questions and compassionate curiosity make me a better writer; their belief in me a better one still.

BIBLIOGRAPHY

BOOKS AND ARTICLES

Baird, Nancy Chappelear, ed. *Journals of Amanda Virginia Edmonds: Lass of the Mosby Confederacy, 1859–1867.* Stephens City, Va.: Commercial Press, 1984.

Bakeless, John. *Spies of the Confederacy.* Mineola, N.Y.: Dover Publications, 1970.

Carter, Isabel, submitted by Stevan Phillips. "My War: Praying for Southern Victory." *Civil War Times Illustrated* (March/April 1991): 12–69.

**Chang, Ina. *A Separate Battle: Women and the Civil War.* New York: Puffin Books, 1996.

**Clinton, Catherine. *Scholastic Encyclopedia of the Civil War.* New York: Scholastic, 1999.

Compton, Marianne E. "A Woman's Recollection of Two Famous Battles." *Manassas Journal* (July 4, 1913).

**Indicates books appropriate for young readers.

Davis, Burke. *Jeb Stuart: The Last Cavalier.* Short Hills, N. J.: Burford Books, 1957.

Ewell, Alice Maude. *A Virginia Scene or Life in Old Prince William.* Lynchburg, Va.: J. P. Bell, 1931.

Freeman, Douglas Southall. *Lee's Lieutenants: A Study in Command.* Vol. I, *Manassas to Malvern Hill.* New York: Scribner, 1942.

———. *Lee's Lieutenants: A Study in Command.* Vol. II, *Cedar Mountain to Chancellorsville.* New York: Scribner, 1943.

———. *Lee's Lieutenants: A Study in Command.* Vol. III, *Gettysburg to Appomattox.* New York: Scribner, 1944.

Jones, Vergil Carrington. *Ranger Mosby.* Chapel Hill, N.C.: The University of North Carolina Press, 1944.

Larson, Rebecca D. *Blue and Gray Roses of Intrigue.* Gettysburg, Pa.: Thomas Publications, 1993.

Leonard, Elizabeth D. *All the Daring of the Soldier: Women of the Civil War Armies.* New York: W. W. Norton, 1999.

Lomax, Virginia. *The Old Capitol and Its Inmates: By*

a Lady, who enjoyed the hospitalities of the Government for a "Season." New York: E. J. Hale & Son, 1867. Available electronically through the University of North Carolina at Chapel Hill's digitization project "Documenting the American South, Beginnings to 1920."

Lowery, Rev. I. E. *Life on the Old Plantation in Ante-Bellum Days; or, A Story Based on Facts.* Columbia, South Carolina: The State Company Printers, 1911. Available electronically through the University of North Carolina at Chapel Hill's digitization project "Documenting the American South, Beginnings to 1920."

McLean, James. *California Sabers: The 2nd Massachusetts Cavalry in the Civil War.* Bloomington, Ind.: Indiana University Press, 2000.

McNeil, Keith, and Rusty McNeil. *Civil War Songs.* WEM Records (WEMCD507A; 507B; 507C), 1989.

**Murphy, Jim. *The Boys' War: Confederate and Union Soldiers Talk about the Civil War.* New York: Clarion Books, 1990.

**Pflueger, Lynda. *Jeb Stuart: Confederate Cavalry*

General. Berkeley Heights, N.J.: Enslow Publishers, 1998.

Ramage, James A. *Gray Ghost: The Life of Col. John Singleton Mosby*. Lexington, Ky.: The University Press of Kentucky, 1999.

Ramey, Emily G., and John K. Gott, eds. *The Years of Anguish, Fauquier County, Virginia, 1861–1865.* Collected and compiled for the Fauquier County Civil War Centennial Committee. Bowie, Md.: Heritage Books, 1998.

Rawlings, Kevin. *We Were Marching on Christmas Day: A History and Chronicle of Christmas during the Civil War.* Baltimore, Md.: Toomey Press, 1996.

**Ray, Delia. *A Nation Torn: The Story of How the Civil War Began.* New York: Puffin Books, 1996.

Rust, Jeanne. "Portrait of Laura." *Virginia Cavalcade* 12, no. 3 (Winter 1962–63): 34–39.

Scheel, Eugene M. *The Civil War in Fauquier.* Warrenton, Va.: The Fauquier National Bank, 1985.

———. *The History of Middleburg and Vicinity.* Warrenton, Va.: Piedmont Press, 1987.

**Smolinski, Diane. *The Home Front in the South.* Americans at War Series. Chicago: Reed Educational & Professional Publishing, 2001.

**Varhola, Michael J. *Everyday Life during the Civil War: A Guide for Writers, Students, and Historians.* Cincinnati: Writer's Digest Books, 1999.

Ward, Geoffrey C., with Ric Burns and Ken Burns. *The Civil War: An Illustrated History* (Companion Volume to the PBS television series). New York: Alfred A. Knopf, 1990.

Wert, Jeffrey D. *Mosby's Rangers, from the High Tide of the Confederacy to the Last Days of Appomattox.* New York: Simon and Schuster, 1990.

PAPERS AND MANUSCRIPTS HELD BY THE MANASSAS NATIONAL BATTLEFIELD PARK LIBRARY MANUSCRIPT FILES

Holden, Belle J. "Reminiscences of the War Between the States." Typescript.

Letter written by Florence to her sister, dated July 24, 1861, near Groveton, Prince William County, published in *Southern Magazine* (Baltimore) VII, no. 5 (May 1874).

Milliken, Ralph Leroy. "Then We Came to California, a biography of Sarah Summers Clarke, written in the first person." Typescript.

Robinson, James. "Disposition before the Commissioners of Claims," February 2, 1872.

Tidball, Captain John, of 2nd U.S. Artillery. War journal excerpts.

TIMELINE

OF THE CIVIL WAR IN VIRGINIA

1860

November 2	Abraham Lincoln elected president
December 20	South Carolina secedes

1861

April 12	Confederates fire on Fort Sumter, Charleston, South Carolina
May 23	Virginia secedes
July 21	Battle of First Manassas (Bull Run)
October 21	Battle of Ball's Bluff
December 20	Battle of Dranesville

1862

March-June	Stonewall Jackson's Shenandoah Valley campaign (Kernstown, March 23; McDowell, May 8; Front Royal, May 23; Winchester, May 25; Cross

Keys, June 8; Port Republic, June 9)

March 9 *Monitor/Merrimac,* sea battle off Norfolk; Confederate troops under General Johnston withdraw from northern Virginia

April 4 Union general McClellan advances his troops up Virginia Peninsula

May 4 Confederates evacuate Yorktown

5 Battle of Williamsburg

15 Battle of Drewry's Bluff

31-June 1 Battle of Fair Oaks (Seven Pines)

June 1 General Robert E. Lee takes command of the Army of Northern Virginia

June 25-July 1 Seven Days' Battles (around Richmond) (Oak Grove, June 25; Mechanicsville, June 26; Gaines' Mill, June 27; Savage's Station,